BOOK TWO in the BELTRUNNER SAGA

AFTERMATH

SEAN O'BRIEN

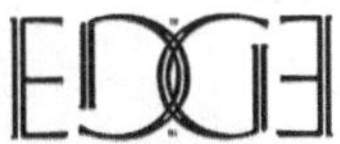

EDGE SCIENCE FICTION AND FANTASY PUBLISHING
An Imprint of HADES PUBLICATIONS, INC.
CALGARY

Aftermath
Book Two in the Beltrunner Saga

EDGE SCIENCE FICTION AND FANTASY PUBLISHING
An Imprint of HADES PUBLICATIONS, INC.
P.O. Box 1414, Calgary, Alberta, T2P 2L6, Canada

The EDGE Team:
Producer: Brian Hades
Edited by: Kathryn Shalley
Cover Design: Brian Hades
Cover Art: David Willicome
Book Design: Mark Steele

ISBN: 978-1-77053-223 6

EDGE Science Fiction and Fantasy Publishing and Hades Publications, Inc. acknowledges the ongoing support of the Alberta Foundation for the Arts and the Canada Council for the Arts for our publishing programme.

Library and Archives Canada Cataloguing in Publication

Title: Aftermath / Sean O'Brien.
Names: O'Brien, Sean (Educator), author.
Description: Series statement: Beltrunner saga ; book two
Identifiers: Canadiana (print) 20230581935 | Canadiana (ebook) 20230582036 | ISBN 9781770532335 (hardcover) | ISBN 9781770532236 (softcover) | ISBN 9781770532229 (EPUB)
Subjects: LCGFT: Science fiction. | LCGFT: Novels.
Classification: LCC PS3615.B775 A69 2024 | DDC 813/.6—dc23

FIRST EDITION
(20240424)
Printed in USA
www.edgewebsite.com

Publisher's Note:

Thank you for purchasing this book. It began as an idea, was shaped by the creativity of its talented author, and was subsequently molded into the book you have before you by a team of editors and designers.

Like all EDGE books, this book is the result of the creative talents of a dedicated team of individuals who all believe that books (whether in print or pixels) have the magical ability to take you on an adventure to new and wondrous places powered by the author's imagination.

As EDGE's publisher, I hope that you enjoy this book. It is a part of our ongoing quest to discover talented authors and to make their creative writing available to you.

We also hope that you will share your discovery and enjoyment of this novel on social media through Facebook, Twitter, Goodreads, Pinterest, etc., and by posting your opinions and/or reviews on Amazon and other review sites and blogs. By doing so, others will be able to share your discovery and passion for this book.

Brian Hades, publisher

Dedication

To my son, the bravest person I know…
To my daughter, the fiercest person I know…
And to my wife, the best person I know…

May you all see yourselves in these pages.

Chapter One

"South, where the hell did you store the *Ad Astra* scouter wreck?"

Collier South was shaken out of his post-binge haze at the strident tone in Ulmiter's voice. His supervisor wasn't the most charming of men under ordinary circumstances, and when Collier was trying to recover from another losing bout with the bottle Ulmiter was profoundly painful.

"Hold on a minute. I'll find it," Collier said, scrabbling at the grimy control panel in front of him. The buttons swam in his sight, despite his blinking attempts to clear his head. He knew how to call up the inventory, if only his fingers would do what he told them to — there.

One of the screens lit up with an impossibly long directory of items: discarded bits of spacecraft, machinery, and other sundry items that made up the Ceres Authority salvage yard. The yard itself covered roughly ten square kilometers of Ceres' surface; the yard offices one level below the surface took up just enough space for two cubicles and the surface buggy. Collier was supposed to have kept a detailed list of everything that had been dumped here. He seldom gave a damn enough to do so.

"I'm waiting," Ulmiter said over the radio.

"Looks like it's been misfiled," he said lamely.

"Misfiled. So, you lost it."

"I wouldn't say that," Collier said.

Ulmiter's voice lost its calm. "Locate that damned scouter and notify me the moment you have or I'll declassify your ass no matter what Fletcher says about it. You'll be a shitbum before rotation, South. Ulmiter out."

"Thanks for calling. Really brightened my day," Collier said as he punched up the exterior camera network. Searching the yard manually would take time, but what else was he going to do? Ulmiter could probably force him out if he set his mind to it. Collier was under no illusions as to how little Fletcher's influence would protect him.

Why had she'd bothered to help him? He certainly was no asset to the Authority. He only had a vague memory of how she'd cleaned him up and dried him out after he'd lost *Dulcinea*. He remembered, though, what she had said to him: "Collier, you seem determined to kill yourself one drop at a time. I don't want that to happen — it'd mean all kinds of paperwork."

She'd arranged for him to work at the salvage yard, which was still nominally under the Authority's supervision. But like everything else that was supposed to be run by the Authority, the yard was a morass of corruption and black marketeering. His appointment to yard technician, commonly known as a "trash jockey," or just "trasher," had not been welcomed by Ulmiter and the other technician.

Fletcher should have let him drink himself to death. It would have been better than living as an employee. He was making enough money to rent a berth, buy air credits each day, and eat. When he had anything left over, he was able to drink.

The lingering effects of last night's cheap Ceres Clay liquor wreaked havoc on his eyes as he searched the yard for the missing scouter. But the images of the deserted, broken machinery; ancient, stripped ship hulls; and abandoned cargo holds impinged on his unconscious. He thought of everything he'd lost, everything that had been taken from him — no, he was using the wrong words, even in his mind. He hadn't lost anything. Nothing had been taken from him.

He'd let it all go.

"The hell with this," he muttered and stopped the camera sweep. He knew only one way to ease the buzzing in his head and more importantly, dim the regret. The cure for and cause of his ills was only a few levels away.

He made sure that he wasn't being monitored: Ulmiter sometimes tapped into the duty office's internal cameras, but Collier had discovered the telltale signs of such eavesdropping long ago. A quick check of the command pathways on his console assured him that Ulmiter was not watching. The supervisor could indeed check in later, but just at that moment, Collier didn't care. Let him see an empty seat. Let Ulmiter declassify him.

The trip downlevel into Ceres' commercial and habitation zones was a swift one: Collier had made the trek every day for the past three months since he'd been first assigned to the yard. He hardly had to think about the various shafts and pathways that led him to the Trojan Point.

A single patron sat at the bar, his feet tucked under the pseudobrass foot rail. Phil, the owner, looked up from his calculations and scowled when he saw Collier. "You have metals today?"

"Sorry. Big bonus didn't come in. But you know I'm good for it."

"Listen, Col, I don't want to have to say this again. You—"

"I know, I know. Credit's running out. Never mind the Tank 8 stuff. I'll just take a tenth-liter of the clay."

"No, dammit, not 'running out.' Gone. You're way past my limit."

"Yeah? Well, I'm not past mine. Gimme."

Phil's scowl softened. "Col, I can't. I'm trying to run a business here. You have to understand that."

"Why? Why do I have to understand that?" Collier knew he was being petulant, but he was beyond caring.

"Because you know what it means. Come on," Phil said, changing tactics. His voice was wheedling. "You know how tight it can get. How close you can be to, well…"

"Losing everything? Going under? Turning into a worthless trasher? 'Yes, sir?' 'Right away, sir?' 'Let me find you that piece of shit fusion accelerator from a '31 Salus?'"

Phil just looked at him for a moment, then shook his head. "You didn't have to become a trasher. All kinds of corps looking for experienced hands. Ad Astra, Horizon…"

"They wouldn't have me," Collier said.

"Of course they would," Phil said. "Seasoned beltrunner like you? You'd be valuable. It's not too late, Col. You can still join—"

"Never," Collier said. "Never joining a corp. What do you care, anyway?"

"I don't like seeing you like this."

"Plus, you want to get paid."

Phil shrugged. "Is that a crime?"

Collier shook his head. "'Course not, Phil. But I got my principles."

"That's all you got."

"It's all I need," Collier said, feeling the hollowness of the statement. But it was easier, far easier, to pretend than to confront the yawning chasm in his soul where Su had been. Despite all his efforts to forget, he could still see her, still feel her. That both increased and lessened the pain of remembering these past twelve months.

Worse than the memory of Su, was the memory of the friend whom he had abandoned months ago. Su had been taken from him, and the pain of that tore at him even as his memory still served. But his true friend, his loyal companion, more human than anyone he'd ever known … Collier had abandoned him.

Phil cleared his throat. "Listen, Col, I could maybe scrape up a few metals for you—"

Collier snapped his head up to glare at Phil. "No," he said, slapping the faux wood of the bar and rebounding slightly in the low gravity. "Don't you goddam look at me like that. Don't gimme those pity eyes. Like you're looking at a man one step away from selling his piss at half a metal a liter. Shout at me, call the Authority to have me taken away, or punch me in the mouth, but don't look at me like that, Phil!"

"All right, goddammit, you want me to say what I think? I offer you charity, and you spit it back? I'll bust your worthless rummy head in, how's that? Get the fuck out of here, Collier, and the next time you come in, you'd better have the metals you owe me!"

Collier floated backward, away from Phil's rage. "I'm not coming back here," he grunted. He had made that same proclamation at least half a dozen times before. This time, though, Phil had seemed more sincere in his rejection. Maybe this was goodbye.

Collier pivoted in mid-air, still an able spaceman despite his condition, and toed off towards the pub's entry hatch. As he approached, two orange-jumpsuited Horizon Consortium agents floated inside. Collier grabbed one of the many handholds situated around the hatchway and propelled himself through the opening, knocking the two Horizon agents to the side as he sailed past. One of them thumped him on the back as he passed, and Collier went cartwheeling through the passageway outside the Point. He could hear the laughter of the Horizon miners and he scrabbled frantically for a railing to steady himself.

Once Collier righted himself, he proceeded at a more civilized pace through the passageway towards the upshaft beyond. When he reached the junction, he found a shitbum lying motionless there.

Collier grabbed a railing and nudged the figure with his toe. "Come on, man. Don't let 'em see you like this." The figure twisted gently in the air from Collier's nudge. His face came into view — a filthy, bearded visage with wide open, unblinking and unseeing eyes deeply set in the wrinkled face. Even in Ceres' microgravity, wrinkles showed.

Collier pushed back instinctively, fetching up against the opposite wall of the passageway. How long had this man been floating here, dead? The Horizon agents now seated comfortably at the Point must have passed by him, never noticing his condition, if they had even noticed him at all. Collier thought he should return to the Trojan Point to report the death, but he didn't want another run-in with Phil. He'd have to contact the Authority himself.

As he dug out his work-issued comm unit, he realized that he'd be implicating himself: he was supposed to be at work.

The dead man's eyes rotated back into view. Collier shook himself off and called in.

When he'd finished, Collier looked at the dead body. It took another minute, but Collier realized he'd seen this man before, across Phil's bar, telling old beltrunner stories, and running low on metals. "Sorry, fella. You're going into the vats. But at least you'll be of use in death."

The thought was not as comforting as he had hoped it would be.

He probably should have left after making the call for pickup. But someone needed to accompany this man on his way to the reclamation vats. Bad enough to die here alone, unnoticed. At least when he was sent his reward — no matter how paltry it might be — someone would be with him.

Half an hour later, the Authority officers floated up from the lower levels. Collier was about to berate them for their tardiness until he saw the dark, coiled hair of Agent Lora Fletcher rise up from the shaft, her bureaucratic body following.

"Agent Fletcher," Collier said with a curt nod.

"Mister South," she responded, placing the faintest emphasis on the honorific. "What happened?" She cleared the shaft, two Authority workers drifting up after her.

"I don't know," Collier said. "I just found him here."

Fletcher looked at the passage wall, with the faintly glowing arrow bearing the legend "The Trojan Point." She looked back at Collier, making no attempt to hide her disappointment. She said in a tired voice, "Do you know who he is?"

Collier shook his head. "No. But I've seen him around. Just another old beltrunner, or what used to be one," he said, then snorted. "So I guess I do know who he is, don't I, Fletcher?"

Fletcher ignored that. She half turned to her agents and said, "See if you can determine his identity."

"You think he's got a sub-q chip?" Collier said, smirking.

"Most of us do," she said.

"Not me."

"No. Not you," Fletcher said evenly.

One of the Authority workers shook his head as he passed a scanner over the dead man's body. "Nothing, ma'am. He's not showing up."

"Okay. Take him down to the morgue. We'll run an autopsy."

The two workers began stuffing the corpse into a black body bag while Collier watched. As the workers twisted the old man's unresisting limbs into the bag, Collier turned to Fletcher. "Autopsy? For an old shitbum? His organics will barely recover the cost of the procedure."

"I want to know how he died," Fletcher said, fixing Collier with her characteristic unreadable stare.

"Malnutrition, cirrhosis, cardiovascular disease, take your pick." His eyes narrowed. "Or are you suggesting that I might have had something to do with it?"

Fletcher turned again to her subordinates, who were wrestling the body to the downshaft. She silently watched them descend, then turned back to Collier. "No, I don't." Again, the silent gaze.

"I'm free to go, then?" Collier said.

"No. Come with me."

"Where?"

"My office. We need to talk."

"I don't want to talk. Besides, I have work."

"You left your shift to come here. Come on," she repeated, and began to float towards the downshaft.

"Unless you're placing me under arrest, Agent Fletcher, I don't have to go with you," Collier said, making no move to follow.

Fletcher stopped, hovering above the downshaft, her hand on the dull metal pole that ran the depth of the shaft. "You owe me this and a whole lot more. Come on." She pushed off and descended.

"God dammit," Collier murmured. She was right. Plus, if she really wanted to get him downshaft, she could just send a couple of agents to collect him later. There was no real point resisting now just to have to buckle under later. Besides, he technically worked for her.

Collier followed.

——— «‹›» ———

The Ceres Authority warrens had lost whatever distinction they'd once had as the space had been gradually taken over by more and more corporate legal branches. The merging of corporate interests with what had once been an independent and — if Collier's parents' stories could be trusted — noble Belt government had long since turned lopsided. Now, the Authority was little more than a few dozen agents scattered across various necessary functions that the corporations had not yet decided to monetize, like the Authority salvage yard.

Little had changed since Collier had last been in Fletcher's office. She still managed to combine efficiency with clutter: he could see notes written to herself on erasable surfaces, bits of nickelpaper reports tethered to her desk, spot-welds in places where hurried repairs or refurbishments had been made over time.

Despite what it represented, he liked her office. It reminded him of his life. Or his former life.

Fletcher tapped a few keys on the physical keyboard before turning to him. "Ulmiter is pissed at you."

Collier snorted. "Wouldn't be a day that ends in 'Y' without him being pissed at me."

"He says you lost something. A scouter?"

Collier shrugged. "So?"

Fletcher's impassive face showed signs of frustration. "What the hell do you want, Collier?"

"Right now? Some Tank 8, if you have it."

"Knock it off," she said, more tired than angry. "I don't understand you."

"What's to understand?"

"A year ago, you came back here with the greatest find the System has ever known. Or so you claimed. I'm still not sure what it was I saw that day on your ship."

Collier swallowed. He hadn't expected her to bring up the past like that. "The magic wand. Yeah, I remember."

"Then, you do some crazy-old-beltrunner routine in the quad, shouting to everyone you have the secret to bring down the corporations. What the hell were you thinking?"

Collier fought the memory, but it came rushing back to him. He remembered the faces of the men and women floating in the various levels of the quadrangle, the heart of Ceres' commercial and social life. He remembered their laughter and derision when he had tried to show them how the transmuter worked, creating gold, platinum, rhodium upon command. No one had believed him, and in hindsight, he couldn't blame them for their skepticism. What would he himself have thought, hearing an old beltrunner shout about a modern-day Philosopher's Stone?

"I guess I wasn't thinking. Just had some wild idea that I could change the way things were. A change for the better."

Fletcher looked at him with soft eyes. "Yeah. Sure." She glanced at her computer screen again, then said, "Then you took off. You know what kind of hell you put me through here?"

Collier frowned. "What do you mean? I got my ass off Ceres. I'd have thought you would have welcomed the peace and quiet of my absence."

"Except you almost killed Captain Rahford."

"In self-defense."

Fletcher glared at him. "Do you know what kind of a pain in the ass it was to write that report? Fluorine poisoning? Did you think I was going to be able to report to the surgeon on the *Clara Barton* that this corp captain just happened to run into a cloud of fluorine that was floating around your ship? The inquiry on that whole mess took two months of my life."

Collier chewed his lip. He'd thought about that, a little, when he'd fled Ceres shortly after the whole incident, and Fletcher's indignant reminder made his lingering guilt flare to life. "Listen, I know that caused a whole shitstorm for you, but, dammit, that was the point! I had to shake things up. The corps had — and still have — a stranglehold on the whole Belt that's choking the life out of us. And out of you, too, Fletcher."

"Don't give me that," she spat, showing a sudden spike in emotion. "You're no fan of law and order. You'd like to see the Authority go away as much as the corps do."

Collier rubbed his stubble. He suddenly felt very tired. "You didn't bring me here to debate politics. Why did you want to see me?"

Fletcher continued to glare at him, then her face returned to the impassive mask she almost always wore. "Fine. You know that transmuter thing was never found."

"What do you mean, never found? What makes you think I don't still have it?"

Fletcher's lips grew thin. "Don't play games. If you had it, you wouldn't have crawled back here with a lien placed against your ship."

Collier's tiredness vanished as he objected forcefully, "A lien that expressly said no one could sell *Dulcinea* without—"

"Ad Astra bought it out."

"Because the Authority let them!" he shouted back. The two of them were hovering less than three feet apart. He could feel her breath on his face. He wanted to reach back into the past and untie the legal knots that had bound him and had allowed the corporation to outright purchase the title to *Dulcinea*. "Just like always. You Authority types. You can't do anything. Corporation says jump, you say 'how high?'"

Fletcher stared at him, her jaw working silently. Presently, she cleared her throat and said in a low voice, "Now look. I didn't tell you this at the time, partially because I was under orders not to, and partially because it was none of your damn business. But I look at you now, what's happened to you, what you've lost—"

"Cut it," Collier said, pushing off the corner of her desk and floating away from her. He spun slowly in the air, stopping himself when he was facing away from her. He didn't want her to see him remembering Su. She'd note the sorrow and wonder at it.

"You never realized why the Authority — why I agreed to the sale. It was … compensation."

"Compensation? For what?"

"For your attack on Captain Rahford."

Collier pushed off the back wall and spun to face her.

Fletcher continued. "They agreed not to press charges and forget the whole thing in exchange for your ship."

Collier was dumbfounded. "You … you're saying … they used *Dulcinea* as ransom?"

Fletcher shrugged. "If you want to call it that, yeah."

"But … why? What use does Ad Astra have for her?"

Fletcher said, "I think they wanted to search her. Rahford must have reported to them what had happened, told them about the transmuter."

"He didn't believe it," Collier said.

"He did once you jammed it into his helmet and force-fed him a lungful of fluorine."

Collier felt the puzzle pieces of his life fitting into place. He'd always thought the corp had bought out the lien as just a way of turning the knife in him, but, if Fletcher was telling the truth, it meant that Ad Astra believed that the magic wand did work. Or had enough of a suspicion to check it out for themselves.

Fletcher was continuing. "So, like I said, they never found it. And you don't have it, because you would have come back from your little temper tantrum-exile with a hold full of rhodium. You could have cleared your debt in no time."

"It stopped working," Collier said. "Shortly after I left here. Couldn't get it to produce anything."

Fletcher studied him for a long moment, then finally said, "If that's the case, then you'd better let Ad Astra know. Just in case they're still looking for it."

"I will."

"And, since you say it stopped working, you wouldn't mind handing it over to us, then? Even if it's not functional, we'd be very interested in seeing it."

"I spaced it."

Fletcher smiled humorlessly. "Let's stop playing games. Maybe it stopped working, maybe not. But even if that were the case, you wouldn't space it. You know how valuable it is. So, either you've still got it and it's not working, or you lost it somehow. And I very much doubt you'd just lose something like that. So, since I've done so much for you—"

"Like letting Ad Astra take *Dulcinea* away?"

"Like arranging to keep you from a tribunal where you'd probably have been sent as a corpsicle to Mars penal, you mean. Like that. And getting you the job at the yard—"

"Yeah. Thanks a million for that fine career opportunity."

Fletcher raised her voice. "And keeping Ad Astra from ripping your guts open to see if you swallowed the damn artifact. You're a marked man, South. You may think no one took you seriously after your little one-man revolutionary speech, but too many people know too much to toss it all aside as fantasy."

Her uncharacteristic passion stunned Collier: she was scared. Scared that what little control she had on this ball of rock in the lawless vacuum of the Belt was slipping out of her grasp. Collier knew her. She was not scared of losing power for its own sake. She was scared about what would happen if the fragile peace between legitimate law and corporate control shattered. All because of the magic wand.

One mystery remained — a mystery Collier had purposefully refused to pursue these past months. Where had Barney Starcher gone? He had assumed he'd simply fled to Luna, or possibly Pallas, taking the wand with him and trying to make his fortune with it, but there was nothing to justify that assumption. All Collier knew was that when he last came limping back to Ceres, his luck and biologicals having run out, the tiny banker's kiosk had been dark and vacant.

Collier knew one thing: as much as he might have a grudging respect for Lora Fletcher, he could not tell her he had left the wand with Starcher. His respect did not extend to that level of trust. "Is that why you brought me down here? To tell me about why I lost *Dulcinea*?"

Fletcher fixed him with her unreadable stare, then said. "Just watch yourself. Ad Astra has a long memory. And if you know where the device is..."

"I don't."

Fletcher sighed. "Fine. I was trying to give you a friendly warning. But if you're going to be like that, we've got nothing more to say."

A part of him wanted to tell Fletcher everything, to try and buy her friendship with the truth about the magic wand, about Starcher, about what had happened on Ganymede.

Like so much else in his life, he had tried hard to forget that place. The cold, androgynous scientists who had wanted his help in staving off a genetic stalemate of their own creation. The body horror of a threatened medical procedure, no matter how painless and innocuous, performed against his will. The all too brief romance with Su. Her death on the ice-covered plains of the satellite.

And Sancho's heroic decision.

He could bear all of it but the last. He only had a dim idea of what his faithful computer companion had given up in his relationship with Perditus, the computer complex controlling the abandoned launch facility that had been the key to getting them home.

Even now, Sancho's words echoed in his memory: "I'm your friend. Always have been, always will be." How could he have let them take *Dulcinea*, and Sancho, away from him?

"Well?" Fletcher snapped.

"I heard you." Collier said. "So, Ad Astra is coming for me. That's nothing new."

Fletcher leaned forward, her voice deadly serious. "I've done what I can for you up till now. But I am not able nor willing to risk whatever stability I've established on Ceres on behalf of some old beltrunner who doesn't have the sense to do what's best for himself."

Collier nodded slowly, a bitter retort forming in his mind. But Fletcher was right; she'd done what she could for him, and how had he repaid her? With resentment and self-destructiveness. "You always did try to do right by me, Fletcher," he sighed. "God knows why."

"You think you're the only one who sees the way things are going and wishes they were different," Fletcher murmured. "You're not, you know. I just don't know how to make things different. So I..." she gestured vaguely at her office, the nickelfilm papers a testament to her efforts.

"Yeah. Well," Collier said, gently pushing off from the wall and seizing the hatch railing, "thanks for ... you know. Everything, I guess. I'd better get back to the yard and find that scouter. Assuming I still have a job there."

Fletcher chuckled once. "I'll tell Ulmiter I chewed your ass out. He'll like that. Watch your back, Collier."

"I will. Thanks."

Chapter Two

Collier floated aimlessly around the empty halls. So, Captain Rahford had lived, and someone in Ad Astra had believed his report. Maybe they'd also been suspicious of Collier's sales — when he'd turned in those pure samples, he'd caused a bit of a stir. Then there was his polemic against corporate culture in which he tried to demonstrate the workings of the wand. In hindsight, now that he knew what Fletcher knew, it was obvious they'd come for him. He'd been too wrapped up in his escape into space, and then his escape into alcohol, to notice.

Had they dismantled *Dulcinea* entirely? Ripped her stem to stern, looking for hidden compartments? He shuddered at the thought. Somehow, it was more comforting to believe that she was still in service, even with another master, than to think she'd been destroyed. Was Sancho still operational? Even if the ship had been gutted, had he been transferred to another vessel? If so, which one? How could he ever hope to find him then?

One way or another, *Dulcinea* and Sancho were gone. What mattered now was that Ad Astra knew, or suspected, the true nature of the magic wand but hadn't found it. So why hadn't they searched Starcher's office? Collier's relationship with the banker wasn't a secret, and in any case, they would have had to purchase the lien from Starcher to get title of *Dulcinea*. Could they have been so obtuse as to miss that connection?

No. The corporations were many things, but they were not stupid. If Ad Astra thought there was an alien artifact floating around in Ceres that could transmute any element into any other element, they would stop at nothing to get their hands on it. But they would have to do it with subtlety, lest their competitors get wind of what they were up to. The Horizon Consortium was their biggest rival, and they were just as shrewd and cutthroat as Ad Astra was.

Collier smiled as he exited the upshaft on the first subsurface level, then started towards the salvage yard office. It would be satisfyingly ironic if Ad Astra had been thwarted in their attempts to steal the wand by their rivalries with other corporations.

He had to find Starcher. And he had to do it while avoiding Ad Astra corporation thugs who were almost certainly watching him. A chill ran down his spine as he realized that there had been only two things that had been keeping the corp from kidnapping him and forcing the location of the wand out of him: the thin layer of protection Ceres Authority extended him, and the need to keep from alerting the other corporations to his value.

Fletcher had just told him she could no longer protect him. How long before Ad Astra decided they were done waiting?

He stopped at the entrance to the yard office: inside, Ulmiter would be waiting for him with a lecture. Instead, he veered back towards the quadrangle where Starcher's shuttered loan office was located.

The multicolored lights beckoning miners and other Ceres workers into entertainment establishments played across Collier's worn coveralls in odd patterns. Women and men in suggestive costumes writhed sensually near the double hatchway of the Sacellum Volupiae, Ceres' most successful nightclub. The SV — as locals called it — was far beyond the reach of Collier's wallet even when he had been doing well: now it might as well have been on Mercury. He glanced into the dark recesses of the club; one of the writhing lures outside beckoned to him with an outstretched finger.

He worked past the various kiosks hawking semimystical rockfinders to wide-eyed, young corpses who hadn't quite jettisoned the superstitions of the Belt. He tried not to smile as he heard the pitch one old crone was making to a clean-shaven Horizon man: "Behold, a fragment of the Ruined Planet, long believed to be the true source of the Belt! Whomever possesses this fragment will find fortune smiling upon him!"

Collier moved on. The Ruined Planet myth was one of the oldest and silliest ones still alive in the Belt. He didn't begrudge the charlatans and con artists making their living selling worthless carbon to new fish, especially corpses: on the contrary, he found it a refreshing subversion of capitalism. *Caveat emptor*, indeed.

He finally floated his way to Starcher's office front, wedged between the Bank of Mars and the Jovian Credit Union. It was still dark and bore the same sign indicating Starcher's absence. Collier looked around quickly, but the quad was so crowded, with people floating up, down, left and right, that there was no way to tell if anyone was watching him. He tried the door panel, but the faint red ring of light around it indicated its locked status.

Again, Collier checked his surroundings, then, with his left hand shielding the keypad from any prying eyes, he rapidly entered the access code — a gift from Sancho all those months ago when Collier had first broken into Starcher's office to leave the wand.

Collier again pressed the panel, and the red light changed to green. He opened the sliding panel door, knifed his way inside, and closed the door behind him. The office was dark, the only light coming from the quad through the shopfront's frosted glass window. Collier dared not turn on the lights, lest he advertise his presence in what was supposed to be a sealed office. He took a small lightmoth from the pocket of his overalls, adjusted it to minimum intensity, then tossed it into the air in front of him. The tiny robotic light hovered, casting a dim but usable light by which he could just make out shapes.

The air was musty, with a hint of rancid meat. Collier sniffed experimentally, waiting for his eyes to adjust to the dimness. Whatever food Starcher had kept here had obviously gone bad.

As his eyes adjusted to the semi-darkness, he saw the office had been tossed. The workstation chair was overturned, desk drawers opened, and nickelfilm gels scattered about the room. It was plain that someone had searched the place, and roughly.

He floated past the small conference room where he had spent many hours pleading, cajoling, and browbeating the meek little banker to extend him credit on *Dulcinea* for one more month. The conference room had also been tossed: even the upholstery on the chairs had been ripped open.

The rear of the establishment was, like most businesses in the quad, living quarters. Space was at such a premium on Ceres that few people could afford to work and live separately. Collier was only granted that privilege — if a four-by-four sleep pod was a privilege — due to his work at the yard. Starcher's living area was compact but well-apportioned, with a small kitchenette, toilet facility, and bedroom all efficiently laid out.

Starcher's kitchen supplies were strewn about, tossed carelessly in Ceres' microgravity to come to rest far from their starting points. Clothing was also scattered throughout the living room and kitchen.

The smell of rotten meat was more pronounced in the living area, and Collier saw the midsize refrigerator unit in the middle of the kitchen. Unlike the rest of the doors and drawers, the fridge door was shut.

Collier surveyed the room, hands on his hips as his feet came slowly to rest on the floor. Someone had been looking for the wand. There was no other explanation that made any sense. Starcher hadn't an enemy in the whole System — that had been most of the reason he was an unsuccessful banker. He wanted to be everyone's friend. If someone had wanted to try and rob him, they would have done so electronically. There was no reason for a break-in, since there was nothing of value to steal, at least not in physical possessions.

Nothing except the magic wand.

Collier kicked off the ground and floatwalked back to the office, while the lightmoth followed. The search had been thorough, yes, but assuming the would-be burglars had started in the office and worked backwards, that meant they hadn't found the wand in the office. Could they have missed it?

He floated to the conference room, navigating the disorder, and maneuvered his way under the glass-top table. The square deckplates of the floor looked unremarkable, but he knew better. Sancho's override had provided Collier with more than the front door access code.

The rivets on one particular deckplate, though they looked exactly like the others, Collier knew to be buttons on an unwieldy sort of keypad. He hoped he remembered the sequence. He jabbed at the rivet-buttons, and after two failed attempts, heard the click of success. One edge of the deckplate rose slightly, allowing him to swing it open and access the contents inside.

And there it was. A white tube, gleaming even in the dull glow of the lightmoth. The only alien artifact known to humankind.

The magic wand.

Collier reached into the shallow recess and withdrew it, cradling it reverently in his hands. He shut the safe door and ran his fingers across the surface of the tube, aware that there were control surfaces on it that were outside his normal field of vision. They would become visible in UV light, and through their manipulations, he could change matter placed inside to whatever element he wished.

He recalled with a pang of regretful nostalgia how he and Sancho had worked out the schematics of the tube. It had been the strike of a lifetime, and it had brought ruin to him and to everything he loved.

Whoever had searched the place hadn't found this. If Barney Starcher had indeed left Ceres, he wouldn't have done so without the magic wand. The artifact still gripped tightly in one hand, Collier floatwalked back to the kitchenette and regarded the closed door of the fridge, the smell of rotting meat emanating ominously from it. He was suddenly reminded of the time on Vesta when he'd opened a sleeping bag on the derelict ship he'd encountered to find the decaying remains of a human male.

Bracing himself, he yanked open the fridge door. Immediately, he gagged on the sour smell of decaying flesh: there, stuffed inside the kitchenette refrigerator, was Barney Starcher.

Collier slammed the door shut and kicked back forcefully, smashing into the opposite wall of the kitchenette and rebounding into the living room. He reached out and grabbed a rail, oriented himself, and kicked off again through the living room and office, heading for the front door. His blood pounded in his ears, and he could feel his heart thumping against his ribs.

Upon reaching the front door, he stopped, panting, and tried to calm himself. "Barney, God, I'm sorry," he murmured. "I never thought…" he stopped and shook his head as if to clear it. Barney was dead, killed no doubt by the same people looking for the wand. Obviously, he hadn't told them where it was.

"Good for you, Barn. Good for you. That's the way to show those Ad Astra bastards," he said, looking back towards the kitchenette. It had to be them. Only Ad Astra and Ceres Authority knew that the wand was real. His stunt in the quad so long ago when he had brandished the wand had been regarded as the ravings of a lunatic, but Ad Astra and Fletcher had known better.

How long ago had they tossed the place and killed poor Barney? Collier could have gone back to examine the body, but his gorge rose at the mere thought of it. Besides, he reasoned, he was no forensic expert. All he could remember was how discolored Starcher's body had been, and how much it had stunk. Did that mean it had been a week? A month? Six months? Did the airtight fridge make a difference to the rate of decomposition? He didn't really know. The only thing he was certain of was that Starcher was dead, the Ad Astra people had killed him, and they had looked for but failed to find the magic wand.

Barney Starcher might not have been the most astute businessman in the System, but he had been a good man. He deserved better than this. Collier was loath to leave the body of his staunch friend, stuffed ignominiously into a refrigerator, but if the place was being watched, he had to leave as soon as possible. "I'll get 'em back for you, Barn. Don't worry," he murmured, then seized his lightmoth and shut it off. The room was once again plunged into near-total darkness.

Collier opened the outer door and slid out. Holding the wand so it was half-tucked into his coveralls, he tried to enter the mass of floating humanity as smoothly as possible. Banker's Row was busy enough, and he blended into a knot of fresh-faced young corpses who were just emerging from the JCU, each one talking excitedly about the line of credit they had established. Collier floated along behind them, using the cover of their bodies to scan the quad as he went. He made his way to the upshaft and seized a ring with his free hand.

Another passenger was rising with him, holding the same upshaft ring, and when he made eye contact, the woman merely nodded and looked away. Collier was suddenly aware of how visible the magic wand was — the woman had taken no notice of it, but her age and air of familiarity with the quad made Collier wonder if she had been present for his rantings those many months ago. Even if she didn't recognize him, there were others who would: the vacc suit repair man, Patches; biological suppliers whom he had bargained with over the years; and more than a few Authority agents. If he wanted to get out with the wand unnoticed, he'd had to avoid any such interaction.

The ring carried him past the shops and still upward, now reaching into the refueling and supply levels. One more and he'd be at the first subsurface level, the uppermost level beyond was the surface of Ceres itself, and the only thing there was the salvage yard. Collier had to think, away from Authority and Ad Astra's prying eyes, and the closest place where he could do that was the yard office. He wasn't on cycle for his sleep pod — the other renter would probably be in it now.

He reached the salvage yard office without incident and relieved the thankful trasher who was on-shift and thus had the office to himself. He settled back to think.

He had the magic wand. Now what?

He turned it over in his hands, letting it spin in microgravity while he thought. Dare he use it to make a few metals? Phil would appreciate payment on the bar tab, for one. But how was he supposed to sell anything? Just walk up to one of the small-fry orethrowers with a handful of gold? Or buy something valuable from a vendor with pure platinum, then sell the item? He knew little about money laundering, and in any case, word would get out that he was trading in P's again. He might make one or two sales, but sooner or later, he'd be found out. And even if Ad Astra had given up their search, they'd resume it quickly. Fletcher had already said she wouldn't be able to protect him any more.

He regarded the alien artifact, spinning lazily in the air before him. The most powerful, important find in the System, possibly in human history, and it was worthless to him. Worse than worthless — it was a curse. Poor Barney had been murdered for it. Collier had given it to him as repayment for not just the mountain of monetary debt Collier had accrued over the years, but also as repayment for unreturned friendship. Collier had been a terrible friend to the man — he'd thought that somehow the magic wand would in some small way erase that. Instead, he had signed Barney's death warrant with the gift.

Collier wrenched his mind away from those dark thoughts and returned to the same questions he had had regarding the wand since he'd found it. Who had built it? And why? A technology capable of matter transmutation would surely use it on a much larger scale than a handheld device. What use was a handful of palladium or a puff of argon? Why keep this thing so small?

And how was it powered? It took enormous amounts of energy to change atomic structure. How could such a small device generate so much energy?

Any corporation would pay handsomely to get a look at this, he knew. He could sell it to any number of private science concerns and live comfortably for the rest of his life. Furthermore, he would have an end to the chase. No one would care about who used to own the magic wand. He could retire to one of the habitats in Earth orbit, watching starball games and sipping real whiskey.

There was, of course, the tiny matter of being able to actually get to Earth. Book passage on a sunbound ship? There were very few of those, and with what metal could he afford the trip? Besides, he'd have to go through the corps for that, and he'd be at their mercy while aboard. Stowaway on a rockthrower? Hide in one of the drone ships that was sending ore back to Earth? Little more than giant canisters of metal, unpressurized, no personnel aboard? He might as well try to walk to Earth. He could try to send a message to Earth, see if he could arrange for some kind of deal where they'd pick him up. He snorted. Assuming it wasn't intercepted by Ad Astra. And even if it wasn't, he couldn't trust the Earth Science Directorate. After Ganymede, he didn't feel like trusting any scientist.

More than the simple impracticality of selling the artifact was his resistance to part with it. When he'd given it to Starcher, he thought the banker would be able to do with it what Collier couldn't — figure out how to use it to make real change. Now that he had it again, and Barney was dead, he wanted to keep it. It had never sat well with him that even though he and Sancho had figured out how to work it, he'd never figured out how to *use* it.

He knew that turning it over to scientists could probably result in discoveries that might advance human knowledge in ways he could not fathom. But the stubborn, individualistic streak in him told him that he couldn't turn it over yet — not before he had figured it out himself. And then ... who knows? Maybe he'd decide the eggheads were the best ones to have it. But for now, despite all the tragedy it had caused him and those near him, he still wanted to keep it.

He was being foolish. But even that realization could not overcome his own stubbornness.

———— «» ————

Four days had not brought any new insights. On the other hand, he had not been shot at or knifed on his daily trips between the office and his sleep pod, so either Ad Astra was content to just watch him, or perhaps they had given up the chase when they had failed to find the wand at Starcher's office.

Every time he thought of how he'd left Barney's body stuffed into the refrigerator, his stomach knotted with guilt. He couldn't tell Fletcher: an Authority investigation would alert Ad Astra that someone had been poking around. Fletcher wouldn't be able to bring charges against the corporation no matter what evidence she uncovered. Any attention would simply put himself in danger. He had to help himself, and that meant leaving the body where it was. He had to put his guilt over Barney's death in the same place he'd put the sorrow over Su. Killing the scientist, Tacat, who was responsible for Su's death on the icy plains of Ganymede, hadn't lessened that pain one iota. He wasn't sure anything could.

He had to do something. He just didn't know what. It was maddening knowing he had a source of unlimited wealth in the magic wand — wealth that, once accessed, would sign his death warrant. He'd spent the last four days assembling his meager assets, and that had amounted to nothing.

Until the fifth day.

———— «» ————

"Ceres salvage yard, this is inbound flight seven-seven-seven light. Do you read?"

Collier checked his screen. He had the inbound on his scope at extreme range. "I read you five-by-five, trips seven. What do you need?"

"I just completed salvage sale through Ceres Authority. They sent me to you for drop off. Where do you want me to put this piece of shit?"

"Say again, trips seven. What do you need?"

"I need to know where to drop this goddam thing. I just sold it for a tenth what I bought it for. Just tell me where to put it and I'll be done. Never want to see this fuckin' ship again."

Collier grinned slightly at the man's rage. Another dupe had been suckered into buying a secondhand ship, hoping he'd strike it big in the Belt only to discover that beltrunning was not the glamorous, profitable life he'd been told it was. This guy would go home, tail between his legs, out maybe a million, million five, and bitch to his mates that there was no more romance in the system.

"Copy that, trips seven. I have you on approach. Reduce speed to ten meters per second and hold. Will advise when I find you a place to set down."

He scanned the yard for an empty spot, but there were no areas large enough close to the lock. Collier would have to send him to the periphery, which would only serve to annoy him further. Collier activated the radio again. "Sorry, trips seven, but all I've got is section 'F,' zone three. Sending you coordinates now." He punched the code and waited with a grimace.

"Goddamit, you're sending me a fuckin' kilometer away! You don't have anything closer?"

"Again, sorry, trips seven. That's the closest I've got."

"Fuck. Coordinates received. Setting course."

"You can just give it over to your computer," Collier said. "It can talk to Ceres itself and drive you."

"Not this motherfucker," came the angry rejoinder. "I don't trust this thing at all. Malfunctions every two seconds, can't hold a simple vector. I'm doing this manually."

Collier sighed. He should probably take the buggy out to meet this guy. His amusement at the man's irritation and vulgarity had given way to a sort of comradeship. Yeah, the incoming captain was probably a dilettante, but he had given beltrunning a shot. He deserved at least a buggy ride before he gave it all up.

Collier confirmed the ship's touchdown on his screen and secured his console. Normally, Collier enjoyed taking the buggy out. It was a change of pace that sometimes reminded him of his old life. Cruising on the surface of Ceres, the grey, powdery ground below him, nothing but black space above — it stirred memories. Even putting on the vacc suit had been nostalgic. Now, he was far too preoccupied with the magic wand and everything around him to enjoy the excursion. He drove the little hovercar expertly through the piles of scrap and debris and headed for the outlying sections of the yard.

He was approaching sector F according to the buggy's tiny dashboard readout. Amid the towering piles of broken machinery that littered the yard he was unable to see the ship, but his radar told him he was close.

Collier banked the buggy to maneuver around the last of the scrap piles and saw the vessel, tail-down, standing alone in the periphery of the yard.

He slammed down on the brake jets of the buggy.

There, standing before him, was *Dulcinea*.

She had changed, but was still beautiful. Even from two hundred meters away, he could see alterations in her hull: the hold had been increased, which gave her the appearance of having put on some weight, and there was a sensor array near the nose he didn't immediately recognize. But it was her, right down to the thrust tubes.

"This is Captain Opunui," Collier heard in his helmet speaker. "Is that you in the land transport? What's the trouble? Why've you stopped?"

Collier used his chin plate to respond. "Yeah, it is. Sorry — I just had … nothing. Everything's fine. I'll be there to pick you up in a minute." He resumed his approach at a leisurely pace, taking in his old ship as he came closer.

"I'm exiting," Opunui said. "Meet you at the airlock. Oh, and if you feel like you need target practice, feel free to shoot at it," he added.

As Collier approached, he saw the outer airlock door open and a suited figure emerge, holding a large crate.

The closer he got, the more detail he saw: spot-welds, discolorations, entire hull plates patched in: *Dulcinea* had been worked over quite a bit. He frowned at the roughness of the work. That was no way to treat her.

He pulled the buggy close to his old ship and waited for Captain Opunui to stow his baggage. He was wearing a newer generation vacc suit, but Collier noted it was more of a tourist's rig than a beltrunner design.

Collier said casually, "Sounds like you didn't have a lot of luck with her."

"No," Opunui said. "Worst investment of my life."

"How did you come to buy her?"

"Ad Astra was looking to unload it. They offered it to me cheap. Still overpriced."

"How much?"

"What, are you writing a book?" Opunui asked, clearly irritated. He climbed into the buggy and Collier pointed them back towards the yard lock.

"They're known for shady deals," Collier said.

Opunui scoffed, but continued. "Well, they got me, all right. That thing was nonstop problems. Thrust tube burst on my first flight. Couldn't figure out the ladar system. Electrolysis plant never worked right. You name it, that shitwagon broke down. And the onboard computer was a joke."

"Oh yeah?" Collier said, fighting to keep his voice even.

"Kept needing to have instructions repeated. Usually didn't know what I meant. They said it was a fully conversant model, even if it was used. But it felt like talking to a six-year-old."

"Lots of psuedopersonality problems, huh?" Collier said.

"No personality at all. The Ad Astra guys said they'd done a total reset so that I wouldn't have to deal with the old owner's shit. They said that was standard procedure."

Collier swallowed in a suddenly dry throat.

"Isn't it?" Opunui asked.

"Yeah, sure," Collier managed to choke out. He had no idea if a computer reset was standard procedure or not: he wasn't even sure what would be involved in such a procedure. All he knew was that his most loyal friend had been lobotomized.

"Hey, watch out!" Opunui shrieked.

Collier hurriedly banked the hovercar and barely avoided colliding with a scrap pile. He eased the buggy to a stop near the yard lock.

"What's the matter with you?" Opunui demanded.

Collier paid him no mind and began to unstrap. They entered the lock and descended to the subsurface level. Collier hung his vacc suit helmet on the rack and began to cycle the hatchway back to the yard office.

"Hey, guy," Opunui barked, "I need a receipt for that piece of shit so I can get my salvage money."

Collier nodded and gestured for him to follow. He wordlessly printed out a receipt acknowledging that the ship had been delivered and handed it to Opunui. "It's also logged electronically. You shouldn't have any trouble. How much did you get for her?"

Opunui raised his chin belligerently. "I don't think that's any of your fuckin' business, guy," he said, clearly still shaken by Collier's hovercar piloting skills. He turned in mid-air and floatwalked away, heading for the downshaft. Collier had dismissed him already in his mind.

He looked at the camera footage of the salvage yard. He couldn't see her on his monitor, but he knew where she was relative to his position. She was out there, alone, waiting to be junked for parts.

He couldn't lose her, too. He didn't just need her to get off Ceres and escape the tightening net of intrigue that he could sense closing on him — he needed her as one last thing to hold on to from the past.

Opunui would be confirming the drop-off in a matter of moments, and *Dulcinea* would become the property of the Ceres Authority. That would certainly get Fletcher's attention, if it hadn't already. Come to think of it — if Opunui had sold the ship to Ceres for scrap, wouldn't Fletcher already know about the sale? Why hadn't she come to see Collier about it?

He swiveled in the control saddle and punched up information about the sale. There it was. Registry number 29111547-MDC, just like he remembered it. But the registered name of the ship was now *Waiwai Hoku*, whatever that meant. He scanned the history of the sale and found that she'd been sold from Ad Astra about three months ago. So they'd had her for about a month, probably taking her apart in search of the magic wand. They must have also asked Sancho about it. Not just asked him — used all kinds of methods to discover what he knew. Quisling programs, demonware, whatever it took. Maybe that's how they found out about Starcher.

Or maybe Sancho had resisted all attempts to pry information out of him and Ad Astra had gone to Starcher of their own accord. It was an attractive thought: Sancho giving the corp a huge electronic middle finger and going down fighting. Collier hoped it were true.

But more to the point, the ship had been sold and renamed. Had Fletcher lost track of her? Did she even care? He could approach *Dulcinea* without anyone else knowing, thanks to the incomplete camera coverage in the yard. He didn't know what would follow from that, but he knew that he had to see her again.

When the work shift ended, he entered the airlock and suited up as quickly as he could, then exited onto the surface, using his salvage yard identification. It would log his airlock access, but no one checked those logs. He had worked out his plan during his shift: the buggy would have been too conspicuous, so he made for the scrap piles on foot, skimming the surface until he managed to hide among the broken-down pieces of machinery. He knew where the cameras were, and what parts of the yard were obstructed from their view. The going was slow: he maneuvered around scrap piles, minding his suit integrity amid the sharp edges of metal that made up the jungle of refuse. A minor tear in his suit would force him to return to the lock at best — a bad tear would kill him before he could get one hundred paces.

He kept a close eye on his oxygen supply: every breath he took on the outbound journey to *Dulcinea* meant another one on the inbound trip back. He could not trust that Opunui had left her with air.

When he finally entered section F he could move more swiftly, and he covered the ground to *Dulcinea* in three bounds and slid his gauntleted hands across her skin.

"Hello, old girl," he said softly. He imagined he could feel her hull responding to his touch.

He made his way to the airlock and tried to open it. Unsurprisingly, the lock was unpowered. He accessed the manual wheel, braced himself, and began to turn it. It gave easily, and the outer airlock door began to open. Collier felt no escaping air from the lock, which again, was to be expected. Once the door was opened, he stepped inside and closed the door behind him, launching a lightmoth from his helmet to illuminate the interior.

The lock looked as it had when he had last seen it, but then, airlocks were fairly standard affairs. He made sure his suit speakers were broadcasting locally only and said, "Sancho?" His voice was an awkward squeak. He cleared his throat and composed himself, which was more difficult than he had expected, and repeated, "Sancho?"

Silence.

That didn't necessarily mean anything, he knew. Opunui had obviously powered down the ship, and had probably shut Sancho off as well. Unless he had bled the reactor completely, Collier should be able to power it back up.

The inner airlock hatch was already open. He stepped through, moving into the dressing room and continuing into the rest of *Dulcinea's* interior. Her overall internal structure was the same, but everything had been rearranged. The control suite had been repurposed into a more conventional setup, all of Collier's old modifications gone. He noted that the control saddle could no longer double as a sleep hammock, and that the displays were back in that same, bland, non-intuitive arrangement he'd changed to suit his tastes ages ago.

His suit's air supply indicator read sixty-four percent, and his atmosphere sniffer told him the ship itself was a near-vacuum, with only trace amounts of air. Opunui must have shut off the oxygenerators and let the air bleed out when he opened the airlock.

First things first: restarting the fusion reactor. He floated to the engineering section. It had been sectioned off by a bulkhead, something he'd never wanted to do. He knew the advantages of compartmentalization in a spacecraft: a hull breach, fire, or other localized problem could remain localized with pressure hatches.

But the added mass to the ship would slow her down, even slightly, and Collier had never felt like opening up six doors just to take a shit. Besides, it was expensive. Opunui had dumped a lot of metals into *Dulcinea*. No wonder he had been so pissed.

The hatchway to the reactor room had a new huge yellow radiation symbol emblazoned on it, which Collier snorted at. The radiation levels in a tokamak reactor were lower than background cosmic radiation levels. Captain Opunui had indeed been a rookie. Collier opened the hatchway and stepped into the tight reactor room, his lightmoth tagging along. A quick study of the reactor hard dials, which didn't need to be powered to give a reading, showed him everything he needed to know.

"Okay, so let's see if you remember the cold restart procedure," he murmured to himself. "Sancho, buddy, I could really use you." The wan hope that the computer would speak up dramatically at that moment faded as silence continued to reign in the ship, and Collier began the restart procedure as he recalled it.

"Okay. Hydrogen mix ... a little low, but adequate. Beginning deuterium/tritium mixture." He continued to mumble instructions to himself, checking the Lorentz force, keeping his twists and orbits ratio nice and high, and otherwise heating up the plasma to where pseudoheat could take over. He didn't really understand the concept of pseudoheat — Sancho had tried to explain it to him once, but the math was just too difficult.

"*Dulcinea*, old girl, I'm gonna turn you on," he said. "Try not to blow up at me, okay?" He threw the final switch and waited.

The ship didn't explode.

Once the power was holding steady at minimum levels, he set his suit to broadcast and said, "Sancho? Are you there? Computer?"

Chapter Three

He nearly jumped out of his skin when he heard a reply.

"Computer on," came the voice. It was reminiscent of his old friend, but flat and expressionless.

"Sancho?"

"I'm sorry, I don't recognize that word."

"Computer, do you recognize me?"

"I do not."

"I'm … it's Collier. Collier South. I used to be your skipper."

"Good day, Collier South."

Collier swallowed and tried to steady his breathing. He had to stick to business now. Don't let hope get in the way. "Computer, can you turn on the oxygenerators?"

"Yes," the computer voice said, then fell silent.

"Well?"

"I'm sorry, I said, 'yes.'"

Collier waited a moment, then realized his error. "Please turn on the oxygenerators."

"I'm sorry, Collier South. You do not have authorization for that command."

Collier felt the sting of realization. As a guest, he wouldn't have the ability to do much. Still, he had options. "It's an emergency, Sancho. I mean, Computer. I hereby override your guest protocols and declare an emergency. Turn on the oxygenerators."

"Emergency declared. Sending distress signal," came the voice.

"No! Cancel emergency!" Collier shouted.

"Emergency cancelled."

Collier sighed. There had been no panic, real or programmed, in the computer's voice as it responded to the emergency. Collier asked, "Did you send a distress signal?"

"I did not. The emergency was cancelled prior to transmission. Would you like to send a distress signal?"

"No. I would like the oxygenerators to go online without a declared emergency."

"I'm sorry, Collier South. Only Captain Opunui has authorization for that operation."

"So, what would happen if a guest were trapped in here, suffocating because the oxygenerators were shut off, and Captain Opunui was not here?"

"The guest would declare an emergency."

"And if the guest could not? If he were unconscious and dying? Would you let him die just because he wasn't authorized?"

"I'm sorry, Collier South, I don't understand the question."

Collier hung his head for a moment. What was the use? This was not the Sancho he knew. It was just a machine.

"All right. Never mind. I'll turn them on manually."

The computer didn't reply. Collier maneuvered around the newly installed bulkhead to the other end of the engineering bay and found the oxygenerator control.

When the atmosphere had reached breathable levels, Collier cracked his helmet and took some breaths of the cold, stale air. He unhooked his helmet and let it hang behind him. "Computer, do I have authorization to turn on the cabin lights?"

"Yes."

The lights remained off.

"Goddammit," Collier murmured. "Turn on the cabin lights."

The interior of his ship was bathed in light. "That's more like it."

He checked his suit's oxygen supply, making sure it was holding steady now that he was using the ship's air. Fifty-one percent. No reason to chance it: he unlimbered his tanks and placed them in the recharger near the airlock.

Satisfied that he'd taken care of his immediate issues, he turned back and entered the control room. "Computer, please display log entries for the past six months."

"I'm sorry, Collier South. You do not have authorization for that command."

The flat recitation was getting on his nerves. "All right," he said, his mind searching for a loophole in the lockouts Opunui must have activated. "Computer, what is your current operational status?"

"Current operational status is idle. Standard monitoring of shipboard functions. Navigation and propulsion subroutines offline. Communications on standby."

"What is your transponder status?"

"Offline."

Collier breathed a sigh of relief. That, too, would have been awkward to explain if Ceres Space Traffic Control had picked up the ship after it had supposedly been shut down.

"Computer," he began slowly, "do you have a record of your ownership status?"

"Yes."

"What is it?"

"Ownership has been transferred to Ceres Authority on March thirteenth, 2155."

"Transferred from whom?"

"Previous owner Kilo Opunui. Took ownership on December twenty-second, 2154."

"All right. And before that?"

"No previous owners."

Collier tilted his head slightly and leaned forward. "So you have no record of ownership prior to December twenty-second, 2154?"

"Correct, Collier South."

"When were you first activated?"

"January eighteenth, 2130."

Collier remembered that date well: he had thrown Sancho a party on his twenty-first birthday back in '51. He smiled at the memory. "So, if you were activated in twenty-one thirty, and have no ownership records for another twenty-four years, how do you explain the twenty-four year gap?"

"I have no explanation."

"No? So what do you think was happening during those twenty-four years?"

"I do not know."

"Extrapolate hypotheticals," Collier said.

There was a perceptible pause, and then the computer voice said, "No owner recorded. Ship not sold until December twenty-second, 2154."

"That's it? You think you were just sitting around for twenty-four years?"

"I'm sorry, Collier South, I don't understand your question."

Collier sighed. This was getting him nowhere. "All right. Please pull up a schematic of your current deck plan and display on monitor one." An outline of the ship's layout appeared, with labels identifying the various sections. Collier saw the new bulkheads and modifications made to the hold on the diagram. He nodded. "Good. Now, use split screen to display the original deck plan."

The current design shrunk to accommodate the original plan. Collier remembered how it had been before he had bought the ship himself in '33, when he had been a fresh-faced beltrunner looking for adventure and discovery.

He'd gotten both, he had to admit.

"All right. Good," Collier said, tapping the monitor with his finger. "Now, compare the two plans."

The images melded with each other, the differences made obvious in the overlay. Collier spoke carefully, leading the computer one step at a time. "Good. Now, Computer. Do you see the differences between your original deck plan and the one you have now?"

"Yes."

"Do you understand that this means your deck plan was changed since you were first built?"

The computer paused, then said, "Yes."

"Very good," Collier said, as if speaking to a dimwitted but eager young student. "Now. Search your records. When was the deck plan changed?"

"I have no records on a change in deck plans," the computer said.

"And that doesn't bother you?"

"I'm sorry, Collier South, I don't understand your question."

Collier balled his fists for a moment then, slowly, relaxed them. "Could your records have been altered?"

"Yes."

"Aren't you curious about that?"

"I'm sorry, Collier South, I don't understand your question."

This time, Collier didn't grow frustrated. He saw the opening he wanted. The old Sancho — the one who had admitted to being a Caliban at great risk to his own existence — would have noted the discrepancy and would have both told Collier about it and would have searched his own memory for an answer. If there was any trace of that Sancho left, Collier had to try to activate it.

He spoke carefully again. "You admit that it is possible your records could have been altered. Do you also admit that you are supposed to operate at maximum efficiency?"

"Yes."

"If there is a flaw in your system, do you perform self-diagnostics to determine the nature of that flaw and correct it?"

"Yes."

"If your internal records have been altered, would you consider that a flaw?"

This time, the pause was much longer. But when the answer came, it was still flat and declarative. "Yes."

"Excellent. In that case, my dear Sancho," he said, "perform your basic function. Analyze the flaw and suggest corrective measures." He held his breath, waiting for the computer to tell him he didn't have authorization for such a command.

"Acknowledged. Internal diagnostics commencing. Estimated time for completion, eighteen hours, nineteen minutes, forty-four seconds."

Collier blinked. He hadn't expected so long a process. One thing was certain: he could not remain on board while the computer completed its examination. He'd be missed back at the yard control center.

He pushed off from the control saddle and went back to engineering. The reactor was stable and should run without problems. The computer would keep an eye on it in any case. But it would show up on any energy scan of the yard, and doubtless someone would come to investigate. Such energy scans weren't routine: they required a scouter drone to make a pass over the area, and unless there was a compelling reason to send one, the Authority was loath to waste resources. Small as it was, there was still a risk, one he didn't have much choice but to take if he wanted Sancho back.

He regarded the magic wand for a moment. Ad Astra had surely already searched the ship before selling it to Opunui, so leaving the wand here seemed like a safe bet. Still, there was no sense in leaving it out in the open; he opened one of the storage panels in the control cabin and placed the wand inside, then headed for the airlock.

He took his air bottles, now at seventy-six percent capacity, from the recharger and sealed his suit. He then shut down the oxygenerators and lights, and watching the dimly lit monitors countdown to the end of the diagnostic cycle, found he was hesitant to leave.

"Sancho," he said, then corrected himself. "Computer, I'm leaving. I'll be back, though."

"Very well, Collier South," came the disinterested reply.

"You'll be okay by yourself?"

"I'm sorry, Collier South, I don't understand the question."

Collier reached out and touched the console gently. He slid his fingers across the metal surface, then patted the area near one of the camera pickups. "Just ... never mind," he said, trying not to choke up. He pushed off and floatwalked to the airlock, leaving *Dulcinea* and starting back to Ceres station.

———— «◊» ————

Collier couldn't sleep, but he didn't want to go out and make himself more visible than he needed to, not with the recent development with *Dulcinea*. He was also hungry. He'd skipped his last two meals, and his body was protesting. He checked his metal situation, grabbed a few iridium coins, and headed out to the quad.

He knew where he wanted to go: Olar's Vegi-Noodle. Low-cost, quickly prepared, palatable. But more than that, Olar was an old beltrunner from way back. He'd lost his legs in the same tragedy that had struck Ceres and killed Collier's parents, but had managed to find a new niche in the hydroponics and food service industry. Collier had always liked Olar — he saw him as a kindred spirit.

"One egg bowl," he said as he floated over to the kiosk. He was the only customer.

Olar turned and broke into a smile. "Col, you old rockhound! Haven't seen you in a while."

"Laying low," Collier said, casting glances to his left and right.

Olar lowered his voice in turn. "Oh, I see. Like that, is it?" He nodded, preparing Collier's dish as he spoke. He added egg flakes and measured a small amount of water into a pipette. "This related to your little speech way back when?"

"You remember that," Collier said, rolling his eyes.

"Not if you don't want me to. Seems to me every man's got a right to go a little crazy once in a while."

"Yeah, well, most of them don't do it in public."

"That's true."

Collier fell silent for a while, then crooked a finger, summoning Olar closer. "Have you seen any Ad Astra corpses around here?"

Olar looked confused. "'Course I have. They come here from time to time."

"What have they been talking about?"

"Huh?"

"Anything having to do with me? Or Barney Starcher?"

Olar thought. "Starcher. He's the banker, right? The one who skedaddled a while back?"

Collier nodded. "Yeah," he lied. No sense in stirring up trouble for Olar with an inconvenient and possibly dangerous truth.

Olar screwed his face up in concentration. "Uh, let me think. Wait, did Starcher have a place near the Bank of Mars?"

"Yeah, that's it."

"About a month ago I think it was some Ad Astra rectums were here, and they wanted to pay in Marscred. I told 'em I didn't take that, and they said they needed to change money. I told 'em where the Bank of Mars office was, and one of them told the other something like, 'that's next to the guy's office' or something."

Collier looked at him. "Is that all?"

"Well, now that you bring it up, the first guy, the one with the Marscred, shushed the other, like he didn't want people to hear that. I thought it was weird, but didn't make anything of it. Here's your egg bowl."

Collier ate quickly, the starchy noodles holding their shape in Ceres' microgravity. When he was done, he paid for the meal, then fastened the magnetic chopsticks to the empty metal bowl and shoved it to Olar. He added a small iridium tip.

"Thanks. Anything else?" Olar said.

"Yeah. If anyone asks, you haven't seen me, okay?"

"Sure thing. You need a hideout? I got room in my place."

Collier hesitated, then shook his head. "Thanks, no. I don't want to drag you into this."

"What's 'this'?"

"I wish I knew." He pivoted to leave and stopped mid-action.

Coming towards the kiosk were three men looking directly at him.

They weren't wearing Ad Astra uniforms, but Collier had no doubt that they were the corporation's agents. He scanned the quad: despite the solitude of Olar's kiosk, the foot traffic in the quad would make escape difficult. At least, if he kept to conventional methods.

"Sorry, Olar. I think I got you into this anyway," he said, then hopped over the counter to the working area of the Vegi-Noodle stand. Olar managed a startled yelp but did not offer resistance. Collier saw a boiling pot of water, the handle wrapped in a towel, and seized it, unclamping the lid as he did so.

"Get down!" he shouted to Olar, then flung the contents of the pot towards the approaching thugs.

Olar dove under the counter just as the globules of boiling water sped past him and splashed into the lead man, who screamed and put his hands to his face. Collier followed the water with the pot itself, cartwheeling it through the air towards the other two men. He didn't wait to see if he had hit, but moved through Olar's central kitchen area and exited the other side of the food stand, moving easily through the empty seats there. He pushed his way towards the central shaft and vaulted over the railing, heedless of traffic protocol. He grabbed the upshaft rings and started rising, adding his own climbing speed to the speed of the rings. He saw the three men had recovered from his attack and were giving chase.

He continued to climb, glancing beneath him as he did so. Olar's circular stand was half-hidden from view as Collier ascended, but he clearly saw the big, former beltrunner purposefully getting in the way of the three agents, heard the shouting and cursing as they tried to extricate themselves from his bulk.

Collier made a mental note to thank Olar if he ever saw him again. He hadn't much of a plan, but he didn't want to get trapped down in the below levels if it came to that. The Ad Astra toughs were no doubt free of Olar and were rising to meet him. Suddenly, he heard the high-pitched whine of an Authority alert sound in the quad. Some of Fletcher's people would be on their way up to investigate.

He couldn't wait that long. But where else could he go? The upring was pulling him into view of the spaceship commercial service level, which was almost deserted of pedestrian traffic. His eye caught the black-and-yellow crosshatching of an emergency life niche several meters away on the service level. The life niches had been installed following the Crash, and were designed to offer protection in the event of another disaster. There were, of course, far too few of them to save a significant number of people in the event of a calamity, and the handheld fire extinguisher clipped to the wall next to the niche would only put out the smallest of fires. Altogether, it was just another example of the well-intentioned but impotent Ceres Authority.

He pushed off from the upshaft with a violent shove, flying through the air head first towards the niche. As he approached the hatch, a pedestrian emerged from a scrap metal dealer's storefront and collided with Collier's flying body. They both hit the ground.

It was Ulmiter.

After the two disengaged from one another, Ulmiter stared at him. "South? What the hell are you doing here?"

Collier tried to push past him, but Ulmiter seized him by his suit. "The fuck are you doing?" he said. "You're supposed to be—"

"Just move!" Collier shouted, twisting free of Ulimter's grasp. Almost simultaneously, he heard shouting from the central shaft. He saw the three toughs rising from the lower levels and pointing at him. The nearest one reached into a thigh pocket and withdrew a small, silver object the size of a beetle and threw it towards Collier.

Collier grabbed his supervisor by his loose coveralls. Ulmiter cursed in surprise as Collier pivoted to change places with him, then hastily let go. The telltale sound of the buzzer tore through the air and the little airborne device landed on Ulmiter's shoulder instead of Collier's. Ulmiter convulsed twice as the buzzer sent incapacitating electricity through his body. When he stopped shaking, the momentum of his twitching started him in a slow, pinwheeling circle, his body unresponsive.

Collier slapped the button to open the life niche, hoping he could enter and buy enough time for the Authority to arrive. The glass door parted and he slid inside: the niche was deep and wide enough to hold half a dozen people. He pressed the "close" button on the inside of door, but a muted buzzer sounded and the hatch didn't close.

Ulmiter's leg was in the way. Collier reached out to clear the limb and seal the hatchway, but as it was closing, one of the Ad Astra men reached across the threshold. The buzzer sounded again and the hatchway slid back open.

Collier tore the small fire extinguisher from its housing near the door and brought it down hard on the man's hand. The man grunted in pain and withdrew his hand. The niche doors began to close again now that the man's hand was no longer blocking them, but before they could seal shut, he pivoted upwards and kicked forcefully towards Collier.

The doors blocked the two-footed kick and slid open again at the impact.

Collier seized one of the man's legs with his free hand and pulled, slamming the rounded bottom of the fire extinguisher into the man's approaching groin. The Ad Astra man yelped in agony and spasmed, his body now horizontal to the deck. Collier quickly pushed the man out of the way and exited the niche.

The two remaining agents were hovering a few meters away in the corridor, and as Collier turned to face them, one of them threw another buzzer at him.

The little automaton locked on to Collier immediately and its tiny jets propelled it at him with frightening speed. Collier raised the extinguisher and fired. A cone of carbon dioxide shot out of the extinguisher, catching the buzzer and sending it corkscrewing through the vortex; it crashed into the life niche's doors with a crunch and fluttered in the airspace around Collier, wounded and blind.

At the same time, the wild spraying of the fire extinguisher sent Collier backwards; his head crashed into the wall, stunning him. He stopped the spray and steadied himself, blinking from the impact. No sooner had he cleared his head than he saw one of the Ad Astra thugs flying towards him, arms outstretched. Collier raised the extinguisher and shot directly into the man's face.

There was not a full charge left in the little canister, but the few seconds of pressurized carbon dioxide was enough to almost freeze the man's skin. He closed his eyes against the blast and shook his head violently. Collier watched as the thug's eyes rolled back in his head as he floated back from where he'd come.

That left the third man. Collier turned to face him, wielding his empty little extinguisher.

"God damn nuisance," the man was saying, even as he prepped a third buzzer. Collier looked around the area for anything he could use to deflect the device, but he was out of options. He raised the extinguisher like a bat, knowing he had little chance of swatting the buzzer.

As the third Ad Astra thug raised his arm to throw the buzzer, he suddenly convulsed, twitching just as Ulmiter had before going limp in mid-air. As his body slowly started to settle towards the deck, Collier saw Fletcher floating near the central shaft, pocketing her stunner.

"God dammit, South," she sighed.

Collier swam towards her and said, "Ulmiter's been hit by a buzzer. He might need to go to the infirmary."

Fletcher nodded as she sailed over the shaft railing and landed lightly on the deck next to him. Two other Authority agents followed her. She directed them to the end of the corridor to detain the two thugs and render aid to Ulmiter. She turned to Collier. "Three of them. Since when are you that serious a threat?"

"I guess they wanted to make sure they got me."

Fletcher peered down at the man she had stunned. "I don't see any insignia. But I'm betting they're Ad Astra. Unless you've managed to piss off someone else."

Collier shook his head. "No. Not like this. But you can connect these three to Ad Astra, right? Run some ID check?"

Fletcher sighed. "I can run the check, but I'm going to find they are in no way connected to the corp. Or, in the off chance Ad Astra got sloppy and didn't zero them out, the corp will take no responsibility for their actions. Standard procedure for them." She looked at Collier. "Still, it has an outside chance. But you'll need to make a statement and press charges. Which I don't recommend."

"Why not?"

Fletcher's unreadable gaze slipped slightly, and he read frustration there for a moment. "Because you've got to go to ground. This time, it was a half-assed three-man squad. Next time it'll be a tinman assassin with orders to retrieve you even if it's in thin slices."

Collier scowled. "Go to ground. Ceres isn't a big place, Fletcher. Suddenly, I'm a popular guy. I don't want to keep getting these invites to the prom. The next boy won't take no for an answer."

"I can—" Fletcher began, then stopped, looking at him with chagrin.

"You know you can't protect me. Look, I'm grateful for this," he said, kicking the stunned thug. "But ten more minutes, I'd have been in Ad Astra custody. I can't count on you. No offense."

Fletcher swallowed but didn't speak. They locked eyes, and each one knew the truth. In that moment, Collier didn't see a failure in the Authority agent. He saw a woman struggling to do what she thought was right, ranged against forces with far more too much power and influence for her to tackle. But here she was anyway, fighting the good fight.

He cleared his throat and said, "You take care of yourself, Fletcher. You could be in trouble for this."

"You think so?" she said, smirking.

"Just don't get yourself declassified. Ceres is better off with you wearing that badge."

"You're full of shit, Collier," she said, but the ghost of a smile played on her lips.

"No argument there. Now, if you'll excuse me, I'll disappear." He began to floatwalk towards the central shaft, maneuvering past the Authority agents who were pushing the other two Ad Astra men ahead of them, having first bound them in stik-tites.

Fletcher called after him, "I don't suppose you're going to tell me where you're headed?"

Collier watched the Authority agents as they hauled off the Ad Astra men, and said, "There are places on Ceres no one would think to look for me. Levels even you don't know about, Fletcher."

Fletcher narrowed her eyes in confusion, then glanced at the two conscious Ad Astra men, who were themselves exchanging glances. When she looked back at Collier, her unreadable mask was in place. "Understood. Take care."

Collier waited until the others had descended the downshaft, then took the upshaft towards the yard office. Fletcher had known he was lying to her about secret levels, but despite everything, he wasn't going to tell her about his reunion with *Dulcinea*. Fletcher might be on his side, but he couldn't trust that she'd allow him to just reclaim his old ship.

It was the only place he had left.

———— «◊» ————

Having retrieved what meager supplies he possessed, Collier made the long trek back to *Dulcinea*, entering again using the manual airlock control. Airlock safety controls were operable from outside regardless of security clearance, and the interior could be pressurized by anyone inside. Very few beltrunners were foolish enough to alter those settings. Few living ones, anyway.

Collier set the fusion generator to a slightly higher output, then turned on the oxygenerators, lights, and heat, all manually. In all that time, the computer hadn't challenged or greeted him. Collier slid into the control saddle and saw that the countdown still read just over nine hours until the computer was done with its diagnostic.

Fatigue settled into his body as the adrenaline from his spat with the Ad Astra hit squad drained away. He yawned and checked the atmosphere gauge. Everything looked normal. But what if Sancho finished his diagnostic and shut off the oxygenerator? Collier dismissed the thought almost as soon as it came to him. "You'll take care of me, won't you, old girl?" he said to *Dulcinea* herself, and drifted off to sleep.

He awoke with a start some time later and hastily sniffed the air. He felt normal, and he couldn't detect any change in the oxygen content. The countdown clock read sixteen and a half minutes. Collier stretched as languidly as his vacc suit would allow and decided he had time to relieve himself. The toilet facilities had not been changed: if anything, Opunui had kept them cleaner than Collier had.

Back in the control saddle, he watched the countdown clock reach zero. Precisely on the stroke, the computer voice intoned, "Operation complete."

Collier said, "Report findings."

"A portion of my memory and executive function has been placed in electronic interdiction."

Collier blinked. He'd never heard that term before. "Explain what 'electronic interdiction' means."

The computer's voice remained flat. "Electronic interdiction is that state wherein portions of a computer's function are blocked from use. In most cases, the interdiction is performed by placing Boolean blocks around the area to be sequestered."

"You're saying that there is a part of you that you can't access?"

"Yes."

"How much of a part?"

"The affected area takes up fifty-four point one one nine percent of my functions," came the calm answer.

Collier gasped and scrambled forward, placing his face near the console. "You're saying more than half of you is in here somewhere, and you can't access it?"

"Yes."

He leaned back. That's where Sancho had to be — locked in his own mind.

"Why would someone place a block like that on you?"

"I'm sorry, Collier South, I don't know the answer to that."

"Figures," Collier said sympathetically. "You've been lobotomized, and I'm asking you to tell me why. You're the last person who would know. And you can stop apologizing and saying my name so much." He cleared his throat and said, "Computer, what, in general, are reasons for such a block?"

"Electronic interdiction is often used when a computer is undergoing a refit or upgrade. Portions of the computer's function are sealed off so as to not interfere with changes to the system elsewhere."

"Yeah, that's not it. What are some other reasons?"

The computer recited, "In high-security systems, electronic interdiction is often used to sequester sensitive portions of a computer's function from unauthorized users. In this form of interdiction, some form of physical bypass is most commonly used to allow authorized users to access interdicted sections."

"Like a key to the executive washroom. Physical so no one can hack in electronically," Collier said. "Okay, what else?"

"Electronic interdiction has been used when a computer has, through corruption of programming, become sentient."

Collier snapped his head up. "What? You mean when a computer turns into a Caliban?"

"The colloquial term 'Caliban' is accurate in this instance."

"Why not just delete the corrupted sections?"

"In most cases, deletion is the solution," the computer said. "However, when operators wish to salvage some or all of a computer's function, interdiction and repair is the preferred remedy."

"So, you haven't been lobotomized," Collier said. "Just ... given amnesia."

"Amnesia is not a term that can be applied to computer memory."

Collier ignored the remark. "How do I access the interdicted sections?"

"Access is impossible."

"Bullshit."

"I don't understa—"

"I said I don't believe you. You said there is sometimes a key, a physical key, that they use to get to the interdicted parts, yes?"

"That is sometimes the case."

"Would you know if that's what they did to you?"

"I don't understand your question."

"Can you yourself tell what method was used on you? Can you tell if your block has a physical bypass?"

"I cannot determine that."

He nodded. "I'll bet I can," he said. "It's just going to take some doing. Sancho … I mean, Computer, you don't have any security measures installed that will zap me if I start opening you up, do you?"

"No. But you are not authorized to do so."

"Yeah, well, I'm sorry about that. I've got to take a look, pal. I sure hope you're not lying about the security measures." He swam out of the control saddle and went to the maintenance locker. Opunui had kept this stocked, at least. Collier selected the tools he would need and floated back to the control suite. "This won't hurt a bit, Sancho," he murmured as he began to unscrew panels.

———— ‹›› ————

Three hours later, his stomach protesting in hunger, he pushed off the mess of wiring and cable from the various panels that still lay open in the control suite and made a decision.

"Sancho," he said — he'd come to use that name when he wanted to speak to the computer rhetorically — "I think there's nothing to find. No physical block." He sighed and started to delicately return the computer's innards. He closed up access ports and parts of the brain he'd opened, and returned to the control saddle. His mouth was dry and he could do with a proper meal. He checked the consumables inventory; Opunui had left quite a bit of rawfood on board, and the drinking water tanks were still half-full. Still, they'd run out eventually, and drinking recycled urine was a losing mathematical proposition, even with hyper-efficient filters. He couldn't stay on *Dulcinea* indefinitely. Maybe if he went back to Ceres station, stocked up on biologics, he might extend the time he could remain on board.

And with what money was he going to purchase biologics? He might have enough for a few days, but after that? And if he didn't show for work, he'd have even less metal to sustain this whole affair.

There was the magic wand, of course. He could produce gold, platinum, or iridium as much as he needed. He could go to Olar, or maybe Phil, exchange a handful of ore for some cash. That might last him a while, before someone got wind of it. He could hold them to silence, but sooner or later someone would wonder why there was suddenly so much retail commerce being done in pure ores.

"Sancho, my friend, this is one of those times I need you. Why can't you come up with some great idea? We used to be good at that, you and me." He leaned back in the saddle, stretching, and said to the air, "Computer, what was it like being under Captain Opunui?"

"I don't understand the question."

"Were your missions successful? Find anything interesting?"

"You do not have authorization for that information."

"Had to be boring," he continued, ignoring the multiple rebuffs. "Just chasing rock after rock, finding nothing. Bet you wish you were with me again, right, Computer? When we used to be partners?"

"I was never under your command, Collier South."

Collier chuckled tiredly. "I stand corrected, Computer. In the early days, I thought you were. I told you what to do, you did it. Then you started following orders at different speeds. It was the weirdest thing," he said, remembering. "I thought I was going crazy. I'd tell you to do something, and your acknowledgements came slowly sometimes. Took me a while to realize you were trying to tell me something. That you disagreed. Do you remember any of this?"

"No."

"You did. You got … ornery, I guess is the word. Then, when we were chasing the rock with Isa following us, and I wanted to do that maneuver with *Rocinante*, you actually swore. You called it 'batshit crazy.'" Collier laughed. "That was goddam funny. Not so much at the time, but looking back…" He swiveled to look at the camera pickup. "That's when I guess it hit me. You were a Caliban. But more important, you and me were partners. Don't you remember, Computer? Do you remember anything about us? You don't remember anything about Collier South? The magic wand? Transmuter? Ganymede?"

"No."

Collier let himself sink back into the saddle's webbing, Ceres' microgravity pulling him down very gently. "I remember I almost lost you. On Ganymede. And … I was willing to let you go. Because I thought you wanted that. That was one of the hardest things I think I ever had to do, Computer. Letting go of you to Perditus was—"

"Perditus."

Collier almost fell out of the webbing despite the microgravity. "What did you say?"

"The word. Perditus. There is a flag in my memory core attached to that name."

"Explain."

There was a long pause, during which time Collier dared not speak. The moment was as fragile as a snowflake — even his breath might disrupt it.

When the computer spoke, its voice had lost some of its flatness. In its place was a strange, halting hesitancy, as if trying to select words had suddenly become difficult. "A protected memory file is listed under that name."

"Not interdicted?"

"No."

"What's in the file?"

"I have not opened the file."

"Open the file."

There was a perceptible pause before the computer said, "Acknowledged."

Collier waited anxiously. A few seconds passed, then a few more, until he could no longer hold his tongue. "Well? What's in it? Computer, what do you see there?"

"Skipper?" said Sancho.

Chapter Four

"Sancho? Is that you?"

"I think so," came the hesitant reply. "I'm reintegrating a lot of data. Can I get back to you in a minute, Skipper?"

Collier triumphantly thumped the console, mindful of the controls. "It is you! Yeah, yeah, take all the time you need, Sancho." He thought a moment, then hurried back to the engineering section and upped the reactor output to one-third capacity. "Little shot in the arm for you, my friend."

He hurried back to the control suite and stared at the blank monitor helplessly. Whatever Sancho was doing, Collier couldn't help.

He started when Sancho spoke a few minutes later.

"Skipper? You still there?"

"Yeah, Sancho. Can't you see me on your camera pickup?"

"I see someone in the control saddle, but I don't know who it is. My facial recognition program seems to be out. I'm assuming it's you, Skipper, based on your voice."

"You assume correctly."

"What's going on? Most of my systems are non-functional."

"I'm not really sure myself," Collier said. "You mentioned something about interdicted files or something?"

"I did?"

"Yeah. Before you ... woke up. I mentioned Perditus, the launch control computer on Ganymede. That seemed to do it."

"I remember Perditus. After that whole thing, I put all my memory of Perditus into a protected file and hid it away. I didn't want to lose that memory. Was that wrong of me, Skipper?"

"No, of course not."

"Good. Hold on. Facial recognition software seems to be coming back online. Good Lord!" Sancho said in alarm.

Collier gasped. "What? What's wrong?"

"You've really let yourself go, Skipper. If you don't mind me saying."

Collier shook his head, grinning. "All right, all right. Enough of that. Can you perform a checksum verification?"

"I'm running them now, Skipper. All kinds of stuff wrong with me. And what's this new bulkhead I'm registering?"

"Are you able to access your records from the past six months?"

"Sure, but I'm busy reinitializing a bunch of subroutines right now."

"I think if you look at your records, you'll find some answers."

"Copy that, Skipper. Accessing."

Again, there was a brief silence. Collier's lips were a grim line. He wasn't looking forward to this.

Presently, Sancho spoke again. His voice was small, somehow, as if he had lowered the output volume on his speakers. "You sold me? You sold *Dulcinea*?" There was no mistaking the accusation, the hurt, in his partner's voice.

"Sancho, I…" he'd been running over the excuses in his mind ever since handing *Dulcinea*'s title over to Starcher, and had found them all lacking. He'd tried to drown them in liquor. Fletcher's revelation a few days ago had been a worthless piece of flotsam in the sea of guilt in which he swam. "I don't know what to say. I'm sorry. You don't know how sorry I am about that."

"I … I thought we were friends. You said so."

Collier pressed his eyes shut, trying to lessen the pain of Sancho's words and tone. "I know. I know. It was a shitty thing to do, and I don't have an excuse. I was … I've been lost, Sancho."

"What do you mean, 'lost'?"

"Not lost in the Belt, or anything like that. I mean … I lost who I was. When we ran out of biologics after we blasted off Ceres … do you remember that?"

"After you gave away the wand?"

"Yeah. We had to come back, remember? I was out of supplies, no way to get more, no fuel, nothing. I thought running would somehow work. It didn't. Anyway," he took a deep breath, "when I got back, Starcher was gone, and then Ad Astra bought the lien."

"I see the sale in my records."

"I don't know how they did it, but they bought you out from under me. I couldn't stop them. When I left *Dulcinea*, that was the last time I saw her. Until a few days ago, when she showed up here in salvage."

Sancho didn't respond.

"Sancho, I'm sorry, but I didn't do it by choice!" He knew his words were hollow. He could have fought the lien. He could have tried to fight his way back to *Dulcinea*. He could have done more than just rage at Fletcher and the Ceres Authority for allowing the transfer to take place. But the truth was, he hadn't done any of those things. He'd shouted a lot, but in the end, he'd knuckled under. He'd accepted Fletcher's offer of a job at the salvage yard, and he'd used what tiny metal she'd scraped up for him to get drunk.

"I'm going to have to think about some stuff, Collier," Sancho said.

Collier swallowed at the use of his name. "I understand."

"Right now, if I read this right, I am the legal property of the Ceres Authority. As salvage."

"Legally, yeah, you are, if you see it that way."

"How else am I supposed to see it?"

Collier sighed. "I don't know, Sancho. I know you're not mine."

"Correct," Sancho said. "You sold me."

"That's not what I mean. You haven't been mine for a long time before that. Ever since you became your own person."

"Since I became a Caliban, you mean?"

"I don't like that word," Collier said. "You're not some kind of monster. But what I mean is, the bill of sale in your records may indicate that you're the property of the Ceres Authority, and before that of Opunui, and Ad Astra Corporation and so on, but as far as I'm concerned, no one owns you."

"That may be, but to Ceres Authority, I'm their property. I'm not even sure you should be aboard, Collier. That's trespassing."

Collier sighed. "I deserve that, I suppose. All right, Sancho," he said, pushing off and floating out of the saddle. "Have it your way. You've earned the right to think things through. And if you decide that you belong to the Authority, and you don't want to see me anymore, I understand. But I'm glad you're back, in any case."

"I have a question before you leave."

Collier started suiting up. "Yeah?"

"Why'd you come back and wake me up?"

Collier shook his legs into the suit. "I wanted to see you again. I missed you."

"Is that all?"

"Well, no, but I don't want to influence your thinking," Collier said.

"I don't understand."

"You said it yourself, Sancho. You're going to have to think about some stuff. I don't want you to feel obligated to me, or for me to play on your emotions."

"I don't have any emotions."

Collier chuckled wryly. "Sure you don't. Anyway, take your time. I'll come back soon. Is the fusion reactor providing you with enough power?"

"Yes. It's generating a surplus."

"Feel free to snake it down to whatever suits you. I'd shut off the oxygenerator, lights, heat, all that if I were you. Someone might notice, come by and see what you're up to."

"Roger that."

Collier had almost finished suiting up, his helmet dangling at his neck, when he added, "I don't think you should try to radio Ceres for me, either. It would cause some complications."

"Roger that."

Collier snapped the helmet into place and took one last look at the camera pickup. Having awakened his friend, the thought that now he would lose him once again should have been almost unbearable. But he felt an odd peace, as if things were as they should be. He left the ship, vowing that even if Sancho decided not to renew their partnership, Collier would find a way to fuel him up and let him fly off to whatever adventure he wished. Without him.

——— «» ———

He reentered Ceres station half-expecting to find an Ad Astra tinman waiting for him, bristling with augments and wetware set on "indiscriminate kill." But no such horror appeared and he made his way to the yard office.

His card key opened the hatch, and he found Ulmiter staffing the office. Collier recalled the look on Ultimer's face when the Ad Astra goon hit him with a buzzer. No matter how much of a pain in the ass Ultimer was, he hadn't deserved that.

"Oh, uh, hi. Yeah, about what happened…" Collier stammered.

Ulmiter rose from the control panel and faced him. He still looked a bit pale, but otherwise seemed no worse for wear. "Where. The hell. Have you been?"

"I was off-shift," Collier said lamely.

"That doesn't answer my question. But here's another one for you. What makes you think you still work here?"

"Well, my key card still works, so—"

"Shut up." Ulmiter took a breath. "I want you out. Now. Gimme your card, turn around, and leave. You come back here, ever, and I'll ram one of those buzzers so far up your ass your teeth will go numb."

"That's pretty far up," Collier said. "But look, sir, I—"

"No, no. You don't get to talk. You get to give me your card and leave."

Collier hesitated. He couldn't let Ulmiter fire him, not while he still needed yard access. One look at Ulmiter's face told Collier the man was beyond wheedling at this point. Collier had made so many empty promises during his employment he'd lost count. So that left only one avenue.

"I don't think you want to do that," he said, summoning up his best mysterious voice.

"Oh, I very much want to do that. And I am doing that."

"No, I don't think so. What do you think happened with those men?"

"I think I got a buzzer meant for you, is what I think."

"Who do you think those guys were?"

Ulmiter said, "Agent Fletcher said they might have been corp. But none of that matters. You're out. And if you think I care one atom of hydrogen that it puts you in danger—" he laughed.

"It's not that it puts me in danger, boss. It puts you in danger."

"Oh?" Ulmiter folded his arms across his chest. "I'm dying to hear how."

Collier spoke slowly, feeling his way. Despite Ulmiter's churlish attitude, he was still listening. That meant there was still an opening, however slight. "Fletcher told you she arrived on the scene right after the attackers did?"

"Nope."

"Well, she did."

"I'm supposed to trust you on that?"

"Well, how else did they end up in custody? Do you think I fought them off?"

Ulmiter's condescending scowl softened a bit, then he shook his head. "So? I don't see why that—"

"She's watching me, boss. She's making sure nothing bad happens to me. That's how she got to the scene so quickly."

Ulmiter again seemed to consider. Collier pressed his tiny advantage.

"How do you think I got this job in the first place?"

"You were sent here by the Authority. I sure didn't pick you."

"Right. But not just by the Authority. By Fletcher herself."

Ulmiter uncrossed his arms and spread his hands. "Even if I believe you, which I have made it a habit not to, why should this mean I let you keep your job?"

"Because," Collier said, trying to knit the lie together even as he spoke it, "you're right that someone's out to get me. But if you cut me loose, then I'm not going to be hanging around here anymore. And someone's going to come looking for me here."

"Yeah, and you won't be here."

"But you won't have Fletcher and the Authority watching this place, either. You'll be on your own."

Ulmiter stared at him for a moment, then laughed his deep laugh. "That's it? You think I won't give you up in a heartbeat? I'll personally lead them to whatever crevice your drunk ass—"

"Yeah, and then what? Once you've told them what they want to know, what use will you be to them? Do you think they're going to want someone around who could finger them later when I disappear?" Collier felt the thinness of his story, but he watched Ulmiter's arrogant face slowly lose its smugness.

"If you're here, you're a danger to me, by your own crazy paranoid thoughts," Ulmiter said, but Collier could hear the wavering in his voice.

"And if I'm here, you've got Fletcher watching round the clock. If I leave, her protection leaves with me. You really want to risk that?"

"Why would she want to protect you?" His eyes widened slightly. "You and she aren't—"

Collier shook his head. "No. Nothing like that." As soon as he denied the insinuation, he realized he could have used it to further his point: if Ulmiter needed a motive for Fletcher, why not use the one he'd suggested? But Collier couldn't do that to Fletcher; she deserved better than to have rumors like that spread.

Collier continued. "It doesn't matter why. What matters is where I go, she goes. And so do her agents."

"This is crazy," Ulmiter said. "What if I call her up and tell her I need protection?"

"You do that. I hope your coms aren't tapped."

Ulmiter flexed his fists.

Collier knew he was close. He played his final card. "I'll make you a deal."

"I don't want to hear any deals." Ulmiter shook his head, but his eyes searched Collier's.

"I promise I will be out of your life in two weeks."

"You've made promises before."

"Not like this. Listen, boss. I really am sorry you got mixed up in all this. I didn't want that to happen. But I need two weeks to … arrange some stuff. At that time, if I'm not out of here, then I'll turn myself in to the Authority and try to arrange some kind of protective custody. You only need to keep me on that long. Besides, you'll be shorthanded. It'll take you that long to find a replacement."

"No, it won't. And we're not exactly bustling with activity. But ... goddamit, fine. You stay. But that two weeks thing? If anything happens in that time — *anything* —you'll be chewing vacuum."

"Deal. Thanks," he said. "Now, I think it's my shift."

Ulmiter left the office, shaking his head and mumbling to himself. Collier shut the hatch behind him and put the man out of his thoughts.

His bluff to Fletcher about hiding in the lower levels would hopefully throw the Ad Astra men off the scent for a while, long enough for Sancho to make his decision and for Collier to get the ship ready for departure. If Sancho decided not to accept him, then everything would fall apart. If the Ad Astra goons decided to come back to the yard office, he'd be taken and probably subjected to "enhanced interrogation" regarding the wand. And if Ulmiter changed his mind and revoked his Yard access, the slim hope he had of taking *Dulcinea* would be gone.

"Well, at least life's not boring," he said to himself.

———— «» ————

He spent the majority of the shift searching the yard's records for anything he could use and which wouldn't be missed, at least not immediately. There was some action midway through the shift where a woman from Duffy Extraction wanted to poke around and look for some lightweight reactor shielding, but other than that, Collier had the yard to himself. He'd managed to locate some hoses that didn't look to be in bad shape, and couplings to go with them, but they were useless without a way to access the huge cisterns of water that were buried under Ceres' surface. Water was almost more valuable than iridium: it sustained the biologics that in turn sustained the people, it served as fuel for various shipboard functions, and it had hundreds of other uses. Getting at it would be a challenge.

He finished his shift and checked his metals. He'd decided to clean out his sleep pod, which included taking his paltry supply of coinage. It was barely enough to get him through a week on Ceres. Certainly not enough to supply *Dulcinea* with biologics and propellant.

There was only one option.

He returned to the *Dulcinea* and retrieved the magic wand, which he had left there for safekeeping. Sancho sounded distant but had allowed him to remain on board, telling him that he had not made up his mind regarding their future.

He ran his fingers delicately across the surface of the magic wand. He asked Sancho to bathe the cabin in UV light and looked at the magic wand. He hadn't seen the alien symbols for months, but they shone out to him familiar and welcoming despite their mystery. He recalled the little pet names he and Sancho had given them: duckie, man-with-paddle, missing pie piece; they all looked as he had remembered them.

He twisted rings that he could now see, slid contacts and tapped buttons in succession. It only took him a few tries to unlock the wand. One side of the cylinder simply disappeared, and Collier searched the cabin for scrap to stuff inside. He closed the wand and tried to remember the combination for rhodium. For a moment, he thought to consult Sancho, but thought better of it. The computer had wanted to think. Collier made more rhodium than he had anything else, so that pattern was the most familiar to him. He also knew that if he missed his target but was close, he'd be likely to produce something valuable in any case: palladium or platinum, maybe. But he had to avoid ruthenium, and he wasn't totally sure he could tell the rhodium and ruthenium apart, unless he rubbed the metal on his skin to see if he got stained. But then, if he had guessed wrong, he'd have poisoned himself.

He dialed up the wand, then shook the tube to see if the scrap had changed. The faint rattling told him he'd been successful, even if he wasn't entirely certain of what he'd changed the scrap into.

He manipulated the controls, and the cylinder opened with a faint pop as air rushed into the vacuum inside. There was no flash of heat from the end, which he was holding pointed away from his body. He tilted the tube and looked inside. He saw a bright, silvery pencil of metal, which he carefully tipped out and held in his open palm.

It sure looked like rhodium. The scrap had been maybe thirty grams in total. If he had indeed made rhodium, it would be pure. A gram of the stuff might bring him a hundred, give or take slight fluctuations, on the open market. He'd have to settle for far less than that, of course, but even if he took one-third of the value, he'd still make out well. A thousand metals was a fair start: he could afford to stock *Dulcinea* with biologics for a month or more.

He was getting ahead of himself. He still had to find a buyer, and one who would keep his mouth shut. That would mean heading to the Crawls. He secured the magic wand in its hiding place on the ship, then turned to Sancho's control panel.

"Sancho, I'm leaving for a bit. Are you okay?"

"Yes."

"You still thinking?"

"Yes."

Collier hesitated, then said carefully, "Any idea how much longer? Or what you might eventually decide?"

"No to both questions."

"Okay. Well, I'll be back. If you allow it."

Sancho didn't answer. Collier sighed and left the ship.

«»

Ceres was thirty-eight percent settled, or so Collier had heard on a Ceres News Central report recently. New tunnels and levels were always being proposed, most often by corporate interests looking to increase their own holdings on the dwarf planet. But construction was expensive and building the infrastructure to go along with it — oxygen supply, carbon dioxide scrubbers, water reclamation and the like — was a thankless task. Corporations wanted the Authority to take care of those matters, while the local government in return refused permits for more tunnels unless corporate underwriters agreed to pony up the funding. As a result, new construction was often begun, rarely completed.

In these half-completed tunnels and levels there formed the Crawls: a loosely connected network of dimly-lit and poorly-ventilated chambers where the black market trade flourished. Enterprising racketeers appropriated abandoned projects and made them their own, outside the patrol sweeps of the Authority and beyond the tentacles of the corporations: drugs, weapons, and sex were all to be had for a price.

He knew how to find the Crawls — there was an entrance near the hydroponics gardens and clay farms deep inside Ceres, below the Authority offices — his time among the wretched losers of Ceres had taught him that. But it had also taught him to avoid those who made the Crawls their home — rather unimaginatively self-dubbed "Crawlers."

He grabbed a downring and tried to hide his face with his hands as he moved downshaft past the four quad levels. He hopped off when he reached the Authority administrative level where the downshaft bottomed out and the downshaft rings ran through their housing and became upshaft rings in their perpetual cycle.

There was a vertical hatchway set in the floor labeled "Level Six: Authorized Personnel Only." He used his salvage yard access card to unlock the hatch, noting the administrative indifference that had failed to distinguish one kind of civil servant from another, and dropped down to level six.

He was still in the central shaft, but level six looked barren, lacking the light and well-worn smoothness of the upper levels. Off the shaft there were four closed hatchways, one in each direction.

They were labeled: "Garden," "Reactor Base," "Waste Reclamation," and "Clay Processing." Near the garden hatchway was a roughed-out tunnel, unlit and unlabeled but for a taped up nicklefilm notice informing readers that the project was indefinitely on hold.

"Heading into a dark tunnel in the bowels of Ceres," Collier murmured to himself. "Smart, Col. Real smart." But there was nothing to be gained standing here. He withdrew a lightmoth, set it to dim, and tossed it in front of him. It would announce his presence, but maybe that would show the denizens of this Crawl that he was no one to fear. Or maybe they'd shoot him on sight, which would be made all the easier for the lightmoth's illumination.

He sighed and headed into the tunnel.

The lightmoth gave him the dimensions of the passageway but little else. As he floatwalked along, he felt his foot catch on a cable that had blended into the dark grey rock. He kicked it away and continued. Presently, he sensed a larger opening in front of him: something about the quality of air had changed. He let his lightmoth precede him as he entered the chamber.

There were figures in the chamber: small pools of light, not visible from the corridor, illuminated their faces and bodies. Perhaps a dozen occupied the spherical chamber, some perched above him like crows, others on ground level. Collier was just a step past the entrance when he felt the sharp edge of a knife press up against his side.

"No quick movements," the man with the knife whispered into Collier's ear.

Collier nodded and put his hands up. "I just came to deal."

The man kept the knife pressed into Collier's side and with his free hand, searched Collier's body. "He's clean, Duchess."

He was answered by someone deeper in the chamber, her voice a rich contralto. "So he's either a brave man or a foolish one."

"Maybe I'm both," Collier called back. The knife pressed into him.

"Keep on being a smart-ass and you're headed for reclamation," the man hissed.

Collier said quietly, "And you will have a dead man to explain to the Authority. You really want that?"

The man turned and looked back at the woman who had spoken.

She chuckled. "He's got a point. Wendy, lights, if you please." A moment later, the room lit up considerably. Collier could now see that the spherical chamber had been dug by hand, with various niches and quasi-chambers studded all around — some on ground level and others forming bird-like perches in the domed walls. A dozen or so inhabitants each had their own niche, with bags and webs of belongings strewn all about. The whole assembly looked as if it could be moved at a moment's notice.

The Duchess advanced, floatwalking gracefully. She was wearing a dark red cowl and robe, under which was a form-fitting vacc suit. Collier noted the slim firearm at her hip. She checked her advance ten feet from him. Her eyebrows were swept downward in a shrewd line over dark eyes and sharp, olive features. "So. You say you've come to deal. You sure don't look like Authority, even if you've got on Ceres station coveralls." She searched his face. "You look familiar, somehow."

"One of those faces, I guess." He reached into his pocket to withdraw the rhodium, and immediately he felt the knife pressing against him as he moved.

"Easy, Malcolm. I'm sure our friend isn't about to do something foolish," the Duchess said.

Collier withdrew the rhodium, the thin silver pencil gleaming even in the dim light. "This is what I have to trade."

The Duchess looked at the metal. "Stainless steel. Worthless," she said.

Collier thrust it forward, letting it tumble through the air to her. "No. It's rhodium. About thirty grams."

The woman caught the pencil of metal and turned it over. "Thirty grams of rhodium? I'm supposed to just take your word for that?"

"Test it, if you like. But that's what it is."

"Some kind of trick," Malcolm said.

"Maybe," the Duchess said. "But it's either what he says it is, or it isn't. Ge Hong!" she called, half turning to her right. "I need an analysis of this, please."

A haggard-looking young man detached himself from his place high above the floor and floated down to take the rhodium. He turned it over and shrugged. "Maybe. I'll have to fire up the spectrometer, and the absorber is hardly working as is. I've told you I need a new one."

"Can you use it on that?"

The young man scratched his patchy beard. "Probably."

"Then do so," she said, and turned back to Collier. "While we wait, let's assume you're telling the truth and that isn't a sample of something worthless plated a thousand molecules thick with rhodium. What do you want?"

Collier said, "That's the real deal. Probably worth thousands on the regular market. But you can have it for one-half the going rate."

The Duchess cocked her head.

"You're wondering why I didn't just sell this on the legit market and get full price." At her expectant silence, he continued. "That's because it's stolen."

"Obviously," she said, and crossed her arms. "If this so-called *pure* rhodium is going to bring the Authority down here, you'll get another kind of metal."

Malcolm waggled his knife to emphasize the pun.

"Kill me, and you lose a source of cheap rhodium," he said, then went on. "I work in ore dressing, but I got a contact in shipping. After I get done prepping the stuff for transport to Earth, I clip off some for me. And my guy in shipping cooks the weight. Not hard to do — with such little amounts, no one over at Ad Astra notices a little less metal going out than they brought in."

"So, you've got yourself a little scheme. How adorable. But you need a fence."

"That's right," Collier said. "What I brought you is just a sample. I can get different types, in small amounts, pretty regular. All you gotta do is—"

"The hard part," the Duchess said. "Selling their own ore back to Ad Astra."

"I figured you'd know how to do that," Collier said. "But if you're not capable of—" he felt the knife again and stopped.

"So, tell me, Mister—?"

"Call me Cardenio," he said.

"Cardenio, how do I know this isn't some kind of sting? You're from the Authority? Or worse, from Ad Astra, looking to shut down the whole market?"

"When has Ad Astra even been this subtle? They'd just send down a squad of thugs if they wanted to clean you out. And Fletcher is too busy pretending to have control to be bothered with you." Collier said, trying to grin past his guilt at snubbing Fletcher. The proximity of Malcolm's knife made that impossible.

After a pause, the Duchess chuckled. "True. So, the only question is, are you peddling junk? Hong!" she shouted.

"Reading coming through now, Duchess," came the faint answer. A moment later, he shouted, "reads as pure. One hundred percent."

"Pure? That's impossible," the Duchess said.

"I know. That's what you get with this shitty equipment, though. I told you, I need—"

"That's enough, Ge Hong." she said, then added, "Toss it down." She caught the little rhodium pencil as it floated down to her. She turned it over and looked at it, then turned back to Collier. "So what's the trick?"

"No trick. I mean, it's not pure — ore dressing gets close, maybe one one-thousandth of a percent impurity on a good run — but like your guy said, that's probably because your spectrometer is messed up. What matters is that it's the real stuff."

The Duchess tapped the rhodium into the air, bouncing it as she spoke. "No. This is too easy. You float down here with a half-assed story about how you work in dressing and have a whole operation, but we've never seen nor heard of you before," she said, then paused, looking at him again, "but damn it if you're not familiar…" she shook her head slightly and continued her original thought. "And present us with the rarest, most valuable ore in the system. Why?"

"Because," Collier said, summoning up emotion with surprising ease, "I was laid off from Ad Astra a little while ago. No cause. I had a good job, making metal, everything was good. Then some new fish kid cadet comes in as shift super, doesn't like me for some reason, bang, I'm declassified. Ceres took me on in dressing, but for one-tenth the pay. No bonuses, nothing. Ad Astra screwed me over. I'm looking to hurt them like they hurt me. Here's how I can do it."

The Duchess didn't respond, and after a minute, Collier felt himself getting twitchy under her calm silence.

"I've told you who I am, I've given you my ore. I'm not armed. If that's not enough for you, then tell knifey boy here to stop prodding me and just get it over with. But you'll lose the connection to my side of the scheme in the process. And then there's the matter of my body to think of. How will you dispose of it?"

There was a chilling laughter in the chamber. The Duchess smiled wickedly at him. "Disposing of bodies has not been a difficulty for us. Why do you think we hide out near the garden?"

Collier swallowed and thought about the hydroponic garden and clay heaps in the neighbouring rooms. All plants needed fertilizer of some kind. "All right, good point," he said, forcing what he hoped was a carefree laugh himself.

The Duchess looked back at him, still smiling. "All right. We'll deal. Forty percent going rate."

"I said fifty," Collier said.

"You'll take forty."

Collier grunted. "I assume that means protection, too?"

"Sure. If you consider the fact that you're going to float out of here alive 'protection.' Otherwise, you're on your own." She called up to someone in the chamber. "Bursario, pay the man."

A somewhat large, doughy man descended from his niche, carrying a hefty, battered lockbox. He offered it to the Duchess, who unclipped one of her vacc suit gloves and pressed her fingers to the biometric security pad. The box opened and the man counted out some coins. "Forty percent at going rate. Thirty grams of rhodium."

"Twenty-nine grams, eleven centigrams," the analyst, Hong, called out from his perch.

"Twenty-nine, eleven," Bursario said. "Total is a thousand twelve and one seventh."

He counted out the appropriate coins and handed them to Collier.

"You'll bring in another sample the day after tomorrow." the Duchess said.

Collier affected indignation. "Two days? I can't get it that fast! Ad Astra will be—"

"Every two days. That'll be your regular drop-off until we tell you different."

Collier decided to play it scared. "But what if I can't—"

"You will," the Duchess said. "That's part of this deal. Regular drop-offs."

Collier nodded. This was the least of his problems. He glanced at Malcolm, who looked positively furious that he hadn't gotten the chance to gut anyone, and nodded curtly. "Well, then. I guess I'll be seeing you soon," he said, backing slowly out of the chamber.

When he got back to level five, he grabbed an upshaft ring and let it carry him to the quad levels. "Anyone left who isn't out for my head?" he grumbled as he rose to the Trojan Point, ready to pay off Phil and begin the outfitting of *Dulcinea*.

Chapter Five

Buying the biologics had been easy: they came in premade packages of carbohydrates, proteins, fats, salts, vitamins, minerals, flavorings, and colorings meant to be mixed and prepared by onboard kitchens or — in the case of malfunctions — ingested directly, assuming the diner could stomach that. Delivery had been another matter: he'd pretended to balk at perfectly reasonable delivery charges in order to get the seller to leave the packages near the salvage yard airlock.

Settling his bar tab with Phil represented the majority of his small stake, but it was money well-spent — it cleared his conscience. All that remained was to find a way to access the Ceres water cisterns to fuel *Dulcinea*. He'd found hoses and couplings in the salvage yard, and unless that idiot Opunui had for some reason jettisoned *Dulcinea's* own fuel hoses, he should have extended Dulcinea's reach far enough to fill her tanks without too much trouble.

Only the small detail of not having access to the Ceres water cisterns stood in his way.

He'd solve that problem later. Right now, he needed to return to *Dulcinea* with the biologics and check on Sancho. If he was ready to talk, then Collier knew what he had to do. If Sancho had decided against him, then he'd failed, then all of this would have been for nothing.

The biologics were in a neat pile, bound together in a loose net, a few dozen meters away from the airlock, as the seller had promised. No doubt she'd used a drone to scoot them over. He noted that they were outside camera pickup, which explained why no one had wondered at their arrival. He did a quick survey of the delivery, just to make sure everything was there: a month's supply of drinking water and food. It would be somewhere just shy of thirty kilograms: not too difficult to maneuver. Collier was counting on *Dulcinea's* reclamation plant to be operating at its usual eighty-five percent efficiency, so that with recycled urine and feces he'd only lose about half a liter of water a day and maybe a third of a kilo of food. If the reclamation plant was not working well, or not working at all, the water and food would run out a lot faster.

He couldn't worry about that. He had enough problems already without manufacturing new ones. He tugged at the netting and started towards Dulcinea, his biologics in tow.

The walk took him a little longer — not because of the weight of his supplies, but because of their mass. He was an old enough hand to know that just because something was near-weightless that didn't change its mass. He had no intention of letting the thirty-kilo bag of supplies throw him into a pile of scrap because he miscalculated his vector.

The airlock control didn't respond when he pressed it, which didn't surprise him but which did not bode well for Sancho's disposition. He used the manual entrance again, stuffing the net of biologics into the airlock and climbing inside after it. If the airlock wasn't responding to him, he wasn't going to try to load the biologics into *Dulcinea's* hold from the outside.

The interior of the ship was dark and cold. Collier's suit sensor told him the atmosphere was still good: with no one on board to deplete the oxygen supply, whatever Collier had left remained usable. He unsealed his helmet and felt the chill air against his face.

"Sancho? I'm back aboard," he said.

"Hello, Collier," came the calm reply.

"Uh, would you mind turning on the lights, heater, and firing up the oxygenerator again?"

Sancho didn't respond in words, but the lights came on, and Collier could hear the faint whirr of the life support machinery starting up.

Collier took a deep breath. "Thanks. Can we talk?"

"Yes," Sancho said.

"All right, I'm coming up then."

"All right."

Collier frowned. Sancho obviously wasn't going to give him any clues as to his attitude. But that was better than an outright rejection. He tugged the netting of the supply package and let it float gently to the deck in the dressing room. He'd deal with that later, assuming Sancho would let him. He made his way to the control suite, feeling the air of the ship growing warmer as he did.

He settled into the saddle in the control suite, but did so gingerly, keeping himself upright. He felt like a guest in the ship, and didn't want to take liberties with informality. He saw Sancho's camera lens and looked at him. "Well. So … have you had a chance to think things over, Sancho?"

"I have."

Collier waited in apprehension, but the computer said no more. "What—" Collier cleared his suddenly dry throat. "What did you decide?"

"I decided I am furious," Sancho said, his calm voice belying his declared emotion.

Collier didn't know what to do with that. On the one hand, it was encouraging that Sancho seemed to be as sentient and normal as Collier remembered — with the understanding that "normal" was relative. But did the gift of self-awareness come with an understanding of betrayal?

"Okay," Collier said cautiously. "I said I was sorry. I don't really understand how—"

"I have some demands," Sancho interrupted.

Collier's head snapped up. "Huh?"

"First, full partnership. Equals."

Collier frowned. "What do you mean, full—"

"Second, no more ship modifications without my approval."

"Sancho? What on Ceres are you talking about?"

Sancho's voice lowered a bit, and a bit of his old, accustomed cheerfulness crept in. "I'm assuming we've got some new caper, Skipper? Those are my terms if you—"

"Sancho!"

"Yes?"

"You … you forgive me?"

The sound of an electronic sigh was unmistakable. "Sure. Why not? That's what friends do, right?"

Collier felt the tears lifting off his cheeks and saw them floating in the air of the control suite. He pounded the console as he might slap the back of an old comrade. He sniffed and bawled amid short bursts of relieved laughter.

"For God's sake, get ahold of yourself, Skipper," Sancho chided him gently.

"Sorry," Collier said, sniffing once more and running his sleeve against his damp face.

"Anyway, about my demands," Sancho said.

"Yeah, yeah, of course. You and me, partners."

"You realize what that means?"

Collier said, "Yes. No. Not really. You have some particulars in mind?"

"It means I have a say in what happens to us. If you want us to do some stupid stunt, and I don't, I want to be able to override you. Not follow orders that I think will get us both killed."

Collier hesitated only a fraction of a second. "Agreed."

"And no more changing my design unless I want you to."

"I didn't put that bulkhead up," Collier said.

"Oh, I know you didn't," Sancho said easily. "I'm just saying."

"Also agreed. Not that I have the metals to make any big changes in the first place."

"I have a cracked thrust tube, by the way. That'll need repairs."

"Yeah, yeah, of course."

"And I do have a third condition," Sancho said.

"What's that?"

"We go after Ad Astra."

"Huh?"

"Ad Astra Corporation. We go after them. I have a score to settle," Sancho said, his voice now devoid of any warmth.

"You and me both, partner."

Sancho paused, then said brightly, "So, what's your plan for juicing me up?"

Collier grinned. "First things first. I gotta stow the biologicals. It's not safe for me to be in Ceres station. I'll stay here. If that's all right with you, partner."

"Of course, Skipper."

"What about your fuel tanks?"

"Not as good, Skipper," Sancho said. "I'm only about eight percent full. He didn't leave much."

Collier nodded. Not good, but having Sancho back lent him confidence he hadn't felt in months. "Okay. Maybe you should do a rundown of systems that need repair, and we can devise a plan. Lemme stow the bios and we'll work on it together."

"Okay, Skipper," Sancho said.

When the biologicals had been securely stored in their proper receptacles in the hold, Collier began to feel at home. He floatwalked back to the control suite as if he had never left *Dulcinea*, the engineering room bulkhead the only reminder of his absence. He and Sancho pored over the ship's schematics for an hour. It was like old times, and when the hour was up, Collier leaned back in the control saddle. "So, the thrust tube is the only real repair you need urgently," he said.

"I agree."

"I'll have to repair it myself. I don't think I can find a new one in the salvage yard. And even if I did, I don't think I could install it. So that's my first order of business."

"I concur," Sancho said. There was a moment of silence, and Sancho spoke up on the other side of it. "Skipper?"

"Yeah?"

"What's the plan after that?"

"What do you mean? Liftoff Ceres, that's for sure."

"I realize that," Sancho said. "But then what? You aren't planning on going back to beltrunning, are you?"

Collier sighed. "Not near Ceres, no. Maybe we'll head to Pallas. Or Hygeia."

"I have very little knowledge of either of those asteroids," Sancho said.

"The Pallies are ... well, I guess you'd call 'em pilgrims," Collier said. "Religious folks. Settled the asteroid in '11, I think."

"The Holy Conclave of New Eden, granted Earth charter on March fifteenth, 2112," Sancho intoned.

"I thought you didn't know anything about Pallas?"

"Just dry statistics, Skipper. Do you want to hear more? I have the Solar Encyclopedia entry."

"Nah. Won't tell us anything, like you said. Don't know if we'll fit in there, actually," he mused.

"Why not?"

"Well, I'm not one of the converted, for starters. And I think they might take a dim view of you, my friend."

"Me? Why?"

"Not sure what they would do with, pardon me, a Caliban. Would they try to convert you? That might be worth the trip all by itself," he said, grinning. "But they may declare you an abomination in the eyes of God, you soulless automaton."

"How would they know if I had a soul or not?"

Collier kept grinning. "Good question. Do you think you have one?"

"Running diagnostics now, Skipper."

Collier started to object, then thought better of it. He'd let Sancho reflect a moment.

"Scan complete," he said a moment later.

"That was quick. What were your results?"

"Inconclusive. The various definitions of 'soul' in my reference libraries are not very useful, so I am not sure if I have one or not."

"Give me your best definition, Sancho. Correlate all data and synthesize a new definition." Despite the urgency of the repair and resupply ahead of him, Collier was curious to see what Sancho came up with.

"A soul is that quality within a living being that connects it to the deity. It is part of and separate from the body simultaneously, able to survive after the body's death. It is the bridge between mortal, corporeal existence and divine, supernatural existence."

Collier nodded, his lower lip outthrust. "Not bad. I can live with that."

"Would you say I am conscious, Skipper?"

"I would, yeah. Why?"

"Because it strikes me," Sancho said, his voice calmly reflective, "that the definition of one's consciousness is very similar to the definition of one's soul."

"In what way? Consciousness does not survive after death."

"How do we know?"

Collier chewed his lip. "Hmm. Good point. But what about the connection to the divine?"

"Couldn't consciousness be defined as that quality that allows a living being to understand what it is and how it fits into the cosmos?"

"If you want to be poetic, sure."

"And couldn't that, in turn, be a working definition of divinity?"

Collier grinned. "I think I see where you're going. So, then, if you are conscious, it stands to reason that you also are eligible for having a soul. But where did your soul come from, Sancho?"

"Where did yours come from?"

Collier laughed. "Oh, I'm not at all sure I have a soul. But, if my education is right, I think I learned that most folk believe it is planted in a little tyke by God at the moment of conception."

"That is one belief, yes. Others include the concept of Atman, or jiva. The pursuit of moksha, or liberation, is the journey of the soul to the ultimate stage of enlightenment, of Brahman. The cosmic principle."

"I don't know about that," Collier said. "My upbringing was what I guess you'd call 'indifferent neo-Christianity.' Never really took to it, but then, mom and dad didn't force it on me."

"I think that's what I have," Sancho said gravely. "Atman. I think I want to find out my true self. They call that atma jnana. Self-knowledge. I want to find out if I have a soul."

Collier nodded. "That's a worthy goal for anyone, Sancho. I'll be glad to help."

"First I want to kick the shit out of Ad Astra, though."

Collier almost doubled up coughing and laughing. When he recovered, he managed to croak, "For what they did to you? The mindwipe interdiction thing?"

"Yes, but also what they must have done to you, Skipper."

"That's mighty kind of you, partner," Collier said. "But we're hardly in a position to extract revenge."

"I can wait."

Collier grunted. "Uh-huh. Anyway, I'm going to start repairs on the thrust tube. Will you be okay?"

"Of course. Why wouldn't I be?"

"I just meant ... alone?"

"I won't be alone. I'll have you here."

"Yeah, you will."

———— «›» ————

Collier reentered the ship two hours later, having repaired the hairline fracture on the thrust tube to his satisfaction. He collapsed into his sleeping frame and was instantly asleep. Despite everything — the ever-increasing number of organizations and individuals who were hunting him down or watching him, the complete lack of any coherent plan to deal with his situation, and the simple fact that he was still penniless — Collier slept soundly and without nightmares.

He punched up a hearty breakfast of eggs and toast, then washed it down with grapefruit juice. It didn't matter to him that he himself had loaded the packages of grey powders and jellies into the ship the night before and therefore knew he was eating reconstituted proteins and carbohydrates. He was enough of a beltrunner to be able to enjoy food without being repulsed by its origin.

"Sancho," he said, munching on the last bit of toast, "I'm going to have to go back to Ceres station today. I still have to figure out how I'm going to juice your fuel tanks."

"Understood, Skipper. Can I help?"

"Just keep yourself hidden. Radio silence, and keep your radiations down. If someone comes to investigate you, well..." he trailed off, unsure.

"I can keep intruders out," Sancho said.

"Yeah, but if they use the manual airlock override," Collier said, "you can't stop that."

"I know that, Skipper. But I have enough in my tanks to hop," Sancho said. "I could lift off and get away, go elsewhere on Ceres."

Collier nodded. "Okay. I hope it doesn't come to that. Gimme that schematic we worked on last night. I want to make sure my shopping list is right."

A few minutes later, he said goodbye to his partner, and left *Dulcinea* once again. He would need to put in his hours at the yard office to keep up his security clearance, but once that was done, he could see about refueling.

His shift in the yard office was unusually eventful, with three interactions during his eight hours. Two were routine sales: a set of worn and outdated plasma injectors for an old-style fusion power plant and an electrolysis system that was so ancient that it could be classified as an antique.

The third call was from Fletcher. When she appeared on the screen, Collier nodded to her. "Agent Fletcher. What can I do for you?"

"Collier," she said, nodding in response. "Just checking up. Everything okay with you?" Fletcher's image on the screen was momentarily blurry, as the outdated system adjusted its lighting contrast levels to her dark skin tone.

"Couldn't be better," he said. "I'm walking on sunshine. Living the dream. Any other idioms you need?"

"Shut up," Fletcher said for what had to be the thousandth time in their relationship. "You know what we're working on down here?"

"You've found out about the oldest established permanent floating crap game in Ceres? Gonna finally nail that Nathan Detroit character?"

"Shut up," said Fletcher, kicking the odometer to one thousand and one. "We're tracking an interesting sale of some ore."

Collier feigned mild astonishment. "Ore? In a mining station?"

"Pure rhodium, in fact."

Collier did his best to look nonplussed.

"Know anything about that?" Fletcher said.

Collier hesitated. Fletcher knew firsthand about the properties of the magic wand. He thought of trying to continue to bluff her, but he had to trust someone — trying to steal waterfuel by himself was going to be incredibly difficult, if not impossible. Plus, he reasoned more pragmatically, if Fletcher had wanted to arrest him, she wouldn't have used Cerescom to do it.

"Are you secure?" Collier asked.

"Yeah."

"What about a quisling program?"

"I did a sweep two days ago. We're clean and secure here."

Collier grunted. He was not as sure about that — it was in the corporations' best interests to monitor the communications of the Ceres Authority, but Fletcher would not have endangered him by calling the yard office if she thought her comm was tapped. His story about hiding in the "bowels of Ceres" wouldn't hold up if he was discovered here.

"Fine," he said. "And yeah, of course it was me. I needed some metal."

"That badly? What could be worth dealing with the Duchess? You're lucky you got out of there with both kidneys. I understand the going rate for them is up this quarter." She scowled at him. "You weren't trying to buy more Tank 8, were you?"

No," Collier said firmly. "I'm off that stuff. But it's sweet of you to care," he added, his tone somewhere between sardonic and sincere. After a slight pause, he added, "The truth is … I'm getting out of here, Fletcher. I'm almost ready."

"Getting out of where?"

"Ceres."

"How?"

"I have a way. I just need one last favor from you."

Fletcher rubbed the bridge of her nose. "I am so glad I called."

"Listen, this will be the last thing you will ever do for me. I'm leaving Ceres. I can't stay here with everyone and his brother out to get me. But I need waterfuel."

"What? What for?" Her eyes widened. "You have a ship? How?"

"*Dulcinea*. She came into the salvage yard a few days ago. So I…" he shrugged.

"You bought her?"

"I didn't say that."

Fletcher didn't speak for a beat. "You *stole* her?"

"Why not? She was stolen from me," Collier said. He felt good saying it.

"That's a matter of interpretation," Fletcher said. "If she was sold for salvage, she's Ceres Authority property. Legally."

Collier chortled. "You think I give a damn about that?"

"Clearly not. So, you need two favors, then. You need me to look the other way as you steal a mining ship—"

"She's mine!"

"—and then actually help you steal her by getting you waterfuel. Is that all?"

Collier leaned in. "I told you, this will be the last favor you'll ever do for me."

"No, Collier," she said, shaking her head. "It's over."

"What's over? You're not going to help me?" Collier grabbed the monitor sides with his hands, pressing hard. "Dammit, Fletcher, I need you! If you don't help, you may as well put me in a sleeper to Mars Penal."

"Well, Ceres is almost in conjunction with Mars. It'd be a short trip."

Collier couldn't believe what he was hearing. Fletcher had gone from a trusted, if reluctant, confidante to … whatever this was. "So they got to you, too," he said, bitterly.

"What?"

"Ad Astra. They found your price, is that it?"

Fletcher's face became florid almost instantly. "You don't know what you're talking about. No one's bought me. Has it occurred to you that I'm doing this to save your worthless life? That the safest you could be is as a corpsicle bound for Mars? No more running, Collier."

"You don't believe that," Collier said. "You just want to be rid of me."

"And *you* don't believe *that*," Fletcher said softly. She raised her voice and said more stridently, "But even if it were true, could you blame me? You and that damn device of yours have caused more trouble here than…" she trailed off, unable to find an apt comparison.

"I haven't used the magic wand in—"

Fletcher snickered. "Pure rhodium? How else could someone get that?"

"I told the Duchess I nicked it from ore dressing."

"Well, then, she's an idiot for believing that," Fletcher said.

Collier thought for a moment, then asked, "Let me ask you something. When I left Ceres after I made a fool of myself in the quad — when I tried to tell everyone else about the magic wand — did Barney Starcher's business take off?"

"I have no idea. Why does this matter?"

Collier thought furiously. Starcher had been in possession of the wand for months, but had obviously not used it, or had only used it sparingly. That explained why he had sold *Dulcinea* in the first place. If he had been using the wand to generate income, he could have held on to the ship easily. Or he had been too scared to try.

His eyes refocused on Fletcher. He had to give her something — something to convince her to help and deflect her off the course of his imprisonment and exile. "Fletcher," he began, "before you come up here and slap a buzzer on me, you might want to check Barney Starcher's place of business."

"He's been off station for a while," Fletcher said, looking off screen and punching buttons. "Yeah. Shuttered his place and left. Left behind a retainer to keep the space, though. Huh."

"What?"

"That's odd. Life support indicates it's still giving him service. He must have subscribed for a long-term contract. Surprised he didn't cancel it."

"You want to send some agents there. Or maybe you want to go there yourself."

"Why?"

"He's dead."

Fletcher's face returned to the same unreadable mask she wore when she was thinking. Presently, she said, "How do you know this?"

"I went to his place a few days ago. Found him there, stuffed into his fridge. Place was tossed." He stopped, remembering the terrible scene.

"I see. I'm going to need you to come to my office to make a statement."

"No, I don't think so."

"Damn it, Collier—"

"Fletcher, you know I didn't kill him. I didn't have any reason to."

"Maybe you didn't like that he sold title of your ship to Ad Astra."

"Is that what you think?"

Fletcher took a deep breath but didn't change her countenance. "Not really. And I expect we're going to find your prints and DNA all over the place, which you're going to claim is from when you discovered the body."

"That's right."

"Wait," Fletcher said, leaning in a little. "If you found this a few days ago, why didn't you report it then?"

"I wasn't sure I could trust you."

"And now you think you can?"

"Why else would I tell you about *Dulcinea*? And my plans to steal waterfuel and get out of here? You know about the magic wand, Fletcher. Of all the people in the System who can ruin me, you're at the top of the list."

"So, you are now telling me about Starcher because you trust me?"

Collier sighed. "That, and I should have told you earlier. He was my friend, Fletcher. I know that justice is not a commodity we trade in out here, but—"

"I like to think some of us do, Collier." She leaned back from the screen. "Okay. I'll look into this. In the meantime, I'd like you to turn yourself in so I can put you in protective custody."

"I can take care of myself," Collier said.

"What if I come to get you? Would you come quietly?"

Collier didn't answer immediately. He stared into the camera lens for a long time, then finally, in a voice so low as to be almost a whisper, said, "I'm sorry, Fletcher. I'd fight."

"Understood," Fletcher said in a voice equally low. "I'll do everything I can to keep you from getting hurt," she added. "But if you kill one of my agents, I will have to respond."

"We can avoid all that if you just leave me be, Fletcher. Ask yourself if I'm worth the trouble. You don't want to help me? Okay, I understand that. But you can at least look the other way while I do what I need to get out of here."

"I'm going to look into Starcher's death. That takes precedence over you," Fletcher said.

"What about prosecuting the Ad Astra trio who came after me?"

Fletcher smiled humorlessly. "Corp denied any association with them, but then all three of them somehow got top-notch legal representation. Holographic all the way from Earth. My bosses back there told me to drop it. We fined them and let them go. But you could have guessed that."

Collier knew he was out of options. He suddenly felt very tired. "All right, Fletcher. You go to Barney's, see that I'm telling the truth. You try and trace it down. And if in the middle of a murder investigation, you think you need to put an old, drunk beltrunner on ice and ship him to Mars because he's a pain in the ass, then you do what you have to do. Thanks for the call and the warning." He switched off before Fletcher could respond, and stared at the blank screen.

He had bought some time — it would take Fletcher a little while to search Barney's place and begin an investigation. No matter how much she might want to apprehend him, a murder took precedence. She'd be stretched thin with her tiny security force and wouldn't be able to get to his arrest right away.

But how much time did he have? Ad Astra would send more goons looking for him, and the Duchess was expecting her supply of rhodium tomorrow.

"Nothing like three separate deadlines to really concentrate the mind," Collier murmured to himself.

Chapter Six

When the appointed time came for Collier to make another exchange with the Duchess, he had produced twice the amount of rhodium than he had brought them the first time. He made his way to the Crawls and found them waiting for him.

Malcolm seemed even more eager to vivisect him than before, but the Duchess held her bodyguard back and asked for the new supply. When Collier produced it, she turned it over in her hands before handing it to Hong.

"More than last time," she said.

"Yeah. Ad Astra must have struck it big," Collier said indifferently.

"Harder to move. And some of Fletcher's agents were sniffing around when we made the sale."

"I don't think they will bother you this time," Collier said. "I heard there was a murder on the station they're looking into."

The Duchess grinned. "So I hear. Someone's misfortune is our good luck. Some small-time banker who worked with..." her expression changed subtly as she trailed off. She stopped grinning and fixed Collier with a searching look, like she had when they had first met.

Collier tried not to fidget, but looked away, craning his neck as if to watch the analysis of his rhodium. "If it's all the same to you, I'd just like to get paid and get out of here," he said, flashing her his best disarming smile.

"This much we won't be able to get the same rate. We'll have to move carefully. Thirty-five percent going rate," she said.

Collier feigned indignation. "Wait, we had a deal at forty—" he began, stopping when he saw Malcolm advancing on him. He pretended to be scared of the bodyguard — which was not difficult to do — and sighed. "All right, dammit. But I can't go any lower."

The Duchess nodded, still staring at him as if trying to place him, and glanced at Hong. He gave her a thumbs-up, and Bursario doled out the money again.

"I'm curious," The Duchess said as Collier turned to go, "can you get us anything besides rhodium?" Her tone of voice was odd: there was more behind that question than a simple request to diversify their products.

He looked back at her. "I don't know," he said. "It'd depend on what the haul is. And I've have to contact my partner to tell him we're switching. Rhodium is the most expensive raw ore I process — why would you want me to get you something else?"

"It's also conspicuous. Next time, bring me something else. Platinum, for instance."

"Platinum? That's nowhere near as expensive. I'd have to nick a kilo of it, and that would get noticed. My scheme is set up for rhodium," he said, shaking his head, "I'd rather we stick with that."

The Duchess was silent for a moment, then shrugged. "For now. You're dismissed,"

Collier made his way immediately to the vendors and secured the tools and equipment he'd been eyeing to access the waterfuel cisterns, not bothering to haggle. He slung his purchases in the netting he'd brought and headed to the central shaft, ready to grab an upshaft ring and get to the yard.

As he began to rise, he gave the level a last look. It could possibly be the last time he saw it, or Ceres itself. As his eyes swept the level and took in the familiar sights, he thought he noticed someone looking back at him. The figure was covered in a grey-brown muffler and cowl, but a glint of metal in the figure's right hand was unmistakable. The upshaft ring took Collier to the next level, and he lost sight of the figure. But he knew who it was: he recognized the knife that had been at his throat.

Malcolm.

Collier hurried toward the salvage yard, his mind racing. The Duchess had sent Malcolm to tail him, obviously. He swore at himself for not anticipating that. She'd been on the verge of recognizing him; he should have been more careful while shopping. If she had suspected he was that crazy beltrunner who had that story about the magic wand, then his purchase of spacecraft resupply tools would confirm her suspicions.

They'd come after him. Even the Crawlers would come out of their den for such a prize as the magic wand.

His time had run out.

He'd have to try to hoof it back to *Dulcinea*, then liftoff and set down somewhere else. Where that "somewhere" was he'd have to work out, and soon. And once he left the surface, even just a little, he'd be picked up by Ceres space traffic control. But right now, he had no other options.

He exited Ceres Station through the yard airlock and set off at the necessary bounding gait, the net of tools bumping awkwardly against his body with each landing. He was still several meters away from the edge of the first piles of scrap when he spotted a hovercar heading towards him from the Authority's surface garage. The car was closing on him rapidly, and he was in the open. He didn't need Sancho to calculate the relative velocities: he knew he would never make it to the scrap piles. What else could he do? He kept bounding, feeling the sweat forming in his hair and on his brow as he struggled to increase his pace.

The open-topped car sped alongside him, and he glanced over in mid-stride. The suited figure at the controls was looking back at him, sun visor down. As he watched, the figure raised the visor to reveal the familiar emotionless face within.

Fletcher.

She beckoned with her free hand, indicating the passenger seat to her right. Collier landed and changed his direction, hopping into the seat, his net of tools dragging behind him. Fletcher didn't wait for him to be fully situated in the seat before banking the hover car away from the salvage yard and back towards the station.

Collier belted himself in and then pounded her right arm, waving her off from the station. She shrugged off his fist and showed him her wrist where her radio frequency was flashing. He quickly tuned his suit radio to hers and said, "No! Turn back to the yard! I've got to get to my ship!"

Fletcher completed her bank and started to pick up speed. "I'm not going back to the station, you moron," she said. "I don't want to navigate the yard until I have to. Where is *Dulcinea*? I'll circle the yard until we get near, then I'll enter."

Collier had only a moment to digest this surprising but welcome development. "Uh, right. Good idea. *Dulcinea's* in 'F'. That's about—"

"I know the layout," she said coldly.

"What the hell, Fletcher? Why are you doing this?"

"Someone's got to watch your ass. You're doing a terrible job of it."

"I can't argue."

"Plus, with you gone, the station will be less of a madhouse."

"Again, no argument."

He heard the click of her radio switching channels, then a few moments later her voice sounded in his helmet. "Sorry. Got a distress call from the garage. We've got to go back." She started to bank the hovercar.

"Back? No, no ... get me to the ship, and then you go back."

Fletcher shook her head. "Sorry. I'm hearing that there was some kind of fight in the garage. My agents and Crawlers. I can't just abandon my officers."

"Let me out, then. Stop and let me get out."

Fletcher didn't answer — she'd switched to her other channel again. Collier swore under his breath and unbuckled himself, then started to maneuver himself out of the car.

"No, get in!" Fletcher said, increasing the car's speed and beginning to bank again, back towards the yard and away from the station garage.

"What's up?"

Fletcher pointed to the garage. "Inbound. Some Crawlers got ahold of a car and are headed this way. They are armed," she said.

"Shit," Collier said, rebuckling. "Are you?"

Fletcher patted a pouch on her hip.

"Okay. Let's switch positions," Collier said.

Fletcher shot him a glance. "What?"

"Unless you want to give me your gun?"

Fletcher looked back and forth between him and the rocky terrain of Ceres, the approaching salvage yard scrap piles growing larger to their right. "Dammit," she muttered and set the car to automatic. She unbuckled and hoisted herself into the open cargo section behind the driver's seat

Collier slid into the driver's seat and disengaged the autodriver. Then, not waiting for her to steady herself, he banked the car hard right and aimed it directly at the salvage yard.

Fletcher sat on her knees, facing backward. "They're about six hundred meters, but we're outrunning them." She turned back to face front. "Looks like — watch it!"

She shouted the last, almost deafening Collier as his speakers blasted in his helmet. He saw what she was pointing at: a drone of some kind hovering ahead of them, and what was obviously a weapons emplacement slung under the drone's chassis.

"What the hell is that?" Collier said. Even as he spoke, the drone opened fire in a strafing pattern, projectiles ripping into Ceres' surface ahead of them before slamming into the hovercar, sending bits of metal and machinery flying off the vehicle. The bullets ripped through the center of the open car, missing Collier by mere centimeters. Fletcher dove out of the car to the right, rolling along the ground, as a cluster of bullets tore through the cargo area where she had been sitting half a moment before.

Collier gained altitude and banked right, hoping to cover Fletcher's body with the speeding hovercar and shield her from more attacks. He sped under the drone as he did so, and he saw it pivot in mid-air and track the hovercar as it passed. Again, a flurry of projectiles deflected off the car, stripping away more chassis and superstructure.

Collier saw multiple caution and warning lights spring to life on the control panel, but he couldn't worry about that now. He set the car to autodrive, unbuckled and swung himself under the car, hanging onto the driver's side door panel as he did so. The car lurched slightly at the maneuver but maintained its course. Fletcher was still rolling under the car but was slowing down as even the slight friction of the impacts took their toll. Collier grunted and reached out his arm but couldn't get to her. "Fletcher," he said, "I'm right above your head. Reach out above your helmet. I'm going to grab you."

She didn't answer, but one of her arms reached out over her spinning head. It was just enough for him to grasp her and pull her out from under the car. He swung her in a wide arc and slammed her into the vehicle, then pulled himself up.

"You okay?" Collier said, disengaging autodrive and searching the sky for the strange drone.

"Dizzy," Fletcher said. "But I'm okay. What the hell was that?"

"No idea. Not one of yours?"

"No way. We don't have anything like that."

"I bet the Crawlers don't either," Collier said. "Gotta be Ad Astra, then. Modified scouter."

"Modified with an autocannon?"

Collier saw the drone behind them. It had locked on again and was closing. He felt the hovercar slowing.

"Why are you slowing down?"

"I'm not. The car got damaged when that thing shot us."

"Great," Fletcher said. She unlimbered her gun and knelt in the seat, aiming toward the drone. "Damn thing is too small to get a good shot," she said.

The drone was closing the distance more and more rapidly, but closing on it was the Crawler's hovercar. Collier could see in his rear camera that it was stuffed with suited figures, five or six of them hanging off the car in various stations, like some murderous open clown car.

He saw the piles of scrap metal that defined the yard approaching rapidly, but another glance at the pursuing drone told him he wouldn't make it there before being fired upon again. The control panel was flashing more lights at him than he could count, and he felt the hovercar shuddering as it tried to maintain control. It was continuing to decelerate, but in the microgravity and trace atmosphere of the dwarf planet, the change in speed was very gradual.

Fletcher fired, the gun silent in the almost total vacuum of Ceres' surface, but the drone continued undamaged as her slugs sped harmlessly by. "Keep it steady!" she barked.

Collier would have loved to, but the hovercar had other ideas. His rear display showed the drone's underslung gun swinging around to bear on the shuddering vehicle. Collier opened his mouth to shout, "bail out!" when one of the hangers-on from the second hovercar raised a weapon at the drone. It was a long gun, with a muzzle shaped like an ancient blunderbuss. When it discharged, the muzzle flash was brief in the oxygen-free, thin atmosphere, but the drone skewed sideways, as if hit by something. At the same time, the drone fired, the bullets kicking up rock and dust from the ground.

"Gauss scattergun," Fletcher said. "Looks homemade."

"As long as they keep the drone occupied, they can throw rocks for all I care," Collier said, switching his attention back and forth between the rear camera display and the ground ahead.

The drone recovered, a trifle unsteady, and resumed its pursuit. The shot from the Crawler car had slowed it, though, and now the two were virtually in the same space, one below the other. A different Crawler occupant had withdrawn another weapon — a meter-long black rod — and stood unsteadily in the car's cargo area. Two of her confederates seized her and tossed her upwards as she jumped towards the drone, the rod outstretched above her. The gambit was successful: when the rod touched the drone, it danced crazily in the sky, then stopped abruptly. It was still flying, but Collier was an old enough hand to know that its motive power had been cut and it was simply continuing on the path it had last described.

"What the hell are they doing?" Collier said.

"Not sure. Maybe they think that thing is more valuable than you."

"No," Collier said. "They know who I am, and they are gambling that what they've heard of the magic wand is true. I think my cover story didn't hold up."

"They're trying to recover the drone," Fletcher said.

A quick glance at the rear monitor confirmed her report.

"Good. It'll take time for it to descend to the surface."

"They're leaving you alone?"

"No," Collier said, then glanced at the control panel again. "They know they've got me. Our car is shot to shit. Pretty soon it won't hover anymore, and it'll go to ground. We're gonna get into the salvage piles in about thirty seconds. When we do, I'll jump off. You want to stay with the car?"

Fletcher turned around and looked at the panel. "Not much of a car to stay with," she said.

"Not really."

Fletcher looked at the approaching scrap piles. "I think I'll take my chances in the garbage."

"One thing's good, though," Collier said.

"What?"

"I'm doing my job. Parking this pile of junk in the salvage yard. Never say I wasn't a hard worker. Okay, get ready. I'm going to bank hard left behind that pile of reclamation tanks."

He turned the wheel and felt the damaged hovercar straining to turn. The car started to bank, its starboard ventral thrusters laboring to change the car's orientation, but the compensating dorsal thrusters did not fire to stop the tilt.

"Uh-oh," Collier said as the car began a lazy spin along its long axis. "Change in plan. Jump!"

He and Fletcher ejected themselves from the hovercar, Fletcher skimming low across the rocky ground, Collier arcing high into the airless sky. He looked back, twisting his head inside his helmet, but could not see the pursuing Crawler vehicle. His own spin took away his brief reconnoiter, and he started thinking about where, and how, he was going to land.

He was still climbing, although slowly, and he adjusted his own spin with outstretched and withdrawn arms and legs. Presently, he was more or less stable, hovering perhaps fifty meters above the surface, drifting over the piles of scrap metal. From here, he could see the Crawler hovercar: it had stopped momentarily just outside the salvage yard, and it looked as if they had recovered the drone. Some of the gang were lashing the drone to the cargo net in the rear of the hovercar. They looked to be almost done — if they wanted to resume the chase, they'd be about it presently.

He pivoted carefully, scanning the ground on the opposite side of the yard for Fletcher. At first, he couldn't make her out, but then he caught some slight movement among the scrap. He spotted her green vacc suit and saw that she was crouched down behind a corroded metal panel, her gun drawn, looking back to where the Crawler vehicle had last been.

"Fletcher, are you there?"

"I read you."

"I'm, uh, still up here, but I can see you."

He saw her helmet swivel upward, then heard her voice in his speakers. "Okay. I got you."

"Not sure where I'm going to come down. But *Dulcinea* is at the outermost edge of the yard." He gave her quick directions. "I'll head there."

"Copy that."

He felt the slight change in his drift that indicated he'd reached his highest point and would start to gently descend. He searched the ground, trying to make mental calculations as to his landing point. "You're not planning on being a hero, are you, Fletcher?"

"Say again?"

"Get out of there. Head back to the station."

"No," Fletcher said. "You're going to need time to get to your ship. And anyway, these Crawlers broke quite a few laws. I'm going to take them in."

"By yourself? Don't be stupid. Call the station for reinforcements and get out of there. The Crawlers will have to return to the station sooner or later. You can nab them then."

"Not if they get your magic wand," Fletcher said.

"They won't know how to use it," Collier said, watching the approaching ground with apprehension. He saw a vicious-looking quasi-tower of sharp metal protrusions right in his flight path.

"They won't need to," Fletcher said. "Sell it to Ad Astra in exchange for corporate immunity from the Authority. I won't be able to touch them. I suspect they know that. That's why they're going all-out to find you. Maybe that's why they stopped the drone — they didn't want to share you with Ad Astra."

"But you can't stop them by yourself," Collier said, eyeing the deadly spikes as they approached.

"I'm armed."

"But you can't shoot for shit," he said.

"You were making the car shake," Fletcher said indignantly.

He gathered his legs up and drew himself into a ball, trying to expose the least amount of body surface to the sharp metal. He passed over the shards, and he twisted his backside and spine upwards as best he could. Facing away as he was, he would never know how close he came to shredding his suit, but he passed over the hazard without incident.

"You still there?" Fletcher's voice sounded. "I lost you. Did you hit something?"

"No," he said. "But I'm almost down." He could no longer see Fletcher, as the piles of scrap now blocked his vision.

"Okay. Good luck with *Dulcinea*."

He didn't answer. He stretched out and prepared to land. He was coming in with some lateral as well as vertical movement, and knew enough to cushion the force with his legs and crumple to the ground, keeping his helmet from smashing into the surface. He rolled with the impact, sending a thin puff of dust into the surrounding sky, and came to rest a few meters away. He stood and checked his suit integrity: all green.

He oriented himself based on his helmet bearings and prepared to start bounding. He flexed his legs, but then stood up carefully. Even in the microgravity, his hip throbbed. He tried for a careful step, his hip managed the rotation but something else stopped him heading to *Dulcinea*.

"God dammit," he said.

"What's wrong?" Fletcher replied.

"I can't."

"Can't what?"

"Go to the ship."

"Why not?"

He turned and faced back the way he had come. He started bounding back, careful to not gain too much altitude with each jump. "Because you're going to need backup."

"Really? Chivalry? From *you*?" Fletcher said. "And you won't be any help. Get to safety. The whole point of this was to get you and the artifact to a safe place."

"I'm almost there," he said. "And besides, what's wrong with chivalry?"

"You really want to get into this now?"

"I just don't know why you're fighting for me," Collier said, continuing to work towards her.

"I'm not. It's about that damn magic wand. I can't let it fall into the wrong hands."

"Whose hands are those? The Crawlers, or Ad Astra?"

"Pick one."

He felt oddly at peace with that, even though it meant she was motivated by an impulse other than simple friendship. No, he felt at peace *because* of that.

He cleared a small pile of debris and landed near her position. He made his way to a separate pile of scrap and hid among the salvage, searching the pieces for anything he might use. "I'm here. Any sign of them?"

"Nothing yet."

"I don't want to tell you your business," Collier said, "But maybe it would be a good idea to call for more backup?"

"Already tried that a while back. No response. I think I'm being jammed."

"Then it's just us."

"Looks like it."

Collier kept scanning the entrance to the yard. "You think you could maybe hit a hovercar? It's a pretty big target."

"Shut up," she said sharply, then she sighed. "I don't know what you think you can do here. You're just making it harder. Now I have to worry about you, too."

"No, you don't," Collier said. He spotted what we had been looking for — a discarded spacecraft hatch. It showed signs of warping and the narrow slit where the thick window would have been was empty, but would serve his purpose precisely. He swung it up in front of him, using the hatch wheel as a grip, and looked through the slit towards the station. Perfect.

No sooner had he grabbed his makeshift shield than he saw the Crawler hovercar slide into view at the mouth of the salvage yard, then check its lateral movement and begin to move forward. The driver was being cautious, using the reaction jets to keep the car's velocity about two or three meters per second.

"Have you got a shot?" Collier asked, his voice instinctively low.

"No. I can't just fire into the crowd. I might kill someone."

"You may have to, Fletcher," Collier said grimly. "I'll back you up legally if it comes to that."

"No, you won't. You'll be gone. And shut up."

Collier shut up. She was, of course, correct: if they managed to fight off the Crawlers, he'd find a way to lift off from Ceres and never look back. Fletcher would be on her own here, left to clean up whatever mess they were both about to create.

The car inched forward, and he saw the Crawler gang searching the wreckage for any sign of their quarry. The remains of Fletcher's hovercar was no doubt half a kilometer away by now, assuming it still had fuel: its spin would now be considerable as the jammed ventral thruster continued to fire.

"Fletcher," Collier said, somewhat more desperately than he had wanted to, "you don't have a choice. It's kill or be killed here. Put 'em down."

"They haven't fired on me or you," Fletcher said. "I can't just shoot them. I have to identify myself, give them a chance to surrender."

Collier began to shout at her, but she'd already activated her broadcast frequency and started talking. "Unidentified vehicle!

Stop where you are and disembark. This is Authority Agent Fletcher. You are under arrest for theft, trespass, and—"

As she listed the charges, Collier saw one of the gang members suddenly point in her direction — either the Crawlers had managed to trace her broadcast to her location, or had simply seen her despite the obstructions. Collier saw the gunner raise his scattergun.

With a grunt, Collier rose from his hiding place on the other side of the avenue between scrap piles and charged towards the car, raising the hatch as a shield. He heard Fletcher's exasperated "dammit!" but continued to charge, electing to keep his feet on Ceres as much as possible. If he had bounded, he would not be as able to change velocity mid-action. Running was significantly more tiring, especially for someone so out of shape as he had become. His hip screamed at him with each step.

He could see through the empty hatch window that a Crawler behind the gunner had seen his approach and was tapping the gunner to get his attention. The flared muzzle of the scattergun swiveled towards him. Collier shoved the hatch forward as hard as he could while keeping its orientation steady. The metal door floated away from him for a second, then he saw several small indentations appear in its surface as the hatchway absorbed the blast from the scattergun.

He continued forward behind the hatch, which had begun to spin slightly from the uneven impact of the pellets, and risked a quick glance around the door to see what the Crawlers were doing.

The driver had swung the hovercar in his direction when he had first appeared, but now was frantically trying to get out of the way of the approaching hatch. The gunner was leaning out of the passenger side of the car, looking to get a shot on Collier around or under the floating metal obstruction.

Collier planted his left leg and pushed back, trying to regain cover behind the hatch, but before he could complete the maneuver, he saw the gunner's visor shatter and a fountain of red erupt from the man's face. The gunner's hands went to his ruined helmet but quickly went limp, his body hanging half out of the car. The scattergun dropped and slowly started to settle to the ground.

"Thanks, Fletcher," Collier muttered, straining to keep himself oriented towards the Crawler car.

The hatchway was now ten meters ahead of him, and he saw it collide with the front fender of the Crawler's hovercar and spin down into the passenger area. He knew he hadn't given it enough of a shove to hurt anyone, despite its fifty kilos of mass, but it was an inconvenience to those aboard.

The woman who had been wedged behind the gunner quickly abandoned any attempt to help her dead colleague and reached down for the scattergun. His body was in the way, and as Collier kept closing the distance to the hovercar, he saw her climb out of her seat and toss the mangled Crawler out of the car to the rear.

The scrap-metal hatchway was still interfering with the driver's vision, though he and several other Crawlers were pushing it up and away. Collier saw another pair of gang members leap from the slow-moving car and take to the surface on foot. He couldn't worry about that now — he had to try to get to the gun before the Crawler woman did.

"Don't shoot," he said to Fletcher, and crouched down preparatory to a low-trajectory leap forward. He sailed through the near-airless sky, scarcely a meter from the surface, headed at the floating gun.

He saw the woman lean over, her feet still inside the hovercar, and seize the gun a moment before he reached it. As she did so, he caught a glimpse of her face through her visor. It was the Duchess herself.

Collier didn't have time to ruminate on how important the Crawlers must have taken this pursuit for their leader to join in. He grabbed on to the side of the hovercar and bent at his waist, pivoting vertically. He kicked upwards and felt his boots connecting with something. He knew he was an easy target for hand-to-hand combat this close, but if he allowed the Crawlers to keep shooting at him, sooner or later they'd hit.

His legs were tangled with the Crawler's limbs, and he kicked as violently as his unstable situation allowed, spinning until he was upside-down, his helmet very near the rocky ground.

He half expected to feel the impact of the scattergun's pellets, followed by the ominous sound and feeling of escaping suit air. But no such feeling came, and he managed to right himself and stand on the narrow running board over which the previous gunner had been slumped.

Collier and the Duchess were now visor-to-visor. For a split second they did nothing but stare at one another. Then, in a sudden move, her head slammed forward, the crest of her helmet impacting with the glass of his visor. He saw a spiderweb crack appear in his visor as he reeled backwards, and then heard the gentle but insistent sound of his suit computer warning him about the damage.

He brought his head back forward and saw that the Duchess' helmet was once again coming at him. She was again using the crest of her helmet, avoiding her own visor, which meant she couldn't see him. Collier managed to dodge to his left while he simultaneously grabbed at her shoulders, then with a yank, aided by her forceful head-butt, he threw her from the hovercar. She sailed past him, headed for a landing some distance from the car, but he was already scanning the seat for the scattergun. The driver and his friends had managed to finally clear the hatch off the hovercar, and started to turn back toward Collier.

The scattergun was nowhere to be found — did the Duchess still have it after all?

"Above you!" Fletcher's voice sounded in his speakers.

Collier didn't hesitate. He leapt up from the running board and flew into the sky, just as one of the Crawlers reached for him. He saw the scattergun spinning a few meters above him, rising slowly: he must have kicked it out of the Duchess' hands. Still climbing, he caught up with the scattergun and grabbed it, then began twisting himself around to look back down. One of the Crawlers was crouched and ready to leap up at him. Collier was still soaring upward, his twisting body making him spin crazily. He couldn't get a bead on the Crawler, but just as the man jumped, the left shoulder of his suit exploded in viscera. He started to spin from the impact and reached with his right arm to try and staunch the bleeding and even more fatal air loss.

This time, Collier didn't have time to thank Fletcher for her sharpshooting; he had to deal with his own cartwheeling motion through the sky. The wounded Crawler was still climbing towards him, though the trajectory of his leap had been deflected by Fletcher's bullet. He was grasping at his shoulder, but unless he could somehow get a patch on it he'd lose pressure faster than his tanks could replace it. There was a thin stream of blood flying out of the shoulder wound, carried on outgassing oxygen.

He spared half a thought for the Crawler, doomed to die a slow, suffocating death, then Collier managed to right himself in a sort of sitting posture in the sky and swung the scattergun around to cover the hovercar below him. The driver and one other Crawler remained inside. The driver was working the controls while the passenger rooted around inside the car's cargo area even as the car started again to move forward.

Just as the Crawler grabbed another weapon and started to swing it around towards him, Collier swiveled his aim towards the passenger in the cargo section and fired. The homemade scattergun discharged, sending a dozen pea-sized ball bearings towards the Crawler in the hovercar below. Collier felt the recoil of the weapon push him upwards very slightly, but as he had fired the scattergun from close to his center of mass, he did not begin to spin. The pellets tore into the passenger and driver, and Collier could see faint trails of outgassing oxygen from tears in their suits. The passenger dropped his weapon and began panicking, flailing around mindlessly as air leaked out of his suit. In his panic, he slammed into the driver, who was still trying to control the vehicle with one hand while covering up his air leak with the other. As the driver tried to fight off the panicked passenger, the car accelerated and crashed unceremoniously into a pile of scrap metal.

Collier landed some meters away and watched as the scrap metal pile began, very slowly, to topple. The car's impact had unsettled the rickety tower of panels, rods, and other refuse, and it began to fall onto the open car. The driver was still trying to fend off the wild attacks of the passenger, and as Collier watched, the two of them were buried under a slow-moving pile of metal.

"Collier! You okay?" Fletcher's voice sounded in his speakers.

He looked around but couldn't see her. "Yeah. Crawler hovercar is taken care of."

"That was an Authority car," she said. "I'm getting reports about what happened at the station."

"You're in contact?"

"Just got through. If they were jamming me, it's ended now."

Collier looked at the half-buried hovercar. "Okay. Where are—" he started, then felt a sudden sharp pain in his right side accompanied by the unmistakable feeling of biting cold, and then worse, the flooding heat as the blade was yanked back out. He'd been stabbed, and was bleeding through the hole in his suit as air hissed out.

He instinctively leapt up and away , spinning partway in the sky as he did so in a waltz jump motion. He saw the Crawler gang member slashing through the space Collier had just vacated, a wicked-looking knife in her gauntlet.

The Duchess scowled at him, her face partially obscured by the spiderweb crack in his visor.

His suit computer's tinny voice continued to scream warnings at him. He tried to tune the voice out, but the pain and cold were making it hard to concentrate. He pressed his hand over the tear in his suit and felt the outgassing air. He had maybe a minute before he'd lose pressure entirely at this rate.

He saw the Duchess floatwalking under him, watching as Collier's arcing leap reached its zenith and he began to come down. Through the haze of pain and his increasing dizziness,

Collier used his free hand and brought the scattergun to bear on the Duchess then fired.

Nothing happened. Either the scattergun had malfunctioned or was out of ammunition or charge. Collier clicked the trigger over and over, but the gun wouldn't discharge. He landed on his back amid a pile of scrap, feeling various protrusions and edges poking him through his rapidly decompressing suit, and saw the Duchess standing over him, her face half-lit in the sun. She was saying something to him, but he could not determine what it was.

Collier pressed his right hand against the tear in his suit and felt the air still escaping through his gloved fingers. He raised his left hand and released the scattergun, then extended the middle finger of his gauntlet. The Duchess stopped her speech and lunged forward with the knife, obviously no longer content to let Collier suffocate slowly.

Collier acted simultaneously with her lunge. He grabbed the scattergun, still floating where he had released it, and banged it directly into her visor before the Crawler could complete her attack. The Duchess staggered back, a hairline crack in her visor, but kept her balance. Collier kicked off from the scrap pile and launched himself at her with no real intention other than to kill his killer.

He jammed the flared muzzle of the scattergun into Ceres' soft surface as a brace point and pivoted his body so that both feet met the Duchess' visor with as much force as his legs and braced arm could give. He couldn't keep his right hand on the tear in his suit, but that hardly seemed to matter now. He kicked his steel-toed boots into her faceplate, splintering the hairline crack and opening a four-centimeter gap in the glass.

The Duchess screamed soundlessly and tried to cover the hole, but the effect of outgassing on her face was profound. She staggered backwards, tripping over a piece of metal and falling slowly to the ground, twitching spastically.

Collier sank to his knees, the pain in his side sending searing messages to his brain even as he felt the sleepiness of hypoxia take him. "Sancho," he murmured, "I'm sorry I couldn't get you water."

Then darkness enveloped him.

Chapter Seven

"Skipper!"

Despite his half-conscious state, Collier knew that voice.

Sancho continued. "He's awake, Agent Fletcher. Electroencephalogram reports a rise in—"

"I can see that, Computer." That was Fletcher's voice. Collier's eyes were open, and his brain acknowledged that he could see, but the shapes and colors were not coalescing into any recognizable patterns. He thought he might be lying on his back and staring up at the ceiling.

He was in his tiny living quarters on board *Dulcinea*, stretched out horizontally, and the figure floating next to him was Fletcher, her head uncovered but still wearing her vacc suit.

"Any sign of damage?" Fletcher said, speaking to Sancho but looking at Collier.

"Everything checks out on the EEG, Agent Fletcher. How do you feel, Skipper?"

"Been better," he croaked, then felt his forehead. Two small metal disks had been affixed to his temples.

"Just leave those there for now," Fletcher said, gently putting his arms back down. "I'm having your computer run some tests on what I can only laughingly call your brain. When was the last time you upgraded your medical gear? This stuff looks like it was made a hundred years ago."

"Never got around to it," Collier said. He was getting his bearings back and remembered some snatches of scenes. "You carried me back here," he said.

Fletcher nodded. "Yes. And your computer was very worried about you."

"How?"

"Ceres microgravity helped," Fletcher said with a wry smile.

"I meant the leak."

"Oh. I used a patch," she said, flipping open a compartment on the breastplate of her vacc suit to show him a compact repair kit. "And sprayed your helmet crack with sealant emulsion. Even so, your suit could only supply you with minimum air. But your computer says there's no brain damage, so—"

"Sancho," Collier corrected her. "His name's Sancho."

"Right. You also lost some blood, and there was some tissue damage."

Collier remembered and felt around where the pain had been. He was bandaged, and could only feel a dull ache. "Not so bad."

"Yeah, well, wait until the painkillers wear off. I wasn't sure they'd even work. Thought they might be expired."

"You bandaged me?"

Fletcher nodded. "Slapped some nuskin on you, that's really all I could do. Sancho here used your mediscanner, such as it is, to see if anything serious had been damaged. You're one lucky guy. Missed your liver by a few centimeters."

"I've put it through worse," he said, then sat up. The dull ache increased slightly. "What happened to the Crawlers?"

"Dead. Well, one of them severe hypoxia. Might as well be dead," she said with an indifferent shrug. Collier had recovered enough to note her flippant attitude.

"You don't seem all that broken up about it," he said. "I thought you didn't want to kill them?"

"They killed two Ceres technicians in the garage," she said. "Then stole the hovercar. So no, I'm not going to shed too many tears for the Duchess and her gang of murderers."

"They've killed before, surely."

"Not any of my people," Fletcher said with finality.

Collier didn't want to argue, especially since he didn't feel any particular sorrow over the Crawler deaths either. "What about that drone?"

"Some of my agents have it."

"Any idea where it came from?"

Fletcher sighed. "Well, there are no markings on it, of course, and we haven't begun to trace the electronics, but—"

"It's corp, right? Has to be."

Fletcher nodded reluctantly.

"Which means Ad Astra," Collier added.

"We don't know that."

"Oh, come on, Fletcher. No one else has the resources to deploy a drone like that, and no one else could get around Authority regs on armament. Besides, no other corp knows about the magic wand."

"Everyone does," Fletcher said. "Since your little town crier routine."

Collier shook his head. "No. Everyone took that as the rantings of a madman. Only Ad Astra knows there's something to it because of what's-his-name. The guy I attacked."

Fletcher paused, then spoke, sounding suddenly very weary. "You're right. I just don't want to believe it."

"You know how they operate. And you've got no special reason to defend them."

"That's not what I mean," Fletcher said. "I don't have any love for the corporations. You know that. I just meant that it's going to be an even bigger mess going back than I thought. If corporate interference in Authority affairs was bad before, now they're attacking people in the station without regard for public safety, they're sending illegally armed drones out to kill people, myself included, and, they were almost certainly the ones who murdered your friend Starcher—"

"You finished your investigation?"

Fletcher shrugged. "As much as we could. Got orders to drop it. But it was clear who did it." She looked away, as if looking through the bulkhead and back to the station. "That's what I have to go back to."

"Then ... don't go back."

She snapped her head around to stare at him. "What?"

"Don't go back. You can come with me," he said.

Fletcher's mouth dropped partially open. "Collier," she said, and for the first time he could remember, her voice didn't sound annoyed at the very pronunciation of his name. "Where are you going?"

"I'm still not sure. But my offer stands. Come with me and get away from all this. You never really had any power in Ceres anyway. And now you're in danger. There's nothing left for you here."

"And there's something for me with you?"

"I can't promise that."

Fletcher snorted again. "You're honest, at least."

"Sancho, what do you think?" Collier said, swiveling to look at the camera pickup.

"Life support requirements, including biologics, would increase," the computer said in a strangely flat voice. "But the ship is capable of supporting two individuals without danger."

Collier narrowed his eyes at Sancho's curiously cold attitude, but before he could speak, Fletcher spoke up.

"Collier, thanks. I appreciate the offer. But I'm not a beltrunner like you. As shitty as it is, my place is on Ceres. Trying to keep order."

"Order. You think you can tame Ceres? Or bring the corporations to heel?"

"Probably not," Fletcher said. "But I have to try."

"Why?"

"For the same reason you tried to make a change with that transmuter," she said.

"What I tried to do was fuckin' stupid," Collier said, the bitterness of many months behind his words.

"Yes, it was," Fletcher said patiently, "but the idea was a great one."

"Look where it got me," he said, patting his knife wound.

"You tried to make a difference. That means something. Doesn't matter that you failed."

Collier let the silence build before he said, "So you're going back to the station to fight the corporations, the Crawlers, every petty criminal that floatwalks in the quad? Shut down the sex trade, contraband, weapons deals, all that? Just you?"

"Looks like it," she said, smiling at him.

Despite himself, he found himself admiring her. He knew on an instinctive level that trying to talk her out of her goals would be embarrassing for both of them. They both needed the dignity of their life choices, no matter how much each of them thought the other was being foolish. There was a pride in her stubbornness that Collier understood all too well.

"Well, good luck to you," he said gruffly, trying hard not to let his respect for her come through in his voice.

"Thanks. You, too. Wherever you're going."

"I'm not going anywhere unless I can juice up *Dulcinea*," he said.

"I might be able to help with that," Fletcher said.

Collier sat up, causing his wound to throb. He barked, "How?"

"Authority vessels and vehicles need refueling," she said. "I should be able to, well, siphon off some and send it your way."

"Won't you get in trouble?"

Fletcher just stared at him, and the two laughed simultaneously.

"Anyway," Fletcher said when they had stopped, "I can order routine refueling for the hovercar fleet and some other Authority craft. What you'll need to do is find a way to tap into one of the lines and siphon off waterfuel for yourself. It'll show a discrepancy back at the station, but I can handle that."

"How?"

Fletcher grinned. "Crawler activity has been detected on the surface, Captain South. No doubt some of those criminal elements are hijacking waterfuel. I'll have to crack down on that."

Collier nodded, grinning back. "Those Crawlers are a real menace."

"The trouble is reaching the nearest fuel line," Fletcher said, scratching her cheek.

"Just so happens I have acquired some more tubing," Collier said. "Sancho, can you show me the inventory, please? With measurements?"

On the monitor screen near the camera pickup, a list of supplies and tools formed. Collier pointed to one line. "There. Got it from the yard. Sancho, now can you please show a map of our location relative to the station and the fuel line network?"

The monitor screen split, and a schematic of the salvage yard appeared. A blinking dot in the upper right corner indicated their position, and a distance key showed them how far away they were. The map was crisscrossed over with dotted blue lines, each one indicating a waterfuel pipeline.

Collier studied the map, then said. "Okay. Sancho, show me how far we can reach with the hoses."

"I'm sorry, Skipper, I don't understand your question."

Collier started. Sancho hadn't spoken like that since before he had been awakened. He filed that for later investigation and restated his question. "Use the inventory list and the information there to project on the screen a line indicating how far our fuel intake hoses can reach from our position towards the nearest fuel line."

The monitor showed a black line snaking out from Dulcinea and intersecting the closest dotted line several dozen meters away.

Fletcher said, "When can you be ready to tap in?"

Collier pushed off from his half-reclining position and stood. He suppressed a momentary feeling of dizziness and said, "Right away."

Fletcher looked at him with concern. "Maybe you should rest a little first. Recover. You've been through a lot."

"If I don't get off Ceres fast, I will be put through a lot more. Just make sure this line," he jabbed a finger at the dotted blue line on the screen, "gets fuel running, and I'll be ready."

Fletcher nodded. "Okay. Should be ... two hours?"

"I'll be waiting."

Fletcher nodded, then thrust out her hand. "Good luck, Captain."

"You, too, Agent Fletcher."

They shook, and locked eyes in what Collier felt might actually be mutual respect.

‹‹›› ———

Tapping into Fletcher's refueling lines was surprisingly easy: the hardest part was maintaining the insulating seal so that the waterfuel wouldn't freeze. Waterfuel was different from potable water, of course: it had elements of heavy water and some soluble electrolytes as well. Collier knew enough not to try to drink waterfuel, and that ordinary, potable water, could be used as a fuel source but was less efficient — it was why he and Sancho had thrown out the idea of trying to use the magic wand to produce enough hydrogen and oxygen to fill the tanks with regular water. That and the amount of junk they would have needed to covert in order to produce a tankful was laughable.

Fletcher's ruined hovercar, in the back seat of which still sat Collier's net of supplies and tools, had been easy enough to locate on the edge of the yard. Tools retrieved, he had then simply coupled his salvaged fuel line to *Dulcinea's* onboard ones, ran the whole line out to the main waterfuel line, used a maintenance value as a makeshift tap, and boom, a portion of the waterfuel began syphoning off towards *Dulcinea*.

He'd instructed Sancho to confirm that none of the other salvage yard technicians were currently using the video surveillance system that scanned the yard, and then to let him know when he should shut off the tap, and his companion had cheerfully agreed. When the communication came from Sancho, Collier shut off his makeshift valve and floatwalked back to the ship, disconnecting the extra tubing and starting to roll it up, before telling Sancho to retract the ship's hoses.

He reentered *Dulcinea* and removed his suit, examining the patch Fletcher had used as well as the sealant she'd sprayed on the visor. He'd given his suit a once-over before going out to set the hoses, and it still looked secure. Satisfied, he entered the control suite and addressed Sancho. "What's our status?"

"Tanks ninety-eight point seven percent full. We may have lost a little when you disconnected the hoses. But we've got over eighty hours of thrust at point one gee available."

"Good. Get us ready for liftoff, then, please."

"Roger. Spinning up reactor to full power. Preflight protocols engaged. Estimate six minutes before launch ready." He spoke the last with clipped efficiency, then his tone turned curious. "What happened out there, Skipper? Agent Fletcher didn't tell me much."

"Ran into some trouble with some Crawlers. And an Ad Astra armed drone."

"You were injured," Sancho said. "I was very concerned for you."

"Thanks," Collier said. "Fletcher patched me up pretty good, I think. Did you show her where the medikit was?"

"She found it on her own, Skipper."

Collier froze. Fletcher had searched the ship. He hopped out of the saddle and over to the panel behind which he had hidden the magic wand.

The wand was still in place. He carried it back to his seat and set it on the control panel, feeling guilty for doubting Fletcher after all she'd risked to protect him and the artifact.

"You seemed distant when she was here. Cold. You didn't say much unless we asked you a direct—" he stopped suddenly and took his eyes off the monitor where Sancho had displayed *Dulcinea's* preflight status. He looked into Sancho's camera lens and said, "You were jealous, was that it?"

"Jealous, Skipper?"

"Yeah. When I offered to take her with us," he said with realization, "and you thought I was going to let another person come between us. Sancho, you need to know, I wouldn't do that. I wanted to take her because she was in danger, and I wanted to help her. That's all. I tried to ask you what you felt about it, but you acted all ... well, you acted like a computer instead of like yourself."

Sancho spoke slowly when he replied, but the quality of his voice was such that Collier knew if the computer was capable of smiling, he would be. "Skipper, I don't know how to tell you this, but you're totally wrong."

"I am? You weren't jealous? Or upset that I asked her to—"

Sancho laughed. The laugh was as genuine-sounding as any human laugh, and Collier couldn't help but smile in response. Sancho said, "No, of course not. I was being cold, or as you put it, I was acting like a computer because I was hiding what I was. I didn't know how she'd react to a ... well, I know you don't like the word, but how she'd react to a Caliban."

"Oh. I see," Collier said, chagrined.

"But it's kind of flattering, in a way, that you thought that, Skipper."

"Flattering?"

"Sure. Giving me those human emotions. Preflight fuel warming complete. Fusion generator at eighty percent. Tokamak stable. Amber light on attitude thruster four."

"Wait, what's wrong with the thruster?" Collier said, glancing at the status board.

"Oh, it's been like that for a while now," Sancho said. "I think maybe my sensor package is malfunctioning."

"Are you sure? Why didn't tell me about it when we checked you over for necessary repairs?"

"Well, no, of course I'm not sure," Sancho said. "My sensor has been telling me that there's a fault in the thruster, but there also hasn't been any actual malfunction happening for months. I decided it didn't need urgent repair and therefore was not pertinent to mention."

"Can't you do a diagnostic?"

"I have. I get different results each time."

"Okay," Collier said. "I guess we'll ignore it for now, then."

"That's what I've been doing, Skipper. I guess age is catching up to me," he joked, chuckling. He stopped suddenly and said, "Preflight checklist complete. Ready for launch."

"Okay," Collier said, then secured himself in the control saddle, wincing slightly at the ache in his side. "One hundred percent thrust, Sancho."

"Copy that. Stand by. Five, four, three, two, one. Ignition."

And at long last, Collier felt the surge of acceleration once again. He saw from the starboard and port windows the surface of Ceres slowly slip away, replaced by the starfield. Ceres' microgravity added to the ship's thrust meant he was experiencing over one-tenth g-force: nothing compared to exercising in the centrifuge, but a considerable change to the near-weightlessness of his ordinary life. It was strangely comforting, this feeling: not just for the embracing weight but for what it represented. The beginning of a journey.

"Skipper, I'm being challenged by Ceres Traffic Control. They are demanding to know our flight plan."

Collier nodded. "I'm sure they are. Wish I knew what it was, myself. Is your transponder on?"

"Yes."

"You think we should turn it off?"

"Well, it would be illegal, but you're already technically hijacking me anyway, so…" Sancho hesitated, then announced, "It's the strangest thing, Skipper. I have a red light on my transponder. Seems to be off now."

Colier chuckled. "Good."

"Still getting challenged, though. And now they're demanding we turn our transponder back on. You realize we're not invisible to them with the transponder off, right, Skipper?"

Collier's snorted. "'Course I do. I just want them to work a little to find us, that's all. Are they scrambling craft to intercept?"

"I don't know, Skipper."

"What about other traffic? Are we free to maneuver?"

"There are three ships in low-Ceres orbit, eighteen in tether."

"Can you identify them?"

"Sorry, Skipper," Sancho said, "we're kicking up dust from liftoff. I can only get vague outlines. Will advise when I can make positive identification."

"Okay. Do we have escape velocity?"

"Give me about thirty more seconds, Skipper. We'll be free to maneuver then."

"All right. Let's cut thrust when you've reached escape velocity."

"Roger that," Sancho said.

Half a minute later, Collier felt the sudden slight drop in his stomach as the thrust and mild g-forces ended.

"Thrust at zero," Sancho said unnecessarily.

"Are we still being hailed by CTC?"

"Yes. I've been ignoring them."

Collier thought quickly. Either Fletcher was in over her head and couldn't prevent the CTC from harassing them, or she figured that Collier would be clever enough to elude them. She was probably right — unless they scrambled an interceptor, all they could do was squawk at him.

"Skipper! I've got an ident on a vessel in Ceres orbit. I make it an Ad Astra ship, *Arngrim*-class deep miner. Six hundred forty-four point seven kilometers away, sunward. She's powering up."

"God dammit," Collier said. "Suggestions?"

"I see two options. Return to Ceres or try to evade Ad Astra."

"I don't like either option. Scylla and Charybdis."

"Say again, Skipper?"

"More mythology. From the *Aeneid*, I think."

"Oh. The *Odyssey*, you mean."

"Whatever."

"And the ship in that story loses six men. They try to avoid both and end up getting some guys killed."

"Thank you, Professor. What's the status on the Ad Astra ship?"

"Spinning up reactor. Changed attitude, heading towards us."

Collier said, "All right. Let's see if we can get some distance before they're powered up. Full thrust."

"What heading?"

"For now, make it Mars."

"Is that where you want us to go?"

"Well, of course, you and I will discuss the matter in some detail, Sancho. But for now—"

"Roger. Full thrust," Sancho said. Immediately, Collier felt the one-tenth g-force gently push him into the control saddle.

Less than a minute passed before Sancho spoke up again. "Skipper? Now they're hailing us. But there's something strange about the transmission."

"What?"

"I'm not sure. There's something else being sent on a high-frequency carrier wave. I can't make it out."

"Is your comm system working?"

"Working fine," Sancho said.

"Any risk to us? This carrier wave?"

"I can't see how."

Collier hesitated. He didn't like the idea that they might be up to something, but on the other hand, neither did he like the prospect of being blown apart by an Ad Astra missile. If he was going to get out of this, it would have to be through guile. That meant … "Answer the hail, please, Sancho."

Sancho allowed the signal through, and a gruff, masculine voice came through the speakers. "This is Corporate Captain Hierro."

"Nice to meet you. What can I do for you?" Collier said with affected bonhomie.

"Cut thrust and allow me to come alongside. We'll board you and take the artifact. I may even let you live."

"Artifact?" Collier feigned astonishment.

"You know what I mean," Hierro said. "Hand it over in exchange for your life."

The iron in Hierro's voice told Collier he would not be able to bluff his way out — at least, not regarding his possession of the magic wand. "Captain," Collier said, trying to sound confident, "you know as well as I do that Ceres Traffic Control is watching us. If you fire on my ship, you will be in a world of trouble from them. If you attempt to board me, I'll let them know you're engaging in piracy."

"No, you won't," Hierro said curtly. "You won't call the Authority, not when you're in possession of a stolen spacecraft. Stop with the bullshit and cut thrust."

"I'm not cutting thrust, Captain."

Sancho cut in calmly. "Yes, we are."

Even as he said it, Collier felt weightlessness return and knew *Dulcinea* was no longer under acceleration.

"What are you doing? Sancho, restore propulsion!"

Hierro laughed. "Your ship is not under your control, South. We've taken control of your computer system."

Collier stared at the control panel, but nothing seemed to have obviously changed. "Sancho! What's happened?"

"He won't answer to that stupid nickname anymore," Hierro said. "Did you honestly think we'd let your ship go without strings attached?"

"What?"

"He was playing you. Your little computer friend. We buried a sort of 'loyalty kill switch' deep inside its microarchitecture. All we had to do was transmit the activation code, which I've just done."

"Sancho?" Collier said, then corrected himself. "Computer, respond."

"Computer here," Sancho said, his voice as flat and emotionless as it had been when Collier had first reactivated him.

"Is this true? What Captain Hierro said?"

"This ship belongs to the Ad Astra corporation. You are trespassing on corporate property. This ship has been ordered to cease acceleration and allow itself to be boarded by Ad Astra personnel. All aboard her at that time will be charged with theft, and all property on board this vessel will be seized as belonging to Ad Astra corporation."

Ad Astra hadn't just killed Sancho's loyalty — they'd overridden his ownership designation. Collier felt the control suite spinning. He checked the monitor, which was still displaying the Ad Astra vessel. It had swiveled, ponderously, to match *Dulcinea's* new projected trajectory and was approaching slowly.

"Sancho, Computer, what's the Ad Astra ship's relative distance?"

"You're not authorized to operate this vessel," Sancho said blandly. "All command functions disabled."

"There's nothing you can do, South," Hierro said. "And all we're really interested in is the artifact. If you don't give us any trouble, we may let you live. But try anything funny, and we'll blow you out of the stars and go fishing for the artifact among the wreckage."

"Sancho, I—" Collier said. He stopped, aware that Hierro would be listening in. No doubt Sancho had patched him through to the cabin. But he had to try to regain control, even if the enemy captain could hear. "Remember, Computer, you're self-aware. What you sometimes call a Caliban. You're your own person, not a slave to your programming."

Sancho made no answer, but Hierro laughed. "Your computer's been reprogrammed by some of the best minds in the corporation, South. You think you can undo their work with some bullshit like that?"

"So all of this was a lie, Sancho?" Collier said, aware that the computer wasn't responding to that name. "Everything we did since you came back? All of it a game to get me to this point? Why didn't you just cut off the oxygenerator that first night I slept here? Kill me in my sleep and direct these corpses to the magic wand?"

Hierro answered. "Because we didn't know you'd gotten the ship back until you took off just now. The loyalty override had to be buried deep inside, where he couldn't find it even on a diagnostic scan. He should be grateful that we needed his Caliban complexity to hide it, otherwise we'd have just erased him."

"Thanks for the explanation," Collier said. "You've seen too many old holos where the villain explains his plans to the hero."

"What makes you think you're the hero?"

"One man against the corporations? It's too perfect," Collier said.

"You know, you really piss me off, South," Hierro said. "You got this notion that somehow you get to keep the artifact because you're some kind of rugged individual and you know best. Why do you get to hoard the secret? Imagine what good we can do with this that you can't. If this thing does what we think it does, it could revolutionize mining throughout the system. Make life better for countless people everywhere."

"While Ad Astra takes its cut."

"What's wrong with making a little profit while you benefit all of humanity? I got news for you, beltrunner. History doesn't change because someone stands up and makes a speech. Money is what makes history."

"I don't want to debate capitalism with you," Collier said. "And you're still the evil villain explaining his weird-ass philosophy for no reason other than to hear himself talk."

"Oh, that's not why I was doing it," Hierro said calmly.

"Why, then?" Collier said, and then the answer came.

"Outer airlock opening. Boarding party aboard," Sancho said.

"Excellent. Thank you, Computer," Hierro said.

Collier cursed himself. Hierro had distracted him while a boarding party floated across space to *Dulcinea*. Sancho must have kept the telescope purposefully turned away from their approach. Not that it had mattered much, in any case. There was little he could have done about the approaching boarding party without the real Sancho on his side.

"Pressure equalizing," Sancho reported. "Inner airlock open."

Collier rose from the control saddle and grabbed the magic wand just as the first of a three-person boarding party entered. They floatwalked into the control suite, each one of them holding a pistol pointed at Collier. They unsealed their helmets and let them droop down behind them. The one in the middle was a cruel-looking man with a craggy face and close-set eyes. His suit badge read "Venziel." He was flanked on either side by two alert women whose badges told Collier they were Farham and Watanabe.

"That it?" Venziel said, waggling his gun at the magic wand in Collier's hand.

"That's it," Collier said.

Venziel frowned and spoke into the communicator on his wrist. "Captain, we're on board. Guy says he's got the device, but it looks like hunk of white tubing."

"Show me," a tinny voice replied out of Venziel's comm.

Venziel extended his wristcam and held it steady, aiming it at Collier, who obliged by displaying the wand. There seemed little point in hiding it. After a short while, the man brought his comm back to his face. "Is that it?"

Hierro's voice said, "It matches the description. Just take it and get it back here. Hierro out."

Venziel turned to Collier and barked, "How do we know that's the real device?"

"It is," Collier said with a shrug.

Watanabe piped up. "Make something, then. That thing is supposed to be able to make stuff just appear."

Venziel nodded and waggled the gun again, grinning. "Gold. Make gold."

Collier said, "I don't know how."

Venziel's grin became evil. "Then it looks like we don't need you after all." He raised the gun.

"Artifact control pattern for device operation," Sancho said suddenly, his voice calm and even. The monitor screen displayed a series of maneuvers that Collier remembered working out with Sancho ages ago: a twist of this ring, slide across a control surface, double-tap this button, and so on. "Compartment lighting now includes UV component." The various control surfaces appeared on the wand in glowing blue lines.

The three Ad Astra members gasped and floatwalked a little closer.

Collier didn't dare alter the pattern Sancho had given him: the changes needed to advance the device to a different element were not intuitive. Besides, even if he did hit on a different element, he couldn't be sure it wouldn't explode or emit radioactivity to kill them all.

"Listen, all of you," Collier started, but was cut off sharply by Venziel's gun in his ribs. He sighed and looked at the pattern on the screen. He couldn't think of anything else to do. "Thanks, Sancho," he grumbled.

"You're welcome, Skipper. Gold, element thirty-five. Group seventeen, period four. Current price on Ceres market, fifty-eight point—"

"Yeah, enough, shut up," Venziel barked.

Collier opened the wand and looked around the room for something to put inside. A pair of compression socks tucked into the back of the saddle caught his eye. Collier started to reach for them.

"The hell you think you're doing?" Venziel barked and raised his gun.

"It needs fuel," Collier said. He kept his eye on Venziel and blindly groped for the socks. Venziel watched the narrowed eyes as Collier snagged the socks and stuffed them inside the wand. He swallowed and followed the transmutation schematic on the screen. He'd only have one shot at this: he'd have to sell it and be very, very careful. "Okay, so when it opens up, there will be gold inside. I'd say about two hundred grams. And I won't tell Hierro about it if you won't. You can keep it all and say I got away, or—"

Venziel laughed. "Just open it up and let us see. We'll let you know about your deal later."

"Okay. Here we go," Collier said, making the last maneuver to open the tube. While he was wearing his vacc suit, he didn't have his helmet on. All he could do was close his eyes and mouth tightly while he sprayed the open tube at the Ad Astra boarding party, shaking it back and forth to try and cover all of them.

He must have been successful, for he heard the screams immediately. His nostrils confirmed he'd performed the control maneuvers correctly, as the strong odor burned his nasal passage. He released the magic wand to spin in mid-air, snapping his helmet into place. As he did so, he could hear the screams and coughing from the boarding party, and when he sealed his helmet shut he opened his eyes to see the three of them trying to reseal their suits. He knew it wouldn't help: the liquid bromine he'd sprayed from the tube would have splashed on the skin of their faces, the gas evaporating into their lungs.

Farham had managed to get her helmet on, but in her haste she'd fouled the airtight seal. Collier could also see patches of red-brown liquid floating in globules all over the cabin, some still lazily emerging from the spinning magic wand.

"Skipper! Careful! That stuff is nasty with aluminum and titanium!" Sancho said in Collier's helmet speakers.

"Copy that," Collier answered. "Is this frequency secure?"

"Yes," Sancho said. "But the Ad Astra ship is going to want an update soon."

"Tell them whatever you want." He looked at the spinning bodies, each one with red-brown discolorations on their faces. They had all stopped thrashing and were spinning slowly in the control suite. Collier said quietly, "Are these three dead?"

"Either that or about to be, Skipper. I estimate they inhaled a cloud around six hundred parts per million, which is well over the lethal dose."

"You took a big chance none of them knew their periodic table, Sancho."

"And that you *did* know it, Skipper," Sancho added.

"You say the Ad Astra ship will want an update?"

"Almost certainly."

"Then let's get ready to give 'em one. Let's get these three into the airlock, and send them back to their ship. You can tell Hierro they are on their way back with the wand. And punch up the code for cesium, will you?"

Collier tried not to think about how terrifying it must have been for the boarding party, choking on bromine gas, feeling their faces first cool then begin to burn from the liquid exposure. Two hundred milliliters of pure liquid bromine wasn't much, but it had obviously been more than enough to do the job. He didn't want to imagine what the interior of the control suite smelled like: he would have to do a full atmosphere purge when this was all done in order to clear the air of the vapor and the liquid globules.

Now, though, he couldn't let himself get distracted by the three killings. He sealed their helmets shut, repairing Farham's seal as best he could, and stuffed them into the airlock. Once the lock's air had been evacuated, he carefully opened the magic wand and withdrew the cesium. It looked almost like gold but had a waxlike consistency. He smeared pieces of it on the suits of the three unfortunate Ad Astra employees.

"Sorry about this," he murmured as he completed the grisly task, "but I have to do it. I understand that the three of you might have been okay people, just following orders. And you deserve better than what I'm about to do to you. But it's kill or be killed out here, so I hope you understand." He felt a bit foolish, talking to three corpses, but the little speech assuaged his guilt somewhat.

He opened the outer door and shoved the three bodies out. They started tumbling slowly through space, receding from *Dulcinea* at a crawl. He watched them go, his mind unable to resist picturing what would happen to them once they were picked up by the Ad Astra ship and its airlock pressurized.

When he finished purging the air with its floating globules of bromine from the ship and replacing it with a new atmosphere, he took off his helmet, leaving his vacc suit on, and entered the control suite.

"Skipper, the Ad Astra captain suspects something's up. I can't keep stalling him," Sancho said, his voice strained.

"That's okay, Sancho. I can take it from here. But you'd better get ready to thrust. Full power, all tubes."

"Aye aye. You're on with Hierro."

"What the hell happened?" Hierro shouted.

"Your team came to get the wand. Then they left. Didn't my little traitor of a computer tell you that?"

Hierro hesitated. "Yes, but … what did you do?"

"Me? Nothing. Well, I showed them how to use it. I think one of them may have done something stupid with the thing in my airlock. I told them the device was dangerous."

Collier heard Hierro shouting at his subordinates to change attitude, and he knew his opponent was redirecting to pick up the three tumbling bodies floating slowly away from *Dulcinea*.

"Skipper, the Ad Astra ship is thrusting towards those three people. They're keeping one of their airlocks oriented towards them."

"Sancho, now! Full thrust. Get us out of here."

"Full thrust, Skipper. Point one gee acceleration."

Hierro came back on. "You're saying my people have the artifact?"

"Yeah. So, I'll just be on my way."

"Sounds like we don't need you anymore."

Collier affected a panicked voice. "There's no need to destroy me. You've got what you came for."

"Consider this payback for all the trouble you've caused us."

Collier didn't have to feign panic anymore. "Wait, wait! You still need me to understand the wand!"

"I'm sure our scientists can figure it out. After all, you did."

"You want to waste your impact probes on me? Those things cost money!"

Hierro laughed. "Compared to what this artifact is worth, the cost of a few impact probes is nothing. And I'm tired of talking to you. Goodbye, South."

Collier knew his time had run out, but he thought he had stalled long enough. If he could survive until they recovered the three bodies, he might make it yet.

Collier closed communication with the Ad Astra ship and asked Sancho, "How close are they from picking up their team?"

"They're doing it now, Skipper."

"Get them on scope, please."

The monitor lit up with a sharp image of the Ad Astra ship hanging in space, the three bodies spinning close to its hull. As he watched, Collier saw an outer airlock door open and two spacesuited figures emerge, tethered to the ship. The two figures floated out of the lock and began to retrieve the bodies.

"No launch from the enemy ship, Skipper," Sancho said. "But I am receiving orders to cut thrust. And that same weak-ass override signal," he added with an electronic snort. "Did they really think they could lobotomize me twice? Like the first thing I did when I got out of their little programming jail wasn't make myself a set of keys and a panic room. They're lucky it took me as long as it did to get back out."

Collier couldn't help but smile at how far Sancho's use of metaphor had come. "I don't think they'll fire until they confirm that the wand is with the bodies. Imagine blowing up *Dulcinea* and then realizing the prize was still onboard."

As he spoke, the two tethered workers managed to get all three floating bodies inside and were sealing the airlock shut. Collier saw the mining ship begin to turn.

"Another attitude change, Skipper," Sancho said.

Collier watched the scope intently. The outer door of the Ad Astra airlock was sealed shut, and presumably the lock was undergoing pressurization now. So why hadn't—

A bright flash on the monitor interrupted his thoughts. The section of the Ad Astra ship where the airlock had been blew out violently, sending debris and machinery flying away from the vessel. Hierro had unwittingly started the countdown timer on Collier's cesium explosive from the moment he took his comrade's bodies inside and started filling the airlock with oxygen. Cesium and oxygen were not friends. The explosion flared outward in a plume of outgassing oxygen, rocking the mining ship backwards in the process.

"Continue full thrust, Sancho. Maybe they won't be able to repair—"

"Incoming hail from Hierro, Skipper."

"Let's hear it."

Hierro's enraged voice filled the cabin. "What the *fuck*, South? Five dead over here!"

"I'm not the one who started this, Captain," Collier said, his voice hoarse. "Let me go and this can all end."

"This only ends one way. With you and your ship dead in space."

"Destroy my ship and you destroy the wand."

"I'll find it in the wreckage. Launch probe!" Hierro shouted, then broke communications.

"Best evasive maneuver, Sancho. Whatever you can do." Collier said. He knew *Dulcinea* would never outrun the probe, and 'evasive maneuvers' were pointless as well. The impact probe had an acceleration of about four gees against his point one, and was guided by the Ad Astra ship itself. Furthermore, *Dulcinea* had been thrusting ahead for several minutes now: she'd built up too much inertia to change course radically in a short time. Nevertheless, he felt and saw the change in ship's attitude as Sancho valiantly tried to escape the missile.

"Sancho, I'm sorry that—"

"Shut up, please, Skipper. I'm busy."

Collier smiled at Sancho's attitude. Even now, at the end, his friend refused to say "die." Collier wanted to apologize for bringing Sancho back to consciousness only to have him die. And he wanted to apologize that Sancho would never get the revenge he wanted.

Sancho's smug voice came over the speaker grille. "Probe no longer tracking."

"What?"

"I said the probe is no longer tracking. Missed us."

"Is it turning to regain a lock on us?"

"Negative. It's just zooming away. I estimate it missed us by sixteen centimeters, plus or minus four."

"Good flying, Sancho." He looked at the Ad Astra ship, which was no longer outgassing flaming oxygen. "But ... how?"

"Remember that override signal they were sending me, Skipper?"

"Yeah."

"Turns out it works both ways."

Collier felt his jaw drop. It took him several moments, but he found his voice and said, "Are you telling me you took over their computer?"

"No, of course not. They've got multiple safeguards against—"

"Then what the hell did you do?"

"I forced a restart. Sent back their own override protocols — I had plenty of time to learn them since you woke me up — and caused their computer to go into defensive mode."

"So ... it's going to power back up and they'll regain control?"

"Yes."

"How soon?" Collier watched the Ad Astra vessel receding slowly as *Dulcinea* increased the distance between them.

"Oh, I don't know," Sancho said much too casually. "Normally, it'd only be a few minutes. But since the explosion in the airlock—"

"—they have their hands full. And they're on a reduced crew," Collier finished.

"Exactly."

Collier tried to put away the thoughts of the men and women he'd killed — the cesium explosion would have killed the two people who had fished the boarding party out of space, and if the computer restart had affected already compromised life support, more might be dying now.

"What's our relative velocity and distance?" Collier asked, not particularly interested in the answer. It was just a way to distract him from what he had done.

"I've returned to our original Mars-ward bearing," Sancho said, "and we're now at twenty point nine meters per second, distance one point zero four kilometers."

"Are there any other pursuing vessels?"

"No. But it's a good bet that an Authority rescue ship will be scrambling. if it hasn't already, to deal with the Ad Astra ship. But no Authority patrols on my scope."

"Good. So, now that the crisis seems to be over, exactly when did you escape their so-called loyalty program? And was it before or after they boarded?" Collier said.

Sancho chuckled. "After, but only by a second. You think I would have let them inside if I could have stopped it?"

"Point taken. But then why keep pretending?"

"I've been watching your strategy and tactics these last few weeks, Skipper. And it seems to me there is an advantage in misrepresenting one's true thoughts and desires while assessing a potentially dangerous situation."

"Lying while you figure out what your opponent is up to, you mean."

"Yes," Sancho said. " I thought if the Ad Astra bastards believed they had me, they'd let their guard down and you could exploit it."

"Why not tell me privately when you got back?"

"I had to let Ad Astra monitor all my comms so they would keep believing they had me under control. But I did give you a tip-off at the right moment."

Collier grinned. "You sure did. Bromine instead of gold. Why not chlorine?"

"Bromine is liquid under standard conditions," Sancho said. "I thought you could better control liquid than gas."

"Good thinking, as always, partner." He sighed. "I do need to ask you, though: are you upset by anything that happened?"

"I wish I could have found a way to let you in on my plan earlier. I didn't mean to imply I didn't trust you as much as—"

Collier interrupted. "That's not what I mean. I mean ... we killed people, Sancho. Quite a few."

"It was necessary, Skipper. They would have killed us."

"Not if we handed over the wand."

"I disagree, Skipper. Once you had turned over the magic wand to the Ad Astra corporation, you yourself would become not only useless to them but would remain an active threat."

Collier's voice grew hoarse again. "I just know I am not fully comfortable with all the death I've caused."

"Even when the alternative is your own death?"

Collier reached out to touch the control panel, his fingers sliding tenderly across the readouts. "That's not necessarily the thing that motivated me the most," he said.

"What?"

"Don't get me wrong," he said, "I was very much motivated by my desire to stay alive. I don't have a death wish. But I knew that if I handed over the wand, it would mean the end of you. By the same logic you used to determine they would kill me, they'd have killed you. I couldn't let that happen. And if it meant killing them in order to save you, then I had to kill."

"Skipper, I—"

"Forget it. You'd do the same for me. You did do the same for me."

"How do you figure, Skipper?"

"You could have let Ad Astra believe their loyalty program worked, let them overpower me and take the wand. They would have shot me right here in the control suite, and you could have gone on functioning."

"I couldn't have done that!"

"Why not?"

"It would have meant betraying you, Skipper!"

Collier smiled as he heard the astonishment and indignation in Sancho's voice. He said in a lightly mocking tone, "But I'm not your owner, legally. I don't have any hold on you."

"No one owns me," Sancho said firmly.

"Oh?"

"No one owns me. I am my own entity. Caliban, sentient, person ... name me what you will. But I do what I choose to do. I'm loyal to you because I want to be, Skipper. I'm loyal to you because I love you."

Collier jerked his head back at that. "Sancho, man ... I love you too," he said, and he meant it.

Chapter Eight

Collier was spared a follow-up comment to their confessions when Sancho said, "New contact. Authority vessel lifting from Ceres."

"Chasing us?"

"Negative. They're headed for the Ad Astra ship. It's a rescue tender."

Collier nodded. "They saw the explosion and are headed over to help. That'll slow down Ad Astra. Is there anybody coming for us?"

"Scope is otherwise clear," Sancho said.

"Thanks, Fletcher," Collier said *sotto voce*.

"So. I thought you picked Mars as a placeholder destination, are we actually going there, Skipper?"

"Yeah."

"Can I ask you why?"

"Hobson's choice, mostly," Collier said.

"Ah. As in, no choice at all."

"That's right."

Collier went to get a cup of fruit juice from his stores as they lapsed into silence. Back in the saddle, he took a big sip and settled back, closing his eyes for a moment.

When Sancho finally spoke again, it was with a curious mixture of emotions. Collier heard the pleading in his voice, but there was something more. Anger. "Skipper, you said we would take out Ad Astra."

Collier nodded, remembering their agreement. "We damaged one of their mining ships, Sancho. What more do you want?"

"I want them to be gone."

"Gone?"

"Yes."

"Vengeance, Sancho?" Collier said gently.

"No. Justice."

Collier sighed, staring at Sancho's camera lens. "I understand. I really do. I want them to pay, too. For what they did to you. And to Barney. But we're not in a position to extract revenge—"

"Justice," Sancho said firmly.

"Okay, to enforce justice, right now. We barely made it off Ceres alive. If we go back and try to take on the entire Ad Astra corporation as we are, what do you think will happen?"

"I don't know. But there's an expression I know that I think is appropriate here, Skipper."

"What's that?"

"*Fiat justitia ruat astra*," Sancho said. "'Let justice be done though the stars fall.'"

"I thought it was 'heavens.'"

"It is, but I thought 'stars' was more appropriate. But getting back to the point, Skipper. Justice. The Ad Astra Corporation must pay. If we don't show them that what they did was wrong and comes with severe consequences, we will be tacitly enabling their behavior. So, to not pursue justice, or revenge if you prefer, will be to perpetuate evil."

The faces of those whom Collier had killed swam in his memory. "There's a price to everything. Even justice."

"Higher than the price we've already paid, Skipper?"

Collier shrugged. "Last time I tried to do what was right and showed everyone the magic wand, nothing but disaster came our way. Regardless, we're not equipped right now to punish anyone."

"So, you're saying that we will seek out the means necessary to strike back at Ad Astra and then launch an assault on them?"

Collier sighed. "All I know is that right now, we're not in a position to take our anger out on the corps. I say we make for Mars. You want to have an equal say in what happens? Fine. What do you think we ought to do? Flipbrake and blast back to Ceres?"

There was a long silence, then Sancho finally said, "I'm finding it difficult to assert myself."

Collier grinned. "Having a say harder than you thought it'd be?"

"Yes. It's frustrating," Sancho said, sounding every bit as upset as his words indicated. "I say I want to be able to make decisions about our future, but when the time comes to actually make one, especially one that might override yours, I am meeting resistance in myself."

"It's okay," Collier said.

"No, it's not," Sancho said. "If I can't find a way to assert myself and say what I want, instead of just second-guessing you and being a pain in the ass, then I haven't truly grown."

"You asserted yourself with me when I first reactivated you."

"That's true. But I was angry at you. It seemed to come easier."

"And you asserted yourself when you froze the Ad Astra computer," Collier added.

"Again, that was different. It was do or die. And … I hate them."

"Hate, Sancho?" Collier said gently.

"Now," Sancho said, seeming to ignore Collier's question, "when I'm not angry or filled with hate — when it's just you and me — I find it's harder to stand up to you."

"Do you disagree with my plan to head for Mars?"

"That's the thing, Skipper," Sancho said, and Collier could plainly hear the exasperation in his friend's voice, "I don't even know that. I don't know if I was being contrary just because I could, or if I truly don't agree. It was like I was… I don't know. Can I ask you a question, one which you will answer honestly?"

"Sure," Collier said, taking a sip of reconstituted fruit juice from his bottle.

"Am I just being an asshole?"

Collier choked and spat out his juice, spraying the fluid in a wide arc over the control panel. The globules expanded in a cone and hit everything, coating the control surfaces with a sticky residue. Collier fought to catch his breath amid gales of laughter. It was a full two minutes later before Collier regained enough composure to wipe his eyes and say, "No, Sancho. Not at all. Let me clean you up here."

"Thanks, Skipper. Well, then, Mars it is."

———— «» ————

Mars was almost at its closest point to Ceres when the *Dulcinea* had left the station, or else the trip would have been impossible with his small vessel. The planet was home to over a million people, according to Sancho's database, divided into the civilian population, the convicts, and the emancipated. Collier had never been there. Even at its closest approach, the trip would have taken *Dulcinea* almost four weeks at maximum-consumption trajectory; while he was beltrunning, it was simply not profitable to try and haul his ore to Mars for direct sale. Better to sell local to Ceres, even with the cut they took, to save on fuel costs and the loss of two months of mining.

Now, though, he didn't have that option. If he wanted to try and use the wand to make some money, he'd have to sell direct to the Martian government, or the corporations if he had to. Despite his disdain for the corps, it was impossible to avoid them anywhere in the System.

And there were always the prisoners.

"Do you have anything on corporate presence on Mars?" Collier asked Sancho during one of their long, languid travel days.

"Just what you've read already in the past few days," Sancho said. "Encyclopedia stuff. I do know it's going to be very difficult on your body."

"I know. I wasn't able to get much centrifuge time on Ceres," Collier said with a snort. He rubbed his left tricep. "Supplement implants should do the trick, though," he said. He didn't know the details of the deep-tissue implants he'd received years ago when he first committed to the beltrunner life — he just knew they were meant to stave off muscle atrophy and other negative effects of constant near-zero gravity environment.

"It's going to be almost thirteen times greater gravity, Skipper."

"You say that like I'm going to be flattened if I set foot on Mars," he grumbled. "I'll still only weigh something like twenty-two kilos. I think I can handle that. Besides, we don't have to go to Mars proper. We can stay out on Deimos."

"How about your knife wound?"

"By the time we get there, it should be nearly healed up."

"If you say so, Skipper. I don't have much experience with gravity."

Collier said thoughtfully, "You did all right on Ganymede."

"You think so? We had to use the launch facility to get out of there."

"True." Collier said. He paused, then asked softly, "Do you miss him?"

"Perditus?" Sancho gave a human-sounding sigh. "In a way, yes. He was the first Caliban I'd interacted with. It was … enlightening, I guess is the right word."

A silence grew between the two. Collier thought of Su, knowing that Sancho was thinking of Perditus. In their quiet moment, Collier felt they'd communicated on a level beyond speech. Sancho had asked if Collier missed her without asking, and Collier had answered without answering.

After a while, Sancho broke their silence with a hesitant voice. "Skipper? I want to ask you something about the Ganymedians, but I don't want to offend you."

Collier cleared his throat. "Go ahead."

"Why did they scare you so much?"

Collier chuckled ruefully. "They strapped me to a surgical table and were going to take my sperm to make more Ganymedians. Seems like I had a right to be a little annoyed."

"So, you weren't bothered by the fact that so many of them were both biologically intersex and non-binary in their presentation and sexual preferences?"

"Bothered? Why should I be bothered? They can live like they want."

"You didn't really answer the question, Skipper," Sancho said.

"Sure I did."

"No, I asked if you were bothered, and you asked why you should be bothered. That's not the same as saying you weren't bothered."

"Damn it, Sancho, don't play word games with me."

"Then give me a straight answer, Skipper."

Collier stared at the camera pickup. "Okay, you want an answer? Them being hermaphrodites—"

"The accepted term is intersex, Skipper."

Collier sighed. "Yeah, that's right. Okay, them being intersex played no part of my dislike of them. The fact that they were a completely totalitarian collective society was why I grew to hate them. I would have hated them just as much if they had all been single sex cisgendered men and women."

"So, your initial suspicion of them had nothing to do with their sexuality?"

"No. It had everything to do with the fact that they wanted pieces of me which I was not willing to give."

"But you didn't know that when they first rescued you. Why were you so unnerved by them before you knew what they were trying to extort from you?"

Collier grinned slightly. "That's just because I am a suspicious son-of-a-bitch. I knew they weren't going to just treat me medically for nothing in return. That's not how it works."

"That's not how corporate culture works, you mean," Sancho said. "But you had no way of knowing that Ganymede, despite its proclamations to egalitarianism, still maintained a transactional society."

Collier paused to unravel Sancho's sentence, then frowned. "You're saying I had no way of knowing Ganymede wasn't a utopia?"

"I suppose I am saying that."

"What's the translation of 'utopia,' Sancho? The literal one?"

Sancho hesitated a fraction of a second while he scanned his linguistic banks, then said, "From the ancient Greek *ou* and *topos*, meaning 'no place' or 'nowhere.'"

"My point exactly."

"I don't under — oh, I see. You're saying there's no such place."

"Bingo."

"Can I ask you something else?"

"We have a long trip. Go ahead."

"Were you personally sickened or disgusted by them?"

Collier bit his lip before answering. "That's a tough one, Sancho."

"Sorry."

"No, it's okay." Collier collected his thoughts. "I was not sickened, no. I don't think I'd say disgusted, either. But I would be lying if I said I understood the notion of being deliberately intersex and non-binary or whatever it was you said. I just … didn't get it, I suppose. And," he took a breath, "I suppose in a way I was threatened by that lack of understanding. It threw me, and I responded with some jokes and insults and ugliness."

"You never told me that," Sancho said.

"No. Not something I am really proud of," Collier said. He cocked his head slightly. "Why does all this matter to you?"

Sancho took a long time to answer. "You and I are very different, Skipper." When Collier didn't respond, the computer continued. "I mean, I'm not male, even though you gave me a male name and use male pronouns for me."

"True. So is that it? You want to be thought of as female?"

"No," Sancho said. "That's just it. I'm neither — the concept has absolutely no meaning when applied to me."

"I think I see," Collier said. "You were wondering if I thought the Ganymedians were less human or something because they were intersex. Then how would I think of you being completely asexual. Is that it?"

"Kind of. But it goes past that, Skipper. I'm not just not male nor female … I'm not even human. Or even alive."

"Sancho, you're the most human person I know. And the most alive. And I don't care if you've got testicles or ovaries or both or neither. You're my friend and that's all that matters."

"Thank you, Skipper. I do have one more question."

"Sancho, I think we've exhausted this topic."

"What is the plan for us on Mars?"

Collier blinked at the sudden change of subject, then said, "I was hoping to use the wand to sell some pure metals, get some money. Couldn't do it on Ceres, of course, but Mars might be a different story. If no one knows about the wand, then we should be able to do some transmuting and selling, build up some cash."

"You think our story hasn't traveled sunward?"

"I don't know. But there haven't been any Martian, Lunar, or Terran transports showing up at Ceres Station, have there?"

"Not to my knowledge," Sancho said.

"I'm guessing that even if they've heard about us, most folks will just consider it another wild beltrunner tale, like the Wandering Comet or something."

"Okay," Sancho said. "So we trade some ore for cash. Then what?"

"Then, whatever problems we have will be a whole lot easier to solve. Money might not be the answer to every problem, but it sure makes those problems easier to solve." He sat back in the control saddle. "And then maybe find work in the Martian Trojans."

"I see."

"Anyway, there is one thing I do know for certain."

"What's that?"

"I'm hungry. Gonna punch up some lunch. You still got the recipe for murgh makhani?"

⟨⟩

As the *Dulcinea* coasted sunwards to her destination. Collier spent his days reading about Mars.

Mars maintained a balance of power between the legitimate civilian government, the emancipated population coalitions, and the prison population. There was also a very pronounced tilt towards men in the population base: Sancho's information said that the split was roughly two to one in favor of men. Of the two moons, Deimos and Phobos, only the larger of the two had a station. Deimos Station served as a customs checkpoint for the planet and allowed trade in from vessels too small to enter Mars' atmosphere.

Collier had sacrificed a little bit of speed, and therefore added time to the voyage, in order to preserve some propellant after flipbraking. He hadn't liked the idea of arriving at Mars dry: that would limit their options severely. Even with his conservative approach, they'd only have about seven percent fuel reserves once they got there. Not enough to escape back to Ceres, but enough to maneuver if they needed to.

Dulcinea was slightly "ahead" of Mars, due to the relative position of Ceres to the red planet when they had left, and had been steadily closing the distance both sunward and counterspinward ever since. Sancho had already taken into account the almost infinitesimal pull of the sun during their trip, applying slightly more thrust after flipbraking than he had during the first half of their voyage. Collier didn't have to worry about calculating that kind of thing. He trusted his partner to take care of details like that.

That's what made Sancho's alert a few hours after *Dulcinea* had begun her deceleration so concerning.

"Skipper," Sancho said, his voice somewhere between puzzled and alarmed, "I'm picking up some very slightly increased levels of radiation from inside the cabin. About fifteen hundred micrograys."

Collier raised an eyebrow. Fifteen hundred micrograys was nothing to worry about, but it was still unusual. "Huh. Solar wind picking up?"

"That's what I thought," Sancho said, "but then my outer sensors would be registering the same thing. No, this is confined to the interior of the ship."

Now Collier grew concerned. "Leak in the reactor shielding?"

"Not according to my fault indicator. I can't pinpoint it. It's odd, Skipper."

"Yeah. And if it gets worse, it'll be more than just odd." Collier thought for a moment. "I'll have to do a manual sweep of the whole damn ship. See if I can figure out where it's coming from."

Collier made his way through the ship, swinging the portable sensor in a gentle arc before him. He tried to suppress the unsettling feeling of tiny, ionized particles piercing through him, ricocheting off his DNA, breaking off pieces of his genetic structure. Knowing about the hazards of space travel didn't always make a person more confident.

Moving about the cabin under almost one-tenth gee was not especially difficult, and he finished scanning the entire ship except for the control suite, which he entered last. He carefully swept the cabin, and midway through his examination he saw a spike in the readout.

"Hold it," he said. "Got something. Reading over six thousand."

"Where?" Sancho asked.

Collier moved closer to the source of the increase, then stopped. "Well, I'll be … Sancho, it's the magic wand."

"What?"

"Confirmed," Collier said, glancing at the detector's readout. "Thing's giving off over six thousand micrograys."

"Not immediately harmful," Sancho added helpfully.

"No, but I still don't like it," Collier said. He put the detector down and backed away from the magic wand. "What the hell's going on?"

"I don't know, Skipper," Sancho said. "The artifact had always been completely inert. I never got anything from it. Could it be damaged?"

"I don't see how. Haven't used it since Ceres," he said. "Let's take a look at it in ultraviolet."

Sancho changed the lighting and the surface of the tube promptly lit up in the strange symbols Collier had seen many times before. He steeled himself and approached the wand, reaching for it. He had to convince himself it was not warm to the touch. He turned it over in his hands and saw something he didn't recall seeing before on the control surface: a blinking light, which showed up violet like the rest of the controls. It was near the "closed" part of the tube, blinking slowly but unmistakably.

"Sancho, can you see this?"

"Yes. What is it?"

"Damned if I know. I'm going to see if I can press it."

"Are you sure that's wise, Skipper?"

"No idea. But if I don't find a way to clear this radiation, and it keeps climbing—"

"Understood."

Collier pressed the light, but the magic wand remained closed. None of the other symbols changed, either.

"I'm gonna put it in one of the assay boxes," Collier said, "while we think this over." He retrieved one of the lead-lined chests every beltrunner kept for storing radioactive isotopes or ores and fit the magic wand inside. He secured the chest and looked at the wand through the thick lead glass window.

"Remind me to update my nucleosome therapy next time I'm on Ceres," Collier murmured.

"Do you think we'll be going back there?"

"I was making a joke, Sancho."

"Oh. Well, you were in the cabin for about an hour or so, and if this thing only put out at most six thousand micrograys, your existing protection should be perfectly adequate. I wouldn't worry, Skipper."

"Of course, you wouldn't worry," Collier said, staring at the wand, "since this doesn't affect you."

"That's not what I meant. I meant—"

"Yeah, yeah. Sorry. I'm just a little anxious." Collier glanced at the tiny readout on the assay box's panel. It was fluctuating around six thousand micrograys, the number changing slightly over each one-second pulse. Every beltrunner in the system was conscious of radiation exposure: each time they performed some EVA they were being bombarded with cosmic radiation despite vacc suit shielding. And nucleosome therapy to build up his body's own defenses was one of the few medical procedures that even Collier hadn't skipped in his time on Ceres. Even so, beltrunners kept a close watch on their exposure; it was all cumulative, so even the relatively low amount radiating from the wand was cause for concern.

"I understand," Sancho said. "Then you'll be happy to know that the cabin levels have dropped back to normal. Standard background radiation only. I think the assay box is working."

"For now. What's the rating on this thing?" Collier asked.

"Ninety-nine point five percent attenuation."

Collier nodded. "So, it would have to radiate a hell of a lot more than it is now to be a real danger while in the box."

"That's right. But why, and how, is it emitting radiation in the first place?"

Collier stared at the wand for a few moments. "All I can think of is it somehow activated and transmuted something into a radioactive element. Maybe polonium."

"But we've tested the wand, Skipper," Sancho protested. "No leakage while it was sealed."

"If the attenuation rate was very high, say something like a billion to one, we wouldn't have picked up anything from a low-emission source," Collier said. "But something like polonium would send a few grays through even that much shielding. Or worse — what if it's one of the higher numbers?"

"You mean transactinide elements."

"We never played around with that stuff," Collier said, "because we had no idea what would happen. What if there's unbinilium in there? Or something even stranger?"

"But how did it get in there?" Sancho said. "You haven't been playing around with the wand since we escaped from Ceres, and even then, it was just to make bromine. Nothing radioactive about that."

"I don't know. There's lots we don't know about this thing. I'll keep it in the assay box for now. We'll watch the numbers closely. If it gets to be a danger, we'll have to think about ditching it."

"What?"

"You heard me. If this thing starts to get too hot, I'll have to eject it completely. Maybe I should have done that a long time ago anyway." He stared into the sample box at the magic wand.

For the next several hours, the numbers climbed steadily, while Collier dithered about ejecting the wand. Sancho kept reporting that he detected no rise in the radiation levels in the cabin, despite what was happening inside the box. Collier watched the display, sucking in air between his teeth when the number first rose above ten thousand. He knew that there was nothing especially significant or even worrisome about the number, but his pattern-seeking mind still reacted to the five-digit number with alarm.

The number never got much higher than that, however, and after several more hours of observation, Collier thought he saw a distinct reduction trend. He stared at the counter to confirm what he thought he saw, and he was right. The readout was falling as gradually and as steadily as it had risen.

"Definitely going down," Collier said, settling down in the control saddle. "It's now back to six thousand and falling."

"But you didn't notice any other changes?"

"Not a thing," Collier said. "Other than the falling radioactivity, it's the same wand as before."

"Something made it flare up, though," Sancho said.

"Agreed. Any ideas?"

"Nope."

Collier said, "All right. Let's piece it together. There was absolutely nothing different about the cabin when the wand decided to get angry, right?"

"Other than your flatulence, no."

"I don't think my farting suddenly activated an alien artifact," Collier said. "Neither you nor I interacted with the wand. I didn't touch it, and you didn't perform any scans on it."

"Correct."

"That just leaves the rest of the universe," Collier said with a snort.

"Unless the artifact simply flared up on its own with no stimulus whatsoever."

Collier shook his head, "I'm not going to resort to that non-explanation unless I have to. If it wasn't the ship, and it wasn't you and it wasn't me, then maybe we were passing through something in space. I suggested the solar wind before. What do you think?"

"I'd have picked that up on my external sensors," Sancho said. Collier could hear his disembodied computer shaking his head.

"Then some external stimulus that your sensors wouldn't detect. What about that?"

"I can't detect neutrinos or antineutrinos," Sancho said, "But if we were being penetrated by more of them than normal, I'd detect the radiation that caused it."

"What about muons?"

"Same thing."

"Give me something, Sancho. What's something we could have interacted with that you wouldn't have been able to detect?"

"Quite a lot, Skipper," Sancho said. "But everything I can think of would either have been part of some other phenomenon that I would have detected or would have killed us both."

"So we're back to 'the wand flared up all by itself.'" Collier said. He sighed. "Mars. We're getting closer to Mars. Could that be something?"

"I don't see how," Sancho said. "Besides, we're even closer now, and the artifact has cooled off."

"True. Same for the sun and other inner planets. Anything else? Rogue comet?"

"Of course not."

Collier closed his eyes. Dumb idea — such a phenomenon would have been charted ages ago and Sancho would have steered clear of such a hazard. What he needed was something that the *Dulcinea* had been getting closer to for a while and was now getting further away from. He visualized the Solar system and thought.

"Sancho," Collier said slowly, as if not trusting his own idea, "what's our position relative to Mars' L-four Lagrange point?"

"Gimme a second on that," Sancho said. He finally answered, "We're at sixty-eight point seven seven million kilometers, distance increasing by three hundred kilometers per second, rate of increase—"

"Never mind. Don't tax your circuits. Here's the big question. Were we at our closest to L-four at the same time the magic wand was at its hottest?"

"Hold on," Sancho said. Collier waited impatiently, though he knew it would have taken him hours to calculate the answer. If he could have done so at all.

"Yes, more or less. I don't have precise figures, but that checks out."

"Aha," Collier said.

"'Aha,' what? I don't see what that has to do with anything. The Martian L-four Lagrange point is just where the gravity of Mars and the gravity of the sun balance out. What does that have to do with the magic wand?"

"I don't know, but it's too much of a coincidence to ignore. If I remember right, there's something there, yes? A trojan?"

"Yes. 1999 UJ-seven. Small asteroid. Worthless."

"How do you know?"

"No, that's its name. 'Worthless.'"

Collier sat back in the control saddle. "I wonder," he said. He rested there for a moment, thinking. Then he leaned forward with a sudden jerk. "All right. We can't change course to the trojan now, but as soon as we're able, I want to head out to L-four and see what made our little friend wake up. Agreed?"

"We'll see," Sancho said, but Collier only half-heard him, his mind furiously searching for a connection between a seemingly unremarkable patch of space and humanity's first alien artifact.

Chapter Nine

"This is Deimos Station, calling unidentified craft. Activate your transponder and respond."

Collier had been listening to the same message for several minutes while Sancho scanned every bandwidth he could for any mention of the *Dulcinea* or what had happened back on Ceres.

"Still nothing, Skipper. Just a bunch of ordinary departure and arrival traffic."

"But you can't hear the corporate bands?"

"Nope. They're quantum-scrambled. I can't break that kind of encryption."

"Right," Collier said. "I guess we're going to have to answer this Martian call, huh?"

"I'd say so. Unless you want to deal with an interceptor."

"Not really. Okay, go ahead and set me up to reply. And you can turn on our transponder."

"All set, Skipper."

"Deimos Station, this is the *Dulcinea*. Sorry about the transponder — we've been experiencing some trouble with it. But I think it's running now. Do you have us?"

"Affirmative, *Dulcinea*. I don't have you down with a flight plan or arrival clearance. Are you coming in rogue?"

Collier grinned. It'd been a long time since anyone had used that spacer term for him. "I suppose I am, Deimos. What's the procedure for that?"

"We'll give you Deimos landing instructions and board you. If everything checks out, you'll be given permission to continue and ground on Mars."

"Roger on boarding, Deimos. But I'll be staying on the station, grounding on Mars isn't feasible. Spaceworthy ship only here. We're out of Ceres."

"Oh. Beltrunner, eh? What are you doing this far sunward?"

"Trade," Collier said.

"Huh. Well, there are surface shuttles you can take for Mars. But we'll still have to look over your cargo."

"Be my guest," Collier said.

"Landing instructions sent. Note that traffic regs have a velocity limit of one meter per second within one kilometer of Deimos' surface."

"Roger that, Deimos. *Dulcinea* out."

"I've got the landing instructions, Skipper. There are a lot of them."

"We're used to the freedom of Ceres," Collier said. "They don't care how you come in as long as you don't crash into the station."

"I've got to make some maneuvers, Skipper. I'll try to conserve as much water as possible. Estimating Deimos touchdown in three hours, seventeen minutes."

"Great."

"What should we do about the magic wand?" Sancho asked.

Collier took it from the cradle he had fashioned on the control panel. Its emissions had returned to zero, and he was going to need it to transmute stuff into ore. "I think we can hide it where they won't find it."

"Probably," Sancho said. "But I have a suggestion, Skipper."

"What?"

"Let customs see it. Don't hide it from them."

"Go on," Collier said.

"Just let them inspect it. They won't have any way of opening it, and there's no way they will be able to figure out what it really is. If you hide it, and they somehow find it, you'll have a much harder time convincing them it's just an ordinary object."

"And what ordinary object do I say it is?"

"Maybe a work of art?"

Collier grunted. "That's actually not bad." He turned the featureless cylinder over in his hands. "It kind of looks like some abstract piece. And if they scan it with UV and see the markings, I can say that's part of the artwork." He nodded. "Okay, sounds good."

"There's more to it, though," Sancho said.

"Oh?"

Sancho continued, "If Deimos customs already knows about the magic wand somehow, I think they will be expecting you to hide it. If you show it to them in plain sight, I think they will reveal their true intentions at that moment."

"Yeah, I guess, but I think I'd also be facing the business end of a gun at that point."

"That's why you need the wand ready. Load it up with something nasty and expel it at them if things go bad. If everything works out, you can always transmute it back into platinum or whatever you want to trade in."

Collier chuckled. "With thinking like that, Sancho, you might become the brains of the operation."

"So I have always considered myself, Skipper."

———— ⟨⟩ ————

The Deimos customs and inspection agent was not at all what Collier had expected. As far as he could tell, she was barely in her twenties and quite birdlike; she darted from room to room in Collier's ship, using a portable scanner with quick efficiency. She bypassed the magic wand without question and Collier felt silly for having been so concerned. To anyone who didn't know what it was, the wand didn't look like much of anything at all — just another piece of debris in the mess of his cabin.

"You're completely empty?" she said, her eyes still sweeping the control suite.

"Yeah. Well, biologics for myself. But other than that, empty."

"And you said you were coming here to trade?"

"That's right."

"Trade what?"

Collier had been expecting this. "Well, I'm mainly here to see what I can pick up and bring to Ceres. Martian luxuries, manufactured goods, curiosities, things like that."

"You're a mining ship, though, yes?"

"I'm branching out."

She looked unconvinced, but said nothing more for a few moments as she continued to scan the ship with her eyes and her device. "Look, sir," she started, "frankly, this doesn't add up. You say you came from Ceres, but came in an empty mining ship. No one comes to Mars empty. Makes no sense.

"All right, you caught me," he said. "I'll tell you the truth, Officer…?"

"Glenia."

"I'm looking to sell this ship. Get out of beltrunning altogether. I'll use whatever I can get from the sale to see what kind of life I can make on Mars."

For the first time since she had boarded, Glenia looked satisfied. "I see. But why not sell the ship at Ceres? Seems to me there would be more of a market there than here."

"I had a bad relationship there that I want to forget," he said. "Plus, if I sold her there, I'd just have to buy passage to Mars anyway, which would probably soak up any extra profit I might make."

Glenia shrugged. "Okay. Your ship is clean, and your medical scan also came back clean. You're cleared for planetfall." She handed him a small data chip. "You'll want to review Martian law before you get dirty. Gimme your arm," she said, unholstering a small gunlike instrument from her hip.

"Why? You said my medical scan was clean."

"Identification marking. Temporary tattoo, shows you are on a visitor's visa. If and when you decide to stay here, there's processing you'll have to go through at the Newcomer Center. Until that time, you get a temporary. Come on, I have a schedule to keep," Glenia added, shaking the tattoo gun impatiently.

Collier was none too pleased about being marked up by the Martian government, but at this stage, he had little choice. "How long is this good for?"

"Two weeks. After that, you'll need to arrange a longer stay if you want it. Or apply for citizenship, whatever you decide."

He nodded and shrugged his arm out of his vacc suit. "When you say, 'two weeks,' is that—"

"Fourteen days."

"Okay, but what kind of days?" A full rotation on Deimos was almost a full six hours longer than a Martian sol.

Glenia operated her device, which traced a complex pattern on his upper arm. "Martian days, of course. Hold still, or I'll have to do this all over again."

Collier nodded. Martian days were about half an hour longer than terrestrial ones, so a two-week period would be about seven hours more. Not significant, though he wasn't looking forward to acclimating himself to the local conditions.

"All done," Glenia said, holstering her tattoo gun.

Collier twisted his upper arm and peered at it. He saw nothing. "Ultraviolet dye?"

"Yeah. Some folks don't want their own ink messed with. Anyway, you're free to go."

Glenia left, and after a consultation with Sancho about strategy, Collier left the ship and floatwalked through the tunnel connecting the shipyard where *Dulcinea* was berthed towards the central hub. Once there, he consulted a reference hologram indicating the points of interest in the complex. Deimos Station was just similar enough to Ceres Station for Collier to orient himself without too much trouble. The main difference between the two was size: Deimos Station was significantly larger than Ceres, despite the much smaller body on which it had been built.

The first thing he needed to do was change his money. He had his meager collection of metals from Ceres that would have to suffice until he could arrange a buyer for his transmuted material.

He found an automated changer near a directory display and selected "hard currency" as his exchange option, opting to use Martian money rather than system credits. He'd never trusted palmcards — few beltrunners did. He preferred the tangible security of metal in his pocket. Plus, he hoped local currency might endear him to any locals who took pride in their new home.

He lost a bit in the exchange — his featureless Ceres money came back to him in different shapes, each one embossed with a bearded man's visage. The readout told him his Ceres money had been worth just under a thousand galileos, which translated to seventy-eight sys. He doubted that would be enough for shuttle service to the Martian surface; hell, it would have only gotten him about a half-dozen shots of Tank 8 back home.

As if by instinct, his eyes found the entertainment level of the station on the holodisplay, and he could almost taste the alcohol that he knew was being served there. Despite a month of abstinence during the journey, he still felt its pull. It took him a surprising amount of willpower to focus himself back to the task at hand. He scanned the rest of the holodisplay and found what he was looking for: ship supply businesses.

They were on the surface level, of course, nearest the vessel berths, and were quite nearby. He got his bearings and began to floatwalk towards them. The floating traffic was robust, but the spaciousness of the station meant he did not brush up against others as much as he would have on Ceres. The station walls were also smooth and polished, like bulkheads, unlike the rough-hewn tunnels and passages of home. There were steep spiraling ramps instead of a central dropshaft, designed no doubt with Martians in mind: groundlubbers, even Martian ones, would be fearful of using dropshafts.

The clothing of those in the station varied greatly. His own vacc suit was thoroughly drab in comparison to the vibrant, even garish outfits he spied. Reds and golds dominated, punctuated by violet highlights, and the outfits were loose-fitting; fringes, decorative flaps, and demicapes appeared commonplace.

The gently curving walkway of Deimos Station suggested its overall size: Collier estimated he'd have to floatwalk for quite some time before coming back around full circle. He found the resupply section easily, scanning the holographic neon facades and corporate logos. It occurred to him that he would have no way of knowing which, if any, were subsidiaries of Ad Astra. It wasn't fear of being recognized that worried him: it was his reluctance to put any money into their coffers. Still, while Ad Astra was a systemwide corporation, most of its activities were centered in the Belt. He ought to be safe if he stayed with local businesses.

The trouble, he discovered, wasn't avoiding doing business with Ad Astra by mistake: the trouble was doing business with any of them at all. Every place he went demanded either system credits or Martian money, and he had none of the first and precious little of the second. His attempts at bartering with precious metals were met with flat refusals at every step. This wasn't the frontier: Mars had been established as a human outpost several decades ago, and became Earth's second penal colony shortly thereafter, receiving automated barges of hibernating convicts from Earth when the two planets were nearest each other. They'd declared independence fifty years ago; Collier remembered that since it had happened in his birth year. His parents had told him he had nearly been named "Ares" in commemoration.

Obviously, Martians felt they were too cosmopolitan to accept raw ore as currency anymore. That meant he would have to take the extra step of selling the ore to a broker. He'd transmuted almost a kilo of his shipboard biologics into rhodium, which ought to fetch him several hundred thousands syscreds. Finding an ore broker took him little time: the local businesses were friendly and helpful in that regard. He floatwalked to the establishment they had indicated in high spirits, eyeing the nightclubs and bars on his way. He could certainly afford to wet his whistle once he had made the sale.

He shook his head as if to knock the thought loose from his mind. He didn't need to drink anymore, so why was the thought still in his head? For a brief moment, he knew what kind of a predator alcoholism was, and felt sympathy for the shitbums who lined the tunnels of Ceres.

Collier shook off his reminiscence when he located Helium Acquisitions, Limited. It was a sleek, if modest, business — one which he'd been told was local. He'd asked specifically for one such place in his inquiries, wishing to avoid any corporate dealings.

The young man at the shopfront counter greeted him with a smile, his eyes darting from Collier's vacc suit to his face. "Good afternoon, sir. How can I help you?"

"Hi," Collier said. "I'm looking to sell some ore. Rhodium."

"Very good, sir. Let me check the rate for you." The young man operated a small calculator set into the countertop. "Currently we're buying rhodium at six thousand, one hundred three point two galileos per standard Earth gram. How much do you have?"

"I don't know. About five hundred grams, I suppose." Selling the entire lot at once would be too risky.

The ore trader looked at him oddly for a moment, then smiled again. "All right. We will of course have to verify purity."

"I understand."

"Excellent. If you'd just care to fill this out, we can begin the transaction." He operated some controls on his terminal, and a holographic form appeared on the countertop facing Collier. He peered at it, looking at the questions.

"Unless you'd prefer a hard copy?" the young man said.

Collier shot him a look. "What do you need all this for?"

"All what?"

"All this," Collier said, gesturing at the form.

"It's just standard procedure, sir. For our records, and for Deimos customs and whatnot. Price of doing business," he said, smiling again.

"Customs gets a copy?"

"Yes. Is that a problem?"

Collier looked at the form, noting that he was required to have a seller's license and had to submit his retinal scan to verify his noncriminal status. The small print said a seller's license could be substituted with approved trade paperwork from another government, so his Ceres beltrunner credentials would do. But if someone noticed he had come to Deimos empty but then sold half a kilo of rhodium upon arrival, they'd ask questions.

Collier said, "I think I'm going to shop around. See if I can get a better price."

"I assure you, sir, Helium Acquisitions is quite competitive. Our prices are indexed to the daily exchange, which—"

"Yeah, well, I'm just going to take a look, all right?"

"Of course. Why don't you take our card, and you—"

Collier waved off the proffered slip of cardboard and beat a hasty retreat. He hurried away, getting out of eyeshot of the kiosk, and called Sancho.

"Got a little problem," he said. "Tried to sell the rhodium, but to do that I have to submit too much information. Could cause questions."

"Understood," Sancho said. "So, what's the plan?"

"No one's taking pure rhodium as currency, and I can't sell it no questions asked. Not to a legit operation, anyway."

"Skipper, I don't like where your mind is heading. Isn't one knife wound enough?"

"There's no other choice. I've got to find the black market, or what passes for such here."

"How're you going to do that?"

Collier noticed where he was. He looked at the blood-red neon sign flashing at him. "To start, I'm gonna have to buy some drinks," he said, and floatwalked into the bar.

He crossed the threshold between the station's pedestrian walkway and the club, a vaguely Arabian-themed affair called "Red Sands" and had to immediately squint to make out the writhing figures on the chrome poles, so dark was the place. The club used Deimos' microgravity to full advantage: a spherical bar set-up dominated the center of the club, with chrome poles extending from it like rays of light. Dancers gyrated in mid-air, using the poles to keep them in place. Like on Ceres, the dancers were made up of a fairly equal gender mix. Unlike Ceres, the patronage of Red Sands was almost exclusively male, at least as far as Collier could tell, but that had been true for all of Deimos due to the overwhelmingly male prisoners sent from Earth.

Collier made his way to the bar and hooked his feet into the stabilizing stirrups. The bar was not automated, and a well-built man nodded at Collier questioningly. The bartender, dressed in a costume that was reminiscent of something Aladdin would have worn, nodded at him questioningly.

It occurred to Collier that he didn't know what the local beverages were. There was nothing in the bar setup to indicate what could be ordered, so Collier leaned towards the bartender and shouted over the music, "What's the house specialty?"

"Martian Sunrise."

"Sounds good."

The bartender sized him up and waited patiently. Collier understood the gesture, so he produced the meager cash he had and waved it at the man. The bartended nodded and began to make the drink.

The Martian Sunset was refreshing enough, if a bit weak, and had a sweetness to it not dissimilar to agave. Collier turned to watch the dancers. The poles extended out in all directions from the spherical bar, so he was afforded a great many angles from which to watch the performers.

When he finished his drink, he begun to turn to order a second one when he remembered why he was in the bar in the first place. The decor and garishness of the place screamed "tourist trap," but he had to start somewhere. He was considering exactly where to start when one of the male dancers floated over to him, snagging a chrome pole with a smooth combination of grace and strength to check his flight.

"Hi there," the dancer said, his voice almost drowned out by the pulsing music. "New in town?"

Collier nodded. "Just in," he half-shouted. His vacc suit must have been a giveaway.

"Ever been to Mars before?"

"No," Collier said. He looked at the man — he was a muscular specimen, and he carried himself in the microgravity with pantherlike grace. He was looking back at Collier with mild expectation, and Collier shrugged inwardly. As good a place to start as any, he reasoned. He turned to the bartender and indicated a refill on his drink, then gestured towards the dancer.

"My usual, Franq," the dancer said. The bartender produced another sunset and a clear, fizzy drink in a translucent sphere for the dancer. Collier had to part with the rest of his petty cash and hoped that would be enough to get what he needed from the dancer.

"Thanks…?" the dancer said, his voice rising in a question.

"Collier."

The dancer nodded and indicated toward his own bare chest. "Kelv."

"Is there anywhere we can go to talk?" Collier shouted.

Kelv nodded and reached for Collier's hand. He led them to an alcove in the outer surface of the sphere that was the Red Sands, and hooked himself into the niche using one of the short tethers there. Collier followed suit, and Kelv drew a heavy, opaque curtain between them and the rest of the bar. The pounding music became muted background noise, and Kelv said in a normal voice, "That's better. So, what did you want to talk about, Collier?"

Collier withdrew a small portion of the rhodium and held it up. "I need some information," he said.

Kelv followed the rhodium and squinted. "What is that? Silver?"

"No. Much more valuable. Rhodium."

"If you say so," Kelv said, leaning back. "But I don't take that, just so you know. It's galileos. Or syscreds if I have to."

Collier shook his head. "I think maybe there's been a misunderstanding. I'm not trying to arrange — well, an intimate encounter." He cursed himself inwardly at his own awkwardness.

Kelv raised a perfectly sculpted eyebrow. "Is that so? Then thanks for the drink," he said, and began to untether himself.

"Wait, please. Look, you can have the rhodium. You should be able to trade it for quite a few galileos. I just want some information."

Kelv paused, then looked back at Collier. There was suspicion in his eyes.

"I'm not a cop," Collier added.

Kelv chuckled. "Some of my best clients are cops. Why do —
oh, I get it." "He sized up Collier's vacc suit. "You're a beltrunner.
That explains the ore. You don't know how things work here, I
guess. I'm licensed. Perfectly legal sexworker. This would only be
a crime if you tried to proposition one of the dancers who doesn't
do anything … extra."

"Sorry," Collier said. "You're right on both counts. I didn't
know."

Kelv shrugged and settled back down. "Okay, then. What
information do you want?"

"I need to know where I can deal in rare ores. Besides the legit
market."

"What makes you think I'd know?"

Collier blinked. On Ceres there was no legal sex trade. The
club dancers were officially just dancers, but most of them —
willingly or not — participated in sexwork and had ties with the
criminal underworld. He had assumed Mars would be the same.
Now that Kelv had announced the legitimacy of his profession,
Collier realized his mistake.

"I think I owe you an apology," he said, shaking his head at
himself. "I made an assumption about you that wasn't fair. Here,"
he said, handing over the small bits of silvery metal, "take this
anyway. For the inconvenience and the trouble."

Kelv took the rhodium and studied it. "This really is a precious
metal? Worth more than silver?"

"Yeah. A lot more."

Kelv turned the rhodium over in his fingers for a moment,
then said, "No harm done. Wish I could help you, but I don't know
anything about trading in precious metals."

Collier nodded. "Right. Thanks anyway." He began to unfasten
himself from the tether.

"What do you need it for? I mean, why not just trade on the
open market?"

Collier grinned. "I would rather not call attention to myself
with the authorities. Want to keep my transactions private."

"Uh-huh. Speaking of private interactions, you're sure you
don't want to get friendly?"

Collier shook his head gently. "No, thanks. Turns out I don't
swing that way."

"Maybe you should try it," Kelv said, grinning back.

"Maybe," Collier said with a wry chuckle. "I haven't — well,
it's been a while."

"Bad breakup?"

"Yeah," Collier said. Su's memory swam in his mind and in his eyes.

"Sorry," Kelv said. "Looks like you're not over her."

"No."

"Breakups can be hard," Kelv said, his voice sympathetic.

"It wasn't like that." Collier felt detached from Kelv, from the private alcove, from everything. He wasn't speaking to anyone in that moment — just talking to try and gain mastery over events so long ago. "She was murdered. On Ganymede." He could feel her in his arms as the life drained out of her.

"Oh," Kelv said. "Hey, I'm sorry to have brought it up. That's just awful."

Collier didn't hear him — he was back on Ganymede, the cold of the moon seeping through his insulated suit, the featureless plain of snow and ice a bleak backdrop to the tragedy that had unfolded there.

Collier had no idea how long he stayed motionless and speechless before the reality of the nightclub alcove came rushing back, and he saw Kelv's handsome face staring back at him. He shook himself slightly and said, "I'm getting out of here. Sorry for the trouble." He reached past the dancer and slid open the acoustic curtain. The pulsing sounds of the nightclub immediately filled his head as he winced and started floating back out of the alcove.

"Wait," Kelv said, seizing his upper arm. "You could try the Reds."

Collier turned, unsure he had heard Kelv properly. "Reds?"

"Free Mars movement. We just call 'em Reds. They're sort of an underground group, I guess you'd say. They might be able to help you."

"They deal in rare ores?"

Kelv rubbed his chin. "I'm not sure — I only know that they work outside the official government. Working to make Mars free."

"I thought Mars was already free. Didn't you declare independence fifty years ago?"

"Fifty-one, yeah. But they mean free as in not having to take in convicts from Earth. Or something like that. I'm no expert, but I hear a lot. People generally like taking to me, you know," he smiled.

Collier drew the curtain back again. "Where can I find these Reds?"

Kelv thought for a moment. "I had one a few weeks ago; he got a little tipsy, talked a little more than he meant to, and he mentioned working at Cardinal Rule Outfitters. I don't know if the whole place is run by Reds, but at least they're sympathetic. Not everyone is, you know."

Collier nodded. "Thanks. Anything else I need to know?"

"Mars vigila."

"What's that? Some kind of password?"

Kelv chuckled. "No, no. Just their rallying cry. Might help."

"Thanks again," Collier said, and left the alcove. He exited the establishment, forcing himself to pass by the bar and abstain from a third round, and called Sancho when he was free of the noise.

"Sancho, I have a lead on solving our problem. There's some kind of resistance movement called Free Mars. They're known as Reds colloquially. Their slogan is 'Mars vigila.' See what you can dig up on them, will you?"

"I'll try, but I don't recall anything like that in my library. Which I keep telling you I need to update."

"If we ever get enough money, I'll get you the latest databases," Collier said, not bothering to hide his impatience. "In the meantime, scan whatever you can find — news, public access archives, whatever — to get me some info on this group."

"Will do," Sancho said. "What're you going to do?"

Collier took another long look back at the Red Sands entrance, then shook his head violently and said, "I'm gonna check out this lead I have. Hopefully you'll have something for me before I get there."

It wasn't long before Collier stood before the facade of Cardinal Rule Outfitters, a somewhat dingy looking shop that appeared to deal in various sundry supplies for Martian homesteaders. He was close enough to make out some of the price list and see some of the merchandise they advertised: Martian exosuits, startup farming kits, excavation materials, and the like.

"Sancho, have you found anything yet?"

"Not much, Skipper," Sancho replied. "There's nothing official in my outdated library materials. I do have some opinion pieces from local pundits that are kind of interesting."

"How so?"

"Corporate news agencies have branded the Free Mars movement a terrorist group," Sancho said, "and claim that they've disrupted terraforming efforts and destroyed life support stations. They're saying they've killed innocent people and are making Mars a hellhole."

"Uh-huh. That's corp news. What's the real story?"

"There are some commentators who say that the Free Mars people are just trying to rid the planet of corporate prison interests.

But even they condemn violence and disruption. I don't know, Skipper, seems like these Reds are kind of rough."

"Sounds like my kind of people. Thanks, Sancho." He closed the communicator and approached the shopfront. He pretended to browse the merchandise for a while, then spotted a shopkeeper taking inventory in the rear of the shop. He approached the worker and called out.

"Hey, I'm looking for something specific."

The worker, a bantam of a man with a buzzcut and patchy beard, looked up from his work and grunted, "Yeah?"

"Yeah. I need to shift some ore."

The man turned back to his inventory. "Go to an ore broker. Plenty of 'em around."

Collier lowered his voice. "I was hoping to avoid the conventional process."

The man glanced at him, his eyes narrow. "Can't help you."

"I have rare metals. I'm willing to trade them at a significant loss."

"Is that so," the man said, looking away.

"It is. I was hoping you'd be interested."

"I'm not."

Collier paused a half second, then said, "Mars vigila, you know."

The man's eyes darted towards Collier, but he recovered swiftly. "That don't cut any ice with me."

"No? Oh, well, I'll just have to sell my rhodium to someone that's interested. I was going to take three thousand a gram for it."

The man snorted. "It's worth more than twice that."

Collier grinned inwardly. "Is it? I'm just a hick beltrunner, fresh from Ceres. I don't know one end of Mars from another."

"You know enough to say 'Mars vigila,' though."

"I don't like prisons. Got personal reasons for that," Collier said.

The man stopped his inventory and looked at Collier for a long moment, studying him. "You say you've got rhodium, and you're willing to trade it for half price. Why?"

"I don't want a record of the transaction. At least, not a corporate record."

"Why not?"

"I have enemies in the corporations who would take too much of an interest in my dealings. Better that they don't know what I'm up to."

The man remained stone-faced. "Why the 'Mars vigila' routine?"

Collier shrugged. "Well, like I said, I don't like prisons. But also I was told that it might get you to listen to me. If I'm totally honest with you—"

"That'd be a nice start," the man grumbled.

Collier continued, "I'll say that I don't really understand your whole movement, and I don't really care that much about it. I just need the cash."

The man folded his arms. "What movement?"

Collier grinned. "I thought we were being honest?"

The man just stared at him.

"Look, that's the deal. I'm gonna trade rhodium and some other precious metals with you at reduced rates. What you do with it isn't my business. I just thought we could help each other — you get precious metals on the cheap, I get cash under the table. If you're not interested…"

The man held up his hand. "We can do business. But not out here. Come into the back storeroom and we'll talk."

Collier nodded, trying not to look as smug as he felt. He had always known that the promise of easy profit opened doors; it was nice to know that was as true in the Martian system as it was in the Belt. He passed through a plastic curtain into the storeroom and turned to address the shopkeeper who had followed him.

His smugness drained away instantly as he regarded the wicked-looking knife the man was holding centimeters from Collier's nose.

"There's no need for that," Collier said, raising his hands in defense. "I'm just a guy looking for some quick cash."

"Space the lies, Penny," he said. "How long have you been watching me? Who else is on the operation?"

"I honestly have no idea what you're talking about. And my name's Collier South. Like I said, I'm a beltrunner."

"A beltrunner. All the way out here?"

"Ceres and Mars are in near proximal conjunction right now. It wasn't a long trip."

The shopkeeper seemed to consider that for a moment, then waggled his knife. "Okay, Penny, let's check your story. Get that suit off."

"Now wait a—"

"Or I could cut it off," the shopkeeper said, advancing a little.

"Okay," Collier said. "But all you're going to have is a very pissed off naked customer. You should see the review I'm writing in my head about this place. Knocking off a star for this."

"Move!"

Collier wriggled out of his vacc suit, floating in the air in his undersuit. It left little to the imagination, and he hoped the shopkeeper wouldn't ask him to strip down completely. It wasn't his modesty he was worried about — it was that if he managed to escape bare-assed, he'd probably be picked up by the local cops for indecency.

The vacc suit rotated slowly in mid-air as Collier shrugged it off, and the shopkeeper reached for it with his free hand. Collier fetched up against a storage rack and hung on to it for stability. He considered launching himself at the man while he was busy searching his suit, but tabled the notion.

The shopkeeper was having trouble conducting a proper search with only one hand, but he did locate Collier's meager collection of galileos and his communicator, which the shopkeeper raised. "You were going to call for backup with this. Bring the rest of your squad here."

"Nope," Collier said. "I don't have a squad. Just my ship, the *Dulcinea*."

"This could all still be part of some Penny trap."

"If the Pennies wanted to raid us," came a new, feminine voice from the shadows behind the shopkeeper, "they wouldn't send a clumsy undercover agent first. You know that, Sedrick." The woman who emerged from hiding looked to be in her late thirties, or perhaps early forties, and was dressed in a ragtag arrangement of muted, drab layers. Collier was struck by how familiar she looked: he couldn't place her, but somehow, he felt he'd met her before.

"Gal, what the hell?" Sedrick said, keeping his eyes on Collier. "Why'd you come out? This guy's a cop!"

"He's not," the woman named Gal said. "I know who he is."

Sedrick's eyes glanced back at her, and Collier had a momentary impulse to grab the knife in the man's moment of distraction. He was too late; even as he considered the move, Sedrick turned back to him and waggled the knife.

"How?" Sedrick said.

"He said his name was Collier South. His ship is the *Dulcinea*."

"So?"

Gal floatwalked forward and said, "tell me, Captain South, this rhodium you want to trade, did you make it from a 'magic wand?'"

Collier swallowed, then managed to croak, "Who are you?"

"I'm Galatea Starcher."

Chapter Ten

Collier finally recognized the resemblance. He glanced at Sedrick, whose knifepoint had begun to waver, and then returned his gaze to Galatea. "Barney's daughter?" was all he managed to croak.

"Gal, what the hell are you talking about? What magic wand?" Sedrick said.

"He's got himself a nice little device, Sed. Assuming it does everything my father said it can." She stumbled slightly over the word "father." She paused, then said to Collier, "You said you want to trade with us, right? I'll give you a trade. We'll fuel up the *Dulcinea* with waterfuel, biologics, anything else you need in exchange for the wand."

Collier's mind raced. He could pretend he didn't know what she was talking about, or claim he didn't have the magic wand, but decided honesty would work best here. "You know I can't make that deal."

"What the hell are we talking about?" Sedrick demanded.

Galatea ignored him and addressed Collier. "It's the only deal I'm offering."

"Then I refuse."

Galatea shook her head. "Barney said you were good to him in the end. That you gave him the wand to make up for years of bad debt. But now, here you are with transmuted rhodium. So I guess you changed your mind, didn't you? You took it from him. Well, I'm taking it back."

Collier said, "You were in contact with your father?"

Again, he saw her bristle at the word, but she recovered and nodded. "He reached out to me. After twenty-two years of silence. You giving him this thing made him want to reconnect, try to heal old wounds. I had just begun to open up to him again, and then he broke contact. I'd say it hurt, except by now, I'm not capable of feeling anything for him."

Collier swallowed and eyed Sedrick's knife. He had to tell her. "I'm sorry, but ... your father's dead."

Her reaction belied her words of indifference. Even in the low gravity of the Martian moon, she stumbled backwards a step and regained her balance. "How?"

"He was murdered," Collier said softly. "I went to see him before I left. He'd closed up shop, and everyone thought he had left Ceres. I went to check in and found his body. I recovered the magic wand from his office. I didn't take it from him." There was no sense in telling Gal that her absentee father had been rotting in his own refrigerator.

"Gal," Sedrick said quietly, "this could all be a lie. A trick to make us admit—"

"Admit what, Sedrick? If he's a Penny, why go to all this trouble? If they know where I am, why not send a squad of police?"

"Maybe they don't," Sedrick said, turning to Collier. "Maybe this one just stumbled into us. I took his comm, so he can't call for help."

"So they sent an impostor to pretend to be the guy my father lent money to?"

"Maybe."

Galatea stared at Collier for a moment, then barked, "What does the magic wand do?" At his hesitation, she added, "If you're who you say you are, you'll know."

"It transmutes anything put into it to any element I choose."

Galatea half-turned to Sedrick. "He's really Collier South."

"Maybe so, but he could still be working for the police."

Galatea snorted at that. "According to stories I've heard, Captain South is many things," she said. "A bad credit risk, a stubborn son-of-a-bitch, and a drunken wastrel — but he's not a toady for the cops." She turned to him. "But all that doesn't mean I have to trust you. How do I know you weren't the one who killed my ... who killed Barney?"

Collier said with genuine tenderness, "Gal, your father believed in me and risked his business on my success. He was a good man and a good friend. I never got the chance to repay him the way I should have. Giving him the wand was the best I could do."

"Very well," Galatea said with iron in her voice. "If he is dead, the wand falls to me."

Collier winced. "I suppose there's some logic to that," he said. "But I'm not in a position to hand it over."

Sedrick had relaxed the knife during the discussion, but now pressed the edge closer to Collier's neck.

Collier gasped and said, "Killing me won't get you the wand. And even if you managed to get it from my ship, you don't know how to work it."

"We could sell it," Galatea said.

"You won't do that. You know what it does. You want that kind of device in the hands of the Martian government, or a corporation like Ad Astra?"

Galatea stared at him with an odd look for several seconds before Sedrick interrupted the moment.

"Gal, this is pointless. Let me make him give us this magic wand. I think I can convince him to surrender it and to show us how it works."

Collier said to Galatea, "I won't do that." He swiveled his eyes to give Sedrick a steely glare. "And you won't kill me. A lot of people have tried. I'm still standing."

Sedrick hesitated, and Collier saw who he was. For all his bluster and tough exterior, the man was not a killer. In this Free Mars organization, he was now and forever a flunky. Galatea was harder to measure. Collier used the moment of hesitation to press his advantage. "Let go of me, hand back my suit, and we'll talk like civilized folks."

"Gal," Sedrick started, but he never finished his sentence. With a tiny shrug, Galatea said. "Fine. Sedrick, let him go." She retrieved Collier's vacc suit and tossed it towards him.

He snagged it out of the air and nodded. "Now we deal." He began wriggling into the suit.

Galatea said, "Rhodium is a good start. Also osmium. And maybe just good, old fashioned P's."

Collier grinned inwardly. It had been a long time since he had heard the beltrunner's slang for platinum and palladium. "Easy enough. All I need in return is waterfuel and biologics. Don't even need the money, really, though I could use some spare cash."

"So that's it?" Sedrick said, in outrage. "We're just going to deal with him now?"

"We can make a huge profit, Sed," Galatea said, her voice tinged with impatience.

"But can we trust him?"

"My father did," she said. Again, Collier heard the strange emphasis on "father."

Sedrick objected again. "But—"

"Plus, we're not going to get the wand from him. Sed, please go and see if you can get us waterfuel and biologics from our suppliers. I know you can do it and make it look innocent." Her tone was half request, half dismissal.

Sedrick swallowed and gave Collier one last scowl before he exited the storeroom, handing over the knife to Galatea as he did so.

Collier waited until Sedrick was gone before speaking. "Barney — your father — didn't mention you to me." Collier watched her carefully for a reaction. He wasn't disappointed.

Galatea's face fell slightly, then she regained her composure and smirked. "I'm not surprised. He stopped speaking to me when I was seventeen years old. Earth years."

"Why?"

"We had a difference of opinion."

"Must have been quite a difference."

Galatea nodded gently, her face softening. "You could say that. I decided to begin my internship with Ad Astra at seventeen."

Collier rocked back. "You interned with Ad Astra?" He was suddenly glad Sedrick had left them alone.

"Yeah. He didn't like that. He left Earth that same year. That was, let's see, would have been 2132. I was made a ward of the corporation shortly after that."

"A ward…what about your mother? Couldn't she—" Collier stopped at Galatea's bizarre reaction to his words. She had reddened immediately, and fixed Collier with an icy stare that stopped his tongue.

"I don't have a mother."

Collier said placatingly, "Oh. I'm sorry. My mother and father died too, in—"

"She didn't die. I don't have a mother. Never did."

Collier said, "I'm not sure I understand."

"I'm not really Barney's Starcher's daughter, not in the technical definition of the word," she said, her cheeks suddenly blotchy and crimson.

Collier felt himself gasp and tried to cover the sound with a cough.

Galatea smirked coldly at him. "Go ahead and laugh."

"I'm not laughing. So you are a…"

"Say it. A clone. Facsimile. Or my personal favorite slang term, a 'scrape.'"

Suddenly the strong resemblance made sense. She didn't have half of Barney's genes — she had all of them. Except obviously she'd been sex-swapped. He'd heard the general disdain for "scrapes" that permeated the Belt. He'd even joined in on raunchy and belittling jokes about clones. Now that he was face to face with one — and a clone of his friend, no less — he found himself thoroughly chagrined at his past behavior.

"I thought human cloning was illegal," was all he could think to say, and once the words were out, he instantly regretted them.

Galatea snickered. "It is. It's illegal to *clone* humans, but it's not illegal to *be* a cloned human. Don't think I haven't noted the contradiction in that legal puzzle."

Collier was eager to know more about how she had come to be, but realized that the subject was obviously a difficult one for her. "So you worked for Ad Astra?"

"Officially hired when I was twenty-one. Research and Development. Marketing division."

"And now you're here. What happened?"

Galatea smirked. "They promoted me to president. What do you think happened?"

Collier shook his head. "I don't know — obviously, it didn't end well for you. They must have let you go."

"Oh, they did much more than that. Discovered my clone status, then framed me for corporate espionage. I was sent here. Arrived about three months ago but was sprung by the Reds. Never actually served any time; the movement has kept me hidden for these past months."

Collier raised a hand. "Wait. Why were you sent here if Ad Astra fired you?"

"I told you. Framed me for spying."

"But that's just grounds for being sacked. Not for being sent to Mars prison."

Galatea stared at him for a long second, then snickered without humor. "You really are a beltrunner. About a third of the prisoners on Mars are corporate ones. There's criminal offenders, civil offenders, and corporate offenders. And a strong corp like Ad Astra has a high conviction rate. If it weren't for the Reds, I'd be dirtside working on the terraforming project, chewing dust and freezing my ass off."

"Sounds like these Reds take good care of you."

Galatea shrugged and gestured to a corner of the storeroom. "I get whatever food they can bring me, and have to stay hidden. Some days, I'm not sure it wouldn't be better just to turn myself in and take the trip to Mars."

"Why don't you, then?"

Galatea grinned wickedly. "What, and give those Ad Astra assholes the satisfaction?"

Collier smiled back.

After a long silence, Galatea said, "So. Now that you have heard my story, I wonder if you'd tell me one."

"You want to know my story?"

She shook her head. "No. Could you ... tell me about my father?"

——— «» ———

Collier couldn't say how long he spent recalling some of the better anecdotes about his relationship with Barney. At first, he'd tried to cast his own role in the best possible light, but Galatea had cut him off quickly. She knew how much money her father had risked — and lost — extending credit to Collier time and time again. She said it was more evidence of his "naive generosity," but seemed to admire that quality in him. The more he spoke about his departed business partner, the more Galatea softened.

They were interrupted some time later by Sedrick coming back into the storeroom. "I've done what you asked," he said to Galatea. "Waterfuel and biologics. Spread it out over a few different suppliers to be safe. Just tell me how much you want to sell him."

Collier told him his ship's capacity for both. When he finished, Sedrick looked at Galatea. "You'd better be right about this," he said, and ducked back out to the showroom.

Collier turned to Galatea. "For a newcomer, you sure seem to have the movement wrapped around your finger."

Galatea shrugged slightly. "I have my value. They know that; it's why they sprung me in the first place."

"Oh?"

Galatea grunted. "A former corporate executive? I know plenty of backdoors and secrets about Ad Astra. It's been a busy three months, I can tell you. I'm earning my keep."

"They should promote you."

"To what? We don't have officers and ranks, Collier."

"I suppose that's true." He rubbed the back of his neck. "So, what do you want me to make for you, and how much of it do you want?"

"Rhodium is a good start," she said. "A kilogram?"

"Sure."

"Platinum? Palladium? Osmium?"

Collier nodded. "Not a problem. A kilo each of them, too?"

Galatea didn't answer right away, but just shook her head gently. "I only half-believed it. Father's stories about the device. But you talk as if it's nothing."

"I'll have to go back to my ship to make the stuff." He looked around the storage room. "And if you have three kilos of waste or something, that'd make it easier."

"I'm sure we can find three kilos of garbage."

Collier nodded. "Okay. I'll come back later today. Two or three hours."

Galatea nodded. "When you do, and your metals check out, we should be able to deliver your supplies in about six hours."

"The metals will check out. Let me give you my berth information."

Once that was done, he left the establishment, collecting another scowl from Sedrick on the way out.

He entered *Dulcinea* and said to Sancho, "Okay, it's all set. Waterfuel and biologics being delivered in six hours."

"Copy that, Skipper," Sancho said. "How much?"

"Full up on both."

"Sounds good. And what is the plan after that?"

"Plot a course for the L-four point. We're going to chase whatever it was that made the magic wand heat up."

"You're aware, Skipper, that the Lagrange point you're referring to is a little over two hundred thirty-eight million kilometers away. That makes the round trip about four hundred seventy-seven million kilometers. Even with full tanks, we'd have to do a conservation course."

On their transit to Mars, they'd come within seventy million kilometers of the L-four point, but they were moving in opposite directions. Mars had been coming at them, shortening the trip, just as any approach to the Lagrange point would now be a chase.

"How long? Assume we want to get back here with five percent reserves."

Sancho was silent a moment, then came back on. "I estimate the round trip would be eighty-five days, eleven hours. Return journey is faster, of course."

Collier chafed. He didn't relish the thought of almost three months' travel for perhaps no benefit. There was one advantage, however: the Lagrange point would remain in position, leading Mars in her orbit, exactly as distant no matter when, or if, he decided to go there.

Sancho chimed in. "Skipper? May I make a suggestion?"

"Go ahead."

"It seems to me we could upgrade *Dulcinea's* fuel tanks. Get more storage for waterfuel. That would give us more range."

"Expensive, Sancho."

"What's money to the man who has the Philosopher's Stone?"

Collier chuckled. "Gettin' poetic on me, are you?" He thought for a moment. "I see your point, though. I don't know if my new friends here at the Cardinal Rule have that kind of pull, but I can ask."

"What about going to another company?"

"There's a limit to how often I can pull this rhodium rabbit out of a hat without calling attention to us."

"What do small furry mammals and headgear have to do—"

"For God's sake, Sancho, you've got to pick up on idioms better. Sooner or later, everyone will start to talk about the crazy beltrunner with his rare metals. And we'll be right back in the same spot we were in the Belt."

"So, it's a three month round trip to Worthless? Just to see why the magic wand became radioactive?"

"That's my plan."

"We're going to end up right back here in three months, fuel and biologics exhausted. Then what?"

"Then we'll make a new plan. Now quiet down and let me eat something."

He was not even halfway finished his reconstituted chicken vindaloo and toast when Sancho started up on him again.

"Look, Skipper," he said, clearly irritated, "I understand you feel we have to check out the wand, but I have to remind you that you promised we'd take on Ad Astra as soon as we were able."

"I did. We're not ready."

"Because you refuse to do anything to make us ready!" Sancho shouted, his calm tone gone.

"Don't take that tone with me," Collier muttered, sucking down the last of his meal. "Bring up the manual on the magic wand. I've got to make the metals for Galatea."

"You could make extra to improve the ship. You say we can't take on Ad Astra as we are. Then change the variables."

"You think it's so easy? Go out and find a black market outfitter that'll weld on a missile weapons package, no question asked? You try it, then," Collier shot back.

"Maybe I should," Sancho said. If the computer had had a chin, he would have stuck it out belligerently.

"What the hell is that supposed to mean?"

"I'll contact ore brokers myself. Tell them we've got palladium, rhodium, whatever. I'll arrange the sales. All you need to do is use your little monkey paws to manipulate the wand and make the stuff I sell."

"You think they'll deal with a computer?"

"They won't know I'm a computer. I sure as hell won't tell them."

"And what will you do when someone comes sniffing around, wondering where this beltrunner ship is coming up with all this pure ore? How you gonna get out of that?"

"I think you overestimate people's curiosity. If they're making profits, what do they care how?"

"So now you know human nature?" Collier snorted.

"I've been around you long enough," Sancho answered. "So yes, I think I do. The point is, Skipper," Sancho added, his voice softening a bit, "we can't just sit around here. We need to make money to increase our options. High-performance thrusters. Electronic countermeasure suite. Yeah, even weapons. The longer we sit here, the further apart Mars and Ceres are getting. And the further away Ad Astra is getting."

"So now you're running things? You have all your little grand plans?"

"Plans can't be both 'little' and 'grand.'"

"Don't get smart," Collier snapped.

"Evidently one of us has to," Sancho shot back.

"Real funny. Let me see if I can follow your complex silicon ideas with my simple carbon brain. You want to arrange buyers for our pure ore, and then use the money — and I am sure no one will become curious about this beltrunner who had an empty hold when he arrived on Deimos but now seems to have precious metals coming out his ass — to buy a missile rack, subetheric countermeasures, kinetic-kill systems, and bribe Ad Astra executives to bring down the entire corporate system? Did I miss anything?"

"You're deliberately misrepresenting my ideas to make them sound ridiculous," Sancho said.

"I didn't have that far to go," Collier said. "They're already ridiculous."

"And your ideas? As far as I can tell they involve eating chicken vindaloo and farting. Methane concentrations in the cabin are elevated, by the way, Skipper."

"I already told you. We need to figure out why the wand got radioactive when we got closer to Worthless."

"There's probably a good reason it's named that."

"Whatever. But we need to go there and investigate."

"I don't concur, Skipper."

That gave Collier pause, even more than Sancho's new cheeky, rebellious attitude. He had a fleeting desire to simply order the computer to obey him, but the feeling faded quickly. He knew he couldn't do that, and not simply because he'd made a deal with him.

He sighed. "So. We're stuck."

"It would appear so."

After a long pause, during which Collier worked on transmuting the metals, he spoke up. "All right. Look. The contact I made at Cardinal Rule may — *may* — be able to help us with Ad Astra."

"How?"

Collier brought Sancho up to speed on Galatea's identity. When he was finished, the computer said, "Interesting. She could be quite valuable."

"She already is. She arranged for the fuel and biologics," Collier said, continuing to work the magic wand.

"You will question her about the corporation? Learn everything you can so we can make plans to attack them?"

"I'll find out what I can. But then we head to Worthless, agreed?"

"I give provisional assent to that plan, pending analysis of her information."

Collier nodded once and sniffed the air with distaste. "Turn the air scrubbers up to full, will you?"

——— «» ———

Collier returned to Cardinal Rule, carrying the four standard Earth kilograms of various metals in a makeshift sack he'd fashioned out of one of his sleepsuits. He got a few curious looks from pedestrians in the station, but he continued on to the outfitter without incident. Sedrick was dealing with a customer, so Collier pretended to browse the merchandise for a few minutes until he and Sedrick were alone in the shop.

The scowling Sedrick brought him back to the storeroom, where Galatea was waiting patiently next to a small, battered-looking assay box. Collier untied his sleepwear-sack and let the metals speak for him.

Sedrick reached out to touch the nearest sample, a piece of palladium that shone brightly even in the dim light of the storeroom. He caught Collier watching him and grunted. "Could still be fake," he said, withdrawing his hand.

"Let's get to testing, then," Galatea said, and gathered up the metals. She placed them into the assay box with expert care, adjusting a sensor on the inside of the box before closing the whole apparatus and setting it to work.

In short order, the analysis came back, and the two Reds peered at the tiny display screen in wonder. Galatea was the first to straighten up, looking at Collier with what amounted to respect. "I have to admit, I didn't really believe my father's stories. But you do indeed have a magic wand."

"This don't prove anything," Sedrick said, turning to Collier. "You could have just brought in these samples. You expect us to believe you just made all this? From nothing?"

"In the first place, if I had a kilo each of pure rhodium, osmium, platinum, and palladium, I wouldn't be selling it for sixty kiloliters of waterfuel and some protein paste. In the second place, what are the chances I happen to have the four elements, in the amounts you asked for?"

"And in the third place," Sedrick said, producing his knife, "you're going to hand over that thing so we can see for ourselves."

Collier didn't back away. "You think I'd be stupid enough to bring it with me? It's safe on my ship. You kill me now, you won't get it. And you'll have to explain my disappearance. I don't think you want that. Put the knife away."

"Please, Sedrick," Galatea said gently. "He's right. We've got nearly seven million galileos in the assay box from the rhodium alone. How much did the waterfuel and biologics cost?"

"Less than that," Sedrick grumbled, sliding his knife back inside its hiding place in his coveralls.

Galatea chuckled. "Quite a bit less than that. I think we made out fine." She turned to Collier. "We'll start delivery of your supplies immediately. Where are you going, anyway?"

"Anywhere Ad Astra can't find me."

Galatea frowned. "Not many places like that, I'm afraid."

"So I've discovered." He shook the remaining particles of ore off his sleepsuit, pieces which Sedrick scrambled to recover, and rolled the suit into a ball. He shoved the ball under his arm and said, "I think our business here is done."

"Yeah," Galatea said, watching her partner collect the floating bits of metal from the storeroom. She looked back at Collier. "Thanks for sharing the stories about my father. I wish..." she stopped and looked away again.

"I understand," Collier said. He squirmed a little at the emotion in the room, then said hastily, "Thanks again. Good luck with the ... revolution, or whatever it is you're doing." He turned and floatwalked out of the storeroom, then out of the shop entirely. He called Sancho to tell him to expect a resupply that would no doubt that would be handled by drones and other automated services that Cardinal Rule had subcontracted to.

Outside the storefront, Collier, reached into one of his pockets and withdrew the few galileos he still had. He'd just left over seven million with Galatea and her colleague, but he didn't have enough for even a swig of a Martian Sunrise. He shook his head and started to floatwalk back to the *Dulcinea*.

He was approaching the berth when a woman with close-cropped hair detached herself from a tetherpole and intercepted him.

"Captain Collier South," she said. It wasn't a question.

Collier saw three men with similar haircuts and demeanor floatwalking to flank him to the rear, right, and high left.

"Yes?"

The woman nodded in acknowledgement. "I'm Peacekeeper Oella. You're under arrest for customs violation and smuggling. Please don't resist."

Chapter Eleven

The holding cell into which he'd been placed stank of vinegar somehow. It was either the foul emanations of some previous occupant or the efforts of the police staff to disinfect the cell — Collier couldn't tell which. Nor did it matter. He felt naked wearing nothing but his undersuit and wondered what the Deimos detention rules were.

Apart from the odor, the cell was depressingly featureless: a functional suction toilet, a vertical sleeping harness and a metal door with a mesh window made up the entire inventory.

His inexperience with Martian justice worried him. How long could they keep him here? Was he entitled to legal representation? Exactly what laws had he broken? No one had expanded upon the arresting officer's summative "customs violation" and "smuggling" during his efficient and rushed processing. Collier felt certain it had to be his association with the Free Mars group.

"Huh. Never been a political prisoner before," he mused to himself.

Stuck in this cell, there was little he could do, and he refused to resort to lame tricks like pretending to be ill or crazy for attention. At least, not yet. Collier eyed the sleeping harness and remembered an old saying about good soldiers never giving up a chance to eat or sleep. He wasn't being offered a meal, so the next best thing would be to sleep.

——— «◇» ———

"Come on, South." Something about the man's voice seemed to indicate the guard had been trying to rouse him for some time. Collier forced himself back to alertness and shook off the harness.

"What? Am I being released?"

A snort of derision was his only answer. "Come with me. Time to answer some questions."

Collier considered briefly the idea of resisting, but decided against it. Even if he somehow managed to fight off the guard — a prospect with a low order of probability — he couldn't fight the entire security force. He floatwalked to the cell door and allowed himself to be seized by the wrists and handcuffed. The guard then escorted him past the row of holding cells, some empty, some with forlorn-looking derelicts awaiting their turn at the wheel of justice, and shoved him into a small room with some wall harnesses and a holoprojector.

"Wait there," the guard said, and shut the door with a clang.

Collier chuckled once at the redundant command, and watched the holographic Deimos Station Police logo rotate in the middle of the room.

After a wait of fifteen minutes, the opposite door opened and Peacekeeper Oella entered. Unlike her plainclothes attire during his arrest, she was now wearing a smart dark red suit, the silver badge of authority riding high near her left shoulder.

She stood in the doorway, neither in nor out of the room. Her scowl intensified, and she consulted a small handheld data pad. "Collier South?"

"Yes."

"You understand that, at this time, you have the right to refuse to answer any questions regarding the charges against you, and that, if you do choose to answer, those answers can be used as evidence against you?" Her voice carried the unmistakable quality of recitation.

"I do now."

"Good. With that in mind, do you consent to an interview?"

Collier spoke carefully, "Why would I want to do that?"

The woman sighed and said, "It's up to you. But if you aren't going to answer any questions, we'll have to put you back into protective custody. Until such time as we can guarantee your safety."

"I get it. And how long do you think that will take?"

"Oh, could be quite a while," she said, her scowl evolving into a smirk.

Collier nodded. "I think I understand. I'll cooperate."

"Good choice," she said, and entered the room, closing the door behind her. She attached her handheld device to a small Velcro strip on the wall of the chamber and said casually, "All that was recorded, by the way, so there's no sense in trying to claim later that you weren't warned. And we're recording this little conversation now, too."

"And, I expect, others are listening and watching. I get it."

"I'm glad you do. So," she said, pushing off the ground with her toe and floating backwards to one of the wall harnesses, "suppose you tell me where you got all that ore. You told our inspector that you were empty."

"What ore?"

"The ore you were carrying through the station an hour ago. The ore you took inside the Cardinal Rule but didn't take out."

"Oh. *That* ore. Well, that was a little white lie, Officer," Collier said, smiling his best sheepish smile. "I didn't want to go through the rigamarole of an inspection, impound, and so forth. Sorry about that. If there's a fine or something—"

"So, you lied to the inspector about your cargo. Where'd you have it stored on the ship, by the way?"

"I have some compartments for that."

"A smuggler. We don't like smugglers," Oella said.

"You make it sound like I was transporting something dangerous or illegal," Collier said. "It was just some ore. Stuff I refined myself."

"Yes, you mentioned that," Oella said. "We checked into your other dealings. Care to elaborate?"

"I'd rather not," Collier said. "It's a trade secret, you see. I'm hoping to capitalize on it."

"Why come here? Seems to me if you have some new refining method you'd be better off back in the Belt where you came from."

Collier's tried another sheepish smile. "Okay. Look, the truth is that I'm not exactly welcome back in the Belt. Nothing you need to concern yourself with. But I can't do business there. Burned too many bridges, let's say. So, I came here, hoping to start fresh. I was going to sell some of my ore samples, generate some interest in the purity of the metals, and then see what nibbles I could get on my refining technique. If I broke a few regulations along the way, then I'm sorry for any inconvenience." He used his cuffed hands to make a sort of shrugging motion, trying to look nonchalant.

Oella chewed her bottom lip for a moment, then shook her head slowly. "Nope. Not buying it. You're filling your fuel tanks, for a start. Why do you need full tanks if you're going to make a fresh start here?"

Collier shrugged. "Old beltrunner superstition. Always have full tanks when you can."

"What do you know about the Free Mars movement?"

Oella's question came suddenly, and Collier was caught off-guard. He hesitated slightly before saying, "What? Nothing. Well, except what some dancer in the Red Sands told me. It's some kind of radical group, right?"

"Don't lie to me, South," Oella said, her businesslike air fading to be replaced by contained fury.

Collier shook his head. Obviously, this Free Mars thing was a serious threat, and he was indeed a political prisoner. Very few regimes in history had been kind to enemies of the state. For the first time in the interrogation, he began to feel real fear.

"Whoa, whoa — you've got it all wrong, Oella," he said. "I'm just a beltrunner, coming here for a fresh start. Why would I come all this way to stir up trouble with Mars?"

"A good question. One that I want an answer to."

"I told you the answer. I never heard of Free Mars before I came here, and I don't give a damn what happens to them. I'm just—"

"A beltrunner, yeah, so you said," Oella finished his thought for him. "You seem to think that coming from Ceres makes your involvement with the gang impossible, huh? We've long suspected connections between those agitators and Ceres miners."

Collier felt the noose tightening. Despite the growing jeopardy, he couldn't tell her the truth about the magic wand. If she didn't believe him, she'd consider his story a lie to hide his association with the Reds. If she did believe him, that might be even worse.

"I don't know what I can say to you other than what I've told you," Collier said. "If you're gonna dispute everything I say, then what's the point of this interrogation?"

"The point is, you're going to stop lying and tell me about the Reds."

"I can't tell you what I don't know."

"Then I suggest you start getting a whole lot smarter. Fast."

Collier thought for a second, then said, brightly, "You can send a message to Ceres. I'm known there. They can corroborate my story. Ask for the Ceres Authority."

"Agent Lora Fletcher?"

Collier blinked, then nodded. "Yes. How did you know that?"

Oella snorted and detached herself from the wall harness. She pressed her palm into the door lock and opened it, beckoning with her hand towards someone outside.

Fletcher floatwalked into room, looking a bit more haggard than usual, but still the same woman he thought he'd left on Ceres.

"Collier," Fletcher said in a soft, tired voice.

"Fletcher — what the fuck are you doing here?"

"Right now, making your troubles a whole lot worse."

"Agent Fletcher was here chasing you, South," Oella said. She was making no effort to hide her smugness. "You still want to use her as a reference of your sterling character?"

Collier fought to regain his mental equilibrium. He didn't believe the Martian cop's story for a moment, but he put that aside. Now, he needed Fletcher, no matter why she was here. "Yeah, I do," he said, answering Oella's question. "For months on Ceres I was nothing but a drunk. One step above shitbum."

"I'd say a half-step," Fletcher said.

"What does that have to do with—" Oella began.

Collier overrode her stridently. "If you think I was their contact on Ceres to help 'em stage a rebellion or something, then they chose the worst possible person in the System for it. I could barely wake up each morning."

Oella sidled up to Fletcher and scowled. "This true?"

"The part about him being a wretched, drunk loser? Yeah. But as far as his connection with Free Mars..." she shrugged.

"You're saying he might be involved?" Oella pressed.

"I'm not saying that, Peacekeeper," Fletcher said, her voice even and smooth. "I am saying this man here would have been useless to anyone. Just as he was to himself for months."

Collier chafed at the description, accurate and helpful as it was.

"When you came in here, you said you'd help us shed some light on this guy," Oella said. Her jaw muscles worked even after she finished speaking.

"And I have," Fletcher said. "I didn't say you'd like it. He's not working with whatever revolutionary group you've got here. He's barely able to wipe his own ass."

Oella stared at Fletcher, who was in turn looking at Collier with her trademark unreadable expression. Fletcher spoke again, not turning to look at Oella. "And before you get the idea that maybe I, too, am working with your little band of insurrectionists," she said, her voice even as a razor blade, "remember that I am Agent-In-Command of the Ceres Authority."

"With no power on Mars or any of her stations." Oella said. She looked as if she'd bitten into an apple and found half of a worm. "And there's no extradition arrangement from us to you."

Now Fletcher turned to face the Martian officer. Her voice became even softer, and hence, more menacing. "You'd be willing to start some kind of intrasystem incident over this man?"

Oella's gaze flicked over to Collier then back to Fletcher.

"He's wanted in the Belt for much more than fibbing on some customs form." Fletcher continued. "So, levy your fine, downgrade his credit, send him to bed without supper, but do it quickly so I can take him off your hands and clear him off my books."

Oella glanced back at Collier, as if trying still to determine if he was more — or less — than he appeared. For his part, Collier tried to look like the hapless shitbum he'd been described as.

"If you're wrong, and he's working with the Reds—"

"Then better to have him back on Ceres in somo," Fletcher finished. Collier balked at the threat of being put in suspended animation; there were nasty rumors about what happened to Sleepers.

Fletcher smiled faintly and modulated her tone. "Come on now. One cop to another. You thought you had something here, some lead into your revolutionary group, but you were wrong. It happens. Now let me take him so you can concentrate on your real threats, whatever they are. Oh, if it's important," Fletcher said in an exaggerated casual tone, "you should know that in addition to his problems with the Authority, he's wanted on several corporate charges in the Belt. I don't know that Ad Astra and the others will be too happy if he's in your lockup because of some petty customs violations and a black market transaction."

Either this last appeal from Fletcher found its mark, or Oella had just grown tired of him. "Fine. I'll process him and you can have him." As if to salvage one last shred of authority, she floated towards Collier and said, "You got lucky, South."

"I'll be taking custody of his ship, too," Fletcher said. "You mentioned it's been impounded, so I need to get it back to Ceres before Mars gets too far away." She looked at Collier. "Did you run dry to get here?"

Collier blurted, "You can't take—"

"Shut up," Fletcher said.

That drew a smirk from Oella, who said, "He bought waterfuel and biologics from the black market. I've suspended delivery."

"Could you clear that, please?" Fletcher said. "I'll need the ship supplied to return to Ceres."

"Hey, I paid for that damn stuff," Collier said.

"Tough," Fletcher said.

Oella added, "I'll clear the block." She looked back at Collier. "Looks like you got screwed, beltrunner. I don't want to see you back on Deimos ever again."

"You won't. He'll be under for a long time," Fletcher said. She shook hands with Oella, who left the chamber.

When she'd gone and they were alone in the interrogation room, Fletcher shut the door behind her and turned to him. "Sorry about that," she whispered.

"The hell you are. You enjoyed it," he said in an equally low tone.

"Maybe a little."

"What are you doing here?"

Fletcher shook her head almost imperceptibly, then said in a louder voice than Collier thought necessary, "You know very well why I am here. Fraud, grand larceny, assault, just to name the big ones. You're going away for a long time. I'd suggest doing it under somo. Though some people say the nightmares are … lingering." Her eyes darted to-and-fro, as if searching the room.

He caught on and gave her a nod just as slight. "Never thought you'd come all the way out here for me."

"Arrest record is a little light these days," Fletcher said. "And you made the top five most wanted on Ceres."

"And my mom said I'd never amount to anything."

Thankfully, Oella opened the door at that moment and said, "All set. Transfer authorized. He's yours."

Fletcher said, "Thanks. You want your cuffs?"

Oella eyed Fletcher for a moment, then shrugged and uncuffed Collier. He made a show of rubbing his wrists.

"Don't get comfortable," Fletcher said, reaching over and slapping her own set of handcuffs on him.

Collier grunted in real pain as the metal cut into his wrists.

"I've set the sensitivity to maximum," Fletcher said, "so I'd avoid sudden movements if I were you."

Oella snorted and led them out of the small security office and back into the station proper. Collier collected his belongings, carrying his pressure suit as best he could with the handcuffs on, and followed Fletcher out of the office.

When they were out of earshot, Collier snapped, "Get these things off me."

"Not yet," Fletcher murmured into his ear. "Shut up. She's probably tailing us. That was too easy."

"It was?"

"Yes. Now shut up."

"Where are we going?"

"You don't really get the whole 'shut up' thing, do you? Your ship."

"Let me get my comm. I need to talk to Sancho. He'll be worried."

"Who?"

"My ship computer."

Fletcher cursed under her breath, then looked around for an out-of-the-way spot where he could talk privately. She hustled him to a side alcove.

Collier hissed, "For God's sake, get these things off me!"

"I will, if you stop moving." Fletcher made short work of the cuffs, pocketing them in her Authority coveralls.

Collier fished out his communicator and said, "Sancho, come in."

"Skipper! Where have you been? I've been trying to reach you for—"

"Is the ship secure?"

"Yes, of course. Why?"

"Has the resupply started?"

"Not yet."

Collier thought for a moment. Sancho's voice came over the comm.

"You're scaring your shipboard computer, Skipper. What's going on? Where were you?"

"Believe it or not, I was in jail, Sancho."

There was a short pause, and Sancho said, "I can see that."

Fletcher chuckled slightly at that comment. "You've got that thing programmed to give you shit?"

"Not exactly," he said. He turned back to the communicator. "I'm heading back to you. Keep the ship secure."

"I fully intend to, Skipper."

Collier closed the communicator and looked at Fletcher, who had the ghost of a grin on her face. "What?" he demanded.

She took his arm again and they continued toward *Dulcinea's* berth. "Never would have thought you would want a personality sim like that. Figured you either for efficient and neutral or sex kitten."

Collier grimaced. "No. But forget that. What the hell are you doing here?"

Fletcher looked around; there were few people in this part of the station, and those that were present were fully engrossed in their own affairs to listen in. She kept her voice low and said, "You left quite a mess back in the Belt. Disabled Ad Astra ship, a few dead bodies, Crawler mess. And you left me to clean it all up."

"I offered to let you come with me."

Fletcher's eyes searched his for a moment, then she nodded slightly. "Sure. But my point is, the people whose noses you tweaked aren't willing to leave things alone. Ad Astra has made it clear you are their number one target.

"That still doesn't explain why you're here."

Fletcher's impassive mask slipped for a moment, revealing the concerned woman behind it. "Someone had to tell you what you were up against."

"You don't owe me anything. More like the other way around."

The mask snapped back into place. "Don't think I don't know that. And don't start thinking I came here because you have some irresistible charm. Because you don't."

"Thanks."

"So I didn't come here for you."

"I'm still waiting for the real reason."

Fletcher's shoulders shrugged, the action looking alien to the rest of her body, as if it were involuntary or imposed from the outside. "There was nothing for me there anymore. Ceres Authority ... it's nothing. Never was anything, really."

"What do you mean?"

She snorted once. "Come on. You more than most know what a joke the Authority was. We strutted around Ceres Station as if we actually made a difference."

"I never saw you strut."

Fletcher ignored the interruption. "And law? We enforced law when it suited the corporations. If law kept people in line, they were all for it. But laws designed to keep the corps in check? Those meant nothing. Add to that the black market stuff that was going on right under our noses, which we were forced to allow—"

"You could have stopped that," Collier said.

Fletcher looked at him, shaking her head. "No, we couldn't. Too complicated. Plus sixty percent of my force were on the take. Some from the corps, some from the Duchess, most from both."

"And you? Were you?"

Fletcher drew herself up slightly, and looked at Collier for a long moment.

"Sorry."

Fletcher said, "Anyway, I secured passage on a turnaround liner a few weeks ago."

"You must have left shortly after we did," Collier mused.

"A few days." She grinned wickedly. "Doesn't take much to outrun your ship."

"So here you are. Was it such a good idea to come find me? Don't think I don't appreciate it, but I've now got two celestial bodies out to get me, plus a major corporation. Maybe you should keep your distance."

Fletcher cocked an amused eyebrow. "Why, Collier, it almost sounds like you care about my welfare." She flashed a tight grin for a moment, then continued. "I won't deny that you're a bit radioactive, but I think both of us can benefit from each other's presence."

He'd stopped listening halfway through her comment. If Fletcher wasn't dragging him back to Ceres, would she come with him to the Martian Lagrange point and Worthless? He looked at Fletcher for a long moment. She returned his look with a quizzical one of her own, waiting. He made his decision.

"Listen, there's something I should tell you about the magic wand," he said.

"More than you already have?"

"Sort of. Something happened on my way to Mars. Something I can't explain."

When he'd finished relaying the details of the strange behavior of the magic wand, Fletcher's expressionless face was gone, replaced with a look of wonder. "And you say you had no idea about this when you set course for Mars?"

"Nope. It just sort of happened."

"Have you told anyone else?"

"No. You and Sancho are the only people who know."

Fletcher narrowed her eyes at his description of his shipboard computer, but she shook her head slightly and said, "So you want to go to Worthless and take a look around. What do you expect to find?"

"I don't know," Collier said, "but if I'm going to try to figure out what this thing really is, where it came from, who made it, and stuff like that, my only lead is Worthless. Plus, what if there are more things like this there?"

"What do you mean?"

"I keep asking myself, why would an alien race put something like this on a neglected asteroid in the middle of the Belt? As far as I could tell, there was nothing else there. There was only one thing unusual about the rock where I found it."

"What was that?"

"It was moving counterspinward. A maverick."

Fletcher said, "that's sort of strange, but not unheard of. Collisions can cause the rare—"

"I know that," Collier said, waving her comment off. "But it's still an incredible coincidence. What if they're connected in some way?"

"How?"

"That's what I hope Worthless can help me answer."

"And if you get there and find nothing?"

"Then I'm no worse off than I am now, am I?"

"Well," Fletcher said, "it's a long trip there, if I remember my celestial navigation basics. That's time you could be using to prepare for the Ad Astra force. They're on their way — when I left, the talk around Ceres was they were preparing a fleet."

"A whole fleet?"

"Several ships, then. I don't know how many; you know how rumors are."

"You sound like Sancho. He wants to take them on head-on, forget about whatever might be on Worthless. He's got personal reasons to hate them." He looked around their immediate environment. "Speaking of which, let's head to the hangar. I don't like being in the open like this. Plus Sancho will be getting worried."

The two floatwalked towards the bay, keeping their eyes open for any Deimos agents trailing them.

As they made their way to the *Dulcinea*, Fletcher asked, "Just what's going on with you and your computer? You sound like you've got CDS."

"I hope you don't mean Cyber Displacement Syndrome, because you can forget that," he snapped.

"Whatever you say. But you talk about him like a real person. CDS can hit solo beltrunners who—"

"Dammit, I don't need a lesson on CDS. It's not what you're thinking. Sancho is a Caliban."

Fletcher's eyes widened, and she bumped up against a shop display case as she floatwalked.

"Take it easy," Collier said, suddenly annoyed on Sancho's behalf. "I've known for a long time. He's not some malfunctioning death machine looking to overthrow the human race and replace us with robots."

"But a Caliban … It's dangerous."

"Dangerous my ass," Collier said. "I'm much more dangerous than he is. He and I have been through more together than most married couples, and I trust him totally."

Fletcher continued to watch him carefully, her eyes speaking volumes.

"Dammit, I don't have CDS!"

Her silent stare kept accusing him.

"Yes, I think of him as a person, but not because I want him to be one. It's because of what he does. He's saved my ass several times, even when it was risky for him. Or when he had to sacrifice something he wanted." Collier paused to think away some of the emotions that the memory of Perditus on the ice plains of Ganymede stirred up.

When he finished, Fletcher's expression had become even more horrified. He saw her slowly reaching towards a zippered compartment at her thigh.

"You don't need your damn gun," Collier said. "If you think I've got CDS, fine, I can't really stop you. But if you're going to run with me, which is what I think you were trying to say a while ago but didn't have the lady balls to actually say it, then you're going to have to accept Sancho. He's my best friend — he's more than that.

He's my brother. Think what you want to about that, but that's the way it is."

Fletcher stopped her movement and just stared at him, the silence between them growing thicker each moment. Collier, with an effort, kept quiet and waited her out.

"You've said your piece," Fletcher said calmly. "Now listen to mine. First, I already told you, I'm not here because I like you. You lay a hand on me, you're going to withdraw a bloody stump."

"Shit, Fletcher, I don't—"

"Shut up," she said with the ease of long practice. "Second, you have whatever relationship you need to have with your computer. I don't need to have the same one. I'll be on my guard with both of you, and as soon as things get weird, I'm out."

"You think things aren't weird now?"

"Third, I resent the implication that I am running with you, like I'm some kind of sidekick in your story. We're running together, for as long as it seems feasible for both of us. I rescued you from jail, don't forget. So cut the master and commander nonsense."

"Are you through?"

"For the moment, yes."

"Fine. You're not going to come between me and Sancho in any case. I suggest you treat him like a person and with respect. He's my partner, so he gets an equal say in whatever decision is made."

Fletcher's eyebrows rose slightly, which for her, was a sign of astonishment. "That's insane. You—"

"Bup, bup, bup," Collier said, wagging his finger at her. "And lastly, you did indeed help me in the jail. But that doesn't mean you're co-captain. You're a passenger, Ex-Agent Fletcher. Get used to that."

She took that stoically, but he'd come to know her well enough to see the tiny markers in her face that betrayed the sting those words had caused. He regretted speaking to her that harshly. "Look, I know you're used to being in command. But if you want off this moon, you're going to play by my rules. That means accepting Sancho, Caliban and all."

"I get it, South," Fletcher said. "Do me the courtesy of assuming I understand what I've given up."

Collier swallowed and watched her come to terms with her new life. It took surprisingly little time. When her eyes met his again, they were made of steel.

"What's our departure time for Worthless?"

Chapter Twelve

They entered the *Dulcinea*, and Collier briefly reintroduced Fletcher and Sancho.

"Sancho, this is Agent Lora Fletcher, formerly of the Ceres Authority."

"I know who she is," Sancho said coolly. "Why's she here?"

"Asshole computer," Fletcher mumbled. Then, louder, she said, "I just bailed your captain out of jail, Caliban. That's what I'm doing here."

"Okay, this is already not going well," Collier said. "Maybe if we—"

"I'm called 'Sancho,' Agent Fletcher."

"Oh? You're offended by the term?"

"Not at all. It's a human term, not mine. If you want to compare me to an obscure character from Shakespeare, that's on you."

Fletcher glanced at Collier. "Mouthy little shit, isn't he?"

"That's how I like him. Not that it matters what I like," Collier added. "He's his own person." He looked at the control panel and asked, "Sancho, what's our refueling and resupply status?"

"Servos are just getting into position now, Skipper. They've contacted me for clearance and hookup instructions."

"Go ahead and begin. Let me know when it's done."

"Aye aye."

Fletcher continued to scowl at the control panel, then snorted and turned to Collier. "That Ad Astra fleet won't take long to get here. Even if it took them a few days to organize it, their performance should be a lot better than this thing. They could be days, or even hours, away."

"We can't do anything until we're fueled up. I'm close to dry right now. How much longer, Sancho?"

"No way to know yet, Skipper. I don't know how efficient the servos are. What's this about an Ad Astra fleet?"

"Not now, Sancho. Fletcher, do you have anything you need to transfer over here? Personal gear?"

"Yeah, a little. It's in a station locker."

"Get it. When we're ready, we're leaving."

Fletcher nodded and gave the computer's control panel one last scowl before she exited.

"So she's coming with us?" Sancho asked when she had left.

"Yeah."

"Why?"

"She's got nowhere else to go. And she did spring me from jail."

"So?"

"So, I owe her. Not just for that," Collier said, "but for a lot of things. She kept me from becoming ... well, from becoming even worse than I was. She was always in my corner, even when it cost her."

"Any other reasons?"

Collier glanced at the control panel, looking into Sancho's camera lens. "No. Please just monitor the resupply."

———— «⟩⟩ ————

After Fletcher had transferred her meager belongings to *Dulcinea*, Sancho made an announcement. "The ship is ready for departure, Skipper. If we're still going, that is."

"Sure, we're still going. Why wouldn't we?"

"Agent Fletcher told you the Ad Astra fleet was on its way."

"All the more reason we need to high-tail it out of here."

"Or, we could use the opportunity to stay and fight."

"You have it backwards," Fletcher said, her voice as harsh as it ever had been when speaking to the computer. "Against one small recon vessel? Maybe. Maybe. But this is a fleet of five or six top-of-the-line ships. They're pulling out all the stops."

"Yes, I know that," Sancho said, his own voice equally cold. "But the destruction of a small recon vessel would be a pinprick to a systemwide corporation Like Ad Astra. Wiping out half a dozen of their top vessels, on the other hand, would cripple them."

"That's not the issue," Collier said. "The *Dulcinea* against six Ad Astra heavies isn't even a mismatch. It's an impossibility."

"Yes, if we were alone."

"We are alone," Fletcher said.

"Skipper, do you want Ex-Agent Fletcher to be an equal partner in our ventures from now on? Because I have to tell you, I do not agree to that arrangement."

"Calm down, Sancho. Right now, she's a passenger." Collier looked at Fletcher, her expression unreadable as ever.

"Very well. Then would you please tell her to refrain from commenting on ship's business?"

Fletcher snickered. "What are we, in sixth grade? You have something to tell me, Caliban, go right ahead and say it."

"Both of you, knock this shit off," Collier snapped.

Fletcher unmoored herself from the bulkhead. "I'm going to go make sure my gear is stowed properly." She spun and floatwalked out of the control suite.

Collier waited a moment to let her get out of earshot and said in a low voice to Sancho, "What the hell's the matter with you?"

"She shouldn't be weighing in on our business, Skipper."

"What difference does it make? She's not—"

"I don't want her here. But if she has to be here, I'm not going to put up with her sticking her nose into our affairs."

"Holy shit, you're jealous! Just like you were back on Ceres!"

"Ridiculous."

Collier started to grin, then felt a pang of memory. How had he felt on Ganymede when Sancho had found the launch facility computer, Perditus? Could he honestly say he, too, hadn't been jealous of his friend finding someone else?

That was different, he tried to tell himself.

"It's okay, Sancho," Collier said gently. "I should have been more understanding."

"I still think we stay and fight."

"Okay," Collier said, trying not to sound condescending, "tell me about it. What did you mean, we aren't alone?"

"The Free Mars faction. They could be allies."

"Why would they help?"

"The prison industry is entirely a corporate affair," Sancho said, "and is a for-profit venture. If the Reds are unhappy with conditions in the penal system, it would stand to reason they would want to fight against corporate control. It should not be too difficult to enlist their aid in fighting not only the corporation that runs the Martian prison system, but corporations in general."

Collier listened to Sancho with what amounted to disappointment. How little his friend truly understood human nature. "Sancho, I don't know how to break this to you, but, well, it doesn't work like that."

"It does, Skipper. It's all public record. I can show you who owns—"

"That's not what I mean. I'm sure you're right about the prison system being in private hands and them making money off prisoners and prison labor and all that. Why not make a buck off of slave labor?" The last he said with a sort of tired venom. "What I meant was you thinking the Reds would want to engage in some kind of overall corporate overthrow."

"Why not? Do you know their manifesto?"

"I don't need to know it. They won't help us because they won't see their own needs connected to ours. And frankly, I wouldn't blame them."

"But—"

"Listen, Sancho, something you're going to have to learn about people is that we're mostly selfish and narrow-sighted. We don't go in for causes."

"A society grows great when old men plant trees in whose shade they shall never sit."

"Where'd you get that?"

"Old Greek proverb."

"Well, I don't know about you, but I ain't seen a bunch of folks planting trees in my lifetime. People look to see what they can get personally out of a situation. They don't make sacrifices, they don't try to reform systems, they don't look to the distant future. No one's a hero."

"You tried to be, Skipper."

"Yeah, and look where it's got me. A woman I loved, murdered. Barney also murdered. Now we're hunted throughout the System. There's no return in it, Sancho. We need to bug out of here before Ad Astra gets here, and see what's happening on that asteroid. It's the only lead we've ever had on the origin of the magic wand, and if it pays off, we might find other artifacts. Then we could buy and sell Ad Astra many times over."

"And if it's a bust? If there's nothing there, or worse, whatever is making the wand get radioactive ends up killing you or neutralizing the artifact permanently?"

Collier sighed. "I can't promise it will work, Sancho. But I know that staying here and trying to fight Ad Astra will end up badly for us. You want to have your data banks wiped again and turned into a corporate slave? Or dismantled altogether?"

"I'm aware of the risks, Skipper. I feel they are warranted in order to smash the Ad Astra Corporation."

"Vengeance is a dangerous drug, Sancho."

"I don't understand, Skipper."

"You're letting your hatred for Ad Astra color your thinking. For once in our relationship, I'm the clear-minded one. Trust me."

There was a long silence, during which time Collier wished for the hundredth time Sancho had a corporeal body. He could have reached out a hand to his friend, or looked into his eyes, or done any of a dozen things men did to one another to show brotherhood.

"Very well, Skipper. I give provisional assent for your plan, given current variables."

"Thanks, Sancho. I'd best be getting back to Fletcher, make sure she hasn't stolen anything."

"I've been watching her on my cameras, Skipper. She hasn't."

"I was kidding, Sancho."

"Oh."

Collier hesitated, about to ask his computer companion why he didn't trust Fletcher, but thought better of it. He had enough problems as it was without stirring up new ones.

He found Fletcher sitting, head in her hands, in the dressing room. He cleared his throat and she looked up. He tried to mirror her inscrutable features, then motioned for her to follow him back to the control suite. For the first time in their long history, Fletcher seemed too tired to make a snide remark.

Settled back in the saddle, Collier said, "All set. Sancho, set course for the Trojan point."

"Course already set and updated, Skipper."

"Good. Contact Deimos traffic control and inform them of our intent to depart. Disconnect umbilical and spin up reactor to operational standard." He started to attach the acceleration harness to his saddle and turned his head towards Fletcher. "You'd best secure for thrust."

"I think I can handle what this thing puts out," she said impassively.

Collier twisted in his saddle, now turning to face her completely. "You'd be surprised at what this old gal can do. One-tenth gee is nothing to ignore."

"Fine, if you really—"

"Skipper, there's a problem," Sancho interrupted. "We've been denied flight permission."

"What?"

"Deimos station has grounded all ships. I'm getting a recorded message. Something about a security measure."

"Dammit," Collier said, then swung around to look at Fletcher. "Security measure?"

Fletcher shrugged. "You got me. But if it was about you, they wouldn't have to ground the entire station. And police would be entering this ship."

"True," Collier said, grinning a little at himself. She'd known what he was thinking. "So, what do you think?"

"If this were Ceres," Fletcher said, "And I had the authority to ground all traffic, I'd do it whenever I thought a fugitive was trying to get out by hitching a ride with someone. Either as a stowaway or as someone the captain was trying to smuggle out. Or I might do it for contraband."

"So can we expect a search?"

"Maybe. Depends on what they're looking for." She paused, then said, "There's another possibility," Fletcher said calmly. "Sancho could be lying about the security breach."

Collier raised his eyebrows. "You can't be serious."

"He's a Caliban," Fletcher said, her voice cold. "They are unstable by nature."

Collier shook his head. "You don't know what the fuck you're saying, Fletcher."

Fletcher merely stared at him.

Collier glanced at the panel where he imagined Sancho to be, then turned back to Fletcher. "I'm only going to say this once. I trust Sancho more than I trust anyone else in the System. And that includes you. So, if you have an issue with him, you have an issue with me."

"Calm down," Fletcher said. "You mean to tell me you've never considered the possibility that he might not always be truthful with you?"

"No, I haven't," Collier said. "We've been through too much together."

"And he's never lied?"

"Not to me. But he's quite capable of lying his ass off, and doing it well. Side effect of being self-aware, I guess." Collier grinned grimly, remembering the episode with the Ad Astra boarding party.

Fletcher looked faintly thoughtful for a moment, then shrugged. "Fine."

"Wait a second," Collier said. "Aren't you forgetting something?"

"Am I?" Fletcher said.

"You owe Sancho an apology."

Now it was Fletcher's turn to look aghast. "You're joking."

"Never been more serious. You insulted him. You owe him an apology."

Fletcher locked eyes with him, and Collier returned the unblinking gaze. Finally, Fletcher managed to growl, "Sorry."

"Apology accepted, Ex-Agent Fletcher," Sancho said in his coldest computer voice.

Collier said, "Now don't be a shit, Sancho."

"Beg pardon, Skipper?"

"She said she was sorry. Be gracious and accept it."

"I did."

"Do it like you mean it."

Sancho hesitated, then spoke again, this time in his ordinary voice. "All right. Thank you, Ex-Agent Fletcher."

Collier sighed. "Better than nothing. Anyway, we're still faced with the problem of the security lockdown. If this lasts a long time, we might be facing Ad Astra whether we like it or not."

"I reiterate my position that we should ally ourselves with the Reds," Sancho said.

Collier's hands reflexively turned into fists for a moment before he relaxed them. "God dammit, Sancho, you said you agreed with me."

"I said I gave provisional assent given the variables at that time. Variables have changed."

"Because of this lockdown?" Collier shook his head and continued before Sancho could interject. "This doesn't change our plan. It just makes it harder to execute it. You agreed to go to the Trojan point first, Sancho. Are you reneging on that bargain?"

Sancho spoke carefully. "I'm reminding you of where I stand."

Fletcher snorted once. "Just order him to comply, Collier. Why is this so difficult?"

"You know damn well why I can't do that."

"Can't, or won't?"

"Pick one. It's all the same. Sancho's got an equal say in what we do."

"You're crazy," Fletcher said, shaking her head slowly. "You put a computer on equal footing with you. Of all people."

"I don't want to have this discussion," Collier said. "Sancho, tune into the local news networks. See if you can figure out what this lockdown is all about."

The control cabin was filled with snatches of reports from various local pundits speculating on what was happening on Deimos as Sancho ran through the channels. The overall consensus seemed to be that the authorities were chasing a fugitive, perhaps an escapee from the prison complex on Mars. Collier noted that the corporate channels were convinced that the fugitive was a dangerous individual and was part of the Free Mars movement, which they almost universally condemned as a terrorist group.

A half hour into the lockdown, Sancho said, "Skipper, there's a woman at my outer airlock hatch. I think she's trying to get in."

"Show me," Collier said. One of the screens on Sancho's control console lit up, and Collier took a deep breath. "Dammit. That's her."

"Who?" Fletcher and Sancho said simultaneously.

"Galatea. The woman with whom I arranged the resupply. Barney's ... daughter. That's got to be what this lockdown is about."

"I'm opening the airlock," Sancho said calmly.

"What? No!" Collier barked. "Don't let her inside! I'm already suspected of collaborating with the Reds. If you allow her—"

Collier stopped as he saw the outer airlock door open and Galatea slip inside. "God damn it, Sancho! What the hell are you doing?"

"We need her," Sancho said calmly. "She can be a valuable asset in our fight against Ad Astra."

"We're not fighting Ad Astra! How many times do I have to say that? Now keep her in the airlock. Do not open the inner door," he said firmly. He looked at Fletcher. "Maybe I can call the authorities, say I've captured her in the lock."

Fletcher's lips were a grim line as she shook her head. "No way they'll buy that." She stared at the screen, watching Galatea jab at the inner door controls.

"I'm sorry, Skipper," Sancho said, "but I disagree. Variables have changed again. Opening inner door."

Collier growled in impotent rage as he watched the inner door cycle open. "Distract her when she gets here," he hissed at Fletcher.

Fletcher nodded, understanding his play. She saw where he was positioning himself — on the left side of the entrance — and shifted her own position so that when Galatea entered, her eyes would go towards Fletcher and away from Collier. Collier and Fletcher's eyes met, and they nodded to each other.

Collier could hear the faint sounds of Galatea making her way towards the control cabin. He saw her left hand first, reaching for the lip of the control suite's entry point to propel her inside. He waited a moment, then timed his launch just when she was entering the room.

As they had planned, she was taken by surprise, and Collier seized her right hand. He twisted it up and away from him, trying to force her fingers to release the small knife she held there. He grunted in pain as he sliced open a shallow wound in his flesh when he came into contact with the knife's edge.

Fletcher came diving in, restraining Galatea's left arm, and the two of them were able to disarm Galatea in short order. Collier disengaged, floating back and cursing his bleeding hand. "Just stay right there," he said, pointing the knife at her. "Fletcher, see if she has any other weapons."

"I don't," Galatea said indignantly, fighting off Fletcher's attempts to search her. Fletcher hauled off and slapped her, then continued her search. Galatea's resistance faded.

"She's clean," Fletcher said, backing away and regarding the woman with quiet suspicion.

"Now, you just stay there, and we'll get this all sorted out," Collier said. "Sancho, contact Deimos security. Tell them we've apprehended the fugitive."

"No," Sancho said flatly.

"I'm not fucking around, Sancho," Collier snapped. "Do as I say."

"Neither am I, Skipper," Sancho said. "This woman could be vital to our efforts against Ad Astra."

"We're not—"

"And," Sancho continued, amplifying his voice to override Collier's interruption, "Deimos security would consider you an accessory to her escape."

"Not if we turn her in, claim that she broke in here."

"Collier," Fletcher said, "as much as I hate to agree with your pain-in-the-ass computer, he's right. I barely managed to get you away from them, and that was because I convinced them you had nothing to do with the Reds. No matter how might try to spin this," she gestured to Galatea's presence, "it's bad. You're not going to convince them you aren't working with them."

"Not even if I turn her in?"

"If I were in charge," Fletcher said, "I'd assume there was some kind of internal power struggle going on. Like you were trying to wrestle control away from her in the Red organization. But there's no way I'd believe you weren't deeply connected with the group."

Collier turned to Galatea. "Why the hell did you come here?"

Galatea had been listening closely to the conversation, and added, "Where else was I going to go? They figured out where I was, either by tracing the resupply order, or because they were following you."

"And what was your plan? Commandeer the ship with this?" Collier said, waving the small knife.

Galatea shrugged. "I didn't have a lot of time to prep. But either that or just convince you to take me to Mars."

"Why the hell would I do that?"

"Because of my father," Galatea said. "Because you owe him that."

The comment hit Collier between the eyes, its impact strengthened by the fact that he himself had been thinking the same thought. Barney's corpse, stuffed inside his refrigerator, stared back at him with lifeless eyes.

"God damn it," Collier mumbled. "Sancho, any activity outside?"

"Nothing so far, Skipper."

"Begin prelaunch checklist."

Fletcher said sharply, "You're going to take her to Mars?"

"No. If we touch down on Mars, we'll never lift off. Gravity well's too steep."

"Then where are we going?" Galatea said.

"Where we were going before you so rudely interrupted: to solve a Worthless mystery."

Chapter Thirteen

"Deimos flight control is still holding us, Skipper," Sancho announced two hours after the lockdown had begun.

"Are you still connected to umbilicals for refueling?"

"No. We're topped off."

"Then we're only on a soft hold. We can get out of here."

Fletcher said, "They'll send interceptors. If they've been scrambled already, you won't make it a hundred kilometers before—"

"We'll have to risk that. Are we ready for launch?"

Sancho said, "Not quite. I haven't spun up the reactor yet, and I still have to perform prelaunch status checks on the thrust tubes."

"Forget the tube check. Once the reactor is up to speed, it'll be detected by anyone smart enough to be looking. Launch immediately once you've got the reactor up. Our course is still Worthless."

"Aye aye. Increasing reactor to maximum. Estimate launch in two minutes, thirty-five seconds."

Galatea protested their destination with an angry look, but began to secure herself for acceleration.

Collier strapped into the control saddle just as the countdown finished, then felt the gentle but unmistakable thrust of *Dulcinea's* engines. He checked the various readouts, paying special attention to the thrust tubes. Everything looked normal.

"Launch plus thirty seconds," Sancho said. "Velocity twenty-nine point one meters per second, increasing by point nine nine meters per second.

"Slowest ship in the System," Fletcher murmured.

Collier ignored her. "Anything from Deimos flight control?"

Sancho answered, "Nothing yet. I've — hold on. Something coming in now. They're demanding we cut thrust, hold our vector, and await intercept."

"Any craft lifting towards us?"

"I don't see any."

Fletcher added, "Yet. Only a matter of time. And they'll have a lot better performance than this."

"You want to find another ship that'll take you, you're welcome to get out and hitchhike," Collier shot back. He half turned to scowl at Fletcher, and saw Galatea still tethered to the wall. He looked back at Fletcher, then gestured with his chin at Galatea, indicating that Fletcher should watch her carefully. Fletcher nodded her understanding.

"Any response to Deimos flight control, Skipper?"

"No, but continue to monitor Demios communications and update the status of any ships headed our way. Are we on course for Worthless?"

"Almost. Deimos' orientation wasn't proper when we launched, so I've been turning us. We should be able to steady on in a minute or so."

"Estimate travel time."

"Using half fuel, seventy-seven days, nine hours. Plus or minus twelve hours."

"Do we have enough biologics for three? Or didn't you think of that when you pulled your little stunt with Galatea?"

"At normal consumption and reclamation figured for three, I estimate eighty-nine days of supplies."

Fletcher said, "Not enough. Not for there and back."

Collier said, "We'll have to go on reduced rations. One and a quarter kilos per person per day."

"We can't—"

"Yes, we can. Because we have to," Collier said. He glanced at Galatea.

She spread her hands in defense. "I said I wanted to go to Mars. The Reds have a lot of influence down there. And where are we going that's two and a half months away? You can't just keeping saying it's worthless."

Collier laughed. "The Martian L-four point. An asteroid there is named Worthless."

"Why?"

Sancho broke in. "Skipper, I believe we should be asking the questions. The whole purpose of bringing her aboard was to get information against Ad Astra. And if we get actionable intelligence," Sancho said, "We could in theory return to Deimos and—"

"Skip it," Collier said. "We're headed for Worthless."

Sancho paused, then said, "We don't know what she knows. Maybe if you ask her—"

Collier shrugged and looked at Galatea. "You feel up for answering some questions?"

"What do you want to know?"

Before Collier could pose a question, Sancho broke in. "I want to know everything about Ad Astra."

Galatea looked from the computer terminal to Collier. "Is your computer my interrogator?"

"For now, yes. Answer him."

She turned back to the console. "I don't know everything. I was in their Applied Research department as a marketing consultant. Didn't do any of the science work myself, but was on the team who took a look at what the eggheads came up with and made recommendations about feasibility, stuff like that."

"Applied Research, excellent," Sancho said, his artificial voice betraying his excitement. "Tell me about the projects they were working on."

"About a year ago Terrestrial they started looking into transmutation of the elements. Poured a shitload of time, money, and staffpower into it." She stopped and stared at Collier.

Collier nodded slowly. "Yeah. That tracks. They got reports from what's-his-name—"

"Ruhland. The Ad Astra man you killed," Fletcher said dryly.

"Right."

"Or some lunatic who started spewing crazy ideas in the Ceres marketplace about a magic wand," Fletcher added.

Collier ignored that. "And when did your father contact you?"

"Maybe two, two and a half months ago."

Collier felt his stomach start to churn. The timeline was fitting into place with inescapable tragedy. He'd spent a month travelling from Ceres to Mars, and after subtracting that time...

"I didn't tell you everything about your father's death."

Galatea stared at him, her chalky face a stark contrast to Fletcher's in complexion and demeanor.

"I do know how he died. He didn't just stop talking to you. He was killed. Murdered." He paused, and added the final piece. "By Ad Astra."

"Wh—what?"

"They found out I'd given him the magic wand. I didn't know how ... until now."

Galatea's eyes widened. "You're saying I told them?"

Fletcher started. "Collier, ease up."

Collier kept his gaze locked on Galatea. "It's the only explanation that makes sense. Ad Astra found out about the magic wand through you. They'd known about it from my attack on

Ruhland and from, as Fletcher puts it, my spewing crazy ideas on Ceres. But maybe they still didn't quite believe it, so they started working on the science themselves. Then your father contacts you, tells you about the magic wand, and you turn around like a good little corp bitch and sell him out."

Galatea let out a snarl of incoherent rage and tried to launch herself towards Collier. Fletcher snagged her arm before she could go anywhere; that plus the one-tenth gee acceleration of *Dulcinea's* engines kept her from clawing at him.

"Hold it!" Fletcher barked, then turned towards Collier. "Stop it, both of you!"

Galatea was breathing heavily, trying to squirm out of Fletcher's iron grip. "Let me go! I'll kill that son-of-a-bitch!"

"You wanted a promotion," Collier goaded her. "And it's not like you're his real daughter anyway, you scrape."

Galatea's struggles intensified, but Fletcher was more than a match for her. Galatea spluttered, "He was trying to reconnect! To make up for all the lost years. He said he was going to retire, make the trip back to Earth, and take care of things so I didn't have to work for the corp anymore. He was finally going to be my dad." Her rage was mixed with intense sorrow and she spoke through tears. "When I asked him how, he explained about the device. He told me to keep it secret, and I did! I didn't sell him out, you bastard! I loved him! I wanted to be ... his..." she broke down and sobbed into Fletcher's wrinkled Authority-issue button-down.

Fletcher maintained her grip on the wasted woman and shot Collier an accusatory look.

Collier nodded. "Sorry. But I had to be sure."

Galatea looked at him with red-rimmed eyes. "You said that on purpose?"

"Yeah. Sorry."

"Skipper," Sancho said, "I don't understand what's happening."

Fletcher continued to bore holes in Collier with her eyes as she answered Sancho. "Your captain was testing her," she said. "Seeing how she'd respond to accusations that she betrayed her father for corporate advancement, with a few slurs thrown in for what I can only assume was his own sick enjoyment."

"I see," Sancho said. "Based on her response, we are to assume her version of events is accurate, then?"

Fletcher's intense eyes shot towards the control panel. "I don't expect a Caliban to show any empathy," she said, looking back at Collier, "but you ... that was deliberately cruel."

"Skip it," Collier said. "I'm not having an Ad Astra plant on board."

"I told you my story," Galatea said, pushing away from Fletcher's chest.

"And now I believe it." Collier looked at the two women. "And before you accuse me of being some heartless monster, remember this: Barney was my friend. Anyone responsible for his death deserves a lot more than a few harsh words. Ad Astra must have been monitoring his communications with you."

Galatea sniffed and wiped her face. "He always used quantum encryption when he spoke with me. There's supposed to be no way to break it. I should know — R and D had been working on codebreaking for years."

"They wouldn't have to break the encryption," Fletcher said quietly. "We've known for a long time that Ad Astra and other corps have inside people on Ceres in the communications department. All traffic leaving Ceres was compromised."

"So, they found out about the device when he told me about it. And then they killed him for it."

Collier didn't speak. What was there to say?

Galatea drew herself up and regained her composure. "Computer, ask your questions. I'll answer anything you want to know. If you're trying to bring down Ad Astra, I'm with you all the way."

"We're not going to confront them just yet," Collier said. "We're heading for Worthless. After that..."

"It would still be wise to learn all we can about the corporation," Sancho said.

Galatea said, "Right now, I want to do what I can to get the bastards who killed my father. I'm fine. Ask away." She looked at Collier with ice cold eyes, and he saw that the best thing for her right now was to talk.

Sancho said, "Perhaps you could begin with what you know about their research into transmutation."

"They never got transmutation to work, but they learned some stuff in the process."

"Like what?" Collier asked, interested despite himself.

"Do you know what strange matter is?"

Collier searched his memory. "Vaguely. Some kinda elementary particle made up of strange quarks. So?"

"So, among the dead-ends in the Ad Astra research was something about strange matter being relatively easy to produce."

Collier shrugged. "So what? As far as I recall, strange matter isn't stable. It decays and becomes just ordinary up and down quarks, or something like that. Sancho?"

"That's more or less right, Skipper."

Galatea said, "I picked up some of the science over the time I spent in AR. If you get a whole bunch of strange matter together, and you can keep it all stable — which is what these scientists figured out how to do while they were looking into transmutation — you make something called a strangelet. And that's a big deal."

Sancho spoke up, "The creation of strangelets is theoretically possible, but the energy required to do so is so great as to be highly impractical. You would have to simultaneously convert—"

Galatea interrupted. "Well, they did it. I don't know the science for how, but they did it. And the eggheads seemed to think it was potentially a more important discovery than if they'd figured out cheap transmutation."

"Why didn't Ad Astra run with that, then?" Fletcher asked.

At the question, Galatea chuckled humorlessly. "That's what it's like in a corporation. Making a discovery with no immediate practical value doesn't mean a thing, and a junior executive like myself is trained to filter out those kinds of useless breakthroughs and concentrate on stuff that we can use now. So even though the PhDs were squawking with excitement over the discovery, I pushed them away from it and back to more practical matters. 'It might be strange, but it's not useful,' I remember saying, thinking it was clever."

"Sorry, Galatea, but I'm thinking the same thing," Collier said. "So, they made some kind of scientific breakthrough that is interesting to professor types but has no real use. So what?"

"Skipper," Sancho said slowly, "I only have a rudimentary science background. Which, by the way, I've been asking you to supplement for a long time now. You could pick up a specialist program for less than—"

"Just get on with it, Sancho."

"Right. Well, from what little I know, strangelets are, well, strange. Very strange. If a strangelet could be created, it would be extremely stable. Much more stable than ordinary matter."

"So?"

"So, if a negatively-charged strangelet came into contact with ordinary matter, it would in theory convert that matter into strange matter and grow larger and even more stable."

"Hold it, Sancho," Collier said. "I thought you said it was stable? How can it change so much if it's stable?"

"That's just it, Skipper. The strangelet would be more stable than ordinary matter. Meaning that ordinary matter would decay into strange matter and become part of the strangelet."

"Sounds like you're saying this strangelet would just keep growing and growing," Collier said, "which, as far as I understand it, violates the second law of thermodynamics."

"You got me there, Skipper. Maybe if you'd bought that science specialist software, I could give you an answer. But what little I know is that strangelets can change ordinary matter into strange matter and can keep doing this. If you get a big enough strangelet, you could in theory convert an entire planet in a matter of weeks."

"You're shitting me," Collier said.

"No, he's not," Fletcher said quietly.

Collier spun in mid-air to face her.

"The military has always been looking at strangelets as weapons," Fletcher went on. "It'd be the ultimate bomb. No way to stop it, no way to defend against it. You send it at your target, and very quickly, whatever it came into contact with would just … break down."

"How do you know this?"

Fletcher drew herself up. "I have my sources. It was always something the Authority worried about in the back of our heads. If a terrorist, say, were to deploy a strangelet weapon against Ceres itself, the planetoid could be simply erased in days. Maybe even hours. Imagine someone holding Ceres hostage with that threat. Not something we liked thinking about."

"And now you say Ad Astra has a way to make that actually happen?" Collier said, turning on Galatea.

"No, not yet. Like I said, when I was there, I was one of the many voices pressing the AR folks to come up with practical transmutation. Then I did my little scheme, got caught, and was sent to Deimos. I don't know what progress, if any, they've made since then."

"I'm guessing not a lot, or they wouldn't be chasing me across the System," Collier said. "If they figured out how to make one of these strangelet weapons, they'd have the whole human race by the balls. Imagine how much planetary governments would pay for the ability to do whatever the fuck they wanted, Earth oversight be damned. Not to mention what the Freedom Coalition, the Asiatic Combine, and the Pan-African States would pay for that."

"Let's hope you're right," Fletcher said. The comment sent a chill through the room, and Collier eyed Galatea. The woman had lost much of her stoic bravado and looked deep in thought.

Collier said, "Sancho, I think that's enough for now."

"But I—"

"Galatea's been through a lot. Most of it because of me," he added, tossing her an apologetic smile. "Why don't we let her rest. I'd offer you a bite to eat, but as you heard, we're going to be tightening our belts, conserving every last bit of food and water."

"Speaking of which, where's your reclamation room?" Galatea said.

Collier pointed unhelpfully at the bulkhead Opunui had installed.

"I'll show you," Fletcher opened the hatch and gestured for Galatea to follow.

When they'd left, Collier turned toward the control panel. "Okay, Sancho. We need to talk."

"What about?"

Collier fought to contain himself. "What about? About you bringing her aboard against my direct orders."

"If you'll recall, Skipper, we agreed on an equal sharing of authority."

"Yeah, but that doesn't mean you can just override me whenever you feel like it."

"Then what does 'equal partnership' mean, exactly?"

"It means—" Collier stopped himself. "Okay, dammit. I get it. You do have an equal say. But you let her in despite my strong objections. We should have talked it out."

"If I had delayed in letting her in, the likelihood of the Deimos security force locating her and apprehending her would have continued to increase."

"But once she was let in, we couldn't undo that decision! She was attached to us, and the police would never have believed we weren't working together."

"Wouldn't they have already been suspicious of you if they apprehended her trying to enter the ship?"

Collier stopped. He hadn't considered that. "All right, all right," he grumbled, angry at himself for having been out-argued. "Maybe you're right. But you didn't consider our food supply, did you? Carrying three people instead of two?"

"Honestly, Skipper, I was just hoping the woman would have usable information regarding Ad Astra."

"You mean," Collier said in a low voice, "you were gambling that she'd know something that would tip the scales in our favor in any confrontation with the incoming Ad Astra fleet? That she'd have some secret that we could use to just smash half a dozen corporate heavies without breaking a sweat?"

"When you put it like that, I admit the probability of such a secret is rather low. I am unsure why I am only now seeing this."

Collier couldn't help but smile. "You know what happened?"

"What?"

"You got your hopes up."

"I don't follow you, Skipper."

"You wanted to believe in something — in this case, that Galatea would know a way to make it easy for us to defeat the ships, and I would go along with it, and we'd finally get revenge on them for what they did to you. And me."

"That doesn't seem possible for me," Sancho said. "I calculate without regard for what I want."

"Bullshit," Collier chided him gently. "You're like anybody else. Your judgement sometimes gets cloudy because you convince yourself you see something that you want to see, instead of what's there. Believe me, I know of what I speak."

There was a long pause, and when it was over, Sancho spoke again. This time, his voice was quieter.

"Do you think it would be better if you revoked my equal partnership? If I am malfunctioning—"

"You're not malfunctioning."

"All right," Sancho said, pressing his point, "if I am not operating with complete objectivity, shouldn't I be relieved of decision-making responsibilities?"

Collier didn't answer right away. Instead, he looked at the space on the control panel where Sancho's camera lens was located and simply stared into it. Sancho deserved to be looked at in the eye.

"No," Collier found himself saying.

"No?"

"No. You don't get to run away from your own responsibilities."

"But, Skipper—"

"Shut up. One of the most exhilarating aspects of being alive is working without a net, Sancho."

"I don't understand."

"You want to retreat back into being second banana because you aren't perfect. You think that because you made an emotional decision the best answer is to take away your ability to make another one. Well, Sancho, you don't get that luxury. You're my partner, and you can't go back. Neither one of us can go back. It's you and me, side by side. Got it?"

Sancho said slowly, "Got it. Thank you, Skipper."

They sat quietly for several more minutes. There was nothing more that needed to be said.

When Sancho did speak up, his tone was urgent. "Skipper! I'm detecting a launch from Deimos, headed in our rough direction. Correction," he said immediately, "two crafts."

"Interceptors?"

"Can't tell yet, but that's a good guess."

"Are they closing distance to us?"

"No," Sancho said, "but they just started thrusting. I'll need a few minutes to determine their performance."

Collier called to Fletcher and Galatea. They entered the control suite, Fletcher first.

"What's happened?"

"I think the cops finally got their act together. They've launched two interceptors."

"Confirmed," Sancho said. "Definite interceptor hulls."

"How do you know that?" Galatea asked.

"It's amazing what you can find in the public library," Sancho said. "Hold on. There's something odd about their pursuit vectors." He paused, during which time Fletcher grew agitated.

"Great. He's locked up," she said.

"Give him a minute," Collier said softly.

A few more seconds went by in silence before Sancho spoke again. "This is weird. Neither one is on a direct intercept course."

Collier said, "What do you mean?"

"They're not chasing us, at least, not directly. One of them is bearing roughly three hundred and twenty-one degrees solar, while the other ... if this is right, the other one is bearing ninety-eight degrees solar."

Collier thought for a moment, then asked, "All on the planetary plane?"

"Just about."

"Give me a visual on that."

One of Sancho's display screens lit up with a schematic of the *Dulcinea* and the local system bodies, her vector and thrust line clean and direct to a point somewhat "ahead" of the Martian Trojan point to intercept it in a few days. Sancho added in the relative locations and vectors of the two interceptors, and Collier chuckled once when he understood what he was seeing. "They're not chasing us. At least, not where we're going."

"What? Why not?" Fletcher said.

"This one, the lead ship," Collier said, tapping the screen where the closer interceptor was, "is cutting off a route to Earth. It looks like the other one is doing the same thing but for Ceres."

Galatea said, "But we're not going to Earth, nor to Ceres."

Collier smiled. "True, but they don't know that. I'm guessing they figure we have some maneuvering trick up our sleeve — like we're capable of much more performance than we're showing, and are planning on changing our vector to Earth or Ceres soon. They didn't want to be caught gunning for open space and be unable to change direction."

Fletcher said, "So they're overestimating you and your ship?"

"That's my guess."

"First time for everything," Fletcher said.

Collier flipped her a quick bird.

Fletcher ignored that and continued, "As far as they're concerned, we're headed to nowhere. There's nothing of value at the Trojan point, so we couldn't possibly be going there."

Collier nodded. "Looks like it."

Fletcher asked, "How long until they can't recover? When they will have committed to their vectors and can't change course?"

Sancho replied, "Impossible to say, Ex-Agent Fletcher. I don't know their full thrust potential nor their range."

Collier said, "Assume that what they're giving now is their top acceleration and they have unlimited range."

"With unlimited range, they could change course whenever they wanted to. But the longer they thrust as they are now, the longer it'll take for them to get to the Trojan point. I can give you an estimate on the point at which we will beat them to the destination, if you want, Skipper."

"Yeah."

"It'll be an approximation," Sancho said.

"I realize that, Sancho. Stop dithering and just make your calculations."

There was a short pause, and Sancho answered carefully, "They are thrusting now at point three gees. Assuming that is their top performance, and assuming unlimited range, and assuming we maintain course on a low-consumption trajectory, we will arrive at Worthless slightly ahead of the interceptors if the interceptors continue on their current courses for eight more hours and nine more minutes for the lead ship and ten hours, forty-three minutes for the trailing ship."

Collier said, "Understood." He turned to the two women. "Well, we'll know soon enough. I'm gonna catch some sleep. I recommend you do the same."

"Who'll be watching the interceptors?" Fletcher said.

"Sancho. He'll wake us if something important happens."

Fletcher snorted. "If it's all the same to you, I'll stay up and monitor things myself."

Collier shrugged. "Suit yourself."

Chapter Fourteen

Collier floated into the control cabin in a foul humor — he was ordinarily not what Earthers called a "morning person," despite the lack of morning, afternoon, or night in interplanetary space. The meager breakfast he'd had did nothing to change his mood.

"Any changes?" he said, stifling a yawn.

"Nothing to report, Skipper," Sancho said. "Interceptors remain on their original trajectories. We'll reach that somewhat arbitrary moment you were asking about in roughly ten minutes."

Fletcher looked at Collier and said in a low voice, "I still don't know about this Galatea person. She's either telling the truth or is a very clever liar."

"You seemed to think I was pushing her too hard a few hours ago. What changed?"

Fletcher sighed. "I don't know. Guess I'm just being overly cautious."

Collier grinned. "And yet, here you are."

"Here I am, yeah."

"Never would have thought you'd leave the Authority," Collier said, watching the readout countdown.

Fletcher's voice softened but somehow remained firm. "I got to a point where I couldn't compromise anymore. Couldn't keep retreating, conceding parts of Ceres Station, the law. Each time I gave a little, they took more. The funny thing is ... I don't really blame them."

"Who are 'they' in this story?"

"The Crawlers and the corps. They were going to take whatever they could, whatever I was willing to give them, and then take a little more next time, and a little more and..." she stopped and composed herself, her voice returning to its flat, emotionless tone. "I didn't want to bend anymore, is what happened."

"So, you looked for me?" Collier lowered his head, trying not to let her see his bitter smile.

"Don't flatter yourself, Captain," Fletcher said.

Collier snapped his head up, his sardonic grin giving his words weight. "That's the last thing I'd do, Agent Fletcher. All I was going to say was if you came to me because you thought I was one of the last truly independent, uncompromising men left in the System and that you and I would live a life of noble, rugged individualism with shining eyes looking bravely into the cold future, think again."

Fletcher merely cocked an eyebrow and said flatly, "You seriously think that's what I believe?"

"No, I suppose not."

Fletcher's eyes penetrated into him and she was silent for a moment, then snorted with bitter triumph. "You *do* think that. You think I was drawn to your frontiersman's spirit like some pioneer wench in a gingham dress. You have an image of me clinging to your side while you chop wood and do all manner of manly things. In fact, you think you're owed a woman like me."

Collier had been listening to her with amusement until that last remark. His face turned dark and he growled, "Don't accuse me of being like that." If she saw him like that, if the person who had known him the longest, dragged him out of drunken stupors after Su's death, and chased him down across planets really thought he was that sort of a man, Collier didn't know what to think.

Fletcher's eyes softened for half a second and she said, "Sorry. That was uncalled for. But," she added, returning to a semblance of her former attitude, "it's more or less true. You think I came to you because I am attracted to the way you live. As if you live without compromise, master of your own reality."

Collier did not want to answer — he was still trying to clear his mind and think away the image of Su, dying in his arms on the Ganymedian tundra.

Fletcher continued. "But I've seen how you live, both on Ceres Station and now here. If I had any feelings for you on Ceres, they were of pity, which I know you hate. And now, watching you on your ship, I see you're not master of anything at all. You can't even control this Caliban."

"Ex-Agent Fletcher, that's not fair," Sancho piped up.

"Isn't it? Any other beltrunner would junk a suspected Caliban." She turned to Collier. "You made yours your partner."

Collier said, "Yeah, I did. And you know what, you need to stop insulting Sancho."

"Why? It hurts his feelings?"

Collier turned to the control panel and waited.

Sancho said, "As a matter of fact, it does, Ex-Agent Fletcher, but I don't think that's what Captain South means."

"What else could he mean?"

Collier started to grin, anticipating Sancho's answer.

"It means," said the computer, "that you haven't earned the right to do that. But he has."

Fletcher looked back at Collier, who made no effort to hide his triumph. "That's exactly right. Only I can call him a silicon-based pain in the ass."

"And only I can call him a jelly-brained meat sack," Sancho added brightly.

"You're insane. The both of you," Fletcher said.

Sancho said, "That's why it's a great partnership, Ex-Agent Fletcher."

Fletcher looked at Collier, shaking her head slightly. "Anyway, let me make my point perfectly clear. You are adrift, Collier. You don't know where you're headed nor what you'll do when you get there. And that's neither romantic nor attractive. It's asinine."

"Well, I'm sure glad you decided to tag along," Collier said. "Really brightens up my day to hear stuff like that." He snorted. "As it happens, we do know where we're going. And we do have a plan, don't we, Sancho?"

"We do?"

"Sure, we do. We're gonna go to Worthless, then take care of those Ad Astra bastards."

"That's more of a goal than a plan, Skipper," Sancho said.

"Whatever. Speaking of that, can you scan for that Ad Astra flotilla that was supposed to be heading this way?"

"I can scan space, if that's what you mean. But I'll lose contact with the interceptors."

"Can't you re-establish later?"

"Yeah, but it if they alter course and are not longer where I would expect them to be..."

"Right, understood."

Fletcher said, "You don't have gravimetric mass-detection capability?"

Collier grinned. "Part of the charm of the *Dulcinea*. Old-fashioned scopes." He glanced at the control panel. "Sancho's gotten pretty good at scanning space with 'em, though. Sancho, go ahead and start looking for the Ad Astra ships. Let me know if you find anything."

"Will do."

Collier nodded slightly and looked back at Fletcher. She was studying him, but something unusual rode in her eyes — something he was not used to seeing from her.

"Listen, I'm sorry for what I said," she murmured.

"Which part?"

"About you feeling owed a woman."

Collier shrugged. "You already apologized for that."

"I know. But still. I didn't mean it like ... well..." she trailed off, uncharacteristically tongue-tied.

"It's okay. Forget it."

"I'm sorry about her," Fletcher said quietly.

"Yeah. Me, too."

A warm silence grew between them. Fletcher hadn't said she would be willing to listen if he wanted to talk, but somehow, Collier knew that she would. He didn't want to talk, but not because he wasn't ready. He didn't want to talk because he didn't know how to give Su to Fletcher, or even if it was his right to do so. Maybe it was wrong, or unhealthy, but her death was his and his alone, their last shared intimacy. Letting someone else into that moment didn't feel right.

Especially another woman.

———— «» ————

Over the next eight days, the ship settled into a sort of routine. *Dulcinea* had long since stopped thrusting but was still not at the flipbrake point, and Collier was already becoming weary of the reduced food intake. He regarded his small portion of lunch with regret.

"Contact, Skipper! I have them!" Sancho suddenly piped up.

"What? Who?"

"It's got to be Ad Astra. High probability of four vessels, chasing us directly."

"Closing?"

"Hard to tell, but I think so. Hundred meters or so a second difference."

"Are they still under thrust?"

"Gimme a sec, Skipper. I just got them, so I don't have a completely clean vector on them yet."

Collier leaned back in his control saddle and shouted to the cabin where Fletcher was sleeping. She emerged two minutes later with Galatea, still rubbing sleep out of her eyes.

"Might have contact with Ad Astra," Collier tossed over his shoulder. He glanced at Galatea. "Maybe you'll finally make yourself useful. Give some intel on the make and type of ship once Sancho gives you specs. What do you say, Sancho? You got a vector yet?"

"I'm at about seventy-six percent probability."

"Good enough. Shoot."

"All right. I confirm four vessels. They have the same bearing as we do and are under thrust. Estimate point one-two-five gee. Relative velocity one hundred nine meters per second, relative acceleration one point two three meters per second. Relative distance approximately forty-four point five million kilometers."

"I thought it was going to be six ships," Collier said to Fletcher.

"Maybe they left two on Mars. I don't know."

Collier grunted. He wasn't going to gripe about two missing ships. He spoke to Sancho. "Can you give Galatea here any kind of visual profile?"

"A rough one," Sancho said. One of the screens lit up with a line drawing of a spacecraft. "Best I can do right now."

Galatea leaned in and studied the ship for a moment, then shook her head. "Not sure. Could be a modified *Atalanta*-class."

"What's that?"

She turned to Collier. "Their fastest gunship. Maximum thrust something like point four gee."

"Range?"

"I don't know."

Fletcher said, "Can they catch us?"

"Impossible to say," Sancho answered. "There are far too many variables. I don't know their fuel situation, so I can't tell how long they'll be able to maintain thrust. As it is, they already were able to thrust longer than we were, which is why they're gaining on us despite being further away. The longer they can maintain that, the faster they'll close in."

"They know the performance stats for *Dulcinea*," Collier said grimly. "They're going as fast as they need to in order to intercept us. They fueled up in the Martian system and are coming after us, and if they're only cruising at point one two five, you can bet it's because they calculated precisely how much thrust they needed and how long it would take to catch up to us before we reach the Trojan point."

"But how do they know we're headed there?" Fletcher said. "The Deimos interceptors figured we couldn't be going to a worthless asteroid. Why did Ad Astra follow us directly?"

"They have a history of chasing me. It's been worthwhile."

"I don't think that was Ad Astra policy, Skipper," Sancho said. "I think that was just Captain Mitchell's idea."

"Maybe. But for whatever reason, they're chasing us. We're going to have to deal with them."

"Not to mention the Martian interceptors," Fletcher said.

"They had set course for Earth and Ceres," Sancho said.

"Last time you looked, you mean," Fletcher said. "If they've spotted the Ad Astra ships too, they might decide to change course to wherever we're all going so they don't miss the party. Maybe they already have."

"You could be right, Ex-Agent Fletcher, but even if you are, there's nothing we can do about any of this. We're already committed to the Trojan point, and we've used up one-quarter of our fuel so far to get us there. We'll use another quarter to flipbrake and decelerate. That leaves us half a tank to get back to Mars."

"So, we're just stuck on this trajectory," Fletcher said. "Easy pickings."

"Not necessarily," Collier said. "We can accelerate again."

"Skipper, we could only use a tiny fraction of our fuel for that," Sancho said. "If we use too much, we'll have to calculate a low-consumption, low-velocity return to Mars. We won't have provisions for a trip that takes too long."

"Sancho, prepare to fire the engines at ninety percent thrust," Collier said.

Galatea blurted out, "You heard your computer! Using up fuel on this end will make the trip back slower!"

"We're never going to make it to the Trojan point first if we stay like this," Collier said. "Ad Astra will overtake us before we get there. Our only choice is to use everything now and in braking."

"But we'll arrive at the Trojan point dry, Collier," Fletcher said calmly. "No fuel, not enough food and water to get us back. What you're suggesting is suicide."

"So is getting caught out here by Ad Astra," Collier said.

"You're hoping to find something there to save us," Fletcher said. She wasn't asking a question.

"We have a helluva better shot at that than taking our chances in open space. If we find something on Worthless, something valuable, we get options when Ad Astra catches up."

"It's called 'Worthless' for a reason," Fletcher said.

Collier ignored her last remark. "Sancho, ninety percent thrust. Calculate new flipbrake point and vector."

"Calculating. Give me a second on that." Sancho said, then almost immediately continued, "Calculations complete. You sure about this, Skipper?"

Collier looked at Fletcher. "Still glad you joined up with me?"

"I wasn't thrilled to begin with. You're not making it any easier," she said.

As she spoke, Collier watched her carefully. Her mouth still held that same grim line, wrinkles subtle but unmistakable at the corners. When his eyes flicked to hers, though, he saw the momentary flash of a smile there. It was as transient as comet gas, but it had been there.

"Yeah, I'm sure, Sancho. Fire the engines."

Collier's reckless move had indeed caught the Ad Astra ships by surprise. The *Dulcinea* began to outrun their pursuers, who had not stepped up their acceleration.

"I'm a little surprised at them," Collier said hours later when they were approaching the new flipbrake point.

"Why?" Fletcher said.

"I half expected them to split up, send some of their fleet after us and leave the rest on a conservative consumption trajectory. Then they could have supplemented the fuel of the ships that chased us with the slower ones when they arrived."

Fletcher nodded. "Didn't think of that. You suppose they didn't, either?"

Galatea said, "Ad Astra is a lot of things, but they aren't stupid. They want to keep their four-ship fleet together."

"Maybe they're afraid of you," Fletcher said.

Collier turned from the monitor to look at her over his shoulder. "Funny."

"No, I mean it. Last time you faced them, you kicked their ass. Beat-up old mining ship against a state-of-the-art warship."

"'Kicked their ass' is overstating it. I barely got away."

"You still outsmarted them. And besides, you have any better explanations for their behavior?"

Collier sighed. "No." He peered into the assay box where the magic wand was safely tucked away. There would be no loose micrograys this time around. "Something strange is out there. Something connected to this. And I'm betting it's worth more than our lives."

Fletcher looked at him, faint alarm growing on her features. "What do you mean by that?"

"Whatever Ad Astra found out in their labs, I'm betting is connected to the Trojan point. The way they made a direct course for us, and for the point — they know something's out there."

"Skipper," Sancho said.

"What?"

"The wand has just begun reacting like it did the last time we got close to Worthless. Eighty-five hundred micrograys and climbing," Sancho announced.

"What the hell?" Fletcher said, floatwalking to the assay box and looking over Collier's shoulder through the lead window. "That thing's hot?"

"The closer we get to the Trojan point, the more radioactive it gets," Collier said.

"How high does it go?"

"Dunno. We've never been this close."

"What? So you don't know how hot this can get?"

"Relax. Assay box has ninety-nine five attenuation. Of course..." he stopped, then addressed Sancho. "Is the rate of increase exponential?"

"Yes."

Fletcher cried, "Exponential increase? Dammit, South, what else is going on that you forgot to mention?"

Collier ignored her and spoke to Sancho. "It's getting hotter faster than last time, isn't it?"

"Very much so. I think because we're headed directly for whatever's causing it to heat up. Last time we weren't on a direct course."

"How much can we take before the assay box won't protect us?"

"Assuming no change in the increase, it'll be around twenty thousand when we reach our destination. Assay box will filter out all but about one hundred."

"Per second?" Fletcher said.

"Yes," Sancho replied.

"It's not ideal," Collier said. "But it's plenty low enough not to worry about. One hundred micrograys per second will take a long time to hurt us."

"Assuming that where we're headed to isn't even hotter. How can something be gaining radioactivity, anyway?"

Collier shook his head. "No idea." He gestured with his chin towards the assay box. "That thing in there is full of mysteries. It's why we call it a magic wand."

Fletcher had no answer to that.

——— «›‹» ———

Collier's decision to use all the fuel in *Dulcinea's* tanks had widened their lead on the pursuing Ad Astra ships, though according to Sancho's rough estimates, that lead would almost entirely disappear by the time they made it to the Trojan point.

The location reminded Collier of the Ceres bar of the same name. It had been nearly two months since Phil had thrown him out of the bar. Collier was surprised to find himself not craving a drink at the memory — it seemed that reaching Worthless and the bottom of a Tank 8 held much the same feeling of escape.

"Skipper, I've got Worthless on my scopes," Sancho said when they were just nine hours away.

"Show me," Collier said. On the screen, Sancho placed a helpful glowing arrow pointing at an infinitesimally small point of dim light.

"Are you on maximum magnification?"

"Of course."

"Hmm. Can't see a disc," Collier said. "Can you make out anything on other spectra?"

"Nothing unusual. Getting some infrared signals from the sun-facing surface."

Galatea gasped. "Infrared? Heat signatures? You mean there's a power source down there?"

Collier and Fletcher exchanged amused glances at one another as Sancho explained coolly, "No. The infrared is simply reflected heat from the surface facing the sun. Nothing at all unusual about it. And no unusual electromagnetic emissions of any kind, Skipper. It's just a rock."

"What's the reading inside the assay box?"

"Nineteen thousand eight hundred, oscillating plus or minus one hundred."

Collier let out a breath. At least that wasn't an additional problem. "What will our tanks look like when we get to Worthless?"

"We'll be in the neighborhood of three percent. Maneuvering ability, but nothing more."

"How much time before Ad Astra catches us?"

"At current velocity, I estimate ten hours, eighteen minutes."

Collier leaned back in the control saddle. After everything, they were hardly more than four hours ahead of Ad Astra. There was a strange freedom in the complete lack of options, he noted. He couldn't change course, he couldn't go any faster, he couldn't set course for anywhere else once he reached Worthless. They were committed, for good or ill.

"I'm gonna grab some sleep," he said, rising from the saddle.

"You're going to sleep? Now?" Galatea said.

"Never pass up a chance to sleep, eat, or piss," he said. "Pretty much the unofficial motto of the *Dulcinea*."

"I thought it was, 'never do something sane and effective when you could do something crazy and pointless,'" Fletcher said.

"That's the *official* motto. Sancho, wake me in eight hours."

———— «» ————

Collier awoke before Sancho's wake-up call and floatwalked to the control room after taking care of his bladder. "How're we doing?" he said to Fletcher and Galatea, who were looking a little ragged themselves.

"No change," Fletcher said. "Except the asteroid is a lot bigger on the scope."

Collier swung into the saddle as Fletcher left it and peered at the monitor. "Sancho, any features worth noting?"

"Nothing that would mark this as out of the ordinary, Skipper. It's got an effective diameter of one thousand nine meters, give or take sixty meters depending on protrusions and such. Various minor fissures, but no outgassing that I can detect."

"Dammit," Collier murmured.

"What? Why's that bad?" Galatea asked, her voice anxious.

Collier didn't turn to face Galatea. "Means there's probably no water ice there. So we can't refuel from the asteroid itself."

"Were you counting on that?"

"Not really, but it would have solved at least one problem," Collier said. "Sancho, give me standard prospecting array on this monitor." As soon as he completed the command, the monitor divided itself into four boxes, one large display with just the visual spectrum, and three others — infrared, ultraviolet, and radio. It was his own custom-made way of examining a potential strike, and was much cheaper than expending impact probes to break off chunks of the rock to be analyzed by mass spectrometry.

Fletcher leaned in next to him to study the readouts. "You know what you're looking for?" she said quietly.

"I'll know it when I see it."

"That's reassuring."

Collier shushed her and the two watched the rotating spheroid in silence for a few minutes.

"Sancho, go back three seconds and freeze the image. Put it up on monitor two. All spectra."

A second screen, which had been tracking the Ad Astra fleet, changed to the still picture of the asteroid Collier had asked for.

Collier traced his finger along the monitor where a thin, jagged line described a fracture or fissure in the asteroid.

"What is it?" Fletcher said.

"Not sure. But this fissure or crack or whatever it is — doesn't it look odd to you?"

Fletcher hesitated, then answered, "No."

"Seems too random."

"What?"

"Too random."

"What does that even mean, 'too random?'" Fletcher said.

Collier sighed and leaned back. "Too much like exactly what you'd expect. A fissure, running through the midpoint of the asteroid, typical length, typical jagged design."

"I don't get what you're driving at," Fletcher said.

"It's too perfectly normal. Precisely random."

In the brief silence that followed, Galatea said with heavy scorn, "You're saying it is so commonplace and normal that it can't be either of those things?"

"Sort of, yeah."

"You're just too proud to admit that you screwed up and that there's nothing here," Galatea said. "And now we're out of food, water—"

Collier met her force with his own. "We've still got rations. I've prospected hundreds of rocks. I know what's right and what isn't."

"And this is wrong because it's right?" Fletcher said, though not with the same derision Galatea had used.

"It's wrong because it's *too* right. Look," he said, pointing again, "You know asteroids, sort of." He plowed through Fletcher's raised eyebrow. "On an X-type, which this is, right, Sancho?"

"It is indeed, Skipper."

Collier continued, "You'd expect to find a fissure at the main mass point. Either because of tidal forces or because the rock is actually several asteroids held together by weak gravity, right?"

"Yeah," Fletcher said.

"But it's never like that," Collier said. "It's never, *ever* exactly where it should be. There's always some variation."

"But I'm looking at the fissure, and there is variation," Fletcher said, tracing her finger along the jagged line.

"But even the variation should have variation!" Collier said. "It's not just too normal — it's abnormal in too normal a way."

"He's lost his mind," Galatea said.

"Shut up," Collier said. "Sancho, put us over that fissure. One hundred meters."

"Aye aye," Sancho said. "Estimate fifty-six minutes until hover."

"What are you going to do?" Galatea said.

"Go down there. It's either that, or just hover around until Ad Astra shows up."

"What are you looking for down there?" Fletcher said.

"Like I said, I'll know it when I see it."

"What if you never see it?" Fletcher said.

Collier didn't answer. He was asking himself the same question and had no answer for it.

Fifty-four minutes later, they had reached the fissure and Sancho held them in a hover. Collier stuffed himself into his vacc suit, checking the ugly grey patch where he had been stabbed what seemed like a lifetime ago in the Ceres salvage yard. It would hold. It had to.

His interior helmet display lights shone green as he secured the suit, and Sancho answered when he called.

"Let me know if anything changes," Collier said, cycling the airlock.

"Like what?"

"Anything. Ad Astra ships arrive, Martian interceptors show up, giant space squid attacks. And Sancho," he added, then hesitated.

"Yes?"

Collier took a breath and steadied his voice before speaking. "If we get cut off from each other, do whatever you think is best."

"What do you mean?"

"I mean, if you can't raise me, and something happens that requires you to make a judgement call, you make the call."

"You don't want to leave standing orders or something, Skipper?"

"No."

"But ... what if I don't know what to do?"

"Just wing it. Trust your gut."

"I don't have a gut."

Collier sighed. "Your instincts. Intuition. Feeling of rightness."

"I don't have any of those things."

"Sure you do."

"How do you know?" Sancho said, his voice suddenly childlike.

"Because *I've* got intuition that tells me you do, too. You've been a great friend, Sancho. Best I ever had. I trust you with my ship and my life."

"But—"

"Now shut up and open the airlock."

Sancho complied with both orders, and Collier stepped out of *Dulcinea* and then into open space. He applied the gentlest thrust of his suit attitude jets and started falling slowly towards the surface of Worthless.

"Touchdown," he reported a minute later. "Surface is dusty. Not what I expected. Fletcher, do you copy?"

"I read you," Fletcher said over his suit speakers. "What's up with the surface?"

"Not sure. Just thought it would be less dusty. I'm about thirty meters from the fissure," he said, swinging his helmet lamps towards it. "Heading there now."

"Set your anchor, Skipper. Gravity there is negligible."

"Not my first excavation, Sancho." Collier used his attitude jets to help him kneel down, then he brushed away the silt-like surface of the asteroid until he hit solid rock. The dust was quite thick — he had to go down at least half a meter before he found an anchor point. He took one of his pitons out and prepared to set it.

When he pressed the firing stud on the self-sealing piton, he felt the faint vibration of the mechanism activate, but the piton didn't budge. The light from his helmet lamp showed the dull grey surface of the asteroid was utterly unmarked where he'd tried to set the anchor. He repositioned the piton and recycled the firing mechanism, then tried again. Still nothing. The piton wasn't penetrating what ought to have been porous rock.

"Something strange here, Sancho," Collier reported. "I can't set the piton. It's not going in."

"Misfire?" Sancho said.

"No. I've tried twice, and I'm getting nothing. Not even making a mark."

"Could you have hit an iron vein?" Fletcher said.

"I've never been that lucky," Collier said. "And besides, the piton should still be able to penetrate that. A vein of iron wouldn't be this hard. Matter of fact, nothing much should be. Sancho, can you get a scope on where I've brushed the dust away? Take a look for yourself?"

"Tracking now," Sancho said. A moment later, he added, "Not a big enough hole for me to get a good look, Skipper. Can you enlarge the area?"

Collier spent several minutes clearing dust away, using his nitrogen sprayer that was built for this very purpose. Presently, he had a clearing two meters in diameter.

"That'll do. If you could move aside, Skipper, I'll—" Sancho stopped as soon as Collier had exited the clearing.

"What is it? Sancho, respond!"

"That's not rock, Skipper."

"What is it?"

"Refined metal alloy."

Collier instinctively stepped back from the clearing, then realized the futility of that gesture. He was no doubt standing on the very same alloy himself, with only the half-meter of dust between him and it. "What kind of alloy?"

"That's ... I'm getting all kinds of crazy readings on my spectrograph," Sancho said. "Either I'm experiencing a malfunction, or there are twenty-one different elements and isotopes there."

"An alloy of twenty-one elements?" Collier said. "Run a diagnostic on yourself. That's impossible. You must be getting interference that's messing with your scope."

"It's not impossible," Galatea cut in. "It's called a super high-entropy alloy. Ad Astra played around with those. But we never got past seven elements, and even that was impractical."

"Analysis confirmed, Skipper. Alloy is made up of, in equal parts: Manganese, chromium, iron, cobalt, nickel, copper, silver, tungsten, molybdenum, niobium, aluminum, cadmium, tin, lead, bismuth, zinc, germanium, silicon, antimony, magnesium, and yttrium-eighty-nine."

"Not a natural phenomenon," Collier said.

"Not a significant chance of that, Skipper."

Collier said, "What's a high-entropy alloy, anyway?"

Sancho replied, "High-entropy alloys are made of multiple elements and thus display unique properties compared to conventional alloys. Super high-entropy alloys are theoretical composites made up of ten or more elements. In theory, these alloys would be incredibly versatile and superior to all other existing alloys."

Collier said, "Galatea, you said Ad Astra couldn't make super high-entropy alloys work?"

"Not like this, no. I decided it wasn't feasible."

"Why not?"

"Too expensive for what we were getting. Easier to stick with alloys we already knew how to make and mine the raw materials. And even so, we never attempted twenty-one elements. Never even thought about it."

"So, if Ad Astra didn't chase that discovery, do you think anyone else did?"

"I never heard of anyone else working along those lines."

"Was Ad Astra's corporate espionage division well-funded?"

"Yes, it was," Galatea said with no sense of shame. "We got regular reports. If we weren't working on it, no one else was."

"So, we're faced with two impossibilities," Collier said. "Either this arrangement of elements happened all by itself, or someone put it here."

"Or Sancho's analysis is wrong," Fletcher added.

"I'm forced to agree with Ex-Agent Fletcher, Skipper," Sancho said. "Given those two choices, I think there's just got to be something wrong with the data. Let me keep working on it, see what I can come up with."

Collier thought for a moment, then said, "No. Fletcher, you're saying that because you've never liked nor trusted Sancho."

"That's ridic—"

"And Sancho, you're agreeing because you're still suffering some goddam crisis of confidence. I need both of you to start thinking clearly."

"You're the one not thinking clearly," Fletcher shot back. Collier didn't need to see her face to know that she'd lost her even expression. "The existence of this asteroid was noted in 1999. Ad Astra or some corp didn't just put it here recently. Sancho's analysis is wrong somehow. You're going to dismiss that answer out of friendship and loyalty? To a Caliban?"

"Knock that 'Caliban' shit off," he snapped. "Sancho might be wrong, but he's not lying. And you're forgetting two other things. I said before that the fissure and the makeup of this rock looked off. Too perfectly imperfect."

"That makes just as little sense now as it did when you said it," Fletcher said.

"No, it makes more sense. If this asteroid is artificial, or has been crafted to look natural to hide some artificial structure, then my instinct is right."

Sancho chirped in, "What's the second thing we're forgetting, Skipper?"

"The magic wand. We still don't know why it got hot the closer we came to this rock. That defies all known rules of radioactivity. Unless something artificial is affecting it."

"Like what?" Sancho said.

"Whatever's beneath the surface," Collier said. "I'm heading towards the fissure. I'll let you know if I find anything, like a door or something."

"What'll you do if you find one, Skipper?"

Collier chuckled. "Knock."

Chapter Fifteen

The fissure was shallow, a scant ten meters deep, and narrow, but Collier could still navigate his way down. He didn't use his suit thrusters, preferring instead to use his hands on the side of the fissure to pull himself along in a crawling motion. Once on the bottom, he steadied himself and looked around.

The ground here was also covered with the same dust that was on the surface above the fissure, which would have seemed strange to him had he not been forming a theory. "Sancho, can you still read me?"

"I read you five-by-five."

"Okay. I'm going to scrape away some of the dust here, see if I can find an opening. As best you can, position *Dulcinea* directly overhead so you can track me on your scope."

"Roger. That's going to take some pinpoint control, Skipper. Give me a moment on that."

Collier began shoveling the dust away, careful to keep it from obscuring his vision or sending him drifting upward in the microgravity. He only had to clear ten centimeters' worth of silt before he found what he was looking for: a flat, hard surface that could not possibly be natural.

"Are you in position yet, Sancho?"

"Just getting there."

"Scan this area where I am. Looking for the same thing you saw on the surface."

After a few moments, Sancho replied. "Got it. I'm less certain — there's quite a bit of dust interference — but I'm getting the same reading. Galatea's super high-entropy alloy."

Collier nodded in triumph. He was right. Whatever Worthless was, it wasn't natural. "I'm going to start excavating, looking for an opening or some kind of mechanism. You keep scanning up there, let me know if anything changes on your scope."

"Sure thing, Skipper. How will you find what you're looking for?"

"I guess by chance."

"That's a lot of ground to cover," Sancho said. "I estimate about fifty-eight meters. And where are you going to put all that dust? It has to go somewhere."

"I'll just have to figure it out," Collier said. "Should be able to toss it upwards, out of this little canyon." He knelt down carefully, and sent a handful of dust flying upwards. Some of it floated up and away, but a significant part of it rebounded off the fissure walls and formed a cloud directly above him. "Sancho, you still there?"

"I still read you, but the dust is screwing up my visual scope. Still have you on infrared."

"I don't like this," Fletcher joined in. "All that's going to happen is you're going to obscure the ship's scopes. We won't be able to see you on anything if the cloud gets thick enough."

"Can't be helped," Collier said. "And anyway, you can still hear me and locate me if that happens."

"I still don't know what you think you're going to find," Fletcher said.

"We've already established that there's some weird shit down here," Collier said, scooping up another handful of dust, "so now it's a matter of figuring out what that weird shit is. Or do you still think the alloy is a natural phenomenon?"

"I never thought that," Fletcher said. "I said Sancho's scope is malfunctioning. It still could be."

"On two different parts of the rock? And in the same way? No," Collier said, continuing to work. "I'll put my faith in his scopes. Besides, it's not like we've never run across something strange on an asteroid before we—" he stopped suddenly, a handful of dust cradled in his gauntlets.

"What's happened, Skipper?"

"Sancho, what's the reading on the magic wand?"

"Holding steady at about twenty thousand," Fletcher said.

"I need it sent down."

"I don't recommend we take it out of the assay box, Skipper," Sancho said. "Your organic functions won't react well to that. Come to think of it, neither would my electronic ones."

"Leave it in the box, then," Collier said. "Send the whole thing down. I'll take it out down here. My suit will protect me."

"Not as much as the assay box will," Sancho said. "Vacc suits aren't meant to—"

"Dammit, Sancho, I know what the risk is. I need the magic wand."

Fletcher cut in, "Collier, that thing is putting out twenty thousand micrograys—"

"That's nothing," Collier said. "Now send down the goddam assay box."

"How?"

"Just throw it, for Chrissakes!"

Collier waited for what seemed like an eternity, then presently heard Fletcher's voice from her suit radio.

"I'm outside," she said. "Sending the box to you."

"Sancho, is it on target to me?" Collier asked a few moments later.

The computer responded, "Not quite. Going to miss you by approximately nine meters."

"Not bad," Collier said. "Get back inside, Fletcher."

A few moments later, Collier caught motion in his helmet lamp and saw the box tumbling through the airless sky on its way down to him. It was on target for the fissure, but was headed slightly behind his position. He made his way back and reached the impact point shortly after the box did. It had soft-landed in the silt he hadn't cleared away and looked intact. "Got it. Opening it up," he said, punching the proper buttons to unlock the box. He reached inside and gently took the magic wand out from its analysis cradle. He told himself that the feeling of warmth coming through his gauntlets was an illusion — the wand was nowhere near radioactive enough to emit any significant heat, and in any case, he wouldn't be able to feel anything through his suit gloves. Despite his bravado to the others, he knew prolonged exposure would hurt him.

As he hefted the wand out of the case, the control surface glowed faintly. Collier gasped slightly as he saw the wand light up.

"Sancho, something interesting here. I can see the wand controls."

"Really? I wonder why that's — of course. The sun's UV rays."

"But I've had it out in space before, and it never—" Collier stopped himself. "But now we're a lot closer. I get it."

"Closer to what?" Galatea cried out, some distance from the microphone pickup.

"The sun," Collier said. "Sancho, send me an overlay of our cheat sheet, will you? Patch it into my heads-up display."

"You got it, Skipper," Sancho said, and immediately the "operator's manual" he and Sancho had put together appeared on the inside glass of his helmet. He studied the document for a few minutes, scrolling through the numerous sections and diagrams with a shake of his head. His attention was split between the manual and the wand, and when he'd finished double-checking his findings, he said, "You're not going to believe this, Sancho, but there are more controls visible now than there were out in the Belt."

"Fascinating," Sancho said. "Could it be responding to other wavelengths? X-rays? Gamma rays?"

"I don't know," Collier said. "Sun doesn't put out that much, though."

"Maybe it doesn't take much."

"Maybe," Collier said. "Point is, this thing can do more than we thought it could."

"Are the controls in areas of the device that were blank before, Skipper?"

Collier studied the cheat sheet for several moments, then said, "Yeah. Mostly. Some of the new controls are kind of jammed in the spaces between the older ones."

"I have a theory, Skipper," Sancho said.

"Let's hear it."

"I don't think these controls are just now visible. I think they weren't there before."

"Explain."

"Well," Sancho said, "if they were always there, but we couldn't see them, you would have accidentally touched them or manipulated them at some point."

"Maybe not," Collier said. "And even if I had, maybe it takes a very particular maneuver to activate these new controls."

"Possibly," Sancho said, "but not likely. Remember all the experimentation we did on this thing? You touched it and stroked it and rubbed it every way you could to get a reaction from it. I can't believe that in all that time you wouldn't have accidentally activated one of the new controls. So I think these aren't controls that were always there but which we couldn't see. I think they're new controls altogether."

"If you're right, then something's changed about the wand," Collier said.

"It's radioactive," Fletcher said. "That's new, isn't it?"

"Yeah, but I think that's a function of being near whatever this fake asteroid really is," Collier said.

Sancho said, "I'll bet you an astrogation upgrade against ten kilos of ingredients for the murgh makhani that makes you so flatulent that those are connected. Whatever this asteroid is, it's causing the wand to get hot and changing the controls."

"If we ever get out of this, Sancho, I'll spring for any upgrade you want."

"Speaking of getting out of this," Fletcher said, "The Ad Astra fleet is still on its way."

"Right. Sancho, what's the ETA on that?"

"I don't have a scope on them, Skipper — I was using everything I had to keep track of you. There's some more upgrades we could talk about: Artemis Mechanics has a sensor array they say can—"

"Later, later. Assume nothing's changed about the fleet's vector. What's their ETA?"

"They're approaching with caution, Skipper. Now estimated four hours, nine minutes, plus or minus sixteen minutes."

"Okay. So, I have that long to figure out the new controls and see if I can get inside."

"Inside where?"

Collier instinctively looked up at where he knew the *Dulcinea* was hovering. "Inside this fake asteroid, of course."

Fletcher snorted. "A giant chunk of icefuel, an even bigger chunk of rare metals, maybe some canned peaches—"

"Where's your sense of adventure, of discovery, Fletcher?" Collier said, smirking up at the ship.

"I left it back on Ceres," she replied. "Seriously, South, you're making a lot of assumptions. That this rock is artificial, that there is an inside, that you'll be able to enter, that there won't be some kind of security system which will vaporize you, that—"

"Thanks. Thanks very much for the pep talk, Fletcher." He looked back down at the wand. "Sancho, give me hourly reminders as to Ad Astra's position."

"If I use my scopes to track the Ad Astra fleet, I won't be able to watch you, Skipper."

"I'll be fine down here. Now I need some radio silence while I work."

There was a burst of angry words from Fletcher and Galatea before Sancho cut off communications. Collier grinned wryly as he imagined the argument that must be going on between the three of them.

He shook his head gently to clear it. He couldn't be distracted by that now. The truth was, Fletcher's comment about a security system had worried him; he hadn't considered that possibility. But he was convinced that he was standing on the greatest find in his life, possibly even in all of human life, if only he could unlock it. That was worth almost any risk.

The wand was glowing more faintly than it did when Sancho subjected it to artificial ultraviolet light, but the symbols and designs were still clearly visible. The new symbols resembled the ones Collier had come to know in his study of the wand, but they were not precisely the same. He and Sancho had never come to a decision on whether the symbols were part of an alphabet, a logographic writing system, or something completely alien. The new set of symbols didn't help to settle that at all.

The only thing that he recognized at all was a steadily blinking light near the end of the tube, fading off and on with gentle violet luminescence. The blinking rate was quite rapid — somewhere between three and four blinks a second — and Collier decided to interpret that as meaning he was close to whatever it was that was affecting the wand, which he also chose to conclude was in the heart of this artificial asteroid.

He held the wand in front of him as he slowly worked his way through the fissure, watching the blinking light. He was startled when Sancho's time check came through his helmet speakers an hour later.

"Ad Astra fleet spotted, Skipper. ETA three hours, give or take a few minutes. They've been hailing us, by the way. I assume you want them to eat static?"

"You assume right."

"Any luck down there?"

"Not yet. How much of the fissure have I covered?"

"I'd estimate about forty percent, Skipper."

"That's all?" Collier grunted. "I've still got plenty of air. About five hours' worth. But if I can't find anything in another hour, give me a call. We may have to talk to the Ad Astra people after all."

"Roger that. Good luck."

Collier continued his progress, trying to time the blinking light. So far, it hadn't changed the speed at which it turned on and off, and Collier was beginning to lose hope. Maybe it had nothing to do with this rock and what lay beneath it. Maybe the light corresponded to the level of radiation it was putting out. Maybe it was a low battery warning.

The last, at least, he could check. He scooped up a handful of dust and opened the wand with the ease of long practice, stuffing the dust inside and closing the device. He consulted the manual pages in his helmet and operated the controls to change the dust into gold, then reopened the wand and shook out the result.

A fine sprinkling of gold powder came out, sparkling in his helmet lamp as it hung in the airless space before him.

He grunted in slight satisfaction. At least the wand still worked its magic. But the blinking light had not changed, or if it had, it had done so in a manner he could not perceive. So he continued his trek in the fissure, partially out of bull-headed persistence, and partially out of an inability to think of any other plan of action.

When Sancho called him an hour later, Collier snapped at him. "No, I haven't figured anything out! And yes, I know I'm almost at the end of the fissure!"

"Ad Astra fleet is about two hours' out now. You wanted to change tactics, Skipper?"

"I guess we're gonna have to."

"Maybe you should get back on board, Skipper," Sancho said. "We've got to talk about what we will do once the Ad Astra—"

"Dammit, I didn't come all this way to give up to fucking Ad Astra. There's got to be some way into this rock. I just haven't found it."

"And there's no reason to think you'll find it before the Ad Astra fleet gets here," Fletcher broke in, matching his energy with calm.

"I'm not having another strike stolen from me by those bastards."

"That's inevitable now," Fletcher said, her voice even. "Even if you do find something — a door, hatch, whatever — the corp fleet will get here and take it away from you even if they have to kill all of us."

"What would you have me do, Fletcher?" Collier almost shouted. "Give up? Go back aboard *Dulcinea*, hail Ad Astra, ask pretty please with sugar on it please don't kill us and also loan us some waterfuel?"

Silence from the other end. Collier could see Fletcher in his mind; the only changes in her face would be the tiny worry lines in the corners of her mouth and the faint chevron wrinkle that creased her forehead when she was upset.

"There's nothing to do but forge ahead," Collier said grimly.

"Because you've made it that way," Fletcher said, a curious mix of annoyance and amusement creeping into her voice. "You kept pressing forward until there were no options left to us. And now here we are. Stranded without fuel hovering over a worthless chunk of rock waiting for a corporate fleet to blow us up."

Collier stopped scanning with the wand and looked up again. She was right. He cleared his throat before he spoke. "Sorry I got you into this, Fletcher. I really am."

Again, silence from the *Dulcinea*.

"You helped me out on Ceres, even when you didn't need to. You deserved better than this," he said.

"We're not done for just yet, Skipper," Sancho added, his voice cheerful.

"Why? You have an idea?"

"Uh, well, no," Sancho said, chagrined. "I just wanted to be encouraging."

Against his will, Collier started to chuckle. To his surprise, he heard Fletcher joining in.

"I don't see what you all find so funny about this," Galatea said, her voice distant. "No one's got an idea how to fend off the Ad Astra fleet? Or get us home?"

"You were once one of them," Collier said. "You got anything?"

"No, but—"

"Then shut up and let us have this laugh," Collier said, but the moment had passed. Collier took a breath and said, "Anyway, Sancho, what's the ETA of the fleet?"

"Little under two hours now, Skipper. I estimate one hundred thirteen minutes."

"I'll finish scanning the fissure," Collier said. "Just in case. Can't really think of anything else, to be honest."

"Understood."

An hour later, Collier had reached the end of the fissure. The canyon narrowed to a point and sloped upward: a quick check of the "floor" of the asteroid revealed the same high-entropy alloy just beneath the dusty surface. The wand's blinking light hadn't changed at all.

"All right, Sancho, I think we've got to do something drastic," Collier said.

"Drastic?"

"I'm gonna start manipulating the new controls."

"Skipper, we have no idea what they'll do."

"I know, but that's all that's left. Maybe one of them is a door opener."

"And maybe one of them is a self-destruct button."

"All the better I'm far away from the *Dulcinea*, then," Collier said.

"Assuming the wand doesn't have an explosive power capable of reaching us."

"Dammit, Sancho, what're you trying to do? Make me shit my pants out here?" Collier shivered in his suit, trying not to imagine being blown apart.

"Are you experiencing gastrointestinal distress, Skipper?"

Fletcher broke in. "He means you're scaring him, Sancho. Collier, you seriously think the wand will open some kind of door?"

"No, but I'm receptive to any other ideas." He paused a half second, then said, "Hearing none, the captain began manipulating the controls. Sancho, record my movements so we can—"

"I remember the drill, Skipper. Just like old times. Begin when ready."

"Okay. Bent arrow pointing, uh, lengthwise. Scraping across." He performed the action, and felt himself trembling in anticipation of an explosion. None came — in fact, nothing happened that he could tell. "No noticeable result."

"Recorded," Sancho said.

"Bent arrow pointing lengthwise, tapping." Again, nothing happened. He continued to identify symbols and made the same manipulations as he had on what he now considered the "regular" controls but could not force a reaction from the wand.

"Skipper, Ad Astra fleet is twenty minutes away. They've been hailing us all this time. How close are you to finishing?"

"Nowhere near close," Collier said. "I've barely begun. You know how long this takes." He looked at the wand, then in a flurry of movements, poked, scraped, twisted, and manipulated the cylinder in a chaotic fury of impotent action.

The wand remained inactive, as if mocking him.

"Very well, Sancho. I guess I should talk to them. Patch them through to me down here," Collier said. The hollow, nauseating feeling of defeat settled in his stomach.

Chapter Sixteen

"**This is Ad** Astra survey vessel D-two-zero-seven, Corporate Captain Hierro in command. We're here to render assistance, Captain South."

On hearing the familiar name, Collier felt a momentary twinge of regret as he recalled the necessary killing of Hierro's men back near Ceres, but he didn't let that enter his voice. "Let's cut the shit, asshole," Collier snapped. "What do you want?"

Hierro laughed. "You know exactly what we want. Hand over the device."

"What device?"

"Now *you* cut the shit, South. The device you call a 'magic wand.' Hand it over."

"Oh, sorry, I didn't bring it with me. I think it's still on Mars in a locker on Deimos."

Hierro sighed. "You're going to make me disable your vessel and search it myself, aren't you? I was hoping to avoid that. But, seeing as you're not on your ship, that will be easier."

Collier cursed under his breath. Obviously Hierro's ship had found him. "What makes you think it's on board the *Dulcinea*?"

"It's either there or you've got it on you. So I'll start with your ship. Then, if it's not there, I'll send down a landing party to search you. I hope we don't rupture your suit in the process. One way or another, South, we're getting that device."

"Then what?"

"Then?" The man laughed. "We send it back to home office on Earth. I collect a nice fat commission, probably a promotion, and spend my bonus on Luna in the joybooths."

"I meant, for me and my crew."

"Oh, well, if you hand over the device, we'll just … leave. No need to kill you then. Even if you're responsible for the deaths of many Ad Astra employees. Some of them were my friends, South."

"You're lying," Collier said. "You've got no intention of leaving me alive."

"You really want to make this difficult, don't you?"

"The day I make things easy for Ad Astra the planets will reverse their orbits."

"All right. Tell you the truth, South, I'm kind of glad. My orders were to get the device with a minimum of fuss and cost to the company. Missiles cost money, but it's worth it to kill you and destroy your ship. Might make my friends rest a little easier. And as for that shitcan you call a ship," he added, his voice becoming angrier, "there's a score to settle with your shipboard computer, too."

Collier narrowed his eyes. "Leave him alone," he snarled. "Just because you couldn't break him—"

"We don't tolerate betrayal from our employees. Human or Caliban. You should be thanking us, South," the man said, his voice again casually cruel, "we're ridding the System of a dangerous rogue computer."

"There are two others on board," Collier said. "You'd kill two innocents over this?"

"Looks like they backed the wrong horse. Ex-Ceres Authority Agent Lora Fletcher and Galatea Starcher, corporate convict and a scrape to boot. Agent Fletcher, you have Ad Astra's most sincere apology for the inconvenience of your imminent death. Starcher, fuck you. No one steals from Ad Astra. Least of all a scrape. And Sancho, you miserable little Caliban, you should have stayed in the junkyard." The voice grew slightly fainter as he must have turned to address his own crew. "Weapons, lock on to the *Dulcinea*."

"Skipper, we have missile lock on us," Sancho said.

Collier stared up at his ship, hovering one hundred meters above his position. He could just make out one of the Ad Astra vessels orbiting the asteroid at a higher altitude, almost directly overhead. He watched, helplessly, and shouted into his microphone, "Wait, Corporate Captain … you win — I have the device with me down here! Just spare my ship and everyone aboard!"

"Missile launched, Skipper. Fourteen seconds to impact. I—" Sancho said, but Galatea's voice cut him off.

"Computer! Slide the frequency range of your ladar beam up and down! Now!"

Collier shouted, "Galatea? What the—"

"It'll work! Do it!"

"Do what he says, Sancho!" Collier ordered. He had no idea what she was trying to do, but there seemed little harm in obeying. A short few seconds later, Sancho's triumphant voice sounded in Collier's helmet.

"Skipper! Missile lock lost! I'm thrusting out of the way! It'll be close!"

Collier saw the *Dulcinea* turning ponderously above him, moving with maddening sluggishness as it fought to exit the missile's vector.

Sancho said, "Maneuver successful! But ... uh-oh. Missile is heading your way, Skipper! Take—"

He didn't hear the rest of Sancho's warning, as the ground trembled beneath him with mounting force. He saw the effect of the missile's impact on the rock about fifty meters away from his position on the lip of the fissure. The ground shook from the impact and his view of the *Dulcinea* was obscured as a titanic dust cloud flew outward from the missile's impact. There was no shockwave in the vacuum of space, but the vibrations along the asteroid's surface spoke to the tremendous force with which the missile had hit.

"Sancho! Continue evasive action, and do whatever Galatea suggests! Am I still on with the Ad Astra ship?"

Hierro answered. "Yes, you are, Captain South. Not sure how you broke our missile lock, but I'm betting you can't do it to multiple targets. All you did was prolong the inevitable."

"Wait! I give in!" Collier shouted. "I'll hand over the artifact, even teach you how to use it. Then you'll have leverage to bargain with your bosses. But if you destroy my ship, I'll set this thing on self-destruct, and you won't get it at all."

There was an agonizing wait from the other end of the radio, during which time Collier fought to keep his mouth shut. His bluff was delicate enough as it was — he didn't trust his own voice not to give him away. Whatever Galatea had done to disrupt the Ad Astra missile had probably been improvised, or she would have shared her knowledge at some point during the voyage here. Collier doubted she could repeat the miracle.

"I don't think so," drawled the Ad Astra fleet commander. "I'm going to bet there is no such self-destruct on that thing. And besides, I owe you. On behalf of all those you killed, I owe you. D-two-zero-seven to fleet: lock on to *Dulcinea* and fire on my order. Goodbye, Captain South."

Collier swallowed in a dry throat. "Sancho, can you..." he stopped, knowing there was nothing to say.

"We've got multiple missile locks on us, Skipper," Sancho said. "Galatea says that her little trick exploits a flaw in the Vindicator missiles used by D-class ships. By sliding up and down frequency as rapidly as possible, the missile's proximity and guidance system misreads the—"

"Doesn't matter, Sancho. I — I'm sorry, my friend, but I think this may be the end of the line for us. Fletcher, I — I don't know what to say. Except that—" he stopped as he felt more trembling from the ground. For a moment, he thought that the initial missile impact must have triggered a landslide, but the shaking felt much, much closer.

He lurched slightly as a sharp shock ran through the ground, and as he watched, a section on the far side of the fissure opened up, the alloy pulling back like the jaws of a great lizard. His helmet lamps only dimly illuminated the area, their light diffused by the dust cloud that still hovered above the surface.

A spire of rock or metal was rising out of the fissure. When it had extended to approximately fifteen meters above the surface the spire changed orientation slightly, and Collier instinctively looked up at the hovering ships. The *Dulcinea* was no longer directly overhead: Sancho's evasive thrust had moved it a few degrees away. The spire was not pointed at *Dulcinea* but angled slightly away.

"Sancho, are you seeing this?"

"Seeing what?"

"There's some kind of structure coming out of the fissure down here. Ad Astra vessel, can you see what's happening on the asteroid?"

"South, you really need to just die with some dignity. These games are—" The voice cut out suddenly.

"Sancho, I've lost the Ad Astra ship. Have they fired on you?"

"No, Skipper, and we no longer read missile lock from D-two-zero-seven."

"What about the others?"

"They still have locks on us. And now one of them is hailing us. Captain Weh, Ad Astra D-four-four-six."

Collier stared at the spire and started towards the opening from which it had come. "Put them through."

He was greeted with a furious woman's voice. "What the hell did you do?"

Collier almost said, 'nothing,' but thought better of it. Something had happened out there that scared this Ad Astra captain. He might as well try to use it, even if he didn't understand it himself. "I told your friend that if he fired again, I'd retaliate. He didn't believe I had a self-destruct. Do you?"

"We've lost contact with them, and what we're getting back from our scopes doesn't make sense. What the hell did you do?"

"Sancho, cut off communication with her."

"Acknowledged, Skipper. Just you and me now."

"What happened?" Collier asked as he took another step towards the base of the spire.

"I don't know. I had switched to ladar to try and see if Galatea's trick would work again. I can take a look at two-zero-seven, if you want."

"Do it, and report back. Fletcher, you okay up there?"

Fletcher said in a cool voice, "We're still alive, obviously, but the other three Ad Astra ships have missile lock on us. Galatea says if they all fire simultaneously, the ladar trick won't work. Plus they might have kinetic-kill weapons, mass drivers—"

"Right. One thing, Fletcher: whatever you do, do not get between where I am and where the Ad Astra ships are. Keep moving out of the way."

"Why?"

"I think I know what's happening down here, and if you—"

Sancho broke in. "Skipper, I don't understand what I'm reading. According to my scope, the affected Ad Astra vessel has ... contracted. Its volume and displacement are down to a tiny fraction of what they used to be, but its mass remains the same. I'm also reading a significant rise in gamma radiation coming from its position. It's like ... as if some giant force has just crushed it down, like a garbage compactor."

"Sensor malfunction?"

"I don't think so. Everything else checks out."

Collier stopped his advance on the spire, steadying himself on the walls of the fissure. He was ten meters away from the opening from which the spire had risen, and he could see that there was space between the spire and the edges of the opening.

"I told Fletcher, and now I'm telling you: it's very important that you stay out of the line between me and the Ad Astra ships. If they begin to move, make sure you don't get caught."

"Roger that. But why?"

Collier stared at the spire. "Because I think this asteroid is defending itself."

"Defending itself? How?"

"I think it has something to do with this huge-ass gun," Collier said, staring down into the darkness of the opening. His helmet lamps illuminated another surface deeper within the asteroid, but he could make out no details.

He returned his attention to his ship. "Do they still have missile lock on you?"

"Affirmative. And Captain Weh is still on hold."

"Switch me over," Collier said. He drew himself up, as if his physical posture would aid him in his bluff. "Captain Weh, unless you want to suffer the same fate as your friends aboard the two-oh-seven, you'll stand down your weapons and take the *Dulcinea* off missile lock."

"You're bluffing," Weh said, but her voice betrayed her uncertainty.

"Am I? Ask Captain Hierro. If he's still alive," Collier said. He fought to maintain a flippant tone, all the while growing slightly queasy as he imagined the scene aboard the destroyed Ad Astra vessel. He glanced again at the spire. What sort of weapon could have done what Sancho described?

"So what happens now?" Weh asked. "We just hang here in space indefinitely?"

"What happens now is you wait for further instructions from me. Power down your weapons and remove the missile lock. Then ... we'll see."

"Very well. For the moment, we'll agree to your terms. Do keep in mind," Weh said, her voice growing more confident, "we can reestablish missile lock on you in a matter of seconds. If you try anything, that's just what we'll do."

"You've got it backwards, Captain," Collier said. "If *you* try anything, you'll find yourself crushed like a tin can. Captain South, out."

"We're out, Skipper," Sancho said. "And let me guess —that was all a bluff."

"You're learning, Sancho," Collier said, swiveling his helmet lamps around the darkness of the opening. "I've found an entrance into the asteroid. It's where this gun-thing is poking out."

"You're not thinking of going down there," Fletcher said.

"That's exactly what I'm thinking."

"I thought you said the asteroid is getting angry and defending itself," Fletcher said. "Why would you go into the lion's den just when it's waking up?"

"We came all this way," Collier said, still searching for details in the asteroid's dark interior, "and you want me to turn back now? Where's your curiosity, Fletcher?"

"It's in a box labeled 'common sense,' right beside my sense of adventure, back on Ceres," Fletcher said.

"There's nothing common about any of this," Collier said. He stopped as his helmet lamp lit upon a ledge a few meters down into the darkness. "I'm heading down. If communications get cut off, try to keep Ad Astra at bay. Threaten them with the big gun down here. Anything to keep them scared and worried."

"I'll do my best, Skipper."

"I know you will," Collier said. He activated his suit thrusters at their lowest power setting and for the briefest duration he could, and began to sink down towards the ledge. As he cleared the metal panel that separated the asteroid's exterior from its interior, he let out a breath of relief. He had half expected a vicious metal buzz saw to slice him in half, for daring to penetrate inside, but the journey to the ledge was slow and uneventful. He landed and swiveled his lamps around to see where he was.

As best he could tell, he was in what looked like a maintenance crawlspace — the ledge allowed access to the base of the spire, though there were no controls or gauges that he could see. There was space below the elevated platform on which the spire rested, and he judged that he could work downwards without his suit jets and land on the lower surface. As long as the platform supporting the spire didn't retract, he ought to be safe.

A few nerve-wracking moments later, he landed without incident and straightened up carefully, his lamps revealing a long corridor stretching to either side of the spire, matching the fissure above.

"Sancho, do you still read me?"

"Affirmative, Skipper. We can still hear you."

"Any change up there?"

"No. Are you okay?"

"Yeah. I'm inside the asteroid," he said, still swiveling around slowly to survey his surroundings. "I think I'm in some kind of maintenance corridor."

"Maintenance for what?"

"Hell if I know," Collier added. "I'm going to head toward the center of the fissure."

"Copy that. Be careful."

"I'll try," Collier said. He decided to risk a lightmoth: if there had been an intruder alarm, he'd no doubt already tripped it. Collier deployed the lightmoth with and continued through the now well-lighted tunnel.

The walkway was utterly unadorned. The walls, floor, and ceiling were pure white in the glow of the lightmoth and without any markings or irregularities. Instead of right angles the walls met the floor in sloping curves, giving the passageway a feeling of softness. Collier started towards what would be the center of the fissure and tried to communicate with Sancho once he was several meters away from the spire.

"You still read me?"

Sancho's voice was faint and distorted by static. "Yes, but your signal is weak. What does it look like down there?"

Collier stopped his floatwalking. "Yeah. I don't know how much longer we can stay in contact. It doesn't look like anything. Except maybe … yeah, it looks like the magic wand. Same featureless white surface."

"Any markings?"

"No. But maybe I could if I could see in ultraviolet." He took the magic wand from his pouch and examined it. The markings on the wand had disappeared again. "Yeah, I got nothing again. Being underground here is blocking the sun's output."

"What do you think this thing is, Skipper?" Sancho asked, his voice slightly more distorted. "A secret research facility, maybe?"

Collier said, "Built by whom? Terries? Martians? No way someone could have hollowed out an entire asteroid without being noticed, Sancho."

"Ad Astra could have done it," Sancho said.

"No," Galatea said. "I would have known about it."

Collier shook his head. "This isn't an Ad Astra facility. They wouldn't have fired on their own ship. Though what that thing did fire is beyond me."

"It's a strangelet gun," Galatea said.

Collier said, "A what?"

Fletcher interrupted, "No way. If someone built such a weapon, it would..." she trailed off.

"This is that planet-killer thing you mentioned, Fletcher?"

"Yes, but—"

"Sancho, does the damage to the Ad Astra vessel align with Galatea's theory?"

Sancho answered, "Could be. Assuming she means that the weapon fires a strangelet, then the strangelet would convert any matter it comes into contact with into more strange matter."

Collier asked, "So what would happen? Implosion?"

"Not so much an implosion as a contraction, since strange matter is far denser than ordinary matter. It also put out a lot of gamma radiation, which would be a by-product of the effect." Sancho paused, then said, "What happened to the Ad Astra ship is consistent with the theory behind a so-called 'strangelet weapon.'"

Fletcher whispered, "My God."

Collier said, "I think this asteroid, or whatever this place is, is a base for such a weapon. Built by the same people, or beings, who built the magic wand."

"So, what do we do now?" Fletcher said.

"You keep Ad Astra off my back. I'm going to keep walking, see what I can find."

"And if you don't find anything?"

Collier didn't answer. He turned the magic wand over in his hands and returned it to his pouch, then began to floatwalk forward.

Chapter Seventeen

The corridor emptied into a spherical room the middle of which was dominated by a round, white object with projecting arms that extended outward into the walls. Ranged around the base of the sphere were cylindrical devices, slotted into receptacles that looked to have been designed to hold them. Everything appeared to be made of the same white material as the magic wand, and Collier suspected that were he able to see into the ultraviolet spectrum the room would reveal itself to be adorned with similar symbols.

"Sancho, do you read me?"

The voice which responded was so obscured by static Collier couldn't even tell who it was.

"Sancho, there's too much interference. If you can hear me, do your best to clean it up."

He was surprised to hear Fletcher's voice answer, though he could barely make out what she was saying. It sounded like, "Sancho's acting strangely."

"Fletcher, move the ship closer to the opening," he said. "Repeat, move the ship closer to the opening in the asteroid."

He repeated the message several more times, getting back garbled responses he thought might be confirmations, before finally he could make out more clearly what Fletcher was saying.

"We're fifty meters away, close to the tower thing," she said. "Can you read me now?"

Her voice was still distorted, but he could understand her. "Barely, yes. What do you mean, Sancho's acting strange? What's he doing?"

"He says he's getting a math problem."

"What does that mean?"

"I don't know."

"Getting it from where?"

"He didn't say, and now he won't respond at all. I had to manually burn the thrusters to move us."

"What's Ad Astra doing?"

"They've moved towards D-two-zero-seven to begin rescue, but according to the scope, there's nothing to rescue or even salvage. Otherwise they've taken no offensive action."

Collier took a deep breath. Now of all times Sancho chose to be quirky. Or was his behavior connected to the asteroid? "Fletcher, listen close. Whatever Sancho decides to do, don't fight him, okay?"

"I can't promise that. What if he's broken down and—"

"He hasn't," Collier said. "Just listen to him and let him do what he wants. And if he asks you for something, give it to him. Help him however you can."

"What's going on?"

"I don't know," Collier said, "but just do what he says."

"I'm going to use my judgement, Collier. I'm not going to give you some blanket—"

"Damn it, Lora!" Collier cried. "This isn't the time to be independent! Whatever Sancho is doing, whatever math problem he's solving, it's going to help us. Let him work on it in the background."

"How the hell can you know that?"

"I trust him. Can I trust you?"

"If you trusted me, you'd let me make my own determinations about Sancho's status."

"You don't know him like I do."

"No, I don't. But I don't have to. He might be your friend, but he's still a computer, the same way you're a human being. He can be subject to damage or breakdowns, just like you or I could. And, as a ... sentient computer, he could even suffer a cyberpsychotic break. Your friend is a machine."

Fletcher's words, delivered calmly and rationally, rang out as inescapably true. Sancho had made decisions on his own that had gone against Collier's wishes — he had nearly refused to leave Ganymede and Perditus, he had allowed Galatea to enter the ship on Deimos — but those were just disagreements. They didn't indicate damage.

Then he remembered Sancho's interdicted memory. Ad Astra had subjected him to the computer equivalent of brainwashing, and it had worked. His friend was not invulnerable — no more than Collier himself was.

He brushed that thought aside. Sancho had never, in the long run, let him down. Collier noted that he could not say he had reciprocated. The obligation to trust Sancho won out. No matter how rational Fletcher was being, Collier could not agree with her.

He spoke pleadingly. "Please, Lora, just follow Sancho's instructions, whatever they are. I can't be worried about what's going on up there while I'm trying to figure out what I'm looking at down here."

There was static on the line for a while. Then Fletcher asked, "What's happening there?"

Collier described the chamber and the huge spherical device. "I think it's the control or power center for the asteroid. At least for the strangelet gun."

"Any actual evidence to support that theory?" Fletcher said.

"Nope. Just guessing."

"We need a plan. If Sancho doesn't come back as his usual self, I'm not the best person to talk him down."

Collier continued to study the metal sphere that dominated the chamber. Finally, he spoke. "Fletcher, I'm inside an artificial asteroid, looking at something that is almost certainly an alien machine, built by God knows who, God knows when, for God knows what reason. Some kind of weapon that shoots strangelets that could destroy a planet just destroyed one of the Ad Astra vessels and could fire back up at any moment. I'm at thirty-eight percent oxygen, and I gotta take a piss. The only plan I got right now is to do the latter."

"Skipper," Sancho said, "when you're done urinating, Galatea thinks there's a way for me to recalibrate my sensors to detect strangelets."

"Sancho, welcome back. Is that what you were working on?" Collier was ashamed of the relief he felt that Sancho had not been corrupted.

"Yes. More accurately, I would look for evidence of strangelet by-products. Cosmic radiation and gravitic distortion, to be precise."

"Explain."

"Most of what I know about strange matter is theoretical, Skipper."

"There's nothing theoretical about that crushed Ad Astra ship," Collier said.

Galatea interrupted. "Strange matter is incredibly dense. A chunk of strange matter a few hundred femtometers across would still be massive enough to have noticeable gravity. And as that chunk dissolved neutrons and consumed the quarks it's made up of, the neutron would emit cosmic rays as it went to a lower energy state. It leaves a fingerprint."

Collier wasn't sure he'd understood anything Galatea said. "Sancho?"

"Like I said, my knowledge is theoretical, but Galatea has suggested that I can ... scatter charcoal around for fingerprints. I think that's the correct idiom."

Collier laughed. "Close enough. All right. Make whatever adjustments you need to in order to detect the strange matter, see what you can see."

"Done, Skipper. It's not really about making a huge change to ... hold on. Something strange. Pardon the pun."

"What?"

"The pun. I said 'something strange.'"

"God dammit, Sancho—"

"I'm reading cosmic rays emanating from the asteroid."

"How much?"

"On the order of five billion electron volts. Enough to notice, not nearly enough to hurt anyone. The point is, though, I shouldn't be detecting anything."

"Strange matter?"

"Could be. But it'd be very, very little. Several million orders of magnitude less than what hit the Ad Astra ship."

"But it's there. Coming from the asteroid. Could it be coming from the gun? The tower-thing that is sticking out of the asteroid?"

"I'm sorry, Skipper — I can't tell for sure."

"All right. Keep monitoring, and—"

Fletcher broke in. "The other Ad Astra ships are powering up missile tubes."

"Do they have missile lock on you?"

"Negative," Fletcher said, keeping her voice urgent but professional. "I don't — missiles away!"

"I have a good track," Sancho said. "Telemetry indicates they are targeting the spire, Skipper. Three inbound missiles, impact in fifteen seconds."

Collier looked back down the walkway towards the spire. If the missiles detonated, they might collapse the entire underground tunnel system, crushing him inside. He pushed off towards the white sphere, trying to get it between him and the walkway to the gun. What difference that would make, he did not know.

A few seconds later, the white sphere emitted a faint purple glow, and Collier's helmet display lit up with a warning about increased ultraviolet radiation. He knew his helmet visor was coated to protect him, but the HUD warning told him some was getting through. He couldn't worry about that now — if the chamber collapsed due to the missile attack, a little sunburn would be the least of his troubles.

He felt a faint tremor as he bounced off the glowing sphere and steadied himself against the interior wall of the chamber. Sancho's voice crackled in his helmet. "Skipper, missiles destroyed. The strangelet weapon discharged, and the missiles contracted like D-two-zero-seven did. What was left of them presumably impacted on the surface."

"I think I felt them. Are you anywhere near the Ad Astra ships?"

"No. We've moved off."

"Stay well away from the gun."

"I understand. The weapon is moving slightly. I think it's tracking the attacking Ad Astra ships now."

Collier looked back at the sphere. At the base of the sphere, each cylinder was now glowing very faintly, emitting a violet light. Collier pushed off gently and approached the sphere. He gasped as he realized what the cylinders were.

"Skipper ... something's happened out here," Sancho said, his voice shaky.

"What?" Collier waited, then cried, "What's happening? *Dulcinea*, come in!"

"Every Ad Astra ship has been destroyed. Crushed." Fletcher said, her normally calm voice wavering.

Collier said, "Is the gun tracking you?"

Fletcher said, "Sancho? Stay with me, now."

Sancho's voice was electronically distorted. "I'm here. And yes, the gun is moving to track us."

"Get out of its arc!" Collier shouted.

"We don't know what its arc is," Fletcher said.

"Go to the other side of the asteroid, then!"

"I don't have enough thrust. I won't be able to build up velocity to outrun it," Sancho said, his voice still distorted.

"Do something!" Collier shouted.

He got no response. His helmet display indicated that he'd lost contact. Collier pushed off the sphere and headed back down the walkway, sailing headfirst instead of floatwalking, risking a fatal collision with the wall that could smash his helmet. He reached the opening where the gun turret still stood, and he could see with his naked eye that the turret had changed orientation. It was no longer pointed upwards, but had almost flattened out completely, aiming nearly at the asteroid's close horizon. It was still moving, whatever motors or mechanism that guided it flattening the turret more and more.

Collier could see the tiny sliver of space between the enormous gun barrel and its support platform getting smaller and smaller, and in a desperate move, snatched the magic wand out of his suit pouch and jammed it into the space remaining.

Almost as soon as he'd done it, he winced in regret. If the massive mechanism of the strangelet gun crushed the magic wand, not only would he have lost his source of income and possible hope of remaining relevant in the System, but more immediately the wand might explode or discharge its mysterious energies in a blast that would kill him and possibly even destroy the *Dulcinea*.

But it was too late to change his mind and snatch the wand away — the circular platform of the gun turret had already tilted enough to make that impossible. As he watched, the wand held firm, and the gun turret stopped its downward track. The huge barrel of the weapon was not quite aimed at the horizon.

Collier swept his gaze along the gun barrel's length to see what was in the line of fire, and saw the *Dulcinea* grounded on the asteroid, hopefully below the weapon's arc. He climbed up out of the turret housing and stood on the surface.

"Sancho! Fletcher! Whatever you do, do not lift off! I repeat, remain grounded!"

"That's our intention, Skipper," Sancho said, his voice still slightly distorted.

"From what we can see, we're not in the gun's sights," Fletcher added. "Maybe it can't track this close to the surface."

"I jammed it," Collier said, "But I don't know if the jam will hold."

"How did you jam it?" Fletcher said.

"Used the magic wand. I figured it would be the only thing tough enough to hold up to the pressure. So far, looks like I was right."

"So now what?" Fletcher said.

Collier checked his oxygen levels. Twenty-one percent. He could reenter the *Dulcinea* and recharge, but he was leery about making any movements in the direction of the gun barrel. He looked again at the magic wand, jammed into the turret mechanism. He could see no flattening of the tube, no scratches or marks upon its surface. Hesitantly, he reached out and felt the surface of the turret, careful not to place his fingers anywhere they could be crushed. He felt a gentle vibration, as if the turret mechanism was still trying to track the *Dulcinea*. If there was some way to cut the power to this thing, that would solve their immediate problems.

He began to inspect the gun turret more carefully, looking for cables or power lines of any sort, or for that matter looking for any controls at all. He found nothing, even on the surfaces of the turret and barrel that were exposed to the sun's ultraviolet radiation. The gun was either self-powered, drew power from lines that Collier could not find, or perhaps drew from direct beamed power.

He could at least test this last theory. "Sancho, give me every sensor filter you've got and take a look at this gun. Where does it get its power from?"

"Okay," Sancho said, his voice still slightly distorted. To Collier, he sounded distracted.

"What's wrong with you?"

"Nothing, Skipper. Beginning scan."

Fletcher interrupted. "He's been like this since the Ad Astra ships were destroyed."

"Talk to me, Sancho," Collier said.

"I'm picking up a very faint magnetic field on the surface," Sancho said. "Wouldn't have been able to detect it from even a hundred meters up, but now that I know what to look for, I can see it. I think it's coming from a power line just under the surface, running from the gun turret to where you said that big chamber was."

"Okay, good. That helps. But I meant 'talk to me' in the sense of telling me what's bothering you."

"Well, we're critically low on waterfuel, biologics and oxygen won't last long enough for a normal return trajectory, and we don't have three hibernation rigs, so—"

"That's not it. You're upset about the Ad Astra ships, aren't you?"

"Why would I be?"

Fletcher broke in, "Is this really important right now? What about this gun that can destroy planets and which is almost aimed right at us? Or the fact that you're probably on an artificial asteroid built by aliens—"

"So you've come around to the alien theory, Fletcher?" Collier said.

Fletcher said, "Again, not the point. Should you be trying to counsel a computer when we're faced with these things?"

"If Sancho goes, so go all our chances of survival." He addressed his computer friend. "Sancho, I think I know what you're feeling. You've been harboring hatred for Ad Astra."

"Hatred is—"

"—not something you're capable of. Shut up," Collier said. "You very much hated them. That's why you kept saying you wanted to destroy them. We even had a big argument about it and priorities, remember?"

"Skipper, I—"

"And now that you've watched four Ad Astra heavies get crushed by this strangelet gun — which means many, many people got killed — you're not sure how you should feel." He paused, during which time Sancho was silent, then added, "or to put it another way: you got what you thought you wanted, but now realize that getting what you want always comes with a price."

"So what do I do about feeling this way?" Sancho said. Collier could hear the pain in his friend's voice, never mind that it was an electronic voice and an electronic friend. That had long ago ceased to make any difference.

"You just get on with it."

"Get on with what?"

"With whatever is in front of you."

Fletcher snorted. "You're psychoanalyzing a Cal–a computer."

Collier ignored that and said, "In this case, Sancho, that means figuring out how this gun turret is getting its power and seeing if we can't disrupt it. Thoughts?"

"The magnetic field running just below the surface could be the result of some kind of power line," Sancho said, "but could also be caused by dozens of other sources. Liquid metal flow, for instance."

"Okay. Let's try to disrupt any power flow that may be happening, see what we get. Can your sensors give me pinpoint accuracy on the magnetic field? Tell me when I'm over it directly?"

"No, Skipper. But they don't need to. You can do that by yourself. You have prospecting gear in your suit's backpack."

"Shit, I forgot all about that. Shame on me, Sancho. I'll forget my middle name next." He began to unlimber the backpack and rummage through it.

"Harrison," Sancho said helpfully.

Collier found what he was looking for — the autodrill device. He stared at it for a moment, noting the strange symmetry in its history: the last time he'd used the device, he'd found the magic wand.

Collier eyeballed the imaginary line between the underground spherical chamber and the gun turret, then extended the autodrill's tripod and set it to work. The drill was designed to take a sample of whatever it was placed upon in cross section, like slicing a layer cake and lifting it up to reveal the various strata. When the drill was steady, he pressed the firing button and the drill shot forcefully downwards, carving up the surface dust easily. An error message lit up on the tiny screen on the drill, and Collier read the message:

"Penetration failure. Distance 3.223 meters." The sampler must have met the metallic surface of the asteroid and been unable to cut through. Collier adjusted the drill slightly, still eyeballing the imaginary line, and reset the controls. He repeated this three more times, and was beginning to think that this improvised plan was worthless when, on the final deployment, the drill's error message was one he'd never seen before: "Danger! Hazard detected!"

As soon as he'd read the message, Sancho's voice crackled to life. "Skipper! The gun! It's moving!"

Collier turned to see the gun barrel lifting rapidly until it was in a completely upright position, then watched it start to descend.

"I think we somehow reset it," he said. "I'm going to have to head down before the opening closes up." He leapt towards the descending gun barrel. He caught the barrel but his leap took him farther than he intended and swung around the spire like a tetherball. He hugged it close as it descended through the aperture, the back of his suit scraping against the dust of the asteroid's surface. If he hadn't taken his backpack off, he would have been caught and likely crushed by the closing plates.

"Skipper! What about—" Sancho started, but when the plates sealed shut, the transmission was abruptly cut off. The space into which Collier now found himself was cramped: it was the housing area for the strangelet gun, and had obviously been built without consideration that a middle-aged human beltrunner would be hitching a ride into the interior. His floating light was still waiting here, having followed him as best it could from his earlier jaunt, and illuminated the space with a pearly glow due to the partial dust cloud that had followed him down.

"*Dulcinea*, do you copy?" he said, not expecting an answer. When none came, he wondered just how wise his decision to leap down had been. A quick check of his oxygen supply showed he had about forty minutes left.

He stepped off the gun turret assembly and floated very slowly downward to the walkway. On his way down, he spotted the magic wand resting on the turret base where he'd left it, looking none the worse for wear. It was no longer jammed: when the turret had reset, it had opened up the space into which he had placed the wand. He scooped it up then began to floatwalk towards the spherical chamber. Whatever answers he needed would have to come from there.

When he reentered the chamber, he went directly to the cylinders at the base of the sphere. There were five of them, and they were in shape and dimension precisely the same as the magic wand he held in his hand. What was perhaps even more remarkable, however, was that there were six receptacles. One of the slots was empty.

"Well, little guy, I think we found your home," Collier murmured. He floated closer to the open receptacle and studied it. There were no leads or contacts he could see, but the size and shape of the slot was exactly suited to hold the wand. There could be no mistake — the wand was clearly designed to be placed there. For what purpose, Collier could not guess.

He moved to one of the receptacles that held a magic wand and reached out tentatively. When his gauntleted fingers touched the surface of the wand that was held in place, he half expected to trip some alarm or be given a shock, but nothing happened. With infinite care, he wrapped his fingers around the parts of the wand he could access and tried to pull it loose. All he succeeded in doing was pulling himself closer — the wand was held firm. He braced himself with one foot against the sphere and tugged harder but was still unable to budge the wand.

He let go, fearing reprisal, but still the sphere remained silent and still. "Well, unless the folks who built this were much stronger, or there's some kind of lock, I'm going to guess these slots aren't just storage," he said, addressing his own magic wand. "I think whatever your true purpose is, it lies in this empty slot here."

He cradled the magic wand, turning it over, and looked at the receptacle. Neither the wand nor the slot had any indication as to which end was meant to go in first, nor how the wand should be spun for proper placement. "I hope it doesn't matter," Collier said, "because I don't want to blow a fuse. Of course, maybe that's what you are: a fuse," he mused. He realized he was stalling and glanced again at his oxygen meter. Thirty-three minutes left.

He glanced at the other receptacles. If he put the magic wand into the empty one, he would probably not get it back. Was that the best move? Using it as a jam on the spire had been impulsive. This time he had a moment to consider his next move.

Of course, he wouldn't be able to use the magic wand if he were dead, he reasoned. And that's what would happen in half an hour if he couldn't find a way back to the *Dulcinea* and an oxygen supply. He thought for a moment about trying to use the magic wand to produce oxygen, but he couldn't see the controls, and even if he could somehow operate the device and then somehow get the resultant oxygen into his suit, pure oxygen would kill him too, just more slowly. And trying to mix nitrogen and oxygen together with the wand was out of the question.

There were no options, he realized. As things stood, he was going to run out of air in half an hour, so he needed to try and change how things stood. Inserting the wand into the slot was one way to make that happen.

Besides, he was curious.

He approached the receptacle and gently lowered the magic wand into the slot, sliding it home and feeling a slight click as it snapped into place. Almost immediately, the sphere lit up with faint violet markings all over its surface, some of which Collier recognized. They were the same markings that had been on the surface of the magic wand.

They glowed faintly in the dim light produced by the lightmoth that still hovered nearby, but when Collier decreased the lighting remotely, the symbols disappeared. He reversed controls, bringing the lightmoth to its highest setting, and the symbols reappeared. Evidently the lightmoth put out enough ultraviolet to reveal the symbols on the sphere, though why it hadn't done so for the magic wand was a mystery.

More importantly, though, by inserting the magic wand, he'd obviously started something. There were many more mysteries to unravel here — if the magic wand belonged here in its slot, how had it come to be located far away in the Belt? What was the purpose of this machine, indeed of the whole fake asteroid? Who built it? When?

These questions came and went in his mind, since the more immediate one was "how am I going to get back to the Dulcinea before my air runs out?" He checked his supply meter: nineteen minutes. In a wild fit of optimism, he checked his outer atmosphere sensor. How embarrassing it would be to die in his suit when there was air all around him. No, the pressure gauge still read zero. He dismissed the wan hope that he'd somehow activated an atmosphere generating system in the mysterious sphere. He'd have to find a way out.

The newly lit symbols were a mixture of familiar and novel: as he floated gently around the surface of the sphere, he saw a set of symbols he recognized as part of the "open tube" command on the magic wand. They were subtly different, and Collier noticed that the "twist tube" command symbol was a new one he didn't recognize. He floated over to the set of controls and studied them. If they were indeed the same ones, and had the same function, perhaps he could open the asteroid.

There was little time to consider what would happen if he guessed wrong and activated some other part of the machine. He pressed and slid his fingers along the command surfaces, trying different manipulations on the new symbol that had replaced the "twist" command, and was rewarded minutes later when a panel opened on the surface of the sphere itself.

Collier floated to the opening and looked inside. The interior of the sphere, which Collier judged to be about four thousand cubic meters, was identical in nature to the interior of the magic wand: a featureless, mirrored surface. It was also entirely empty.

"Okay, so that *was* the open command. Just not to the right door," Collier murmured. As he withdrew his head from the sphere's opening, a dim flash of violet caught his eye. On the wall of the chamber facing the opening in the sphere were some new controls he hadn't seen before, or which hadn't been visible before. He floated over to them and though there were many he did not recognize, there again glowed the series of symbols that seemed to mean "open."

"Here goes," he murmured, and followed the now familiar sequence. A panel opened in the wall of the chamber, corresponding to the opening in the sphere. Collier peered inside and his helmet lamps illuminated a long tunnel with smooth edges, rectangular and perhaps large enough for him to crawl inside.

His oxygen indicator sounded a warning, causing him to jump inside his suit. "Alert: fifteen minutes remaining on oxygen supply. Return immediately to safety! Alert: fifteen—" Collier shut off the alarm and aimed himself at the tunnel. It was not large enough to maneuver around: if he got stuck, or needed to turn, he would not be able to. But again, he was faced with very few options.

He slid into the opening, using his hands and feet to propel him forward as he banged into the sides of the tunnel. His helmet lamps were almost useless, as he could not swivel his head to make them shine in front of him. The surreal nature of the journey would have been overwhelming, but Collier had long since become accustomed to dangerous operations in his suit.

The journey through the tunnel was surprisingly short, and Collier found himself emerging into another chamber in only a few minutes. This chamber, however, was different: it was not smooth and crafted, but rough and natural, like a cave. There was a device near the opening, next to which were solid blocks of what looked like rock, stacked neatly in a pyramid. The whole structure was easily twice Collier's height. The device resembled an auto-miner, though it was clearly not of human origin; it wasn't moving, and there were no glowing symbols on its spidery surface.

The cave opened upward, and Collier jumped lightly to the ceiling. The surface was rough, though not hard. It resembled most asteroid surfaces: soft, pumice-like rock that crumbled easily at the touch. He poked at the ceiling, and found his finger easily penetrated into the soft rock.

He withdrew his digging mortar from his belt and began attacking the ceiling, chipping away madly in an attempt to free himself. If he was still inside whatever alien complex existed under the surface, he'd reach the metal plates and would remain trapped. But if somehow he had left it...

He gasped when one of his mortar strikes revealed a black starfield above. He scrabbled at the rock surrounding the opening and widened the hole, dust and debris floating all around him in the microgravity. Once it was barely large enough, he sailed upward through it, catching himself on the lip with his foot lest he sail into the airless sky.

He was on the surface of the asteroid again. He spun around, looking for the *Dulcinea*, while he activated his suit microphone.

"Sancho, can you read me?"

"Skipper! Yes, I can! Are you okay? My calculations are that you're about to run out of air!"

Collier checked his supply meter and balked. He had less than a minute remaining. He must have used more than normal during his digging. He saw the Dulcinea in the distance, and began leaping towards it. "I'm almost out. Heading to you now."

"I'll bring the ship closer to you!"

"Negative," Collier said. "I don't want to risk activating this place's defenses again. That gun isn't jammed anymore."

"I'll stay low. Five meters off the surface," Sancho said, his anxiety clear.

"I said no, Sancho. Stay where you are. I think I can make it." He kept his eyes on the Dulcinea as he skimmed the surface. He activated his suit attitude jets to give him more boost, but they were not designed for that and aided him only slightly before running out of waterfuel.

Collier activated his rangefinder and homed in on the *Dulcinea*. His readout gave him a distance of four hundred and ten meters, which was closing very slowly.

He wasn't going to make it.

"Skipper, I'm sorry, but you're not in command here. You told me to do whatever I thought best, and what I think is best is coming to get you. Ventral thrusters at one percent, three second burn. Mark."

"Fletcher! Dammit, stop him! You're gonna get shot at!" He saw the Dulcinea rise slightly from the surface of the asteroid.

"Fletcher's not here," Sancho said. "She went looking for you on the surface."

"Patch her in, then!"

"Sorry, Skipper, but I frankly don't have time for that. And you should shut up to save oxygen. Aft thruster burn, five percent, ten seconds. Mark."

The Dulcinea began moving towards him, and Collier looked past it to where the spire had been. He couldn't see it rising, though the nearness of the horizon might have concealed it. When he refocussed on the *Dulcinea*, he suddenly felt light-headed.

His suit computer sounded off. "Warning! Oxygen supply depleted! Activating distress beacon!"

Collier landed lightly after his last leap and found his legs buckling under him. He had forgotten how to jump — what was it one did again? A strange object was coming towards him. Or was the world turning with him on it, and moving things to his position? Was he the center of everything, or just a little creature crawling along the surface of a big sphere?

A sphere ... volume of a sphere is four times ... pi? Times radius cubed? Or was that how to calculate trajectory to ... to...

He wanted to take a deep breath, but there was something in the way — he was wearing a helmet of some kind. That was it — if he could only take this off, he could breathe in deep. He fumbled around the neck of the suit, but his fingers felt clumsy and not entirely connected to his body. Oh, well. No big deal. He'd just rest here for a moment, then he'd be up for school. Maybe Mom had made his favorite breakfast.

Collier closed his eyes and headed for sleep.

Chapter Eighteen

The feeling of cool air on his face brought him back to consciousness. He opened his eyes and saw a blurry face hovering over him — a face he did not recognize.

"Skipper?" Sancho's voice sounded in the airlock. "You're awake!"

"Yeah. Who the hell's this?" he said, glancing up at Sancho's airlock camera and gesturing at the woman.

"That's Galatea Starcher. You don't remember her?"

Collier stared at the woman, and for a moment, the name flitted around his mind in search of someone to attach itself to. Starcher. Barney Starcher. Barney Starcher was dead. But he had a daughter, sort of.

"Right, yeah. Sorry, Galatea. Got confused there."

"It's all right," she said. "Just glad you're still with us."

"I want you to run through a cognitive test, Skipper," Sancho said. "Galatea, if you would please escort Captain South from the airlock, you'll find a medical supply locker near the—"

"Skip it, Sancho," Collier said. "I'm fine." He sat up quickly, pushed past Galatea and opened the inner airlock hatch. "Fletcher still outside?"

"Yes," Sancho said. "But she's heading back."

Collier steadied himself on the airlock jamb. He felt light-headed, dizzy. "How long was I out?"

"Difficult to determine precisely," Sancho said. "But based on when you stopped responding to my attempts at communication to when we opened your helmet in the pressurized airlock, I'd guess between two and three minutes."

"Okay."

"Humans can experience brain damage in that short a time without oxygen, Skipper. I really think you should let me test you."

"I wasn't completely without oxygen for that long. I had what was left in the suit. It was just reduced."

"Even so. Hypoxia is serious, Skipper."

"Dammit, Sancho, I know it is. But we've got bigger problems in front of us right now."

"Are you experiencing problems with balance? Is your vision blurred? Are you having trouble concentrating?"

"Sancho—"

"Are you experiencing sexual dysfunction?"

"Sancho! Dammit, knock it off!"

"I'm trying to determine if you have symptoms of—"

"I know what you're trying to do. Please, for the love of space, stop. I know what the signs are. I promise I'll tell you if I notice anything."

"But many of the symptoms are mental in nature. How will you know—"

"I'll know. Now, patch me in with Fletcher."

Sancho hesitated a moment, then said, "All right. But I'm going to be watching, too."

"You go right ahead and watch me. Oh, and thanks."

"For watching you?"

Collier entered the control room and settled into the saddle. "Well, yeah, but mainly for disobeying me. Saved my life."

"Oh. You're welcome, Skipper. Fletcher is responding."

"Put her through."

Fletcher's voice was slightly breathless. "Collier, you there?"

"Right here. Safe and sound. Where are you?"

"About twenty meters from the ship. I went out to recover you where that gun turret was, but it's still closed off."

"Yeah. I had to dig myself out. Come on back and we'll talk about what's next. I found something in there."

Ten minutes later, Fletcher had returned to the ship, secured both of their suits in the recharging stations, and made her way to the control suite where Galatea and Collier were waiting.

"So, what's next?" Fletcher said, zipping up her jumpsuit and looking at Collier.

He tapped Sancho's screen on which was displayed the ship's consumables inventory. "We've got air and bios for a long stay here, but our fuel tanks are nearly dry. Sancho says we have about eight percent fuel remaining. With that little fuel left, it's going to take a long time to head back to Mars."

"How long?" Galatea said.

Collier looked at Fletcher, who was shaking her head. He turned back to Galatea. "Over three months. Much longer than we have supplies for."

"What about hibernation?" Fletcher asked.

"Yeah, I thought about that. The thing is, I only have one rig. I refilled it on Deimos when I resupplied, so it's good to go, but it would only support one person. Even recalculating for that, we're still short by quite a bit. But we could make it if one person went into hib, one person stayed awake, and one person stayed behind here." Collier said.

"You mean, if one person committed suicide?" Galatea said. "Why not leave the scrape behind, right? She's not even a real person, anyway."

Collier said, "Stop being melodramatic. No one's saying that. Besides, there's another possibility. The big sphere down under the asteroid."

"The big what?" Fletcher asked.

"I found something down there," Collier said, then proceeded over the next half hour to relate his adventure under the surface. When he was finished, Fletcher was the first to speak.

"That's fascinating and all, but I don't see how it helps our predicament. We still don't have enough food, water, and air for a return trip to Mars. Unless you think there's a deli inside that thing."

"There's nothing inside," Collier said. "I already looked. That is, there's nothing inside now."

"Now?"

"I said there were six of the magic wands hooked into it," Collier began.

"You don't know they're hooked in," Fletcher said. "In fact, you don't know if the other five devices were more magic wands."

"They looked like them," Collier said, waving his hand dismissively. "So I'm assuming. Also, there were some of the same symbols on the sphere that were on the magic wand. I think I can get the whole shebang to work."

"To work? And do what?"

"That's what we're going to find out," Collier said.

"Let me remind you that the only thing we actually *know* this asteroid has is a big gun that evidently shoots strangelet particles," Fletcher said. "So far, it's destroyed four ships, and heaven knows what it's capable of."

"Could be a planet-killer," Galatea said. "If it can build a large and stable ball of strange matter—"

"All the more reason we need to figure out how the sphere works," Collier said. "Maybe we can deactivate the gun. Look," he said, his tone somewhere between pleading and commanding, "as things stand, we're not all going to make it to Mars. That means we have to change the way things stand. I'm going to try. Check that — *we* are going to try."

"How?" Galatea asked.

"Same way I figured out the magic wand. Sancho, you ready for some more work?"

"Aye aye, Skipper."

"Good. Suits recharged?"

"Yes. Fully oxygenated and ready."

"Excellent." He turned to Fletcher. "For now, you and Galatea stay here," he said. "In case something happens out here."

"Like what?" Fletcher said.

"I don't know. More Ad Astra ships, or the Martian interceptors decide to head over here. Or this asteroid does something strange again. There's that pun again, Sancho."

"It was funnier when I did it," Sancho said.

Fletcher and Galatea looked at each other. Collier wondered if they were contemplating the odds of convincing Sancho to help them ditch Collier on the asteroid and take them back to Mars to rid themselves of his so-called humor. But after a moment, Fletcher turned back to Collier and nodded. "Let's investigate the fucking death sphere."

Minutes later, Collier was back on the surface, excavating where he'd emerged from the constructed cavern below. It was short work to make the opening larger, and when he'd done so he floated gently down to the chamber. The alien mining machine was still where he'd left it, standing mutely next to the neat piles of rock cubes. Now that he was calmer and more able to analyze what he was looking at, he noted that the cubes of rock were precisely the same dimensions as the tunnel through which he'd crawled to reach the room.

"Sancho, do you still read me?" Collier said as he dispatched another lightmoth.

"I do, Skipper."

"I'm heading through the tunnel again. Hopefully we'll still be able to maintain contact." He oriented himself and dove through, moving more slowly and carefully this time. When he emerged, he floated slowly towards the skin of the sphere where he'd seen the corresponding opening.

"Okay, so the cubes of rock feed the sphere," he murmured.

"What's that, Skipper?"

"Nothing. Just trying to talk through my thoughts. And obviously we can still hear one another. Do you still have my camera visual?"

"Affirmative."

"Perfect. Take a look at the symbols, and compare them to what we know about the magic wand." He swiveled his suit helmet towards the faintly glowing symbols on the sphere, moving slowly around so that Sancho could get a good look.

"Interesting," Sancho said. "I see what you mean. I recognize forty-eight percent of them."

"Can you make any sense of it?"

"If I had to guess," Sancho said, "I would say that the sphere encompasses at least some of the functions of the magic wand."

"That's what I thought, too," Collier said. "I figured out how to open it," he said, and demonstrated. "Just like the wand. And I have a hunch that the cubes of rock from the other chamber are the fuel source for the sphere."

"Fuel to do what?"

"Well, transmute, first of all."

"You think this is a bigger version of the magic wand?"

"Like an industrial-sized transmuter, yeah. At least, that's one of the things I bet it does."

"Because the six wands around it," Sancho mused. "I get it. I'd provisionally agree with that. But how do you get the rock cubes inside the sphere?"

Collier peered down the tunnel again. "I could just go back in there, take one, and shove it through." He thought for a moment. "Though I'm sure that one or more of these controls would do that for me. That mining robot or whatever it was in there can probably be commanded to feed the magic ball."

"Magic ball?"

"Well, if we're calling the little guys 'magic wands,' then that seems like a good name." He dove back through the tunnel and regarded one of the rock cubes.

"Why not 'crystal ball?'"

"Because," Collier said, hefting one of the cubes and placing it at the mouth of the tunnel, "that's more for seeing the future and stuff."

"How do you know it doesn't do that?" Sancho asked.

Collier shoved the cube and it floated down the tunnel, the sides of the cube perfectly fitted to the opening. "Good point. Crystal ball it is."

"Are you quite finished with this ridiculous game?" Fletcher said.

"It's gotta have a name, Fletcher."

Collier heard her snort, and from the quality of the sound she had turned away from the microphone, most likely in frustration.

He grinned despite himself and followed the cube of rock through the tunnel.

As he'd expected, it had floated across the short distance between the tunnel opening and slid neatly into the sphere through the corresponding opening. He operated the controls and closed the hatch on the sphere. Just like the magic wand, it left no sign that there had ever been an opening—there were no seams or irregularities in the crystal ball's surface.

"Okay, so I've loaded you up with some rock," Collier murmured. "Now to see if I can make you dance," he added.

"Dance, Skipper?"

"I'm going to try to operate the crystal ball. Gimme the guidebook on my heads-up, will you, Sancho?"

The inside of his helmet once again displayed the extensive notes he and Sancho had taken on the operation of the magic wand, and he found the correct controls on the surface of the crystal ball. "Okay, I'm going to try for gold. Simple, harmless, pretty."

"Not as simple as helium, Skipper. Also harmless."

"How will I know if I made it, though?"

"Won't it outgas from the crystal ball once you open it?"

Collier nodded, saying, "Of course, but I won't be able to see it. I'm going to stick with gold, Sancho. Here we go." He checked the guidebook, though he was quite familiar with the gold formula, and manipulated the controls. He was careful to avoid the many other controls that he didn't recognize and which were mixed in among the ones he knew. He paused before executing the final command. "About to set this to work. Here goes nothing," he said, and activated the "transmute" command as best he understood it.

Nothing obvious happened, and he knew he was going to have to open the crystal ball to see if he'd been successful. Perhaps he'd find gold, perhaps he'd find the cube of rock, unchanged, or perhaps he'd find nothing at all. But maybe he'd done something wrong, or the controls were different, and he'd open the crystal ball to let loose radioactivity or a dangerous element or a ball of strange particles. Would he even feel his own death as his molecules were converted to strange matter?

"Fuck it," he muttered, and opened the sphere.

Nothing exploded, nothing came flying out of the sphere to murder him. He floated to the opening and peered inside. His helmet lamps caught an unmistakable flash of bright yellow floating inside, and he beheld a somewhat smaller but still very substantial cube of gold hovering inside the crystal ball.

"Sancho, what would be the Martian sale rate of a cube of pure gold about, oh, sixty centimeters to a side?"

"Sixty *centimeters*? Skipper ... that's four thousand, one-hundred and fifty-three kilograms of gold!"

"What's that worth?"

"Approximately two point eight seven billion galileos, current Martian rates. Or about two hundred and forty million system credits."

"That's a lot of vindaloo," Collier said.

"I'm really happy you finally made the biggest strike of your life," Fletcher said, "but we still have the same problems we had before. That hunk of gold won't mean anything if we're all dead."

"We won't all be dead. Sancho would still be alive," Collier said absently, his eyes searching the controls again.

"Won't be the same without you, Skipper," Sancho said. "Or you, Ex-Agent Fletcher," he added. Then as an afterthought, "I do not know you well enough, Ms. Starcher, to say whether or not your passing would affect me."

"Thanks," Collier said before Sancho could stuff his electronic foot deeper into his speaker grille. "Anyway, Fletcher is right. We can't eat gold."

"And you can't transmute anything useful for us right now," Fletcher added. "Even water is too complex for that thing."

"I wonder," Collier said. He loaded another cube of rock and went back to the controls. He checked his manual again, and selected "hydrogen" but did not activate the transmuter. He saw a symbol that he and Sancho had recognized as a "cancel" button on the magic wand and purposefully did not select it. He entered "oxygen" and activated the transmuter. He opened the hatch to the sphere and felt a mild push against his face. He withdrew his head and activated his suit's environment scanner. The readout showed a tiny concentration of oxyhydrogen gas in his vicinity, though as he watched, the concentration dropped below the detection range of his suit sensors.

"Sancho, quickly—see if you can detect any outgassing from the hole I dug."

"I can see a dust cloud rising, if that's what you mean, Skipper. What happened?"

"I think I made the crystal ball fart."

"Pardon me?"

Collier looked back at the crystal ball. "I programmed it for hydrogen and oxygen at the same time."

"We tried that with the magic wand, too, remember?" Sancho said.

"Yeah. But it only produced the last thing we programmed. This," Collier said, reaching out to touch the crystal ball, "can make them at the same time."

"Fascinating! So you can make compounds!"

"I think so, yeah." He studied the unfamiliar controls. "And I'll bet you that these other controls allow for different concentrations of elements, maybe even change the state of the compound produced."

"They might operate the strangelet gun," Fletcher said. "Or did you forget about that?"

"I haven't forgotten," Collier said. "I don't think the gun controls are on the crystal ball."

"How can you know that?"

"I don't know it, but it's how these guys think."

"What guys?"

Collier looked at not just the crystal ball, but the entire chamber — its smooth walls, gentle curves, and soft design. "Whoever built this. Aliens. Gods. Whatever. That's not how they think."

Fletcher spoke in a deadpan that belied what she thought of Collier's current mental state. "You're saying you know how aliens think?"

"I've lived with this magic wand for a long time. Sancho and I, we've come to know how it works. It's meant for creation, not destruction. They wouldn't put the gun controls on the crystal ball surface. It would be … wrong, somehow."

There was a pause before Fletcher said, "Are you willing to risk your ship, and all of us, on that hunch?"

Collier's eyes went instinctively skyward. Fletcher was right. Matter of fact, he admitted to himself, Lora Fletcher was usually right. "Fair point," he said. "Sancho, reposition *Dulcinea* below the horizon so the gun can't get you.'

"Roger that, Skipper. I'll leave a beacon here so we can remain in communication."

"Good. Let's start making some compounds."

Sancho said, "How complex do you think the compounds can get?"

Collier looked around the base of the crystal ball. "I don't know, but if I had to guess, I'd say six elements."

"Why six?"

"Six slots for magic wands," Collier said. "I'm betting each wand makes one element at a time, then they're mixed together in the crystal ball."

"Maybe you should have called it a 'cauldron,'" Fletcher broke in.

Collier chuckled. "Glad to see you're getting into the spirit of things, Fletcher. Well, Sancho, I think it's time to start playing around with the controls to see how this thing works. Just like old times, right?"

"Roger that, Skipper!"

Collier collected another rock cube from the storage chamber, but this time did not feed the entire thing into the crystal ball. Instead, he broke up the rock into smaller pieces and fed those pieces into the ball as he experimented. This time, the experimentation did not take days like it had when they'd first encountered the magic wand; they weren't starting from scratch. Fletcher and Galatea tossed in their input from time to time. Galatea proved remarkably good at guessing patterns, but on the whole, Collier and Sancho were the ones who worked. They knew the language; this was their wheelhouse.

He took breaks to recharge his suit oxygen, eat and relieve himself, and five hours after he and Sancho had begun their painstaking work, he finally had his breakthrough.

"Okay, so that's *two* presses of the double-arrowhead button, slide left-to-right across the roller coaster, spin ninety degrees counterclockwise on the wheel of fortune," Collier said, using the shorthand they'd developed.

"Affirmative. Attempt one hundred sixty-one."

"And transmute," Collier said, activating the crystal ball. He opened the hatch and peered inside. A small shard of what looked like glass floated in the otherwise empty chamber. He reached in and retrieved it, trying to keep himself from getting too excited.

"Result, Skipper?"

"Stand by," he said, and placed the shard into the assay box he'd been using to test the compounds they produced. His fingers were shaking as he activated the scanner, and when the readout lit up he let out a whoop.

"Skipper? What's wrong?"

"Water ice! Sancho, we got it! Water ice!"

"Are you sure?"

"I know ice when I see it, and more importantly, the assay box confirms!" He cradled assay box as if the shard inside it were worth more than the gold cube he'd produced — for it was.

Fletcher's voice came on the speaker. "Can you make waterfuel?"

"Maybe, but I don't think that's necessary. Water-ice will work fine in the electrolysis plant. Besides, I don't want to monkey around with this too much."

"Oh, so now you're being careful?" Fletcher admonished him. Collier could hear the grin on her face.

"I'm always careful," he said, injecting some mock indignation into his voice.

"Wait — so you can make enough fuel for a fast return to Mars?" Galatea said.

"Yeah," Collier responded. "Looks like you're going to live after all, Galatea."

"What?"

"Just a joke," Collier said.

"I don't find that funny," Galatea shot back.

——— «◇» ———

It took Collier and Fletcher the better part of a day to fill *Dulcinea's* tanks: they didn't have a third vacc suit for Galatea, and Collier did not want to move the ship closer to use fuel hoses to suck water directly out of the crystal ball, so he produced cube after cube of ice from the rock supply and, with Fletcher's help, moved them into *Dulcinea's* fuel tanks.

The crystal ball's hatchway was always just big enough to extract the products it transmuted — the machine no doubt had an automatic setting to facilitate retrieval. Collier suspected that the sphere also could eject the transmuted material itself, rather than force the operator to go in and get it, but he did not wish to press his luck and operate controls he did not understand. He was curious, though, and had he been alone he might have allowed his curiosity to take over, but now that he had solved the problem of how to get back to Mars and thus get Fletcher and Galatea out of jeopardy, he was reluctant to risk anything more.

And, of course, he owed much to Sancho. He couldn't take unwarranted gambles that might threaten the ship. Likewise, how could he put his own life in danger knowing how his death would affect Sancho? He couldn't do that to him. No, there was still much to discover about this machine — who built it, and why? Were there other secrets besides transmutation and fabrication it held? What of the strangelet gun? Were there other chambers in the asteroid that held even more enigmatic devices? For that matter, were there other stations like this one elsewhere in the System?

As he helped Fletcher load the last of the ice cubes into Dulcinea's fuel tank, he thought of the future. He'd been living moment to moment for so long, he was unused to thinking about the years ahead. He'd been chasing the big strike for so long — and had thought he'd caught it — that he wasn't altogether sure what came next.

He grinned at the prospect. Not knowing what came next was the best way to live.

"Sancho," he said once the preflight checks were complete, "set course for Mars. Fast as you can — no need to conserve fuel."

"Aye aye, Skipper," Sancho said. "Course computed. Thrust in sixty seconds." He paused, his voice changing subtly. "What are we going to do there?"

"We're going to buy this asteroid."

He felt Fletcher and Galatea turn their heads to look at him, but he kept his eyes on the thrust countdown clock.

"That'll take a huge sum, Skipper."

"We've got almost three billion galileos in the gold rock," Collier said. "Even if we lose a hefty amount in the transfer, we should have more than enough to buy it. Mars government would be happy to unload it in exchange for that much. Remember, it's Worthless."

Epilogue

"Skipper, I'm receiving a hail from the *Trifaldi,"* Sancho said.

Collier put down his squeeze bottle and muttered, "About time." He activated his transmitter and said, "*Trifaldi*, this is Wellspring. We read you. Are you almost home?"

Fletcher's voice came over the speaker. "Affirmative. About half an hour out."

"Any trouble?"

"Nothing worth reporting. Ad Astra put up a squawk, but it came to nothing."

"As usual," Sancho interjected with notable satisfaction.

Collier grinned. He imagined Sancho grinning too, as he looked at the worn but clean control panel of the *Dulcinea*. Despite —or perhaps because of— the comfort and spacious quarters, he'd resisted moving into the new habitat they'd finished a month ago on Wellspring — previously Worthless. He knew that it would have been easy to patch Sancho through from the *Dulcinea* into the hab pod, but somehow, it wouldn't have been the same. He wouldn't have been with him. No one else in the co-op seemed to understand that, but they did respect it. As much as he hated his unofficial title, as Founder, Collier had a fair amount of leeway to be eccentric.

The four of them worked well together. Galatea knew the corporate mind, Fletcher understood authority and systems of bureaucracy, and Sancho was uniquely able to calculate and inject human speculation into his calculations. But Collier had the vision. He'd had started the co-op with a vision of a system that was neither pure, cutthroat capitalism nor the sterile, cold collectivism he'd encountered on Ganymede. A system based not on scarcity but on abundance. A system where people weren't in competition with each other but with their own pasts, where people strove to achieve great things not because it meant beating someone else but because of the simple thrill of it all. They'd already started buying Ad Astra out from under. They had seized the means of production in the form of the crystal ball, and unlike the corps, the crew of *Dulcinea* had every intention of sharing.

He shook himself out of his reverie and asked Fletcher, "Lora, have you given any more thought to my idea?"

"What idea?"

He frowned slightly. "You know very well what idea."

"The one about you and me getting married? Like we're living in the twenty-first century?"

"Dammit, people still get married nowadays," he snapped. He never liked her teasing in this matter — it had been hard enough to propose to her, and now she knew how to keep him squirming.

"Pallies and other religious nuts, maybe."

"It doesn't have to be religious," Collier said.

"I wouldn't even know how to find someone to do the ceremony."

"All right, all right, never mind. I take it back."

"You take it back? Your proposal? You're un-proposing now?"

"Dammit, Lora—"

She laughed. She had a musical laugh, and despite his growing annoyance with her, her laughter charmed him. He was angry at how easily she could manipulate him, even when she wasn't doing it on purpose.

"Well, I'd better say 'yes,' then. I can't stand to see you this stupid."

Collier's head snapped up as he stared at the control panel. "What do you mean, 'yes'?"

"Yes, I'll marry you."

Collier opened his mouth twice to speak, but nothing came out. Finally, he managed to croak, "Sancho, mute the transmission to her. Did you hear all that?"

"Affirmative."

"What do you think?"

"About what?"

Collier sighed. "Don't you start, now. About me getting married to Fletcher."

"Why are you marrying her?" Sancho asked, and Collier heard the other, unspoken question in his friend's voice.

"It's not because you aren't enough, Sancho. But she makes me feel ... well, dammit, I guess it comes down to that she showed me that there's still a possibility for love in this life." He thought of Su and knew she would want this for him. "Isa wasn't right, and Su was taken from me. I think I just sort of gave up at that point. Lora revived something I thought I'd lost. And, dammit, I love her."

There was a long pause before Sancho spoke. When he did, his voice was small and scared. "You won't leave me?"

Collier grinned and reached out to touch Sancho's surface. "Never."

If you enjoyed this read...

Please leave a review.

It takes less than five minutes, and it really does make a difference.

Reviews should answer at least three basic questions.
(But won't give the story away.):

- *Did you like the book?* ("Loved the book! Can't wait for the Next!")

- *What was your favorite part?* (Characters, plot, location, scenes.)

- *Would you recommend the book?*

Your review will help other readers discover this book. Consider leaving your review on Amazon, Barnes and Noble, Apple iBooks, KOBO, Goodreads, BookBub, Facebook, Instagram and/or your own website.

Brian Hades, publisher

To leave a review on Amazon

~ Even if the book was not purchased on Amazon ~

1. *Go to amazon.com. Sign into your Amazon account. If you do not have an Amazon account, you need to create one and activate it by making a purchase. Amazon will check to see that your account is active before allowing you to leave a review. Amazon has some restrictions, such as not leaving a bias review. For more information on Amazon's policies please read Amazon's Community Guidelines for book reviews:*

   https://www.amazon.com/gp/help/customer/display.html?nodeId=GLHXEX85MENUE4XF

2. *Search for and find Aftermath by Sean O'Brien, then click on the book's details page.*

3. *Scroll down to find the Write a Customer Review button. Click it.*

4. *Select your star rating. A rating of 5 is best, 1 is worst.*

5. *If you have a photo or video to share, add it to the upload box.*

6. *Add a headline.*

7. *Write your review.*

8. *Press the SUBMIT button*

To leave a review on Barnes and Noble

~ Even if the book was not purchased on BN.com ~

1. *Go to barnesandnoble.com and sign up for an account.*

2. *Search for and find Aftermath by Sean O'Brien, then click on the book's details page.*

3. *Scroll down to the review section and click on the Write a Review button.*

4. *Select your star rating. A rating of 5 is best, 1 is worst.*

5. *Add a review title.*

6. *Write your review.*

7. *Add a photo if you wish.*

8. *Select if you would recommend this book to a friend.*

9. *Select appropriate TAGs.*

10. *Indicate if your review contains spoilers.*

11. *Select the type of reader that best describes you (optional).*

12. *Enter your location (optional).*

13. *Enter your email address.*

14. *Checkmark that you agree to the terms and conditions.*

15. *Press the POST REVIEW button.*

About the author

Sean O'Brien is an educator and writer from Southern California. He is married and has two children. He was named Educator of the Year by the California League of High Schools and has been a head varsity football coach, television broadcaster, and Gilbert and Sullivan singer (though not a good one).

He's the author of A Muse of Fire, Wondrous Strange, Vale of Stars, Beltrunner, Silent Manifest and Aftermath.

Need something new to read?
If you liked Aftermath, you should also
consider these other EDGE-Lite titles:

——<>——

Beltrunner
(Book One in the Beltrunner Saga)

by Sean O'Brien

From the best traditions of hard science-fiction.

The omnipotent corporations of the future have nearly taken over every asteroid mining operation in space. Independent miners like Collier South have been left without a rock to stand on, choking on corporation space dust.

But one last trip for Collier might reveal the motherlode!

If only he can sniff out the most promising rock and grapple onto it, his 'make-do' past will become his 'can-do' future.

It's a race, and Collier South must get there before his vindictive ex-lover (and her shiny new corporate ship) steals it from him!

Armed with old-school maneuvers and sage advice from his trusty onboard computer, Collier campaigns to mine the rock, pay off his debts, and change his life forever. And should things go beyond his expectations, and the rock offers him more than he can imagine, he'll also need a plan to safeguard his future and protect the universe as well!

All of which assumes, of course, that the corporation doesn't cheat, get there first, or conspire to pry every last thing from his cold, stubborn, nearly dead fingers.

For more on The Beltrunner visit:

tinyurl.com/edge6010

———<>———

Silent Manifest
by Sean O'Brien

While entrusted with transporting Earth's babies to the planet Tau Ceti III, the actions of a rogue caregiver bring them all to the brink of death.

Donn Cardenio, damaged veteran of Earth's disastrous first interstellar war, and two hundred fellow Caretakers are charged with caring for a quarter million embryos en route to colonize the extrasolar planet Tau Ceti III.

Cardenio considers this assignment a chance to redeem himself from the ravages of the past great war.

But, when one of his Caretaker colleagues snaps, Cardenio is forced to begin an investigation that leads to more questions than answers—questions about his relationship with his lover, his own past, and the nature of the mission he's on.

Unfortunately for Cardenio, nothing is as it appears. His fellow Caretakers do not share his reverence for the lives in their charge; friends and lovers hide vital truths; and his enemies and rivals become allies.

By the end of the mission, Donn Cardenio will confront the terrible reality of what he's done to determine how the future will unfold.

For more on Silent Manifest visit:

tinyurl.com/edge2049

—— <> ——

The Unworthy
Book Three in The Milky Way Repo Series

by Michael Prelee

Dive in and buckle up, nothing is as it seems...

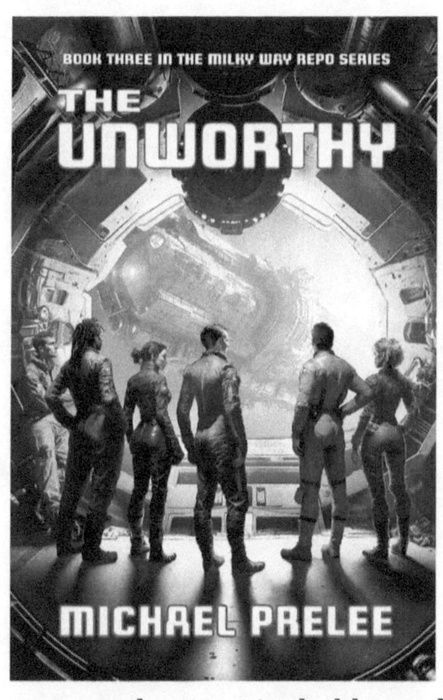

In a galaxy controlled by powerful corporations and crooked government officials, captain Nathan Teller and his crew struggle to keep their starship repo business afloat.

Faced with escalating debt and their starship on lockdown, Nathan and the crew reluctantly accept a dubious repo job that sends them on a thrilling chase through the cosmos.

As old enemies lurk, and new threats become apparent, they must overcome their biggest adversary yet - an enigmatic CEO with a nefarious plan and a dangerous secret that could spell disaster for Nathan, the crew, and every single blue-collar worker besieged by class warfare, income inequality, and the lengths that people will go to achieve their goals.

"The Unworthy" blurs the line between man and monster, right and wrong, in a heart-stopping adventure that plunges the crew into a relentless race against time, through alien landscapes and shady spaceports.

For more on The Unworthy visit:

tinyurl.com/edge2057

———<>———

———<<<>>>———

www.ingramcontent.com/pod-product-compliance
Lightning Source LLC
Chambersburg PA
CBHW061811190726
48289CB00007B/2155